WHEN RIVER LOVES DEBORAH

YONG KIM

When River Loves Deborah

YONG KIM

When River Loves Deborah

FIRST EDITION

©2025 Yong Kim. All rights reserved. No part of this publication may be reproduced, stored in a retrieval system or transmitted in any form by any means electronic, mechanical, or photocopying, recording or otherwise without the permission of the author.

This is a work of fiction. Names, characters, organizations, places, events, and incidents are either products of the author's imagination or are used fictitiously. Otherwise, any resemblance to actual persons, living or dead, is purely coincidental.

ISBN-13: 979-8-9927769-0-4 (Paperback edition).

ISBN-13: 979-8-9927769-1-1 (Ebook edition).

Library of Congress Control Number: 2025906053.

Printed in the United States of America.

3M3G Books, LLC, 8 The Green STE A, Dover, DE 19901.

Cover design by Miblart.

For Linda, the love of my life.

Love recognizes no barriers. It jumps hurdles, leaps fences, penetrates walls to arrive at its destination full of hope.

—Maya Angelou

PROLOGUE

July 2012

She said loneliness could kill me. Not in metaphor, but real, premature death.

Her words possessed me. I spent a decade chasing it. A fortune. An army of engineers. All for that elusive cure for loneliness. Now, I've found it, and you're the first to know.

Turns out, it had been in front of me all along. I just couldn't see it, hidden behind a veil so thin it blurred the line between the happy ending I craved and the tragedy I attracted. I hadn't realized they could live in the same moment, both drawn from the same story.

I see a puzzled look on your face. I'm not explaining this well, am I? Let me try again, this time with an example. Consider the way we romanticize love stories. They're often wrapped in imagery like this: a perfect couple, tying the knot in picturesque Lake Como. They sway together at the center of the dance floor, surrounded by impeccably dressed guests. White, peach, and pink rose petals float in the air while butterflies spiral skyward. As the final note of the song drifts into the breeze, they breathe the word "Forever." The happy ending. The ever after we're expected to swoon over.

But what about the untold story? I mean, the one that begins after the fairy lights dim, the last tipsy guest wobbles away, and everyday life tiptoes in? The sequel that never made it to the screen.

Daily tasks arrive not with fanfare but with fatigue. The whims of life test their affection, gradually turning it into irritation. Their bodies, inseparable in another time, now retreat from one another. Without even noticing, loneliness creeps in and nestles into the corners of their hearts. What began as a happy ending no longer resembles one.

It sounds gloomy, I know. Maybe even unfair. And I'm sorry if I've made you frown. It's not my intent to diminish romance. Of course, there are stories that unfold in the opposite direction: unlikely beginnings, two improbable people, and a love that only deepens along the winding, arduous journey. Those stories exist all around us too.

Where am I going with this?

Every story teeters between enchantment and heartbreak, a space where loneliness takes root. It was there, in that very space, I found the cure waiting.

PART I

1990 — 1994

1

RIVER

Fall 1990

M ost memories dulled with time. But some carved themselves deeper, sharper. Brighter, even. Like the day I met her. It wasn't the cinnamon-scented air brushing against the crimson banners, or the rustling leaves twirling across red-brick pathways. It was that I hadn't been looking for her. Or anyone at all. Yet she arrived, unannounced.

UNDER THE AMBER haze of early evening, I strolled through Harvard Yard with Pete. Clusters of students lounged on the lawn, filling the space with the burgeoning energy of a new academic year. In front of the Memorial Church, a small group had gathered, celebrating German reunification with a peaceful song I vaguely recognized but couldn't place. The black, red, and gold of their German flags blended with the trees draped in honey and russet hues.

"Do you think South and North Korea could unify soon, given what's happening in Germany?" Pete asked.

"Unfortunately, I doubt it. The dictatorship in North Korea will do whatever it takes to stay in control."

"That's tough to hear." A slow sigh escaped him. "But I'll hold out hope for peaceful change."

I appreciated his genuine interest in my Korean heritage. I was used to mentioning Korea only to be met with blank stares or the casual lumping together of all Asian nationalities. But he was a refreshing anomaly. His layered grasp of Korean history and the region's intricate geopolitical dynamics stood in stark contrast to the usual indifference I encountered.

Although I had known him for only a few weeks, I had already grown fond of him. When I had first walked into our dorm room in Straus Hall, he had hovered awkwardly behind his parents, who were busy making up his bed. He was of average height, with a cherubic face, blue eyes behind browline glasses, and dirty-blond hair that flopped across his forehead. His T-shirt and jeans paired incongruously with the fancy watch on his wrist, an heirloom I later discovered was worth as much as a sports car.

I introduced myself briefly, not wanting to intrude on the family moment unfolding nearby. As I unpacked my suitcase, I couldn't help but overhear their conversation. His parents explained in detail why he should never mix colored shirts with whites in the laundry—unless, they guffawed, he wanted his white shirt to turn baby blue. He responded with a bellow, arms thrown up, reminding them "for the hundredth time" that he was eighteen. I caught his exasperated glance that seemed to say, *Parents, right?* We shared a brief smile before he turned back to them.

For a moment, I wondered how I would react if my own parents were here with me on Welcome Day. In one sense, I was relieved they weren't here. It gave me a chance to show the other freshman boys I was more mature. Like someone who didn't need hand-holding. But at the same time, I found Pete's interaction with his parents endearing. That easy bickering and banter I wished I had with my own.

Pete Ames came from an affluent, blue-blooded town outside Philadelphia. Yet he lacked the entitlement or prejudice I might have expected from someone with his background. He favored old, frayed T-shirts and sneakers worn down to a dull gray, ignoring the pristine polo shirts and khakis his parents had bought for him. He rarely mentioned his family's wealth. I didn't find out until weeks later—through our dorm proctor—that his grandmother was the heiress to Ames International, one of the oldest and largest privately held companies.

The first few weeks flew by as Pete and I tried to learn the ropes and figure out where we fit in. While there were plenty of social events for freshmen all over campus, he spent most of his time tucked away in our dorm room. At first, I assumed he was uncomfortable around new people, taking longer to adapt to a new environment. Unlike me—who had left South Korea at eleven and spent the last seven years in boarding schools—he had never lived away from home. I could empathize with how overwhelming it might have been to adjust to a communal setting.

But as I got to know him better, I realized he wasn't struggling. He simply cherished solitude. He would return to our room to read, study, or stare out the window for hours, then scribble something in his notebook with a contented smile. I understood the beauty of that tranquility. Years spent alone, far from home, had taught me to treasure it. Before long, I was joining him in those serene stretches of time. In that silence, an unspoken harmony found us. Just a glance and a smile between us, and our connection deepened.

We did talk, though. And whenever we did, we talked like friends who had known each other for years, not just weeks.

One night, we lay in the dark, the silence floating between us.

"Hey, River, are you still awake?"

"Just about," I said, rolling onto my side to face his direction. "What's on your mind?"

"Do you think everything happens for a reason?"

"What do you mean?"

"Like how you and I ended up as roommates, out of all the freshmen. I mean, I'm from Philly; you're from Korea."

"I do wonder if our choices are truly our own. Or just steps we take along a predetermined path. Why do you ask?"

"I feel like we'll be special friends for a very long time. I can't explain why."

"The feeling is mutual. And I can't explain why either."

WHEN PETE and I arrived at Annenberg, the freshman dining hall, we joined a table filled with familiar faces. Most of them were from Phillips Academy, colloquially known as Andover. That year, fifteen of us from Andover found ourselves at Harvard. I hadn't been close to all of them, but four had been part of the tangled, intimate story of my adolescence.

Tom Wood, New England's top tennis player, had been recruited for his blistering serves. Jack Hur, a violin prodigy originally bound for Juilliard, had chosen the academic path instead. Abigail Fields, a debate team legend, had been named "Most Likely to Be the First Female President of America" in the Andover yearbook. And Kate Sawyer, a future Hollywood star, had Broadway credits before freshman orientation. But that evening, someone new sat at the table.

"Everyone, meet Deborah Noe. We go way back. NASA Space Camp, fourth grade!" Tom gestured toward the stranger.

"It's great to meet you all. I'm Deborah from LA," she said, her smile wide and open. She greeted Jack and Kate, seated beside her, with hugs—like old friends reunited after years apart—then waved to Abigail, Pete, and me from across the table.

The introductions passed easily around the table. Each person offered a genial welcome to her, with laughter erupting in response. Then it was my turn. She shifted toward me, an inviting bow forming at the corner of her plush lips. Her deep brown eyes met mine, and in the stretch between heartbeats, I felt unmoored, as though gravity had stepped aside. Time slowed, each second dragging as I searched for the right words. I opened my mouth, but no sound came out. After what felt like ages—and with Pete's subtle nudging—all I managed was "Hi, I'm River Jung . . . from Seoul, Korea," my cheeks burning as the words left my mouth.

"Seoul is on my bucket list. I'd love to visit someday."

"It's . . . quite nice there," I mumbled, the word landing flat and final. My head lowered as the conversation moved on to other topics.

Throughout dinner, I barely touched my food, my senses tethered to her. She dressed more formally than most of us: a navy pencil skirt that fell just below the knee, paired with an alabaster turtleneck. Not LA at all, I thought. Milan, maybe. Slender and assured, she carried herself with a graceful vitality. I pictured her finding freedom in long-distance runs or improvised dance routines. From time to time, she brushed her dark brown hair off her shoulder, discreetly yet with the care of someone tending to something beloved, like a florist adjusting exotic blooms. When she spoke, her voice flowed with a melodic rhythm, each word sprinkled with earnest enthusiasm. She moved through the conversation with effortless charm. Convivial and confident, but never pretentious. Every time she smiled or laughed, her already radiant skin seemed to glow warmer. And in the spell of that laughter, the rest of the room seemed to vanish. All that remained was her, every detail imprinting itself onto my heart.

As the group delved into topics ranging from German reunification to The Game between Harvard and Yale, I felt myself shrinking at the table, unable to form a single word. Every time I glanced at her, my thoughts scattered, the letters of the alphabet jumbled in my head. Flustered, I stood up, interrupting the conversation. "Sorry, I should get going. I'm a bit behind on my math problem set." Pete followed suit, exchanging goodbyes, even though he was only halfway through his plate.

On our way back, I walked faster than usual, with Pete silently keeping pace. I lost all awareness of my surroundings, my mind still replaying the sound of Deborah's laughter. I had no recollection of how I arrived at Straus, as if I had been transported from Annenberg in one large stride.

When we returned to our room, I tumbled onto the bed, letting out a guttural sigh.

"Are you all right?" Pete asked, sitting down at his desk.

"Do you believe in love at first sight?"

"Excuse me?"

"Love at first sight. Do you think it's real?"

"That's random." He raised his eyebrows. "I don't know. I never really thought about it."

"I think I found the one. And I don't even know her."

"You what? Hold on." He got up, raising his palm at me. "You were just talking about your math problem, and now you're telling me you've found *the one*?"

"I know how it sounds. But I've never felt anything like it before."

"Is it who I think it is?" He hesitated, cautiously measuring his words, and in that brief pause, my nerves coiled. "Is it Deborah?"

The moment her name left his mouth, I buried my face in the pillow as a rush of heat swept over me. Instead of responding, I groaned, turning onto my side to meet his gaze.

"So it is Deborah!" He chuckled, stepping back to lean against the desk, arms casually crossed over his chest.

"That obvious?"

"Well, she was the only new factor at dinner. And you were acting weird."

"I didn't mean to. I just felt tongue-tied. Do you think she noticed?"

"She probably thought you were deep in thought over that math problem set. Nothing sexier than a Korean guy lost in calculus, right?"

"Great, just great," I said, scrubbing my hands over my face. "She probably thinks I'm a nerd."

"I doubt it. You've got that suave, movie-star appeal. I've seen girls checking you out all over campus. Being into math just adds to your mystique."

"Is that supposed to make me feel better?"

"Did it?" He winked, seemingly enjoying my discomfort. "So what do you want to do about it?"

His question hung in the air. My history with the opposite sex had been mostly confined to high school flings and casual dates. None of that had prepared me for the intensity of this feeling.

"I don't know. Has anyone ever made you feel this way? Do you have any advice?"

"Sorry, I'm kind of a novice when it comes to romance."

He stepped back, leaving me alone with the tangle of my thoughts, then put on his headphones to listen to Haydn, Schubert, or whichever composer struck his fancy before studying. I tossed and turned in bed, procrastinating on going to Lamont Library to work on my infamous math problem set.

Then, abruptly, he took off his headphones.

"Oh, by the way, Tom seemed to be salivating over Deborah. Granted, he doesn't have your charisma, but you snooze, you lose."

Before I could respond, he put his headphones back on and flashed me a mischievous grin. Though his comment made me want to sink into the floor, it was nice to see him show a lighter side. It made me feel even closer to him.

IN THE FOLLOWING WEEKS, our dinner table resembled a game of musical chairs. Some days, new faces joined us while familiar ones mingled at other tables. Other days, it was mostly our original group. Deborah joined us sporadically, and when she did, she was engaged with others in whatever the topic of the day was. I would wait for the perfect moment to chime in, but by the time I crafted something witty in my head, the conversation would shift to another topic. It felt like I was in a game of double Dutch, ready to leap in yet paralyzed by trepidation of tripping over the rope and derailing the momentum. I didn't want to be the kind of guy who made her think, *Let's not invite him next time.*

This meant I still hadn't talked to her, which only increased Pete's pity for me.

"Time's running out, my friend. She's in high demand."

"I see that," I said, tugging at my hair. "I don't know what's happening to me. I just freeze in front of her, like I've forgotten how to think, talk, or even walk."

Given how little I knew her, I began to question whether I was infatuated with the idea of her more than with the person herself. At eighteen, how could I distinguish projection from something real?

IN JUST A FEW WEEKS, the campus transformed into a majestic quilt of fallen leaves, as if the ground had stolen the trees' finest attire. While most creatures prepared for winter by growing thicker fur, the trees seemed to do the opposite, standing naked, wistfully waiting for their leaves to return.

On Halloween evening, after a dinner tinged with disappointment due to Deborah's absence at Annenberg, Pete and I retreated to our respective sanctuaries—Straus for him and Lamont Library for me. While Pete found his academic cadence in our dorm room, I thrived surrounded by books at the library. My habit of frequenting the library had been solidified during my four years at Andover. Dr. Paul Sinclair, my first-year English teacher, had encouraged me to claim a personal corner at Oliver Wendell Holmes Library. He had advised me to make it a daily ritual, regardless of whether I had work to do. Following that, the library had become my second home on campus.

Naturally, I continued the routine in college, finding my niche in a corner on the second floor at Lamont. Something about the large window beside the desk and the low foot traffic kept drawing me back, between the day's demands and again after sundown. The other regulars respected the pattern and left my desk undisturbed.

Darkness had already cloaked Harvard Yard, save for the streetlamps casting polka-dot patterns on the ground. The brisk air crept in around my exposed neck. As I approached Lamont, I saw a group of students dressed as Star Wars characters, marching toward whatever party they were heading to. I gave a cursory thumbs-up to Darth Vader, who held hands with Princess Leia, and Yoda, who stood at least three inches taller than Chewbacca. During my childhood in Korea, Halloween was an unfamiliar concept, which made it one American tradition I didn't participate in. Yet in that moment, a twinge of regret crept in. Maybe I should have gone to one of the campus parties.

Stepping into the library, the thought faded, overtaken by the warmth of the air and the calming scent of musty books. I brushed my windblown hair from my eyes and scanned the lobby. Then, almost as if life had orchestrated a surprise visit, there she was, emerging from a corner.

Deborah.

The brilliance of her presence knocked the breath out of me. She walked in my direction, her eyes fixed on the book cradled in her arms. Time momentarily slowed to a crawl—before racing ahead frantically. My pulse skipped a beat and my feet stayed rooted in place. Just as I hesitated, she looked up, her eyes meeting mine. A glow spread across her face as she closed the distance between us. I had fantasized about this one-on-one moment ad nauseam. Yet despite all my mental preparation, here I stood with a blank mind.

"River, right?"

"Oh, hi."

"I'm Deborah. We sat at the same table at Annenberg a few times."

"Yes . . . from LA."

"Good memory. Are you on your way out?"

"I just got here. Trying to get some work done."

"On Halloween?"

"Not very Halloween of me, I know."

"You must be one of those overachievers who give Harvard a bad rep."

"No, no. I'm not like that," I said quickly, waving my hand. "I just—"

"I'm just messing with you."

"Oh—okay."

"I'm heading to check out the festivities in Harvard Square. Want to come?"

"Right now?"

"No, in ten years," she replied with a straight face, then dissolved into laughter. "Yes, right now, silly. Come on. Let's go." She walked ahead.

I stood there, caught between desire and apprehension. I hadn't even brushed my teeth after dinner, let alone checked the mirror to see if I looked presentable. I also hadn't armed myself with clever topics or insights that might showcase the intellectual depth to match hers. The thought of her seeing me in this unprepared, unpolished state sent a wave of vertigo through me. But missing any chance to be near her terrified me more. With a quick breath to ground myself, I capitulated, allowing excitement and nerves to propel me into the unknown.

Outside, we walked side by side, neither of us speaking, with only the rustle of fallen leaves underfoot breaking the stillness. The temperature had dropped, but it hardly mattered. Walking next to her sent my internal temperature skyrocketing.

As we entered the square, Halloween lights and decorations greeted us in a sea of coppery sparkles.

"So tell me something," she said, her voice bright.

"Are you supposed to be a cat or a panther?" I pointed to her red headband with two triangular ears perched on top. She wore a black sweater and coat, black pants, and red ballet flats that matched the headband.

"Oh, this?" She tugged at the headband with a teasing smile. "I didn't have time for a proper costume, so I grabbed this little gem at a corner store for two dollars. What do you think?" She paused midstep, clawed the air, and mimicked licking her paw.

"You're purr-fect."

"Purr-fect?" Her eyes met mine for a beat, eyebrows lifting. Regret hit me instantly. Humor had never been my strong suit, yet it often found the worst possible moments to appear. "Wow, didn't see that coming." She covered her mouth to muffle her cackle.

"I'm sorry. I don't know where that came from," I said, rubbing the back of my neck.

"You surprised me, and I like surprises. All right, let me guess what you're dressed as." Her eyes scanned me from head to toe. "A Brooks Brothers mannequin?"

"You got me." I went rigid—neck slightly bent, one arm outstretched—striking a pose like a mannequin.

"Not bad, but you need to stop blinking."

"First day on the job," I said, refraining from blinking. "I'll work on it."

"You'd better. Customers are already fleeing the store!" She gave me a playful shoulder bump.

We wandered through the labyrinthine streets of Cambridge. Our footsteps fell in sync, as if we had found our own rhythm. The easy pace of our walk matched the placid flow of our conversation. With each step on the cobblestones and each line of dialogue exchanged, the anxieties that had clung to me dissolved into the evening air.

She shared the twists and turns of her first month on campus—adjusting to her classes and meeting an array of intriguing personalities. "Did you know we have a classmate who Hula-Hooped for over twenty-four hours straight? With her brother!"

"Now I feel like an underachiever." I grinned. "Did you grow up Hula-Hooping with any siblings?"

"I have two sisters. We were inseparable growing up. Matching Halloween costumes, synchronized dance routines, even a failed coup against our piano teacher. And no, none of us could Hula-Hoop to save our lives."

"The way you talk about your sisters, I can tell how much you love them. They must've shaped a big part of who you are."

"They've always been my best friends. And occasionally, my therapists."

"Where do you fall in the hierarchy?"

"Take a guess."

"I would say . . . oldest?"

She folded her arms, pretending to be offended. "So I give off bossy vibes?"

"Not at all. Quite the opposite. You carry a composed, unassuming confidence. There's an effulgence in you. Something graceful that draws people in and makes them feel safe."

"Effulgence? I haven't heard that word since the SATs. Either you like showing off, or you're a sweet-talker."

"Sorry it came across that way," I said, running my hand through my hair diffidently. "English is my second language. I learned it from literature and academic journals rather than casual conversations. So sometimes, my speech sounds more structured than instinctive. If my wording ever feels formal or peculiar, now you know why. I get a little self-conscious about it."

"It's kind of refreshing, actually. I don't think I've ever met a teenage guy who talks like you. You speak like someone who thinks before they talk. It makes what you say feel real."

I looked at her, disarmed by her warmth. Her words made my heart feel adrift. Like it had slipped free and floated ahead of me. "That means a lot. I've always worried about my English. How I might sound awkward. So, thank you."

"I think we all get self-conscious about something, but sometimes the very thing we try to hide is what makes us uniquely us."

"And yet, we spend so much time trying to conceal the parts of us that others might cherish." I looked down briefly, then back at her. "Okay, circling back—did I get your birth order right?"

"Not even close. I'm the youngest."

"Okay, the conclusion was off, but I stand by my observations."

"Your delivery was convincing. I'll give you that."

"I'll take it." I smiled, grateful. "So—where are your sisters?"

"They both go to Stanford. I almost did too. My dad hoped for a Stanford legacy, but I wanted to blaze my own trail."

"That's impressive. Not everyone has the courage to go against family expectations."

"Well, it's not like I chose not to go to college to start something on my own!"

"Still . . . I find it admirable."

What if she had gone to Stanford? The thought of never having met her sent a shiver through me. It felt like fate. How the paths of two people from different backgrounds had converged, each person making the same decision independently and unknowingly. Was this what Pete had meant when he asked if I believed in things happening for a greater purpose?

"What do you think of the East Coast so far?"

"I really love it. It's a world away from LA. Less diverse, sure, but so much richer in history. And the colors . . ."

"They're breathtaking, aren't they?"

"They're almost surreal! I've never experienced a fall like this before." She slowed her pace, seeming to savor the last few days of fall. We stopped at the traffic light, turning toward each other.

"So, you love the New England fall, but are you ready for a real snowstorm?"

"Believe it or not, I'm kind of excited about my first proper winter." She clapped, her feet bouncing with energy. "One of my favorite movies is *Love Story*. So much snow! It makes the winter in Boston so poignant. Have you seen it? Probably not your typical guy movie, though."

" 'Love means never having to say you're sorry.' How could I forget?"

"You've watched it!" She beamed, placing a hand on her chest. "Remember the scene where Oliver sits alone on the bench after Jenny dies?"

"Yes. I wondered what it would feel like to lose the love of your life that early."

"It would break me," she said, pressing her hand briefly to her cheek. "But I would rather have found my true love, no matter how it ended."

"Me too. Even if only for a day."

My eyes met hers, and for a moment, something in her gaze held me captive, as if she were saying, *I see you. All of you.* I wanted to pull her into my arms right then, but the light turned green, waking me from the world where only the two of us existed. Lacking the courage and the right timing, I steered the conversation somewhere safer as we crossed the street, surrounded by throngs of costumed students. "By the way, you said *Love Story* isn't a guy movie, but it's one of my favorites, too. I hope you're not judging my masculinity."

"Of course not. Who gets to decide what's masculine or feminine, anyway?" Her smile returned and lit up her face. "Now, your turn."

"Sorry?"

"I feel like I've been talking this whole time. Tell me who you are. You got thirty seconds. Go!" She pointed at me with her index finger, like a drill sergeant issuing commands.

"Who am I?" I fiddled with the strap of my backpack, stalling as I thought of how to answer. "Let's see . . . I grew up in Korea as an only child. I've always been quiet by nature, but endlessly curious, often driving my parents crazy with philosophical questions about life. They used to call me an old soul."

"An old soul . . . it fits you," she said but didn't explain further. "Did they spoil you since you were the only child? I used to envy my friends who didn't have siblings. No hand-me-downs!"

"My mother, maybe, but I promise, I'm not a mama's boy. As for my father, he was barely around. He runs a beverage production and distribution company called SOL in Korea. It's a family business he inherited from my grandfather. Work kept him away, long hours, constant travel. And when he was home . . . my parents fought." I rarely divulged the darker parts of my past, especially with someone I was so eager to impress. Yet, to my surprise, the unfiltered words tumbled out. "When I was eleven, my parents decided to send me to a junior boarding school in America. My father had big plans for me to eventually take over the family business. He wanted me to study and gain experience in the US so that I could help grow SOL into an international player in the future. But part of me wonders if it was less about the education and more about getting me away from their fighting. Perhaps it was both," I said, my gaze drifting toward the distant skyline.

"And?"

"Well, that's how I came to Boston. I spent three years at Fay and another four at Andover. And now here I am, studying economics." I stopped walking and turned to her, sensing I hadn't quite satisfied her question. "Did I miss something?"

"Yes! You came to America all by yourself when you were eleven. That's extraordinary. There must've been a million amazing stories between then and now. Epic adventures, culture clashes, lost in translation! Yet you've just glossed over them all."

"I thought you asked me to give you a thirty-second elevator pitch, not a documentary."

"Mister, that was definitely longer than thirty seconds. But . . ." She tapped her chin. "I'll admit it worked. Color me intrigued."

"So am I off the hook?"

"Not yet. Wait." She pulled up her coat sleeve to check the time on her watch. "Oh no. It's past ten. My friends are probably wondering where I disappeared to. I should get back."

"May I walk you back?"

"Only if you can keep up with me. I used to be a cross-country runner in high school." With a hint of challenge, she walked briskly.

"Four years on the varsity soccer and lacrosse teams at Andover." I caught up to her and even walked past. Then, without warning, she broke into a run, her red headband held tightly in her hand to keep it from falling. I chased after her, wearing the biggest smile of my life.

The next day, I looked for her all day—outside lecture halls, by the library steps, across crowded courtyards—like a daisy waiting for the sun to rise. But it wasn't until dinner at Annenberg that I finally saw her. The moment she came into view, I released the breath I had been holding all day. She glanced up, caught my eye, and gave a quick wave before returning to her conversation.

I hovered in place, torn about what to do next. Maybe I could casually squeeze into the seat near her. But the idea felt uncharacteristically reckless. The thought of her discomfort—the tension in her

features as others gawked and spun theories about my intentions—
sent a shudder through me. Or maybe I would play it cool, as though
last night's walk had been entirely incidental, devoid of deeper meaning. Back in high school, guys swore by "playing hard to get." But I
couldn't bring myself to pull that kind of posturing with her. She
deserved an act of valor.

Maybe there was a middle ground. A way to show her she was on
my mind without causing a scene. I settled at the edge of the table,
making sure she had an unobstructed view of me. Every few minutes,
I stole glances in her direction, hoping she would notice. But she
seemed lost in her own world, chatting and laughing with her
friends. After about fifteen minutes, she stood up, picked up her tray,
and left with her friends without a backward glance.

Having lost my appetite, I returned to Lamont and found myself
unable to sit still at my desk. I kept getting up, going downstairs, and
lingering in the lobby every thirty minutes or so, hoping to see the
voluminous dark-brown hair bouncing through the hallway. But she
was nowhere to be found. As I walked back to Straus that night, I felt
like one of the empty benches in the Yard, stuck in place, waiting for
someone that might not come. The hard truth was I couldn't
complain about things not happening when I hadn't even tried to
make them happen.

On Saturday, Pete headed to Greenwich for his uncle's seventieth
birthday. He had invited me along, but I wasn't keen on being the
only outsider at a family gathering.

That evening, for the first time since school had begun, I found
myself alone in my room, lying wide awake in bed. I tuned the
tabletop radio to WHRB, the Harvard student-run station. The faint
crackle of the radio evoked the afterglow of a fireplace. The nostalgic
tones of Frank Sinatra's "The Way You Look Tonight" filled the air.
With each note of the song, my thoughts drifted to Deborah's eyes
shining like the thousands of stars outside my window. I imagined

myself sprinting to her dorm, calling out her name with a voice that echoed through the courtyard—serenading her with the song as she peeked out the window. If only I could sing like Frank Sinatra. But even if I had his voice, would I go through with it?

Before college, while my friends had been absorbed in video games and parties, I had secretly devoured romance novels. I had kept this indulgence hidden. After all, I'd had a reputation to uphold as a fearless striker on my soccer team. Despite this, I couldn't get enough of the undeniable chemistry between lovers, the inventive— if sometimes corny—tropes, and the thrill of plot twists, even when predictable. These stories stretched my imagination and filled me with emotions that real life rarely stirred. I longed to live like those characters. Yet as my timidness around Deborah showed, living my own life like a romance novel proved to be a far greater challenge. Was it the fear of rejection, the desire to appear perfect in her eyes, or the insecurity that she was out of my league? Perhaps it was all of these.

EARLY SUNDAY MORNING, I went for a run along the Charles River. I had a love-hate relationship with running, despite playing sports throughout my boarding school years. I dreaded putting on my shoes and stepping out the door. Yet I craved the feeling of accomplishment, the calm and clarity that settled in my mind afterward. It was ironic how the hardest things to start often brought the deepest satisfaction, while the easiest pleasures gave way to emptiness once they ended.

The chilly morning air seeped through my T-shirt, but after half a mile or so, the exertion warmed my body. When I reached the Cambridge Street Bridge, about two miles in, I turned back toward campus. More runners had joined the trail by then, and a mutual camaraderie seemed to pass between us—simple nods of acknowledgment for resisting the comfort of a bed on a Sunday.

With about a mile left to Weld Boathouse—a familiar landmark signaling my return to Harvard Square—I heard a voice: "Too slow." It was the voice I had been desperate to hear every waking moment, the sound that made my knees buckle with its mere presence. Deborah appeared out of nowhere, like a sunrise fairy, and ran past me as if I were standing still. She didn't slow down until she had put about fifty yards between us.

"You weren't kidding when you said you were fast." I gasped for air as I caught up to her.

"What happened to all that soccer and lacrosse training at Andover?"

"I guess I'm having a slice of humble pie for breakfast."

We ran back to campus, basking in a comfortable silence. My tired legs surged with renewed energy, as though her presence alone had the power to revive me. If she was enjoying my company even half as much as I was enjoying hers, I would consider that a win.

We stretched for a few minutes in front of her dorm, Hollis Hall. After finishing, she stole a quick glance at her watch. "I'd better head inside. It was nice running into you!" She saluted and walked toward the building.

I watched her silhouette shrink with every step. I wished time would slow, just long enough for her to stay in view. But hadn't I been wishing all along? Wishes alone wouldn't change anything.

"Deborah!" I called out impulsively just as she was about to step inside.

She turned to face me, her hand lingering on the door handle.

"There is a cozy brunch place near Quincy Market."

"And?"

"They make corned beef hash from scratch."

"Okay . . . ?" She tapped the doorknob lightly with her fingers.

"Their eggs Benedict is also scrumptious. I don't know what your schedule is this morning—"

"You got me at eggs Benedict. Meet me here in thirty minutes." She turned and walked into Hollis without another word. But as she did, I caught the faintest hint of a grin. I buried my hands in my hair, trying to process what had just happened. Had I just asked her out? I stood, momentarily stunned yet also relieved and a little proud. Then I scampered, with my arms pumping. But suddenly self-conscious, I halted and glanced up at the windows in Hollis, praying she hadn't witnessed my impromptu solo performance.

DEBORAH EPITOMIZED the essence of fall in Boston. Draped in an ivory crewneck sweater and a camel coat, she exuded timeless elegance. She had a knack for blending classic and contemporary elements, often pairing natural-toned outfits with bold accents—gold jewelry, colorful bracelets, a flash of red on her lips. She carried a tote bag or a handbag, never a backpack. Her footwear choices were equally distinctive, favoring ornate pumps or boots over sneakers. In many ways, her fashion sense reflected her personality: ebullient, expressive, and independent.

Standing next to her on the Red Line T, I treasured the smallest nuances she revealed during our conversation. The way her lips turned up at the corners when she described her roommate, Amy Sanz, who played cello in the orchestra. The way she moved her hand, as though sketching out an invisible diagram, while explaining cellular metabolism. And the way her shoulders shook with laughter every time the train jolted to a stop and our bodies collided together. Each time that happened, I had to resist the urge to hold her and never let her go.

By the time we arrived, the restaurant was already buzzing. Established in the sixties, it had retained much of its original charm, with rustic maple planks on the ceiling and walls that had weathered the decades in a way no modern craftsmanship could replicate.

As we settled into our seats, a waitress in her fifties approached with a carafe of freshly brewed coffee. "Coffee?" she asked, her raspy voice the product of too many cigarettes and years of raising her voice over noisy diners.

"Yes, please!" Deborah said, overjoyed. She stirred two sugar packets and two creamers into her coffee, then, with a delicate exhale, blew across the surface to cool it. "No coffee?"

"No, I don't do well with caffeine. It makes me feel jittery."

"So what do you drink in the morning?"

"I enjoy drinking skim milk."

"You 'enjoy' skim milk?" Her fingers made air quotes around the word *enjoy*.

"I am drawn to its subtlety." I meant it as a lighthearted deflection, but the blush spreading across my face betrayed me. Here was Deborah, a woman of sophistication who likely understood the intricacies of bean varieties. And here I was, proudly boasting about my lactose tolerance. As I started sinking deeper into this absurd sense of inadequacy, the waitress returned, offering a welcome reprieve from my nameless crisis.

"Do you lovebirds know what you want?" She looked at each of us in turn.

Lovebirds? I let out a nervous laugh but didn't correct her.

"I'll have your eggs Benedict. I've heard amazing things!" Deborah said without even bothering to look at the menu.

"It's divine!" the waitress said, fluttering her eyelids before turning to me.

"May I please have corned beef hash with poached eggs?"

"Another excellent choice!" As the waitress collected the menus, she said unprompted, "I've seen a lot of couples over the years, but there's something special about the two of you. I predict a long future together!"

Deborah's lips parted in surprise, then curved into a half smile. When I let out a quick chuckle, she joined in with a stifled laugh, covering her mouth with the back of her hand. Strangely, though, the waitress's exuberant assumption filled me with an unexpected sense of pride. Was this how I would feel if we *were* lovers and a stranger complimented how great we looked as a couple?

Deborah took a sip of water, eyes still glinting from the laugh, then met my gaze. "Do you want to pick up where you left off the other day?"

I was more interested in hearing her story, but I suspected she wasn't letting me off that easily. "Any specific era or event you want me to cover?"

She rested her finger on her lips before leaning in to whisper a suggestion. "Tell me about your first kiss, using the five W's—who, what, where, when, and why."

I searched her face, trying to gauge her seriousness.

She gave a mischievous smile, undeterred.

"I thought you would ask me about something more benign. Like my favorite food."

"That comes after the kiss. Priorities."

"Right . . . well, here is the thing . . . my first kiss was with six girls."

"Six girls?" she shrieked. "I didn't ask how many girls you've kissed. And even if that was my question, that seems like a lot for your age. What are you? Casanova?" There was a flicker of astonishment in her eyes but also something else I couldn't quite place. Impishness? Disappointment?

"I heard you right. Please bear with me, as it requires some explanation." I cleared my throat. "During the summer of 1989, I volunteered in Jamaica after Hurricane Gilbert had devastated the island."

"I remember seeing all the pictures of the damage. It was horrifying. But I'm impressed. I didn't realize a New England preppy would be into humanitarian work."

"To be honest, I had originally signed up because I needed more community service to enhance my college applications. But upon arrival, witnessing the destruction to the infrastructure and the pain of Jamaicans humbled me. Volunteers were there out of an altruistic desire to help, unlike me, whose motivation was self-serving. I felt like a fraud. But I worked extra hard to make up for it, taking on tasks even the most dedicated volunteers tended to avoid. Typically anything to do with the sewer system or temporary toilets. They would say, 'Give it to River. He'll do anything.' After that, I felt I had earned the badge . . ." I paused, glancing up at her. "Am I boring you?"

"No. I was expecting a drunken kissing scene, but this is surprisingly riveting so far. And you know I love surprises."

In that moment, the waitress returned with a big tray. I had forgotten how starving I was after the early-morning run. We dug into our food as if we had just completed a weekend-long fast.

Deborah took her first bite of eggs Benedict. "Oh my, this is heavenly!" She took another bite, humming softly, her eyes closing in delight. From what I had observed each time I sat nearby her at Annenberg, she had a knack for making even the simplest dishes seem piquant. She could relish a piece of toast, elevating it to the status of a delicacy. "So keep going. I'm patiently waiting for the kiss scene."

"It's coming. I'm saving the best for last," I said, reaching for a napkin to wipe my mouth. "After long days of work, volunteers would gather around the campfire in the evenings, chatting until we gradually disappeared into our tents. One night the group discovered that I had never kissed a girl before. They found it fascinating, like I was an extinct animal . . ." I trailed off, suddenly hesitant, unsure if I wanted to share this with her.

"Go on," she said, as if she had heard the voice inside my head. "Don't leave me hanging."

I exhaled, then leaned in. "That night, just as I was about to sleep in my tiny tent, a French college girl urged me to come outside. Thinking something had happened, I rushed out. When I asked what was wrong, she told me to follow. I did and found five more college girls waiting at the campfire."

"Seriously?"

"Seriously."

"Then what?"

"The six girls circled around me, placing me in the center. Without a word, the girl from France, who seemed to have orchestrated this whole shenanigan, stepped forward with a piece of black cloth and blindfolded me." I drew out the suspense, watching as Deborah's lips formed a perfect O. "A few seconds later, I felt a pair of lips on mine. Then another pair of lips, and another, until all six pairs had touched mine. When it was over, the French girl removed the blindfold. She returned to her place in the circle and kissed the girl next to her. One by one, the other girls followed suit. After the last kiss, she said, 'You may go now.' "

"Scandalous!" Her hand flew to her mouth, a gasp escaping her lips. "Was this some kind of voodoo French ceremony? Or did you just make that up?"

"I would never lie to you. Interestingly, the next day they all acted as if nothing had happened. Like it was just a dream." I leaned back with a slight smile, relieved to have made it through the story.

"Oh my, look at that huge grin on your face. You enjoyed it that much?"

"Not exactly, but I did get a rush of ecstasy."

"A rush of ecstasy?" Her eyes narrowed. "You really do have a way with words. Only you'd describe a first kiss like a literary event."

"But to be frank, I was also disappointed. I had been saving my first kiss for someone special."

"You don't have to pretend to be a hopeless romantic with me. Just own it. You're a player." She shook her head before sipping her now-lukewarm coffee.

As I stared at her lips grazing the edge of the mug, a spark of intrigue stirred in me. Who stole her first kiss? Would I be jealous? Oscillating between curiosity and hesitation, I couldn't resist the urge.

"And you? What about your first kiss?"

"My story is so tame compared to yours. I dated a senior when I was a sophomore. He asked me to his senior prom, and I was the only sophomore girl invited. In my naivete, I felt flattered. After the prom, there was a tradition where all prom attendees would run to the pool and dive in. So my prom date and I jumped into the pool, holding hands. When we emerged from the water, he held my face and kissed me." Her cheeks blushed.

"That's how I would've liked my first kiss to be."

"Trust me. You wouldn't have. Walking to the sundae shop in a dripping wet dress afterward was anything but romantic. I looked like a disgraced mermaid!"

AS WE STEPPED out of the restaurant, I realized what had held me back in the past weeks: overthinking and putting too much pressure on myself to impress her. Each risk I took—asking her to breakfast, sharing the story of my aberrant first kiss—gave me a rewarding sense of assurance. I found myself becoming more authentic, engaging with her naturally. This newfound confidence led me to propose a change of plans. Instead of heading back to Cambridge, I suggested we stroll to Boston Common and Newbury Street. Her enthusiastic "Yes!" was all the encouragement I needed.

It turned out to be an unseasonably warm November day, though a bit overcast. Most of the leaves had fallen, but a few clung stubbornly to the branches. They shuddered with each passing breeze, one that carried the scent of Lancôme Trésor, the perfume she wore. I had first encountered it at the duty-free shop in Gimpo Airport. Its distinctive bottle shape and elegant notes of rose, lilac, and peach had etched into my memory. Something about that scent had the power to fly me through memory, then return me to the now.

While sauntering through the Common, she seemed fully immersed in the present moment. The brownstones along Beacon Street, a family of ducklings browsing the ground of the Public Garden, and toddlers toppling over picnic blankets—all seemed to fade into a backdrop of contentment around her.

"You seem so sanguine. The stress of life doesn't seem to affect you. What's your secret?" I asked.

She let a few steps pass before responding. "There's no secret. What I love most about life is its unpredictability. It keeps me guessing and anticipating."

"I struggle with unpredictability. I crave control."

"I hear you. Control feels safe. But maybe unpredictability unsettles you because it asks you to trust that you're enough."

"I'm enough?"

"Yes. Wherever life takes you, trust that everything you need is already within you."

"But there's still so much I want to improve. So many ways I could grow into a better version of myself."

"Wanting to grow isn't the opposite of trusting yourself. I think real growth begins the moment you embrace who you already are."

I reflected on her words. I didn't fully understand them, but they seemed to come from somewhere deep—somewhere untainted. Like the center of her heart. "If you've made peace with life's unpredictability, where do you think it's taking you?"

"You mean what I want to be when I grow up?"

"Yes. Even knowing not everything goes to plan."

"Well, my dreams have changed a lot over the years. Including wanting to be a tangerine when I was four."

"As in ... the fruit?"

"It's the cutest fruit!" she said, giving me a playful look. "But seriously, I thought of being a diplomat, a secret spy, maybe even a politician. Anything to make the world better. Eventually, I realized that being a doctor would let me make a real, immediate difference. After college, I plan to go to medical school. Still undecided between surgery and psychiatry. One heals the body, the other the mind."

"You would be a wonderful doctor."

"You think so?" She slowed her pace just enough to wait for my answer.

"Without a doubt. You have this special gift of making a person feel seen and heard. I've observed how people feel at ease when they're with you. They share their thoughts willingly even without you asking. It's your superpower, your magic touch."

"Are you trying to flatter me again? Do you talk like that to every girl?"

"No, I mean it. I wouldn't say something I didn't believe."

"All right, I'll take the compliment. But if I could choose anything in the world, I'd be a jazz singer, performing on a local stage where the audience feels close. Like old friends."

"What's holding you back? Can you still go for it?"

"Oh, I tried. School plays, musicals . . . I was all in. But let's just say my enthusiasm far exceeded my talent."

"I'm sure you're the kind of singer who takes the audience's breath away. I would love to hear you sing sometime."

"Not unless it's your dying wish!"

WE LEFT the garden and headed toward the crowded Newbury Street, where *real* couples meandered hand in hand. In their eyes, what did Deborah and I look like—lovers, friends, something in between?

"Come with me!" She gestured for me to follow as she led the way into a nearby store. Inside, her eyes drifted over the hats, each a burst of color, from burnt orange to ocean blue to basalt black. Her fingers traced their shapes, brushing over wide brims and tall, pointed peaks. She picked an oatmeal-colored merino beanie from a rack adorned with ten or so other colors.

"What do you think?" She placed it over her satiny hair and posed in front of me. The beanie accentuated the depth of her eyes, pulling me in like magnets. Her lips, lush and sumptuous, seemed to glow with a richer shade of red. I couldn't tear my eyes away from her, completely entranced.

"You look resplendent," I said.

Her eyes widened before she quickly looked away. "You and your vocabulary," she whispered under her breath, a faint flush creeping across her cheeks. She took off the beanie, put it back, and headed for the door. "Let's go before I end up spending hours in here."

When she walked out of the store, I grabbed the beanie and went to the counter. I paid quickly and darted outside. Scanning the bustling street, I spotted her browsing a display in front of the clothing store next door.

"Sorry for the wait."

"There you are." She turned, and her gaze dropped to what I was holding. "Did you buy something?"

"For you." I handed her the bag. "It's going to get much colder soon."

She was quiet for a moment, eyes fixed on the gift. "For me?" Her face lit up, a bashful grin spreading. She pulled out the beanie and ran her fingers over the delicate fabric. "How did you . . ."

Without another word, she wrapped her arms around me, and my heart lurched forward. My hands hovered for a moment before settling on her back. Was there proper etiquette for how long a hug should last or how tightly I could hold her? I didn't care. I held her close for as long as she allowed, cherishing the softness of her hair against my chin and the way her body fit snugly with mine. Like two long-lost gloves finally reunited.

After a few moments, she pulled away abruptly. I could hardly bring myself to make eye contact after letting myself get so wrapped up in our closeness. Did it even mean as much to her? Should I have been bolder, dared to kiss her instead of just hugging? It would've been the perfect first kiss in the middle of idyllic Newbury Street, just as I had read about in romance novels. Instead, I gestured to the pathway, and we resumed our walk.

BY THE TIME we returned to campus, it was almost three. We found ourselves standing in front of Hollis, facing each other.

"Thanks again for the brunch and the beanie." She looked into my eyes, seemingly expecting me to say something. Perhaps something unexpected, given her penchant for surprises.

I searched for the right words, sifting through an imaginary dictionary, but all I found was the quickening of my pulse.

"All right, I should get going." She let out a small sigh, her smile fading. "Don't expect me to show up at your room with European girls tonight."

She gave me a quick hug before walking toward her dorm. I wavered, but as she reached for the key in her bag, I impetuously dashed over and grasped her hand. Startled, she turned back to me. Without waiting for a response, I pulled her into a tight embrace. To my relief, she didn't resist the sudden gesture. Unsure of what to do next, I leaned in to kiss her forehead. But in my clumsy haste, I miscalculated the distance, and my lips landed on her eyebrow instead.

I froze, my eyes wide in disbelief. The heat surged through me, like I was trapped beneath an unforgiving blaze. Without daring to attempt a second try, I turned and bolted away. Each step felt like an escape from a prison of my own embarrassment, the ground beneath me sinking as I sprinted toward Straus. Life had handed me a gift and I flinched.

THE ANTICIPATION of seeing Deborah again at Annenberg that evening filled me with both excitement and dread, my heart fluttering like a hummingbird's wings. Had I made her uncomfortable? Had I tarnished something budding between us? At one point, I almost turned around, considering skipping dinner altogether. But my analysis paralysis was pointless, as she never showed up. Despite my initial relief over not having to encounter her, dismay crept in with the realization that I would have to face these feelings again the next day.

After dinner, I headed to Lamont. I had finished all my work, but I still craved a space to steady the unshakable thoughts circling my mind. As I walked across the Yard, the distance to Lamont seemed to grow with each step. What a difference a few hours made. I had barely felt any fatigue after taking more than ten thousand steps around Boston with Deborah. Now, each step dragged like I was carrying boulders.

The library swarmed with students catching up on work. Their furrowed brows and skin dotted with beads of perspiration reflected the regret of weekend indulgence and procrastination. I reached my unofficially designated desk on the second floor. It was just as I had left, except for a small, old book claiming the center: *The Art of Love*, by Ovid. Someone must have left it behind after reading. I glanced around, but the only movement was pens dragging, pages turning, chairs creaking. When I picked it up to move it aside, a white envelope fell out. To my surprise, it was addressed to me. I unfolded the paper to find a letter written in cursive, the handwriting a juxtaposition of confident strokes and shapely curves.

I saw this book at a used bookstore and thought of you. —Deborah.

As I read the note, I felt like an orchestra percussionist who had just missed his cue at the most crucial moment. She had been here all along, while I had been foolishly waiting for her at Annenberg. I stared at her handwriting and reread the line. My mind spun with a hundred questions. Without a single answer, I put the book in my backpack and ran. Through the corridors, down the stairs, through the lobby, and outside. I didn't know what I was doing, but I knew where I needed to be.

When I arrived at Hollis, the old crimson brick building glowed, bathed in marigold light spilling from every window. She had to be in there. I stepped up to the door and reached for the handle. It was locked. I rattled it once, then again, but it wouldn't budge. I leaned in and pressed my ear to the wood, listening for footsteps. But there was only silence. I looked up again. Any one of those windows could've been Deborah's. Desperate, I shouted, "Deborah," but my voice cracked, barely audible. I tried again, this time filling my lungs with air. Louder, more forceful. "Deborah!"

My voice bounced off the building, cutting through the night. Soon, a second-floor window creaked open, and a girl in a bathrobe leaned out, gripping a hair dryer like a makeshift megaphone. I recognized her from campus but couldn't recall her name.

"What's going on here?" she called out, her voice sharp and demanding.

"Hi, I'm looking for Deborah."

She squinted down at me, her expression shifting as recognition flickered across her face. "Ah, the eyebrow guy!" she said, giggling.

I blinked and reached up to my brow. Then the memory snapped into place—*of course*. The blunder. Embarrassment surged through me all over again. I could turn away now, pretend this never happened. But I had already missed too many chances.

"Yes, that's me. Could you please ask Deborah to come down?"

"Before I help you, I need to know why. Enlighten me!" Her voice rang out across the courtyard, further pulling at the seams of my restraint.

More windows opened, and curious faces peered out. The scene quickly resembled a circus, with children eagerly awaiting the spectacle. Finally, I spotted Deborah's face at a window on the third floor. Standing beside her, tugging at her sleeve, was a girl who had to be Amy, her roommate. Had she been there all along, hidden from the commotion below?

The girl in the bathrobe followed my gaze and let out a dramatic gasp. "Speak of the devil—there she is." She leaned farther out the window, pointing the hair dryer upward. "Hey, Deborah! Guess who's out here asking for you!"

Deborah stepped closer to the window, squinting down into the courtyard like she wasn't sure whether to laugh or call campus security. Then she cupped her hands around her mouth. "River, what are you doing out there?"

"Hi, Deborah."

"You know there's a door, right?"

"It's locked. Could you come down?"

"I'm in my pajamas."

"Just for a minute? Please?"

"What is this about?"

"I have something important to tell you."

"Like what?"

Nosy faces turned, heads bobbing like spectators at a ping-pong match, following our voices as they ricocheted off the brick walls.

"I would prefer to tell you in private."

"You've got an audience here. Don't leave them hanging."

"It won't take long."

"Then just say it!"

I glanced down at my feet, let out a deep sigh, and looked back up at her window. She leaned slightly over the windowsill, patient but expectant. Was I ready to cross a line where my heart would have nowhere left to hide? It was now or never. Go big or go home.

One, two, three...

The timeless melody of "The Way You Look Tonight" flowed through me as I channeled my inner Frank Sinatra. I sang of admiration, of the beauty in seeing her in the simplest of moments. My voice trembled, a ghastly quiver escaping my lips. My hands dithered around my body, not knowing their proper position. But I continued singing into the darkness, lost in the moment. As the final notes of the song faded into the night, a sharp whistle jolted me back to reality. The courtyard reverberated with the sound of clapping and enthusiastic cries of "Encore!"

Did I really just do that? A wave of mortification washed over me. The fight-or-flight instinct lit up inside me. And flight didn't hesitate. I had barely spun around to make my escape when a door creaked open behind me and closed with a faint thud.

"River, wait!"

I turned to find Deborah ambling toward me, her coat draped over her pajamas. In that instant, the unfolding scene seemed to swallow the murmurs of the rubberneckers from Hollis, transforming the courtyard into a soundproof room. She stopped about a foot away and studied my eyes. Her face was inscrutable, a blank canvas showing neither smile nor frown. I averted my eyes from hers, still stinging from my daft performance in front of her dormmates.

"That was unorthodox," she said.

"Sorry, I didn't mean to embarrass you." I exhaled deeply, startled by how long I had been holding my breath. "I got the book you left for me at Lamont. I wanted to thank you in person."

"You couldn't wait until tomorrow?"

"I could have, but . . . there's something else I wanted to say. I was afraid I might not have the courage by morning if I didn't say it tonight."

"What is it?"

I glanced up at the night sky, recalling the words I had rehearsed so many times, before returning to her. "Deborah . . ." Gently, I reached out, taking her hands in mine, their warmth a comforting contrast to the cool evening air.

"Your eyes . . . deep oceans I would dive into. Your hair . . . soft cashmere wrapping me in its embrace. Your lips . . . a haven for my soul. And your nose . . . your nose . . ." I mumbled, my mind drawing a blank mid-sentence.

Her expression shifted, one eyebrow arching.

The words I had rehearsed unraveled in an instant, scattered by nerves and the weight of her gaze. This wasn't how I had imagined it. Certainly not like this, with my carefully written lines abandoning me at the crucial moment. Now, all that remained was my bare heart —unfiltered, unpolished.

"Sorry," I murmured, a flush creeping up my neck. "Please let me start over."

Her lips pressed together, somewhere between a smile and a sigh, like she was still deciding what to make of me. Then she whispered, "Go on."

I forced my breathing to steady, though the tremor in my chest betrayed me. "Something—I'm not sure what exactly—but something shifted the day I met you. Since then, time slows down when you're near. Yet in that pause, the world transforms. More alive, more vibrant . . . just more everything. And somewhere . . . somewhere, there's music playing in the background. My steps feel light, like I'm tap dancing, even though I've never learned how. All these beautiful words—the ones you would tease me for as 'SAT words'—tumble out in a rush to wave at you. I whistle. I hum. I don't recognize myself anymore. And oddly enough, I don't mind. In fact, I think I like this new version . . ."

I faltered, heart thudding, watching her face for any sign I hadn't already lost her. But she didn't look away. So I kept going.

"When I'm away from you, time thickens. But it's a different kind of slow. Minutes dragging into hours, hours dissolving into days. Every sound, every taste, every touch disappears, as if I forget how to feel without you. A day without seeing you, I'm just a body. Cells, molecules, atoms. I don't know . . . I wither inside."

My hands clutched hers as the words spilled out uncontrollably. Her eyes, wide and glimmering, flickered with surprise before softening into something gentler—something like tenderness.

"Do you know? You're the last thought in my mind before I close my eyes, and the first when I wake up. Sometimes, you're there even before I open them. I'm still trying to understand what it all means. But somewhere between the elation of being near you and the ache of missing you, I've been reborn, rediscovering everything about life. I want to be with you and feel this way every day. That's what my heart tells me. And . . . I would like one more shot at my first kiss. Not the voodoo circle I got lured into. Not the gaffe with your eyebrow. A proper kiss."

She parted her lips, as if to speak, but instead, she closed her eyes. I hesitated, then held her in my arms, breathing in her scent of Trésor, lavender, and evening dew. I ran my fingers through her hair and caressed her cheeks. I cupped her chin with both hands, delicately, as if the slightest pressure might vaporize her.

At last, I kissed her. The instant our lips touched, all my senses exploded like fireworks—ferocious, electrifying, teasing, tingling. Sensations I never knew were mine flooded through me, all of it overwhelming in the most delicious and addictive way. When I finally pulled away from the spark, she kept her eyes closed, as if she were still somewhere else, not quite back yet. Then, slowly, she opened them—those eyes I lost myself in. She looked at me for what felt like the entire time between our first meeting and now, folded into a single, fated second.

"What took you so long?" she said, reaching up to hold my burning face. Her face drew closer, her wispy breath brushing my skin. She held her face just an inch from mine for a second. Then she kissed me back. This time, instead of an intense jolt, the world floated. Weightless, like I was drifting on clouds woven from the softest goose feathers.

We stood in the middle of the courtyard, ignoring the sound of oohs and aahs from Hollis, kissing, and caressing under the moonlight.

2

RIVER

Winter 1990–Winter 1993

Although I had been trained as a debater in school, I struggled to answer questions like, "What's your favorite . . . anything?" They felt too neat, too final, in a life that thrived on messiness, contradiction, and restlessness. My answers shifted like tides. And I often forgot what I had once said. Which made it all the more difficult to choose the one moment I kept returning to, even years later.

WHAT ABOUT THE first time we made love?

The night before our first winter break, Deborah invited me over —or maybe I invited myself—to her room in Hollis. Amy had flown home the previous day, which meant Deborah had the room to herself for one last night before heading back to LA the next morning.

Earlier that evening, Pete had given me a sly grin. "Should I not wait up tonight?"

His teasing threw me off. I stumbled over my words, my face flushing burgundy. "We're just hanging out."

"Sure." He pretended to zip his lips.

On the walk over, my mind swirled—anxious, excited, unsure of what might unfold. But when I spotted her waiting in front of Hollis, a calm washed over me.

"I missed you," I said, stealing a quick kiss.

"We just saw each other like an hour ago at dinner."

"One hour is an agonizingly long time to be away from you."

She laughed under her breath and held the door open. But her smile vanished in a blush when a group of girls walked out, one of them whistling, "Ooh, someone's got a secret!"

Deborah rolled her eyes before slipping her hand into mine and pulling me inside. "Hurry, before the audience returns." We sprinted like lecherous teenagers, suppressing laughs, up the stairs and down the hallway. As soon as we stepped into her room, she placed a hand over her heart.

"Why did that feel like a heist?" A laugh fluttered out. "Well, welcome to the tiniest penthouse!" She swept her arm dramatically around the room.

Her room was even smaller than the one Pete and I shared. In a seemingly miraculous feat, matching beds, desks, and closet spaces filled every inch of the cramped room. Two iconic Gustav Klimt posters graced Deborah's side of the room: *The Kiss* and *Lady with a Fan*. On Amy's wall, Polaroid pictures from high school days were tacked in a row. The rest of the room, though, felt stripped back, as if the limited space discouraged any attempt at further decoration. At least the floral scent was a welcome change from the pungent odor of gym socks in the guys' rooms I was accustomed to.

With no sitting area, we perched on the edge of her twin bed, making casual conversation, from Amy's unmatched talent for making her bed to Deborah's struggle to pick just ten cassette tapes when packing for college. I rose and approached the shelf, curious to get a better sense of her taste in music.

"New Kids On The Block?"

"Hey, don't judge. Every genre has its charm."

"I was actually going to say I like them too."

"Do you really?"

"They're great. Don't judge."

"Who's your favorite New Kid, then?"

"I go back and forth between Donnie Wahlberg and Jordan Knight."

She raised an eyebrow. "I was testing you. Thought you were just humoring me. But turns out you actually know your stuff."

"Do I get an A?"

"The test isn't over."

"There's more?"

"Wait and see." She grinned, picked up another tape, and slid it into the boom box. A few mechanical clicks, then Billie Holiday's soulful voice filled the room.

While she adjusted the volume, I wandered over to the window. The glass felt cold against my fingertips as I leaned forward, gazing out at the inky courtyard below. Not long ago, I had stood there, pouring my heart into a love song, my imperfect notes resonating in the cool air, while Deborah had observed from this spot. Where had that boldness come from? A shiver coursed through me at the embarrassment. Still, it had brought me to this moment.

She came up behind me, wrapping her arms around my waist and resting her head on my back. "What's in that brilliant mind of yours?" she whispered. "Lie down with me, and bewitch me with the English you learned from romance novels."

She took my hand, giving a slight tug. My heart lifted as I followed. She lay down first, tapping the spot next to her. I joined her and rested my head on half of the pillow, adjusting my position a few times. She pulled me in closer, even though we were already so near. Her calming scent lingered in the fabric between us, wrapping around me and slowing my pulse. With our cheeks so close, I could almost feel the zephyr from her blinking, the faint rustle of her long eyelashes brushing with each flutter. For a moment, I was no longer in a dorm room but beside an oasis, the tranquil sound of waves lapping against the shore revitalizing every corner of my soul.

"You have the most marvelous eyes. There's so much compassion in them. I want to live there."

"I could get used to this. Keep them coming."

"Oh, I'm just warming up."

She laughed, her breath warm against my cheek. Then she went quiet, as if a memory had come back to her. "Have I told you . . ." she murmured, her fingers absently tracing the buttons of my shirt. "When I was growing up, I was a total bookworm with huge glasses. I never thought much of my eyes. Or myself, really. I don't think you would've liked me during those days. Kids called me a geekazoid."

"You must've been the most gorgeous geekazoid."

"I'm embarrassed to admit it, but I wanted so badly to be part of the popular crowd. Unfortunately, the girls were mean. Really mean."

"I never understood why those kids are called popular girls in American culture. In Korea, we would call them *yangachi*. The closest translation would be *punks*."

"*Yangachi*. Did I say that correctly?"

"Yes. If I didn't know better, I would think you were from Seoul."

A tiny laugh escaped her, pink rising in her cheeks. "In high school, I swapped glasses for contact lenses and started paying attention to how I dressed. I carried myself more confidently. And suddenly, I became the popular girl. I became *yangachi*."

"You are not *yangachi*. You are *yeosin*, which means *goddess* in Korean. It's often used to describe a woman with spellbinding beauty, intelligence, soul . . . a word made just for you."

"Don't you see any flaws in me?"

"No."

"Not even a tiny bit?"

"I couldn't even if I tried."

"But you've only known me a few months. How can you be so sure? I'm afraid your bubble will burst when you realize I fart too."

"I bet it smells like roses."

"It actually smells more like lilacs," she said, and we erupted into laughter.

"And you have an unrivaled sense of humor."

I ran my hand through her hair, the lustrous strands slipping between my fingers. Shifting closer, I brushed my nose against hers. Our foreheads touched, faces aligning like two pieces of a puzzle meant to fit. For a moment, we simply breathed each other in, eyes barely blinking. My hand drifted upward, and my index finger began to trace the lines of her face—from her forehead to her brows, down the gentle slope of her nose, across the delicate groove of her philtrum, and finally to the contour of her lips. When I reached them, she opened her mouth and playfully bit down, as if my finger were a Christmas candy cane.

"I just had the urge to bite you. I love your hands. They were one of the first things I noticed when we met. Oh, and your abs." She poked my stomach. I winced with exaggerated pain, then caught her hand and held it in mine. We surrendered to the moment, lying there with our fingers laced, our bodies intertwined like roots beneath the earth, whispering words of affection until sleep took us.

When I opened my eyes the next morning just before sunrise, I couldn't believe she was lying next to me, sound asleep. My heart overflowed with awe and admiration for her mere existence. I wanted to touch every part of her, but I lay still, breathless, careful not to wake her. As coral shades streamed into the room, gingerly nudging away the dawn, she opened her eyes. She blinked a few times, a smile spreading across her face like the morning star breaking through the fog. "Good morning, my *yeosin*," I said, caressing her hair. Then we kissed slowly, so tenderly, our lips brushing against each other, moving to our necks and shoulders. In that moment, the world seemed to hush. Just our heartbeats.

The kiss grew more incandescent and urgent, as if we were never going to see each other again. I was both surprised and relieved when she whispered to me, "I want you, River." Frantically, we unwrapped each other's layers without exchanging a single word. Under the warm blanket, our raw bodies tangled timidly and clumsily at first.

But soon, they found their way instinctively, attuned to each other like lifelong waltz partners. It was fragile yet exquisite. Abrupt yet eternal. We were each other's firsts, and we vowed to be each other's lasts.

EVEN THOUGH I was madly in love with Deborah, saying those three magic words, *I love you*, eluded me during our early days. Despite the numerous moments of intimacy—when the warmth of her body shielded me from all the noise in the world—the words hovered on my lips.

In my Korean family, love existed as a silent understanding, intricately woven into our daily lives yet never spoken aloud. I had grown up learning that love was demonstrated through gestures rather than declarations: my mother's hours spent cooking my favorite dishes and my father's rambunctious bragging to his friends about my academic achievements.

To me, saying *I love you* required an extraordinary moment. One that would live on even when memories began to blur. I held out for that moment. But another question loomed. Deborah hadn't said it either. She showered me with relentless affection, stealing kisses in public, holding my hand like letting go wasn't an option. Every moment felt like a small adventure she didn't want to miss. Still, the words remained unspoken on her lips. Maybe she was waiting for me to go first, or she was on her own journey to discover what love meant.

Our first Valentine's Day arrived, and we celebrated at an Italian restaurant in Back Bay. The low ceilings and soft candlelight cast an intimate spell over the room. All evening, the words would tango on the tip of my tongue but remain stubbornly lodged there. Each time I glanced at her and parted my lips, her eyes lit up. But instead of confessing my heart, I found myself asking if the linguini was too al dente or whether we should share dessert.

The next morning, when I went to Hollis to pick her up for

breakfast, she greeted me with a kiss that quieted my worry over whether I had let her down the night before. Still, a loud regret persisted. Though I was waiting for the perfect moment—or maybe seeking absolute confirmation that our feelings were mutual—my love for her was unequivocal. She deserved to hear those words from me.

A week later, thick, pillowy snow blanketed Cambridge, transforming Harvard into winter Elysium while the rest of the country welcomed the first signs of spring. Braving the endless snow drifting down, Deborah and I trudged through the Yard toward Lamont. She was bundled up in the beanie I had given her, paired with an olive scarf she had taken from my closet. The only part of her visible in the snow was her arresting brown eyes, twinkling like a lighthouse beacon cutting through the storm.

"Do you still like this weather?" I asked, my teeth nearly chattering.

"What's not to like? I'm walking next to a hot guy!"

Her laughter danced and curled into the frosty air. I looked around the serene snow-covered campus, picturing us as two impressionistic figures in a painting. Perhaps this was the day I had been waiting for.

A few minutes after we settled in at our usual desk at Lamont, I muttered something noncommittal and slipped outside to set my impromptu plan in motion. Just beyond the library doors, I approached one of the snow-removal workers and asked if I could borrow an extra shovel for a few minutes. He raised an eyebrow.

"It's for my girlfriend."

"What, are you rescuing her from the snow?" he chortled.

With the shovel in hand, I plodded to the side of Lamont where I could partially see Deborah through the window. I had a vision of what I wanted to create, but nagging doubts about how it would turn out held me back for a second. Regardless, I began shoveling. After about fifteen minutes, I had to pause, flinching as pain shot through my back. I had underestimated how physically demanding this task would be. It had all seemed straightforward in my imagination. Still, I pressed on. By the time I finished, sweat drenched me despite the biting cold.

As I returned to the desk, she scrutinized me from head to toe, squinting slightly. "You were gone for a long time. Did you get lost in a romance novel again?"

I took off my hat and coat. Strands of hair stuck to my forehead, and damp spots speckled my sweater.

"Or did you go to the gym in this weather?"

Instead of answering, I took her hand and gave her a light tug out of her chair. "Close your eyes and come with me."

She hesitated, her feet dithering around the chair, but eventually relinquished to my pull. With her eyes closed, I guided her to the window near the desk.

"Now, open your eyes."

She took a deep breath before opening her eyes. The moment she saw what was outside, she let out a sharp cry, her hands flying to her cheeks. In the pristine snow, bold letters spelled out *River loves Deborah*, encircled by a heart.

"Oh, River . . ." Her gaze stayed fixed out the window, fingers tightening around the edge of the frame. "That's a lot of shoveling. I suddenly regret not being named Jo."

"Imagine Bartholomew and Alexandrina. I would still be out there with the shovel."

She laughed through tears. Was this the reaction I had hoped for? But this wasn't the grand finale.

"I have one more thing for you."

She turned around, her eyes glistening. I pulled a crumpled piece of paper from my pocket. The melted snow had softened it to the point of near disintegration. The letters were no longer legible; the ink had bled into chaotic streaks, rippling like tie-dye across the page. But it didn't matter. I had memorized every word and held on to their meaning. After briefly clearing my throat, I intoned a poem by Elizabeth Barrett Browning: "How do I love thee? Let me count the ways. I love thee to the depth and breadth and height my soul can reach, when feeling out of sight for the ends of being and ideal grace . . ."

When I finished reciting the sonnet, I couldn't imagine saying anything other than those three magic words. But just as I was about to speak, she raised her finger, silencing me. "Read it for me again, but with a proper British accent this time," she said through her tears, her shoulders shaking as she laughed and cried in perfect synchronization.

Oh, how do I love thee, Deborah?

I reached for her and pulled her into my arms. "I love you," I whispered, my voice thick with the effort of holding back tears. "I've loved you from the moment I saw you. And I'll never stop loving you."

She remained silent in my arms. My pulse quickened as I waited on pins and needles for her response to my confession. Had I been too presumptive in projecting my love on her? Just as doubt began to creep in, she buried her face in my shoulder.

"I loved you first. And I love you more."

Her words landed like warm summer rain, flooding me with an overwhelming sense of relief and tenderness. The corners of my vision blurred, the library dissolving into just her—her whisper echoing in my mind, her scent threading through the air, and her embrace wrapping around me like a woolen blanket. No one had ever said those words to me before. She was my first. My first real kiss, my first lovemaking, and my first *I love you*.

FROM THAT MOMENT ON, saying *I love you* to her became as natural as breathing. I threaded those three words into the fabric of our days— murmuring them against her skin, calling them across crowded rooms, floating them into the closing moments of nights we never wanted to end. Deborah, in that unspoken way of hers, expressed her love through gentle touches, teasing grins, and adoring gazes in unexpected moments.

We built our own little world in Cambridge, tucking pieces of ourselves into every street, every corner—in whispers, in glances, in secrets only we understood. Where others wrestled with a gauntlet of pressure and pretense behind ivy-covered walls, we found a sanctuary of riant laughter and boundless joy. Gradually, our world expanded, reaching beyond the city's cobblestone streets. In search of new experiences, we seized every opportunity to chase adventures during holidays and long breaks. We explored the windswept beaches of Cape Cod and hiked the rugged trails of New Hampshire's mountains. Each journey we shared helped us discover more about each other, deepening the foundation of our love.

Over Fourth of July weekend after our sophomore year, we woke before dawn and boarded a train bound for NYC. We wanted to lose ourselves in the melting pot of humanity—to be engulfed in its unstoppable current, to soak in the city's electric energy. As the train rumbled toward Penn Station, we mapped out how to make the most of our short time there.

"Let's go to the Financial District and explore Wall Street," she said.

"I thought you wanted to visit the Met?"

"I do, but I have a hunch Wall Street might feel strangely like home to you."

By late morning, we found ourselves in the heart of Wall Street, dwarfed by the soaring majesty of the World Trade Center and the storied facade of the New York Stock Exchange. Awe and exhilaration coursed through me. I couldn't believe I was finally here, standing amid it all, with the woman of my dreams by my side.

"When I first came to America, the Twin Towers were the first landmark I saw through the plane window as we descended into JFK," I said, looking up at the towering skyscrapers around us gleaming against the pale blue sky. "That was the moment I realized that I was no longer in Korea. I wondered what my life in America would become, what the future held in this foreign world."

"And here you are, full circle. Can you picture yourself working in Manhattan after college?"

"I don't know . . ." I hesitated. In my mind, my future had always been in Korea, following my father's footsteps at SOL. It was a path I had never doubted, until her question stopped me in my tracks. "Can you see me here?"

"With your suit and leather briefcase? Absolutely! Just don't forget about people like me in scrubs while you're off closing billion-dollar deals." She gave my arm a mock punch, then trotted ahead. Her laughter rang out, so infectious it could bring a smile to even the most stoic face on Wall Street.

Our hands entwined as we navigated the crowded sidewalks, like birds in flight weaving through a dense forest. Around us, professionals surged forward while tourists crawled, cameras raised. Street vendors called out in a chorus of voices, waving miniature Statues of Liberty and snow globes with tiny Central Parks inside. As we wandered toward Tribeca, her question tugged at my mind. What if my path didn't align with the one my father had envisioned for me? What if my destiny was here—in NYC or somewhere else entirely— charting a course different from joining SOL after college? And not just exploring these new possibilities alone, but with Deborah. Was this why she brought me here—to open my eyes to a world of alternate possibilities?

Later, on the train to Boston, she explained why she had suggested Wall Street. She remembered me studying for my macroeconomics final exam, when I had mused aloud what the New York Stock Exchange must've been like during the 1929 crash.

"I can't believe you remembered. Thank you. I don't think I would've gone on my own. But it was magnificent. My heart is still racing from all the energy."

"See? I had a hunch Wall Street would captivate you once you saw it in person." She lifted her chin, looking triumphant. "But I feel like I'm always playing a guessing game with you. You need to start telling me what you want. Where you want to visit, what you want to eat . . . no more of this 'Whatever you want, Deborah.' "

"But I like what you like."

"River!" She slapped my lap playfully, shaking her head with exaggerated irritation. I pulled her into my arms, squeezing so tightly that I almost feared I might break her rib cage. How much I loved her.

It was beyond measure, beyond reason. My love for her felt infinite.
Immortal.

⁓

OF COURSE, not every day was filled with *I love you* or glittering
adventures. We had our little pinches too. What about that time I had
to spend the night at Abigail's place?

My trip to Wall Street with Deborah had shifted something in me.
It opened my eyes to career options other than joining my father's
business in Korea. During the winter semester of my junior year, I
decided to throw myself into securing a summer internship in investment banking. Among our friends, Abigail shared my interest in
corporate finance. We ended up in many of the same classes and
spent hours after lectures prepping each other for the grueling
internship interviews ahead. Before long, we both emerged as final
candidates for the prestigious mergers and acquisitions group at
Windsor Pearson.

The recruiting team invited us, along with other finalists from
different schools, for Superday at their Midtown office. The top floor,
where the interviews were held, offered a sweeping view of Hoboken
across the Hudson through expansive windows. But the decor was
plain—professional, not extravagant. The interview process consisted
of a series of two-on-one sessions with different bankers. Some questions were behavioral, while others were technical, including various
methods to value a business. After a marathon afternoon of interviews, their team took us out to dinner, which, in disguise, was a
continuation of the evaluation process.

During dinner, I caved to the pressure to fit in. I smiled, nodded,
adopted words I rarely used, mimicking not just the confidence—but
the arrogance—of those around me. The performance felt familiar,
and not in a good way. It brought back those early days in America,
when I had tried too hard to belong, concealing the parts of myself
that didn't fit. Then one of the bankers made a crude comment about
the young waitress, and the other candidates laughed on cue. Across

the table, I caught Abigail's face—jaw clenched, eyes flicking away. Something in me recoiled. But I bit my tongue and stared down at my plate, pretending to focus on slicing through a steak that bled too much. From that point on, I began to withdraw—uneasy in a room where bravado and entitlement passed for charm. Windsor was the crown jewel of Wall Street, the most coveted internship on campus. And yet I felt conflicted. It was like I was auditioning for a team destined to win a championship, only to realize I would have to bend my core just to hold the trophy. I found myself questioning whether that discomfort was a weakness—some failure to adapt or connect— or a warning that I wasn't cut out for the job.

Dinner stretched past ten before it finally wound down. By then, I had missed the last train back to Boston, where I was supposed to attend a concert with Deborah the next morning. I scrambled for alternatives—wondering if I could catch a late bus in Chinatown, find a budget hotel outside Manhattan, or even stay up all night at Penn Station. Abigail, planning to stay at her parents' house in the Upper East Side for the weekend, offered me a guest room for the night. With no good options, I gratefully accepted.

Her three-story historic brownstone was lavishly appointed with a private garden, balconies on each floor, and a rooftop terrace with a full view of Central Park. Art deco furnishings and sculptures of different sizes and shapes filled the living spaces to the brim, while paintings by artists from multiple eras adorned the walls.

Her parents spent the winter at their vacation house in West Palm Beach, while her brother immersed himself in the challenges of his first year at Princeton. So it would just be the housekeeper, Abigail, and me. After a tour of the house, she asked me to join her in the English basement, which had been converted into a private movie theater. As she debated which movie to watch from the hundreds of videotapes lined up along the walls, I excused myself to make a quick phone call. After rushing upstairs to a third-floor guest room, I called Deborah. I explained what had happened and apologized, knowing I might miss the concert—and that I would be staying the night at Abigail's.

"You're finally funny. Good one," she said, her laughter cracking through the line. "Are you back at Straus now? Should we debrief over waffle fries, if you're not too tired?" When I didn't respond right away, I caught the faint hitch in her breath. "Wait. You're serious. You're still in New York. Alone in the house with Abigail." Her voice stayed even, but I could hear the tightness just beneath the laugh.

"Not entirely alone. Her live-in housekeeper is here too." I softened my tone, choosing my words carefully. "I couldn't find a nearby hotel. Ones that were available were outrageously expensive. I figured I would rather save that money and treat you to a fancy dinner."

"I'm not sure whether to be entertained or concerned."

Her words suspended in the air. I switched the phone to my other ear, unsure what to say. Before I could summon the right words, she broke the silence, her voice deflated. "All right . . . enjoy your intimate sleepover with Abigail. I guess I'll enjoy the lonesome concert with an empty chair."

"It's not like that. Abigail is a good friend I've known for years. You know that. Plus, you wouldn't want me roaming the streets at night, in the middle of a cold winter, would you?"

"Of course not. I'm just not sure how I feel about you cuddling up at Abigail's alone."

"I'm not cuddling up. Calm down."

" 'Calm down?' Of all the words you could've reached for from your romantic vocabulary, that's what you chose. I see."

"I'm so sorry. That wasn't what I—"

"I have to go. I'm late for Brooks Aldrich's party."

A mechanical beep replaced her voice. I just sat there, staring at the receiver, shaking my head. I wished I could travel through the phone line to her room and hold her—to show her I belonged to her. But the harm had already been done.

Had I anticipated this outcome, would I have made a different choice? Maybe. Deep down, I might have glimpsed her reaction for a split second, but I had ignored the tiny voice in my head. Staying at Abigail's had seemed rational. Practical. It hadn't occurred to me how my actions might come across. That was my mistake. Instead of easing her discomfort, I made her feel like she was overreacting. Still, her doubt—however slight—left me feeling misunderstood.

Abigail and I had been part of the same friend group since freshman year at Andover. We had also worked together on *The Phillipian*, the school's fabled newspaper. Most students outside our circle found her intimidating and kept their distance. They perceived her as a cold, self-absorbed snob. Unlike the rest of us, who all had nicknames, no one ever dared to call her anything but Abigail. Absolutely no Abby or Gail. It was as if even her name demanded a certain distance. Behind the scenes, though, they dubbed her the "Ice Queen" as she moved through the campus with a face that rarely showed emotion. What they didn't realize was that she spent her summers volunteering at a Women Against Abuse center in Brooklyn, and that she had also penned a series of articles critiquing the institutional barriers women faced when reentering the workforce after maternity leave.

Though Abigail and I became close friends, nothing ever happened between us during our Andover days. I wouldn't even have called it platonic. The idea of being more than friends never even crossed my mind. Or hers, I presumed. She mostly dated country-club boys whose last names were etched into Ivy League buildings. I couldn't fathom being her type.

When Deborah and I started dating, I disclosed details about my female friendships, including Abigail, Kate, and a few others. Deborah found most of them innocuous, but for some reason, she didn't feel comfortable about my friendship with Abigail. "You just don't see what I see," she would say. In hindsight, given her sensitivity, I probably should've been more cautious when I accepted Abigail's ostensibly benign offer—at least, as I saw it—to stay the night at her house.

One more thing: Brooks Aldrich III, the host of the party Deborah was attending—and late for. He was the quarterback on the Harvard football team. A recipient of All-Ivy awards three straight years. Girls and boys worshipped him, except for Deborah, who would say, "Brooks? Gross. Dumb as beef jerky." Regardless, she knew all too well my kryptonite: my irritation with the boys who hovered around her.

Although I could never be angry with her, I did find myself feeling sulky whenever random guys tried to catch her attention. Whether they showered her with compliments, cracked jokes, or flaunted their triceps, she always responded the same way: unintentionally, with that radiant grin of hers. It left them delusionally convinced they stood a chance. Despite her reassurances, "You're the sole protagonist in my love story," I couldn't help but feel a flicker of jealousy stemming from my own insecurity.

That said, the important takeaway was this. Deborah hardly ever lost her temper with me during our time at Harvard. In fact, describing it as "losing her temper" didn't capture the situation fairly. *Being upset* or *disappointed* were more accurate descriptions. And each instance occurred because I downplayed something she cared about, like my overnight stay at Abigail's. Or because I said something asinine, like "Calm down."

The next morning, I snuck out of Abigail's house and took the 5:00 a.m. train to Boston. I arrived at Sanders Theatre with five minutes to spare before the concert started. Students, faculty, parents, and locals packed the hall. Among the sea of faces, I found Deborah in the middle section, absorbed in the program. That familiar halo— the molten glow that always seemed to drape her tresses—led my eyes straight to her.

I trotted over to the section and squeezed past patrons already comfortably seated, my words of apology stumbling out in quick succession. Beside Deborah, her wool coat reserved an empty seat. I moved her coat onto my lap and sat down next to her. She pretended not to notice, her gaze fixed on the stage. She looked ravishing in her French braid, round pearl earrings, and a twill winter dress. My heart surged with an insatiable desire to hold her, yet the inability to do so knotted my stomach. The concert was about to start, but the silence between us was unbearable. I turned to her, offering my best attempt at puppy-dog eyes.

"I couldn't sleep after you hung up. I stayed in the guest room all night and left at four in the morning to catch the first train and be here. I'm sorry." When she didn't respond, I lifted my fist. "If Brooks laid a finger on you last night, I'll break his—"

She finally turned to me and raised a finger to my lips. "Shh!"

I tried to plant a quick kiss on her fingertip, but before I could, she pulled it away. The theater darkened, except for the stage. I spotted Jack among the first violins on the left-hand side, while Amy was with the cellos on the right-hand side. Just as the orchestra was about to begin, Deborah leaned into me, her voice a soft whisper: "I didn't go to the party." Then she reached out and squeezed my hand, our secret handshake that meant *I love you.*

I turned to look at her, squeezing her hand in return. When I saw a tiny crease form at the edge of her lips, I moved closer and kissed her in the dimly lit theater filled with the mellifluous sounds of Rachmaninoff.

I DIDN'T GET the internship offer from Windsor, but Abigail did. Doug Avons, the director of the mergers and acquisitions group, expressed concerns about my "cultural fit."

"Mr. Avons, if you may, could you please clarify what you meant by that?"

"I mean, I can't really see you at our firm."

I could practically hear him snort, eyeing his watch, itching to end the call. I was tempted to retort, "Great, I wouldn't have accepted the offer even if you gave it to me," but instead, I thanked him for his time.

In the following weeks, more rejections piled up, and with each one, my confidence plummeted. Then, just as I began to question whether I was good enough, I got the news of an offer from Sterling Greenough when I returned to my dorm. After a stretch of uncertainty, the offer felt like a turning point. Deborah's face surfaced instantly, even before the news had fully sunk in. She had witnessed the setbacks and the self-doubt. Now all I wanted was to share the moment with her. I ran across campus and waited at the Science Center, jittery with excitement. About half an hour later, she emerged from her physics lab, ponytail slightly askew, a thick binder hugged tight to her chest. I jogged up and took the weighty binder from her, tucking it under my arm before she could protest.

"Guess what?"

"You're actually an alien poet. From Neptune."

"How did you know?"

"I have my ways. And don't worry. Your secret's safe with me."

"Thank you. But I've got something even better."

"Better than a boyfriend from Neptune? Okay, now I'm intrigued."

"So guess again."

"Wait . . . you've got that look. No way. You got an offer?"

"Sterling said yes."

"River!" she squealed, launching herself at me and wrapping me in a hug so fast I nearly dropped her binder. She knew how much Windsor's rejection had shaken me—how close I had come to giving up on the whole investment banking path. "Of course you did. I knew it was only a matter of time. I can't wait to see my handsome boyfriend strutting down Wall Street in a svelte suit!" she teased, beaming as she linked her arm through mine.

We stepped out into the open, where twilight had mellowed the evening, signaling the finale of winter's early darkness. A cool breeze tousled our hair as we walked, still buzzing with adrenaline.

"Come on." She tugged me toward Harvard Square. "Let's celebrate at our favorite Mexican place. You're buying. Interns still make bank, right?"

"I might go wild and finally splurge on the overpriced guac."

"Easy there, Rockefeller."

I smiled and followed her lead, the future suddenly wide open. I was grateful for the offer, for the momentum, and for her unwavering belief in me. But even then, an inexplicable hesitation gnawed at me. Something I didn't yet have the words for. She had plans to return to STEMFusion in Boston, where she had spent the past two summers. They promised her a stellar recommendation letter for the medical schools she intended to apply to in the fall. While the thought of joining the bustling sea of finance professionals in NYC thrilled me, the idea of being away from her hampered my excitement. Those ten weeks of internship would fly by, yet they would also mark the longest stretch we would've been apart since we started dating. What if something were to happen to either of us that would test our relationship? I had absolute faith in the strength of our love, but was it worth taking that risk?

Even contemplating these questions felt foolish. At my core, what I yearned for most was sharing every mundane aspect of daily life with her, under the same roof. Though we spent ample time together on campus, our respective dorms held us back from fully exploring the next level of our relationship. The prospect of spending that summer together in Boston—waking up and going to bed side by side every day—excited me far more than anything NYC had to offer. It would be like a pilot test for what our future together might look like after graduation. Regardless, none of this internal discourse mattered if I couldn't secure an internship in Boston, leaving NYC as my only option.

Thankfully, my niggling trepidation dissipated during the final week of decision-making. I received an internship offer from Harriott Group, a boutique investment banking firm in Boston. I accepted it immediately, turning down Sterling and NYC—much to Deborah's surprise. She asked more than once if I was sure, if I might regret walking away from Wall Street. But I was sure. Nothing else mattered.

3

RIVER

Summer 1993

Our decision to live together during the summer of 1993 felt like a three-month overture to a life we intrinsically knew was ours. A trial, a rehearsal, a glimpse of the future we dreamed of calling our own someday. We savored each day—even the muggy, mosquito-ridden ones—hoping summer might linger just a little longer.

We rented a barebones studio in Revere Beach. Despite the name *Beach*, this was no Malibu. Revere, just north of Boston near Logan Airport, was a working-class town, home to many immigrants from Central and South America. There, we could simply exist—unburdened, unguarded—escaping from the Harvard elitists and MIT brainiacs in Cambridge. We were anonymous in Revere. Just two people in love.

The beach was a three-minute walk from our apartment. The Wonderland T station, the last stop on the Blue Line, was an additional ten minutes away. In the morning, we would stroll along the beach toward the T station, the salty ocean air lifting around us. Then we would ride into Boston together. After work, we would meet in Downtown Crossing—sometimes trotting over to Chinatown for a five-dollar dinner special—then commute back home, sharing the details of our day.

We were ravenous for each other. We made love almost every night. Sometimes it felt like working, eating, and sleeping were just necessary breaks before we could return to each other. Was it the looming uncertainty of our final year of college? Or simply the sheer intensity of our love?

When the summer heat kept us awake at night, we would escape to the empty beach, sitting together on the coarse sand, gazing at the sea that resembled a giant navy-blue curtain swaying in the breeze. The ocean's lulling cadence, the soulful calls of seagulls, and the occasional hum of passing vehicles blended into an invisible choir, crooning to us.

"Did I mention you're the most beautiful thing in this universe?"

"Only about twenty times today. You said it thirty times yesterday, darling." She laughed under her breath. Somewhere along the way that summer, she had started calling me *darling*. I liked how it sounded—caressing, almost like a hug. There was a timeless, reassuring quality in the way she said it. Like a vow that our love would last. After all, I had only ever heard married couples call each other that.

"Hey, Deborah . . . may I ask you a random question?"

She raised an eyebrow.

"How many children would you want?" I pretended it was idle curiosity. Light, trivial, just a passing thought. But living with her that summer had intensified my desire to build a life together. I often found myself daydreaming about our future as wife and husband—a life where we raised a family and grew old side by side. I couldn't fathom it unfolding any other way.

"Children? That is random indeed," she said with an amused glint. "Hmm . . . I'd say three. Just like me and my two sisters. You?"

"Maybe . . . five?" My answer came spontaneously, not as a product of weeks or months of contemplation. Yet it felt right, if somewhat exaggerated. I could easily picture her surrounded by a lively brood of beautiful children, each one a reflection of her spirit.

"Whoa, Mister. Good luck finding a wife."

"You don't want to be my wife?"

"Not if you're going to make me produce five children!"

"Fine. Let's say I'm the lucky guy who you decide to marry and we end up having anywhere between three and five kids. Do you think people will see how much we love each other?"

"They already do. Haven't you heard? People call us *conjoined twins* around campus."

"I think it's because you keep following me around."

"Oh, is that how it is? Just wait till I'm on the other side of campus." She pretended to pull away, arms crossed in a mock indignation.

"You know I can't escape your gravity." I reached for her hand, drew her back into my arms, and kissed her cheek.

"Great. Now I can't even pretend to be pouty." She rolled her eyes, and we broke into laughter.

As our laughter faded, I tucked her closer against me. "If we did have those three to five kids, I think I would want them all to be girls."

"All girls?"

"All girls. I refuse to share your magnificent bosom with any other boys."

"Ew." She slapped my shoulder. "Do you have some twisted version of an Oedipus complex I wasn't aware of?"

"You didn't know?" I smiled. "In all seriousness, I worry that I might turn out just like my father. The idea of having a son who may feel the same kind of distance from me as I have with my father . . . it unsettles me."

"Oh, darling. You're going to be a wonderful father."

"I don't know. Growing up, my father and I barely spoke," I said, my eyes drifting toward the ocean. "Even at dinner, we would just sit in silence. It felt so stifling that sometimes I couldn't even taste my mother's food. While I was at Andover, he visited me only once. He didn't even make my graduation. There was a boardroom crisis that couldn't wait."

"I'm sure he wanted to be with you."

"I never understood why things between us had to be so difficult. I suppose I still have a lot to unpack when it comes to my father."

"You know he loves you very much."

"I can't put my father and *love* together in the same sentence."

"His love for you lives in his heart. You must see that," she said, her hand folding around mine. "Sometimes, what's left unsaid means more."

"Does it?"

"It does. Unspoken words are the loudest truths."

"Maybe you're right."

"I'm always right."

"I know. And there's something else I know for certain."

"Yeah? What is it?"

"If you were my wife, I would want to be the kind of husband who always puts you first."

"You'd better."

"Someone once told me that when you get married and have children, the kids become the couple's top priority. But if you decide to marry me someday, you, Deborah, will be my priority, even over our children. That's my promise to you." I meant every word, even if it was said in the spur of the moment. Maybe it was ingenuous to make such a promise without experiencing firsthand what fatherhood might entail, but in my heart, I couldn't imagine loving anyone—not even my future children—more than Deborah.

"I'm liking this pitch. Almost makes me want to marry you on the spot." She leaned her head against my shoulder. We let the silence settle, breathing in the lukewarm ocean air. I gazed up at the star-filled sky, imagining if three to five of those shimmering lights in the sky could be our future daughters.

"Do you think life envies our love the way our classmates do?" I asked.

"If anything, life adores us. It brought us together, didn't it?"

"It did."

"Then what made you ask?"

"Sometimes, I wonder if I can possibly be any happier. Yet the next moment comes, and I find myself even happier. It feels like happiness keeps expanding when I'm with you. But that's when I get scared too."

"Scared? Why, darling?"

"I cannot shake the feeling that this might just be a dream. Nothing in life ever grows upward endlessly. It meanders sideways or even regresses. I worry that life will find a way to take this away from me in its jealousy." I scooped up a handful of sand and let it slip through my fingers.

"My worrywart . . ." She shook her head. "Our love is stronger than anything life can throw at us. So stop worrying, and just enjoy this moment with me. Now!"

She was right again. But no matter how hard I tried to immerse myself in the present moment with her, that nagging worry knocked at the corners of my heart. Barely conspicuous, yet persistent.

As Deborah and I wrapped up our magical summer and geared up for our final year of college, the hard reality of difficult life choices awaited us. What would happen to us after graduation? What would become of us?

Her path was clear: apply to medical school, spend four years there, follow it with a three-to-five-year residency depending on her specialty, and begin her career as a doctor. My path had also been predetermined. My father had a rigid plan for me to return to Korea and eventually take over SOL Corporation. Though SOL was a respected midmarket company in Korea, it was a mere blip on the global stage. My father expected that I, with my Andover and Harvard education and as the only son, would be the one to elevate SOL and aggrandize the family legacy.

Growing up, I had thought his plan would be my destiny. I never questioned it. But falling in love with Deborah altered my path. The future dictated by him no longer appealed to me. I began to envision myself in different industries or career paths. Above all, I saw my life with Deborah. Even at twenty-one, I knew that I wanted to spend forever with her—and our three to five daughters. Nothing else mattered to me but being with her.

The day after finishing my summer internship, I boarded a plane to Korea for a weeklong visit with my parents. Unlike previous trips filled with my mother's delicious food and much-needed rest, this visit was going to be emotionally challenging. I was going to confront my father—the man who had unilaterally mapped out my future.

People feared my father. He was an authoritarian with a temper like a ticking time bomb. When he exploded, people scattered like mice in a basement at the first sign of a cat. At SOL, *good enough* held no place. Even a hint of incompetence was met with contempt. Years ago, when an account manager missed a customer call on a Saturday —resulting in customer churn—my father forced the entire sales team to come into the office every weekend until the number of missed calls dropped to zero. Despite his harsh methods, he was a masterful strategist, often outmaneuvering much larger competitors. In the domestic market, SOL consistently led with the largest shares, surpassing US players in the nonalcoholic-beverage category.

Early on, people recognized him as a child prodigy: he was solving algebraic equations by the age of seven. But his brilliance couldn't protect him from the trauma that haunted his childhood. When he was eight years old, his only brother tragically contracted a severe case of smallpox and passed away in the midst of the Korean War. Two years later, his mother died during what was supposed to be a routine procedure to treat her abdominal pain.

Was it his traumatic childhood that toughened him? Maybe. It was a challenging time for many Koreans who spent their teenage years in the postwar fifties. But while others' hearts gradually thawed over the years, his seemed to remain frozen.

After graduating at the top of his class from Seoul National University, he completed his mandatory military service and then joined SOL. When my grandfather insisted he train under the apprenticeship program, my father refused. Instead, he boldly requested the position of vice president, despite having no management experience or knowledge of the business. Remarkably, within three years, he increased SOL's revenue by 200 percent through aggressive expansion and by taking unprecedented risks in new categories.

During the 1970s, when he assumed control of the day-to-day operations from my grandfather, South Korea underwent a significant economic transformation. He gobbled up local mom-and-pop beverage distributors, often forcing them to relinquish control after engaging in price wars. Renowned as one of the shrewdest businessmen of his generation, he commanded both intimidation and respect—sentiments I shared. Despite the deep resentment I harbored over his stifling control and frequent absence, I couldn't deny the blend of apprehension and admiration I felt toward him.

My parents' marriage was also a result of my father's determination. When he began his career at SOL, my mother was still a sophomore at Ewha Womans University. They met accidentally at a small restaurant, where my father, inebriated, made such an unflattering first impression that it repulsed my mother for quite some time. With his salesmanship and persistence, however, he eventually won her over. She dropped out of school and married him at just twenty-one, a decision she regretted to this day. It wasn't the marriage she felt contrite about, but leaving school with only one year left.

Although most women of her generation never set foot on a college campus, many of her acquaintances—wives of CEOs and politicians—displayed an unmistakable air of arrogance. In social settings, my mother often avoided conversations about her educational background, deftly changing the subject or stepping away whenever someone inquired about her college experience. Perhaps to prove her worth to both the other wives and herself, she worked tirelessly, fiercely committed to being the devoted mother.

She took me to piano lessons, math tutoring, and writing camps. My bookshelves overflowed with essential literature for young readers, and each day came with two nonnegotiable hours of reading. Every meal she prepared was an elaborate culinary masterpiece, often leaving my friends drooling over my lunch box. She dressed me in clothes tailored from the finest fabrics, which I vehemently resisted, as they appeared far too formal compared to my friends' casual T-shirts. Admittedly, I relished how the girls in school seemed to pay me more attention than my friends—evidenced by the surprise notes and gifts that arrived at my desk. Maybe my mother sought to fill the void left by her contentious marriage through the compliments I received for my academic prowess and appearance— qualities to which she contributed significantly.

THIS TIME WAS NO DIFFERENT. During my stay in Korea, she insisted on preparing all three meals—sometimes even four or five, including afternoon and evening snacks. She even took me to a tailor to get new suits for my senior year. I reminded her that she had already bought me two pairs the previous year for my internship interviews. Nevertheless, as the tailor measured me, my mother gazed at me as if actual stars were glued to her eyes.

Each morning, she would ask what "we" should do for the day, even though I couldn't imagine any young man in his twenties spending the whole day with his mother. Occasionally, she would whisk me away to a high-end café, where ladies exchanged banter over expensive drinks. I could sense her delight as her friends doted on me, even calling me the "movie star from Harvard." My mother would wave her hand dismissively. "Oh, no, he still has much to learn and grow," she would say, barely containing her smile.

As my departure date approached, she lamented, almost in a panic, that she had only a few days left with me and still hadn't cooked this or that. "I don't want to look at the calendar," she would say. Guilt washed over me, as I couldn't wait to reunite with Deborah in Cambridge.

On the last night of my stay in Seoul, we went out for a family dinner at my father's favorite restaurant near his office. The restaurant owner, familiar with my father's regular visits, had reserved a private room for us, with sliding doors adorned in traditional patterns. The privacy turned out to be a good thing because, within five minutes of sitting down, my father's voice had already risen to full volume.

"What do you mean you're not coming back?"

"I've thought a lot about this. I don't want to work at SOL. I need to carve out my own path. I want to figure out what's right for me."

"What nonsense is this? Is this what America taught you? To disrespect your parents?"

"I'm not disrespecting you. I'm just—"

"You're a privileged, ungrateful, spoiled punk." His spittle sprayed across the table. "You've been coddled too long. You have no idea what real hardship looks like."

My fists clenched under the table. I almost shouted that I had been surviving on my own in a foreign country since I was eleven. But I bit back the words and held my ground in silence.

"Any sane person would jump at the chance to run SOL!" He banged his hand on the table.

I flinched at the clatter of the teacups and utensils, but I took a deep breath to steady my nerves before nodding in agreement. "There must be many highly capable and experienced executives at the company. Could you appoint one of them as your successor instead? Why does it have to be me?"

"Are you stupid?" He looked at me, flabbergasted. "How did you even get into Harvard with such shallow thinking? Do you not grasp the importance of trust and loyalty? These external hires are mercenaries. They don't care about the legacy. They're not invested in building something that lasts. They're just here for the big paycheck and to pad their résumés for the next move!" His face ballooned like an angry pufferfish as he unleashed his tirade.

While my father and I were embroiled in a heated debate, my mother remained silent. Did she also wish for me to return home—for the sake of preserving the family legacy?

"No more of this Western complacency. You'll return after graduation!"

"No, I won't." A flicker of fear slipped into my voice, but I pushed through, speaking louder now. "I want to be with Deborah even after college."

He blinked, as if he had misheard. "Borah who?" He shot a glance at my mother. "Who is he talking about?"

"Deborah. River's girlfriend," my mother said, her voice subdued.

He turned back to me, brow furrowed. "You have a girlfriend? I sent you to America to study, not to chase after girls." He reached for the bottle of whisky on the table and poured himself a glass, the sound sharp in the silence. He held it for a moment, then took a long sip. The heat was still there, but now it carried a different edge. Measured. Tactical. "Ah, I get it. I was your age once." He gave a tight smile. "But don't waste your time on some random girl. I've already made arrangements. The granddaughter of the SGY Electronics chairman is eager to meet my handsome, Harvard-educated son. If she's not to your liking, there are others. I thought you were really abandoning the business. A girl problem is easy to fix." He waved his hand, as if tossing his worries into the ether.

White-hot rage surged through me. "Deborah is not 'some random girl.' You don't know her, and clearly, you don't care to. But I'm going to marry her. And I'm not coming back. Not for you. Not for SOL."

The words echoed through the walled room. A fleeting glance at my mother revealed her shock. Her mouth hung agape as she darted her wide eyes between my father and me.

My father's fury flared anew, his face reddening instantly. "You ungrateful punk!" His palm shot up, poised to slap me, but paused midair. Instead, he pointed at me with a finger that sliced through the air like a blade. "The way you're talking to me is unacceptable. You're coming back to Seoul. You're not marrying anyone except one of the ones I've arranged. That's an order. No one disobeys my order. This conversation is over." Turning to my mother, he grumbled, "You raised him like a pathetic runt. Weak! Call the driver to bring the car.

I'm leaving." He grabbed his jacket and stormed out, the door slamming behind him.

My mother hesitated, torn between following him and tending to her "pathetic runt." In the end, she grabbed her purse. Just as she reached the door, she turned back to me, her voice heavy. "I hope you know what you're doing. SOL isn't just a business. It's the heart of this family. Your grandfather fought to keep it alive through the Japanese occupation, only to face the devastation of the Korean War right after. Decades of sacrifice, pain, and struggle went into saving SOL. And now you're walking away?"

As the door slid shut behind her, the silence in the room grew deafening. I sat alone, my body shaking uncontrollably. I kept replaying the moment I stood my ground. Where had this defiance come from? Had I finally cracked the shell of my adolescence? Or was it just love—so blinding it outshone the fear?

Soon, the waitstaff entered, setting down dish after dish, an extravagant spread meant for a family. I stared down at the abalone soup, my tears mingling with the intricately prepared broth.

Despite the newfound voice I had claimed in confronting my father, a part of me still held out hope for reconciliation. I fantasized about bridging the abyss that had stretched between us for years. I pictured a relationship remade—like the ones I saw in other fathers and sons, where laughter came easily over sports banter or weeklong road trips. I ached for him to see me as a son worthy of his respect and love, even if I chose a life that fell short of his towering expectations. The thought of losing that connection—of never getting the chance to rewrite our story—only intensified the resentment already simmering inside me. Would he ever understand the grief tied to the future we would never share? Or the disappointment I carried for both of us?

The next day, I headed to the airport alone, bound for America to begin my final year of college, unaware of the peril that awaited me.

4

RIVER

Spring 1994

During our final year, Deborah secured a single at Adams House, while I shared a double with Pete across campus at Eliot. But I spent most of my time at Deborah's place. My presence was so constant that the other Adams residents joked I should be granted honorary status.

Throughout the fall semester, her space transformed into our makeshift war room—cluttered with textbooks, medical school brochures, and company pamphlets strewn across every surface. Whether I was perched at her desk while she sat cross-legged on the bed, or we were sprawled on the floor surrounded by a sea of papers, we spent countless hours imagining our future. Every conversation was a puzzle to solve, each decision a deliberate piece shaping our shared vision. Even with all the uncertainty and so much we couldn't control, we believed in a life that tied us together.

"All done!" She stood from her chair, her fingers riffling through a thick stack of letter-sized envelopes neatly arranged on the desk. Each envelope, meticulously prepared with typed pages, held the potential for her future. "Twelve schools . . . that was a lot of essays to write," she exhaled the words, her smile wide with hard-won relief.

"You did it!" I high-fived her, a surge of pride swelling in my chest. "Any of those medical schools would be lucky to have you."

It was well past midnight on a Friday, and her applications were due in a week. Over the past two months, she had poured herself into assembling application materials, gathering recommendation letters, and crisscrossing the country for interviews. Meanwhile, I had juggled my own interviews, meeting with investment banks and consulting firms in the same cities. Although I had a full-time offer from Harriott Group in Boston, I couldn't commit yet—not without knowing where her path would lead.

"What if I can't find a job in the same city?"

"I highly doubt it, darling. Who wouldn't want a hot, brilliant stud like you?" She wrapped her arms around my waist, pulling me closer. "But even if you don't find a job, you can stay home and wait for me. Buck naked, just an apron on, ready to serve dinner!"

We tumbled onto her bed as our glee spilled into shared kisses. We were two souls tightly bound, navigating the discomfort of an unpredictable future. Each application she completed, each job interview I faced, was a purposeful step forward. Though the future remained a riddle, we clung to the belief that somehow, life would guide us to the same dream. Being together.

As SPRING CREPT IN, the last remnants of old snow bid their farewell. The campus stirred to life, shedding winter's gray scale. Under the returning sun, ancient trees along the Yard stretched their limbs skyward, their budding leaves unfurling in a tapestry of green. A faint sweetness of blooming flowers hung in the air, braiding with the earthy tang of thawing soil.

Deborah and I could barely contain our excitement, the anticipation of acceptance letters and job offers surging between us like an oncoming wave. We would huddle on a weathered bench or in a secluded café corner, lost in endless what-ifs, circling back to the same questions we had debated for months. Our conversations felt like a ritual. Almost like a disguised prayer.

"Let's say you're on Wall Street and I'm across the country. How would that work?"

"I'll fly out every weekend."

"What about all those models-and-bottles parties in the Hamptons you've been dreaming about?"

"Hmm . . ." I tapped my chin like a chess player weighing his next move. "Very tempting. But I would still take scrubs and stethoscopes. Especially if they come with you."

"Are you sure about that?"

"Yes. But promise me. Please stock the fridge with skim milk."

"For your late-night debauchery with romance books while I'm trapped in the lab?"

"You know me so well."

"You're such a party animal. But if you spend all your money on plane tickets and those steamy paperbacks you insist are literature, how will you ever afford my engagement ring?"

"Your engagement ring? Hold on. Is that your subtle way of saying I've made it to the final round for future husband?"

"The race isn't over. But let's just say you've been in the lead for a while, and you're still holding strong."

"In that case, does Tiffany accept frequent-flier miles?"

We would dissolve into laughter before steering the conversation toward specifics—our first apartment, daily chores, even the grown-up subject of shared finances. The future was no longer some distant abstraction. It felt close and tangible, almost within reach.

On the first morning of our final spring break in college, everyone in our friend group scrambled to load the van Tom had rented for our road trip to Quebec. An uncontainable energy filled the air as we readied ourselves for the final adventure of college.

I was helping Deborah with her suitcase when the resident tutor from Eliot House rushed over, his footsteps hurried and frantic.

"River, you need to take this call from Korea. It's urgent."

Urgent?

Gripping Deborah's hand, I stumbled after him. When we reached Eliot, Deborah hovered beside me, eyes full of worry as I picked up the phone. The moment my mother's sobs reached my ear, I felt myself deflate.

"Your father had a stroke . . ."

Her words hit me like a punch to the gut. I dropped the phone, momentarily startled, trying to comprehend the reality of the situation.

I turned to Deborah, my voice shaking. "I need to go to Korea immediately. My father is in serious condition."

"Oh, no." She wrapped her arms around me, her body coiled with the effort of not crying. "I'm so sorry."

"Please don't worry." I forced a smile, suppressing my shock. "I'll be back before you know it. And we'll have the best final semester."

Inside the cab, I waved until she vanished into a distant speck. A knot of anxiety twisted in my chest, even as I held onto the thought of our reunion just weeks away.

～

NEARLY THIRTY HOURS LATER, I arrived at Seoul National University Hospital. The cardiologist briefed me on my father's condition, explaining that he had faced some critical moments.

"He'll be okay, right?" I asked, unable to imagine a world where he wasn't.

"Let's wait and see."

I sent my mother home, as she had spent the last three days at the hospital, hardly sleeping or eating. Alone in the room with my unconscious father, I grappled with the weight of his condition and the possible causes. Was it all the alcohol he had consumed over the years? He could drink like a whale, sitting in one place and imbibing day and night for days. Or was it the tribulation and pressure of keeping the business going? SOL was where he spent most of his waking moments. How ironic would it be if something he loved so dearly was what caused his heart failure? Or was I partly to blame? Had my rebellion and defiance contributed to this? If I was complicit, could I ever exonerate myself?

I studied his face, as if it would tell me the answer. I had never looked at him closely before. Every wrinkle and crease on his face seemed like a badge of honor, each one carved by battles endured well beyond the years he had lived. The story of impossible climbs and devastating descents. Lying still in the hospital bed, he seemed defeated at last. There was no menace or aggression, just a naked emperor, frail on his pedestal, without his crown. His once-commanding fist, capable of breaking through the thickest walls, now lay supported by needles and catheters. I touched his hand tentatively, like a child reaching for a starfish for the first time.

"Father, do you regret that we didn't spend more time together?" The question slipped out, barely audible, as if meant only for me. "I think I do."

When I left Korea at eleven, I was just a child. Now, I returned as a near adult. While most of my friends had learned essential life skills from their fathers, I had taught myself: how to ride a bike, shave, tie a necktie, shine shoes, start a fire with a stick, change a flat tire, and ask a girl to a dance. I had traveled to more countries, tasted more cuisines, and experienced more international traditions than my father ever had. Most importantly, I had found the love of my life. All of it by myself.

"You've missed witnessing them, Father." A lurching ache sliced through my chest. Yet I didn't resent him. I still pined for his love. A nod, a thumbs-up, a pat on the back. Just anything to show me his approval.

∼

"Is . . . that you . . . River?"

I must've been asleep when I heard his voice. Exhausted and dazed, I thought I was still dreaming. His words were slurred, a thick line of drool spreading across the pillow. He slowly opened his right eye, with the left eye still shut.

"Father, yes, it's me, River. I'm here." I wrapped my fingers around his right hand. His left lay still—lifeless. A long silence followed. I scanned him, fearing he had lost consciousness again, but his right eye continued to blink ploddingly.

"Sooin?"

"Mother is at home, but I can call her right now."

"No . . . leave it . . ."

Tears brimmed in my eyes as I took in his frailty, his haggard cheeks etched with a doleful expression. Where had the father I had known disappeared to? Where was the fiery passion, the boundless ardor, that once defined him?

"SOL . . . that's yours . . . take care of it." His voice strained, each word dragged out as if thick sludge coated his tongue.

I bowed my head, tears falling to the floor. With bated breath, I looked up at the ceiling before turning back to him. "Father, I'm sorry."

"I need . . . you to . . ."

"I can't. I need to be with Deborah in America." I wrenched my face away, the weight of anguish crashing down on me.

"Don't you . . . dare . . ." he stammered as his face flushed deep scarlet, veins bulging at his temples. Suddenly, the vital signs monitor erupted into frantic beeping, its previously steady green lines now flashing red. His body convulsed uncontrollably. The room spiraled into a blinding white haze. Doctors and nurses rushed in. I tried to lunge toward his bed, but someone grabbed my arm, pulling me back. Amid the chaos, the sharp commands of doctors cut through the air. My legs gave out, and I crumpled to the floor.

IN THE HALLWAY, a middle-aged doctor with tired eyes behind black rectangular glasses delivered the news that my father had passed. I jerked his hand from my shoulder, the words not yet sinking in. He tried to hold me still, but I tore free. I punched the wall. Then again. I kept punching until two security guards tackled me to the ground. As I writhed beneath their grip, inescapable guilt closed in around me. Even with his final breath, my father's thoughts had clung stubbornly to the legacy of SOL. There was no parting wisdom, no confession of regrets, no cherished memory shared. Just an unwavering fixation on ensuring SOL's future, with its destiny resting solely on his son's shoulders. Had my defiance been the final blow that hastened his end? If I had yielded, if I had offered him the solace of obedience, would he still be alive? The thought that his final moments might have been clouded by anger and disappointment, rather than peace and love, pierced me with unbearable anguish. I had robbed him of a tranquil passing.

"River!" My mother stumbled down the hallway, with only one shoe on. The other was nowhere to be found. Her hair was a tangled mess, escaping its confines in wild strands. Streaks of mascara ran down her cheeks, mingling with raindrops that dripped from her hair. When she saw me being pinned by the security guards, she collapsed onto the floor, as if her soul had escaped from her body. The security guards released me, and I rushed to her, wrapping my arms around her shoulders.

"I never meant for this to happen. If only I had obeyed him . . . it's all my fault." My words came out in a choked sob, each sentence pried from the depths of my despair.

She stared at me in disbelief, the weight of my confession likely too heavy for her to process. What could she do in this moment aside from holding me tightly? Disown me? Lose yet another man she loved?

~

IT ALL HAPPENED SO QUICKLY.

My father's funeral took place three days after his passing. Almost everyone from SOL, along with political figures and leaders from other companies, attended the wake at the funeral home. Each time I bowed to them, I wondered if they knew how I had enraged him to death. Yet without a hint of it, almost all of them solemnly said, "My deepest condolences. He was a great man, one of a kind," as if they had all learned how to pay respect from the same textbook.

In the crowded dining area where guests and visitors were offered customary yukgaejang and soju, conversations shifted to the upcoming baseball season, opinions on President Kim's first year in office, and the tensions between North Korea and the US over the inspection of nuclear facilities. Life, it seemed, marched on indifferently.

After his funeral, my mother and I returned to what was now her place. It was a three-bedroom apartment in the Jamsil District, where all the facilities had been built for the 1988 Olympics six years ago. Thanks to the Olympics, Jamsil had become one of the most modernized areas in Seoul. My parents had never felt the need for a big house since it was just the two of them while I studied in the US. Instead, they had opted for a place that was easy to access from anywhere and comfortable even for foreigners. Did they think I was a foreigner? Was I?

My mother and I sat at the dining room table, staring at the reflections of the chandelier bouncing off the table's surface. The apartment was always immaculate, a testament to the pride my mother took in creating a warm, inviting place for the family. It had a modest layout, with a narrow kitchen, a dining area just big enough for a four-person table, and a cozy living room. The decor was simple: an array of Korean porcelains my father had collected over the years, and a scattering of old framed photographs—awkward snapshots of the three of us in places like my father's office or the temple my mother frequented. Aside from those, there were no notable artworks or paintings.

After a long stretch of heavy silence—the haunting sadness of the day clinging to us like a fetid odor in our clothes—we retreated to our separate rooms. Once I was in my own room, I collapsed onto the bed. In my isolation, a restless need to see Deborah consumed me. I reached for her voice, for the comfort of her sweet words, for the solace of her embrace. But there was nothing to reach, only silence answering back.

Despite the raw ache of missing her, I hadn't called her since arriving in Korea. I imagined her keeping vigil by the phone, afraid to leave its side in case it rang the moment she looked away. Yet the forceful guilt, shame, and burden I carried kept me from reaching out. My mind conjured my father's face, contorted in a way that made it seem as if it might burst like a watermelon struck by a slingshot. I couldn't forgive myself for how my father's final moments had unraveled. I didn't deserve to receive Deborah's love in light of my transgressions. And there was my mother, alone in her room, without so much as a single "How are you?" from the only son she had always put first. I loathed myself for failing to be there for her. Curling into the corner of my bed, I pounded my head with my fist.

"You did this. It was all your fault."

AFTER TWO DAYS of isolating myself in my room, I emerged at 5:00 a.m. I went to the bookcase where my father kept all his CDs, selected one of Mozart's, and played it on the living room stereo. I sat on the sofa, letting the music swathe me. Soon, I heard my mother stirring, walking out of her room. She went to the kitchen, brewed two cups of barley tea, and joined me on the sofa. The nutty aroma filled the air as the melody of the violin enveloped us.

"I never enjoyed classical music, even though your father loved it," she said. "I prefer music with more bass and drums, like jazz."

I handed her my cup, trotted to my room, and returned with Miles Davis's *Kind of Blue* CD in hand. "This might be better," I said, sliding the disc into the stereo. The mournful trumpet of "So What" swelled in the space, each note like a poem of loss and longing. The music wove its way around us, offering bittersweet comfort in the face of overwhelming grief. For a few precious minutes, the ache in my chest eased.

My mother smoothed her sleeve—though it didn't need

smoothing—before turning her gaze toward me. "I know you are still mourning. So am I. But I want you to know that you had nothing to do with his death."

"I had everything to do with his death." Tears began to pool in my eyes.

"No, that's not true." She let out a deep sigh. "He had been under a lot of stress these past few years. He slept too little, drank too much, and yelled more than he listened. His body could only take so much."

"Still . . . if I had only listened to his wishes . . ."

"No, River. He was proud of you. Whenever he heard other people talking about their children, he would scoff at them. 'Let me tell you about my son.' "

I might have heard him say those things from time to time, but they never fully sank in. I had dismissed them as a matter of ego, rather than genuine love for me. How had it come to this—me, slouched on the sofa, lost in a catatonic daze, hearing about my father's love, not from him but filtered through my mother's words?

"You must understand. SOL means something deeply special to many Koreans." She placed her teacup on the table beside the sofa. "Your grandfather distributed SOL beverages freely to tens of thousands of children and women after the Korean War, when poverty had gripped the country and public water was unsafe. He helped save so many lives. Koreans remain loyal to SOL because it represents hope and miracles. That is the legacy your father wanted you to carry on." Her eyes glistened, tears threatening to spill over. Were they for the pride she felt for my father or for the ache of missing him? Or, perhaps, a final plea for me to reconsider my future, to see it differently than I had. "SOL has not been in a good place for a few years. Competition is fierce, and issues keep popping up. SOL's employees see the writing on the wall, and they are scared. They have families to feed, but they just lost their fearless leader abruptly. They need a new leader right away."

"But what am I supposed to do here? I don't know a single thing about the business." *And what about what I want?*

"You will figure it out. Just like your father did when he took over.

You have his determination, intelligence, and grit. You have his blood." She looked at me reassuringly. "But SOL doesn't have much time. We cannot just sit here and mourn. The situation is bigger than you, me, or your father. The company endured unimaginable pain and sacrifices for decades, far worse than this. Whether you are ready or not, and whether you want it or not, there are things you must do. And it is not just for your father." She spoke in a calm, composed voice, projecting a strength that, in that moment, seemed to surpass even my father's.

"Mother . . . what do you want me to do?"

She rested her hand on my shoulder. "Right now, you are the head of the household. And I need you to start acting like one. Can you do that for me?"

The head of the household? I didn't even know how to navigate being twenty-two. But I understood what she was asking of me—to vanquish my own wants and desires. The fear of what this meant for me and Deborah swallowed me. I could almost feel the crumbling ledge beneath my feet, the wind circling, ready to pull me under.

"HELLO, DEBORAH . . ."

I called her at 9:00 a.m. Korean time, knowing she would be in her room after dinner on the East Coast. She picked up immediately. Her breath hitched the second she heard my voice.

"River!" A sob broke through, sudden and unrestrained, as if she had glimpsed the first sliver of light through a tiny pinhole in a pitch-black cave. "I thought I was losing my mind trying to reach you. You said you'd call, but you never did . . ." Her voice faltered as she struggled to steady herself before speaking again. "Your mother finally answered the phone the other day, and that's when I heard about your father. My heart broke for you. I love you so much. I miss you."

Her voice cradled me, each word filling every void in my soul. I could picture her angelic face overwhelmed by tears, her eyes swollen and red, her cheeks tender and blotchy, and her nose raw from constant tissue wiping. Even so, she would remain achingly exquisite.

"I'm so sorry for keeping you in the dark . . ."

I had vowed to remain composed on the phone. Before I knew it, light fractured across my vision—abrupt, disorienting—like my body was short-circuiting under the weight of it all.

I recounted the events since my arrival at the hospital. I confessed the torturous guilt I carried for my father's death, a burden that grew heavier each day. I shared how the pressure at SOL kept mounting, with eyes on me, waiting to see if I would rise as the successor. And how the sheer heaviness of it felt like it could crush me. "Forgive me for showing up like this. I just feel helpless."

"I know it feels like a lot right now. But you're not alone. I'm right here. Everything's going to be all right."

"I don't know . . ."

"You don't know what, darling?"

"I don't know if I'm strong enough for us."

"Don't say that. You're the strongest person I know."

"But this means I have to be in Korea."

"Then I'll move there after graduation and do whatever you need. We'll get through it together."

"Please listen. Korea won't be kind to you. To us. I'll be at work seven days a week, just trying to save the company. You'll spend most of your time in a country where you have no one, all by yourself. You'll suffer greatly. I saw what my mother went through when my father was rarely available at home. What it did to their relationship . . ." *You will resent me.* I let out a slow breath, releasing the air along with the dread that had been trapped in my chest.

"It's okay. I'll keep myself busy. I'll learn Korean. Or maybe teach English. I'll figure it out. And I can run over to your office every evening so that we can have dinner together. It'll be fun."

"But I can't let myself be the reason you sacrifice your future. I've already caused so much heartache to my family. I don't want to drag anyone else down, especially you."

"What are you talking about? I'm not 'anyone else.' All that matters is for us to be together. Remember? Five daughters?"

"Three to five."

"Yes, three to five, but I'm willing to go up to five for you. You'll never get a deal like this. Ever. Let's forget about our plans in the US. I don't need to go to med school. I can start from scratch in Korea. All I need is you and our five daughters."

"What about your dream? You've worked so hard your whole life to become a doctor. I don't want to take that away from you just so that I can fulfill my filial duty. I just can't."

"I don't understand what you're saying right now. What do you mean, you can't?"

"I've already let my father down. I can't bear the guilt of asking you to give up your dream for me. I love you, but I have no choice."

"River . . . you do have a choice. I'm willing to give up everything to be with you. That's my choice to make. But when you decide for me, it feels like you're taking that away."

"I'm sorry. I just . . . I need time to take care of this. My family and the company . . . they need me."

"I understand. I know how much this weighs on you. But you don't have to face it alone. I'll stand beside you, like I always have for the last four years, and help you carry it. We can get through this together."

"Deborah, please."

"Okay . . . then tell me how long you need. Three months? Six? I'll wait as long as it takes."

"I don't know . . . probably longer than a year. Maybe more. But Deborah . . . you're not hearing me. I'm saying . . . we can't be together right now. We have to see where life takes us."

"I . . . I don't understand. What do you mean we can't be together? Please tell me you don't mean what I think you mean. Tell me I misheard you." When I stayed silent, her voice grew louder, desperate, as if raising it could make me understand. "Just say something. I don't believe you. You're still mourning. You're hurting right now. This isn't the time to decide something like this. Let's talk when you're back for the spring semester."

I shook my head, tears dripping onto my chin. In that unraveling, I remembered lying beside her in bed, tracing every detail—the strands of her hair, the contours of her face, the curve of her neck, the lines of her hands—committing each to memory. With unwavering certainty, I had told her we were destined to be together.

Now, those memories felt like a blur, a single scrawl in chalk on rain-washed pavement. Or just a spectacular lie I had spun for her.

"Hello? River? Did you hear me? We have two months until graduation. That's plenty of time for us to figure this out and plan."

"Deborah . . ." There was no turning back. I had already decided that I had to do this. To deviate now would be in vain. If I saw her, touched her, or kissed her, I wouldn't be able to carry on with what I was supposed to do for those who needed me at SOL. "I'm not returning for the spring semester. I'm not going back to America. And I don't want you to come to Korea. We should . . . we should go our separate ways. If we're meant to be together again someday, we will be."

My chest hollowed as I imagined her frozen, the phone pressed to her ear, disbelief shadowing her face.

"What? This isn't real, right? Tell me this isn't happening. How? Just last week we were talking about . . . I don't understand. I really don't." A strangled whimper tore through the phone, followed by a desperate whisper. "Please, River. You're supposed to tell me that we'll be together until the end of time. You promised. Always be together. No, this isn't the River I know. My River wouldn't do this to me. My River loves me more than his life. I know you, River, and this doesn't feel like you. Please tell me it's some kind of terrible mistake or lapse in judgment . . . whatever it is. Please . . ." She gasped between each sentence, her pleas broken by uncontrollable sobs that stole her breath.

I dug my nails into my skin and bit my lip until I tasted the metallic tang of blood, a deep, red reminder of her heartbreak. Every part of me wanted to reach through the phone, to hold her, to soothe her pain, to tell her I was wrong—to erase every sentence I had spoken in those last minutes of darkness, in that spiral of despair. But instead, I thrust a knife into her heart.

"I'm sorry. I love you, but we cannot be together."

"No! No, River! You can't tell me you love me and do this to me. And this is how you do it? Over the phone? Not even in person? Tell me again this is what you want."

"This is what I want. I'll let you go."

The finality of the words felt like locking away the key to our future and hurling it into the deep ocean. As I hung up, her screams reverberated through the receiver. In that moment, with a chilling clarity, I realized it. I was my father's son: ruthless, heartless, a killer in every sense.

PART II

1994 — 1998

5

RIVER

Fall 1994

The streets of Seoul glowed in a kaleidoscope of color. Trees blazed to glory in sepia and vermilion. Leaves tumbled like confetti, chasing one another down the sidewalk. Brisk air carried the shy sweetness of persimmons and chestnuts. It was the only place outside Boston where I had seen foliage so breathtaking. Here, too, fall felt fleeting yet majestic. Yet each leaf and each scent was a tormenting reminder of the treasured moments I had once shared with Deborah. The beauty of Seoul's fall was life's merciless way of entwining me in memories of that poignant chapter.

The first six months in Korea had been cutting. I had wrestled with guilt and heartbreak, all while buried under an avalanche of responsibilities at SOL. On my first day at the job, Dr. Sangtae Nam, a board member, had told me that running a business was like jumping out of a plane and assembling a parachute on the way down. After experiencing it firsthand, I had to disagree. Jumping would've been the far easier option.

At just twenty-two, I stepped into the role of CEO at SOL. The media had a field day, pouncing on, dissecting, and scrutinizing details from my avoidance of military service to the bitter share-holder disputes.

In South Korea, all men aged eighteen to thirty-five were required to serve two years in the military. But for me, being away from SOL for two years wasn't an option. The company needed me urgently. Fortunately, there were a few alternative routes to fulfill the mandatory military service requirement. One such option was to work at companies considered essential to the Korean economy, such as SOL. After months of negotiations, the Military Manpower Administration granted me an exemption on the condition that I worked at SOL for at least three consecutive years. If I left before then, I would be immediately enlisted. Regardless of the arrangement, the public saw my exemption from the military service as privileged treatment. The accusation weighed heavily on me, even though I was working more than twelve hours a day, seven days a week to keep the company afloat.

In addition, there were the 25 percent owners at SOL. These consisted of two private equity firms, LCK Capital and Infineon Capital. My father's will stipulated that his shares, totaling 75 percent ownership, would be divided between my mother and me—35 percent to her and 40 percent to me. It also stated that the largest shareholder, which would be me, would assume the role of CEO. The firms, however, contended that there were more qualified candidates who were better suited to lead the company, given my lack of management experience. They insisted that the CEO selection process should be conducted properly by the board of directors, made up of a representative from each firm, Dr. Nam as an independent member, and my mother and me as the newly instated members. After a tense voting process, I was appointed CEO with a narrow three-to-two vote. But the rift was undeniable. The atmosphere in the boardroom had already soured from the start.

It wasn't just investors who denounced my appointment as CEO. Nearly all tenured employees at SOL questioned my leadership. In Korean culture, age-based seniority still held authority. Elders demanded respect from those younger. About half the staff had been with SOL for over twenty years—some for over thirty. Every executive was at least twice my age. For many, reporting to someone younger than their own children felt unnatural.

The first few months felt like survival training. The hardest part wasn't facing the skepticism of seasoned executives. It was confronting my own self-doubt. Studying economics, interning at a reputable investment bank, and devouring books on management had built a theoretical foundation. But expecting these to prepare me for leading a complex organization was as unrealistic as expecting to pilot an airplane after reviewing an instructional manual.

Nowhere did my insecurity and inexperience echo louder than in decision-making. SOL employees expected me to have answers, make high-stakes calls, and project confidence, even when I felt anything but sure of myself. Only the hardest decisions reached the CEO's desk. If they were easy, someone else would've handled them. These choices demanded swift action, often without reliable data. The pressure to avoid missteps was immense, but I learned hesitation brought its own risks. When I stalled, the company stalled. But even when I acted, I wasn't spared. Mr. Joonan Kang, our CFO, would say, "Are you sure, sir? Your father wouldn't have done that, sir." His comments gnawed at me. At least he addressed me as *sir*.

The first true test of my decisiveness came during my inaugural quarterly business review with the senior executive team. SOL's product portfolio strategy had reached a critical crossroads when Mr. Sunghan Shin, VP of sales, raised concerns about a territory conflict. His sales team struggled with two nearly identical lemon-lime flavored products, Joa and Spark. Joa, a beloved drink since the Korean War, held a special place in the hearts of many Koreans. However, the product development team believed it was becoming outdated. To combat the imports, which had flooded the market after President Kim's policy to open the country to more foreign companies, the team had decided to develop Spark. With a similar taste but added fizz and an eye-catching design with bright colors, Spark was meant to rejuvenate our market presence. My father, aggressive and impatient, had pushed the team to launch it immediately, forgoing any input from the sales teams.

Unfortunately, Spark didn't deliver the anticipated outcome. It provided some additional revenue but cannibalized Joa sales. A diner ordering a lemon-lime drink at a restaurant wasn't going to order both Joa and Spark. In fact, the restaurant would carry just one of them, not both. This created major contention between the sales teams responsible for each product. The two internal teams competed fiercely for market share, but their rivalry inflicted more harm than any external competitor ever could.

Mr. Shin urged that I had to provide strategic clarity on this issue before the big holiday season. When I asked him and Mrs. Soah Kim, VP of marketing, what options I had, they gave me five different choices. These ranged from maintaining the status quo to killing one of the products. They explained the pros and cons of each option and pleaded with me to make the decision by the end of the week. My head spun.

That evening, I went to dinner with Mr. Kang at a nearby restaurant known for its hearty beef bone soup, seolleongtang. From the outside, no one would have guessed it had stood there for decades. The storefront was nearly anonymous, the name barely visible in small, faded lettering above the door. Inside, vapor clouded the windows like a steam sauna. The scent of long-simmered broth blanketed the air, fused with red pepper paste and minced garlic—flavors that clung to hair and clothes well into the next day. A handful of metal tables sat packed tightly together. The menu listed only three items, scrawled in handwritten letters on a grease-smudged wall.

Mr. Kang and I sat across from each other at a corner table near the window. He had worked alongside my father for more than thirty years—long enough to have seen it all. Decades of meetings, unrelenting debates, and late nights had left their mark: a bald crown fringed with graying hair, deep grooves etched into his forehead, gold-rimmed glasses perched on his nose, and a paunch that hung over his belt.

"Mr. Kang, what do you think I should do?"

"What do you want to do, sir?" He looked at me, his glasses fogged up from the hot soup.

"Aren't you the CFO? I thought you were supposed to help me."

"Yes, I'm here to help you, sir, but you're the one who makes the final decision." He flashed a grin that reminded me of Dr. Sinclair from my days at Andover, who had often worn a similar expression while watching me wade through a concept, just on the brink of a breakthrough. It was a grin that seemed to say, *Don't expect me to spoon-feed you.*

"But you've been working with Mr. Shin and Mrs. Kim for decades. You must know these things." Dismayed, I put down my spoon and looked out the window.

"You should eat first, sir." He pointed at my untouched soup with his chopsticks. "You can't make important decisions when you don't supply your body with fuel. That's what your father used to say, sir."

I grabbed my spoon angrily, scooped a big chunk of rice, and dunked it in the soup. I mixed the rice with the soup and took a big bite. The hot soup burned my tongue and the roof of my mouth, but the warmth spread quickly through my body. I grabbed a piece of kimchi and shoved it in my mouth. The tartness and spiciness of the kimchi woke up my taste buds. Without saying a word, I focused on supplying my body with fuel, as he had suggested. I had forgotten that the last food I had eaten was a piece of rice cake in the morning. I lifted the entire bowl, tilting it to my mouth. I gulped down the last drop of soup and set the bowl back on the table with a thunk.

"There you go. That's how you eat! Sir." Mr. Kang clapped, the way an adult might for a child who finished their vegetables.

I wiped my mouth with a napkin. "Mr. Kang . . . actually, may I call you Mr. Kangster?"

"Excuse me, sir?" He was in the midst of slurping his soup and almost spit it out.

"Kangster. Like a gangster. You're one of the most tenured people at the company. And you must be tough like my father. Let me call you Mr. Kangster. A decision made." I offered him a warm glance, hoping to dismantle any invisible barriers between us and earn his trust as an ally. I needed all the assistance I could get from his wealth of wisdom and experience. Also, hearing about his decades-long working relationship with my father had fostered an unspoken kinship with him—like that of a distant uncle—even though we weren't blood related.

"Is this an American thing, sir?"

"Well, if we're going to spend every waking moment together, we might as well have some fun." I shrugged. "Now, back to the issue with Joa and Spark. Here is what I propose. I think we should phase out Spark. From what I've seen so far, the company has too many problems to tackle. Employees are distracted and unclear about our priorities. We need to narrow our focus, choose a few key initiatives, and commit fully to them. I may be younger than your children, but one thing I firmly believe is that concentrating on a single goal and pursuing it rigorously is the way to win."

All or nothing. I paused before finishing my sentence as Deborah's face suddenly flashed in my mind. It was a frequent occurrence—whether in the middle of a meeting, during a shower, or while exercising. Memories of her would unexpectedly surface and squeeze my heart for a second. Since our breakup, I hadn't spoken to her at all. After I had told Pete I wouldn't be returning to campus, he had graciously packed up my belongings and shipped them to me. Harvard had also mailed me my diploma. Despite not completing the final semester, I had earned enough credits for a bachelor of arts degree in economics. Consequently, the last time I had seen Deborah was the day I had rushed off campus. That final glimpse of her brown eyes, filled with concern and tenderness as she had watched me hop into a cab, seared itself into my consciousness. If I had known that would be our last moment together, would I have gotten into that cab?

I shook off the intrusion. "So please remove Spark from our product line. Instead, put all the resources into Joa. It doesn't make sense to split the team between the two products and not be the best in either. Joa is one of the most beloved drinks in Korea. We must double down on it. We can repackage, refresh its flavor, and go after competitors head-on. What do you think?"

I knew that was what I wanted to do, but I still had my doubts and concerns. For instance, what would we do about the younger consumers who thought Joa was for their parents' generation?

"Are you sure, sir? Your father wouldn't have done that, sir."

"Mr. Kangster! With all due respect, is that going to be your response to everything? You said the same thing last week. And the week before." I crossed my arms, a petulant child bristling with frustration.

"Ha! You sound just like your father right now, sir. Whenever he was about to make a decision, I would say the same thing. It drove him crazy when I told him his father—your grandfather—wouldn't have done that. The truth is, I never worked with your grandfather at all, being so low on the totem pole. But I still said it to your father just to get under his skin." He laughed heartily, and I let out a short burst of laughter myself. "There you go, sir. I think that's the first laughter I've seen from you. So is that your final decision, sir?"

I watched him slurp the last of the soup, tiny beads of sweat forming on his shiny forehead. They said not to judge a book by its cover. That was the case for Mr. Kangster. It turned out he wasn't as provincial as I had thought.

MY LIFE in Korea became a cycle of work, fuel, and sleep. Meanwhile, most of my friends were settling into their first jobs, starting graduate school, or traveling the world. Pete told me Deborah had been accepted to nearly every medical school she applied to—including Harvard. But she couldn't bear to stay there. In the end, she chose UCSF, hoping for a fresh start in San Francisco. I pictured her opening her acceptance letters alone in her room. That wasn't how it was supposed to be. Last winter, I had bought a stethoscope with her name engraved on it as a gift for when she got accepted. My plan had been to ask her to listen to my heart with it and then propose, promising her my lifelong devotion. I had even chosen the perfect spot—a secluded cove near Rockport. Now, that plan felt like a relic from another life.

When Pete told me that Deborah had lost so much weight from her already slender figure during the last semester, I wept discreetly.

"She decided to stop shining," he said.

My sin was unpardonable.

6

RIVER

That year, life revealed the raw, profound reality of loneliness. A concept far more blistering than the solitude I had once mistaken for the same.

During my boarding school years, solitude had become an unyielding presence—so familiar I never thought to question it. In the space it left, I learned to be self-reliant, my days shaped by a discipline my peers hadn't yet learned. While my classmates chased girls and parties to no end, I found solace—perversely, of all things—in the struggle to survive in America: learning English faster, blending in without seeming like a cultural misfit, and excelling academically.

After meeting Deborah in college, my once-solitary world blossomed into one of brilliance and glory. Even the simplest things, like the taste of tap water, seemed to explode with flavor in her presence. I laughed like I had only just learned how. I even hummed a song walking out of my econometrics final exam—notorious for its level of difficulty—while others lamented. Was this the real me, the person I had been all along?

Yet losing her didn't revert me to the person I once was—the one who found comfort in solitude. Instead, it pulled me into a different existence: loneliness. Once I had experienced what my life could be with her and then lost it, I came to understand that loneliness was far more complex and debilitating than solitude. While solitude was a peaceful state of being alone without the ache of emptiness, loneliness brought a deep sense of pain and desperation. It was a force that dragged me beneath the ocean's surface and held me there as I gasped for air, sunlight rippling just above. Close enough to see, but too far to reach. Life introduced me to the black hole of loneliness not by throwing me into darkness, but by letting me taste all of life's beauties, only to snatch them away in a single, merciless sweep.

THOUGH SEOUL BASKED in more than two thousand hours of sunlight that year, each moment felt engulfed in darkness without Deborah. The passage of time became meaningless: weekday, weekend, dawn, or dusk. It all dissolved into a shadow that elongated within me.

Somewhere along the way, the hard parts of my job only got harder. No one—and no book—had warned me that the CEO title came with brutal silence, incessant second-guessing, and a thousand invisible bruises. And of course, there were no pats on the back, no sympathetic words of support. Most days, it felt like a battle fought alone, with my biggest enemy being the voice in my head, constantly questioning if I was cut out for this. No matter what decision I made, it seemed to be met with pushback and frustration. When I felt cornered, turning to the board wasn't an option. It would only validate their doubts about my capability. Reaching out to the executive team? That would cause more confusion than clarity or alignment. But that was the job. The dirty secret of being a CEO. No applause, no lifeline. Only the burden of making decisions no one else was willing to make, and bearing the consequences. Still, I kept moving forward.

What drove me wasn't just the weight of familial obligation. Or the unshakable guilt over my father's death. It was the desperate need to avoid spiraling into the loneliness that came with missing Deborah. The more intense and stressful my job became, the less I dwelled on the heartbreak. I pushed myself relentlessly, determined to keep the pain at bay by elevating every aspect of my performance. In the process, I reveled in honing my craft, and with each new skill, my confidence grew. The burdens were heavy, the challenges constant. But every lesson at work helped me forge a path toward not just survival, but growth.

WHAT MANY DIDN'T REALIZE about the beverage industry was that, at its core, it was all about sales and distribution. Yes, the products had to taste great and have attractive packaging to a certain point, but if they were not on supermarket shelves, in convenience store refrigerators, or at restaurants, it was game over. Vendors fiercely battled for prime spots, like the coveted endcap displays at supermarkets. They all knew just how critical that visibility was to their success.

This industry dynamic split SOL into two distinct factions. One group focused on developing and marketing products, while the other handled manufacturing, distribution, and sales. The former, often graduates from top schools, carried an air of elitism. The latter, seasoned veterans from the school of hard knocks, were fiercely loyal and bled blue through and through. When I took over, these two groups abominated each other, constantly pointing fingers when things went wrong. The tension was at its peak, creating numerous challenges at SOL. Even after almost a year in my job, I had no idea how to bridge the gap between those in tailored suits and those in factory uniforms.

After another exhausting day of marathon meetings, I came home at midnight and collapsed onto the sofa, still clad in my navy-blue suit. Once polished and sharp, my suits had grown worn—wrinkled at the elbows, shiny at the seat.

My mother came out of her room to greet me. No matter the hour of my return, she made it a point to be awake, either waiting for me or stirring from sleep. She would always ask about my day and make sure I had eaten properly. Had she done the same when my father had returned home late from work?

Over the past year, she had been an unfailing source of light. Since leaving home at the age of eleven, I had rarely spent time with her or gotten to know her during my formative years. Before this, all I understood was that she loved preparing meals for me when I visited from America and would send me back with scarves and gloves, making sure I stayed warm in Boston. But since my father's funeral and my painful breakup with Deborah, we had developed a new routine of listening to jazz together when I came home late from work, even if only for ten minutes. In a way, we subtly consoled each other for the loss of our respective loves.

"How was your day?" she asked, taking my suit jacket from my hand. I could already tell she would have it dry-cleaned tomorrow. After letting out a long sigh, I began explaining the mounting tension between the two groups at the company and how their refusal to collaborate was stalling progress. "They're depleting my energy. I feel stuck."

She listened in her usual unhurried way, nodding attentively. In that measured tone she used when suggesting anything about the business—seemingly never wanting to undermine my confidence— she asked, "When was the last time you visited the factories?"

"Not since I was first appointed last year, to introduce myself to Mr. Cho. But it was brief because I had a lunch meeting right after."

Mr. Suhyun Cho, our VP of operations, oversaw all aspects of manufacturing, distribution, and logistics. He often found himself at odds with Mrs. Doyun Lee, our VP of product development. Mr. Cho had started at SOL right after vocational school, never attended college, and worked his way up from a forklift driver to his current role. In contrast, Mrs. Lee held a PhD and had been recruited from a competitor. Their vastly different backgrounds and approaches made for frequent clashes.

"So not since your first month at the job?" She looked at me with a half-smile.

"No. Was I supposed to visit again?"

"When your father first joined SOL, your grandfather was adamant that he spend considerable time at the factory. Although your father was not thrilled about it, he complied. He often said that his initial visit marked a watershed moment for him in his career. Even with his demanding schedule, he made a point to visit different factories, returning each time with fresh ideas."

"So...should I visit too?"

Instead of answering, she patted my shoulder, then walked back to her room, my jacket folded neatly in her arms.

SOL OPERATED factories and warehouses across five provinces. The closest to our Gangnam headquarters was in Anyang—usually an hour and a half away, though morning traffic often stretched it past two. At dawn the next day, I set out for the Anyang site. The company provided a car and driver as part of the CEO perks, but I didn't have the heart to wake him that early. Instead, I caught the bus.

There was a distinctive intensity to a Korean morning, an orchestrated urgency that came alive even before sunrise. Car horns blared impatiently, scooters zipped through tight gaps between lanes, and commuters bounced on their toes, eyes flicking between their watches and the approaching buses. Everywhere, a single refrain echoed: "Hurry, hurry"—the unofficial anthem of the city's waking hours.

I transferred buses midway and arrived at the final stop by 6:50 a.m. From there, it was a short five-minute walk to the factory, a hulking gray structure indistinguishable from the others in the industrial park. What it lacked in aesthetics, it made up for in motion. Semitrucks rumbled in and out of loading docks, their high-pitched beepers slicing through the morning air as they reversed into place. A tall chimney exhaled steam in burly bursts—dense as cotton candy at first, then dissolving into a sky that woke later than the factory. Outside the main entrance, workers in orange vests and hairnets gathered in loose clusters. They traded barbed jokes and easy laughter—the kind of camaraderie forged over years of shared battles.

Inside, the reception area bordered on austerity. The space stood in sobering contrast to the polished marble and fresh-cut flowers of our Gangnam lobby. There were no elegant artworks or sleek furniture to please the eye. Just a few HR notices taped to the wall and a crooked row of "Employee of the Month" photos, their corners peeling away from the wall. Down the hallway, a sparse break room revealed metal lockers and plastic tables, lit by tired fluorescent tubes. The air carried the sting of cleaning chemicals, eased by something sweet—boiled sugarcane, maybe.

I didn't know where to go. This was a world that reminded me—just as the media often insinuated—that I had lived a sheltered life. As I wandered past the lockers, uncertain of my next step, I nearly collided with a man in his thirties, dressed in a green vest.

He looked me up and down, askance. "Here for a job interview?"

"Not exactly . . ." I scanned the room before facing him again. "I'm looking for the factory manager."

He narrowed his eyes. "Your name?"

"River Jung."

He froze for a moment, his brow furrowed in thought. Then, his face turned ashen as he seemingly realized who I was. He immediately bowed to me at a perfect 90-degree angle—and held it longer than I felt comfortable with. The exaggerated respect was automatic, reflexive, almost military. It was strange, being treated with deference not for anything I had done, but for a title. Or maybe this was simply how the factory operated: a strict adherence to hierarchy.

He guided me to the end of the hallway, stopping at a blank office door without a nameplate. "Here you go, sir." Another bow, then he hurried off, as if relieved to be done with the encounter.

Mr. Hyunsoo Cha, the manager of the facilities, appeared to be in his late forties or early fifties—an age I was never good at estimating. His face was marked by deep creases, with acne scars and a square jaw. His thick forearms suggested a life of hard work in the field. He emitted a strong odor of cigarettes and soju, as if his pores were saturated with it. He was the type to steer clear of in a bar fight.

His office was unadorned, giving the impression that he had just moved in. There were no photos on the walls and nothing in the bookcase. The only item on the desk was a worn notebook that looked like it had been rescued from a trash bin. The space spoke loudly about the man behind the desk: no frills, no pretense, no interest in making anyone comfortable. He studied me up and down, his demeanor exuding a "Fire me if you don't like me—I don't give a damn" attitude. He was trying to intimidate me. And it worked.

"What brings you here? This isn't a place for people with soft hands . . . sir." He frowned. I could almost hear him wondering, *What's this young punk doing here?*

"Mr. Cha, I'm here to work on the line. I want to understand how beverages are produced and sold, from start to finish. And I want to do it with my own hands." I showed him my hands, hoping he would see they weren't soft, though they bore the marks of gym workouts rather than hard labor.

"Don't you have more important work at headquarters? Like meetings with other executives over a round of golf? Sir?"

"My intuition tells me this work will be more beneficial for SOL. I'm here to learn, not to cause trouble. Also, I'm not a golfer. I prefer sports that leave me with bruised shins. Or a black eye." The last part came out harsher than I intended. Unnecessary. But I wanted him to know I wasn't just some kid in a suit from Seoul.

"Is this some sort of CEO test that the board of directors asked you to do, sir?"

I shook my head without speaking, hoping the gesture alone would show I was serious. He regarded me for a moment, his expression unreadable. And just like that, a silent standoff locked into place between us.

"Do you have a pair of nonslip work boots, sir?" he finally asked, blinking first.

I allowed myself a small grin, knowing I had won the stare-down. Rather than answering, I lifted my pant legs to show him my boots.

"Good, sir. But you're still in an expensive suit. That won't do." He stood up and gestured for me to follow. "Let me get you proper work gear that real people wear when they go to work. Sir."

MY FIRST JOB was in the returns section of the warehouse, sorting through what others no longer wanted. Consumers could be ruthless: one dented can, a torn label, a scuffed box, or just a change of heart, and back it all came. Sometimes, entire cases of Joa were returned just because the packaging had a scratch. Perfectly good product, wasted. Warehouse workers painstakingly sorted through the mess, salvaging undamaged goods for resale—something machines still couldn't do.

As my shift began, I found myself immersed in a sea of returned products. With a kink in my back, I set to work, grabbing each item, inspecting it, and sorting it into one of two bins marked with a big happy face or a big sad face. I continued this monotonous task, interrupted only by a thirty-minute meal break in the staff cafeteria. In addition to the meal break, I had two additional scheduled fifteen-minute breaks during the day. Aside from those brief respites, it was a relentless cycle of inspecting and sorting. On the contrary, the office workers at headquarters enjoyed far more flexibility—freely stepping out to run errands or grab coffee from outside cafés, even though coffee machines were available on every floor.

Although Mr. Cha didn't introduce me as the CEO to the warehouse staff, news of my presence quickly spread. The workers kept their distance, eyeing me as if I were an extraterrestrial. I kept my head down and worked as hard as I could, hoping my effort would speak louder than any title. By the end of my eight-hour shift, my entire body was sore. Even with my eyes shut on the bus ride home, I could still see the glint of cans and bottles flashing behind my eyelids, my arms tightening reflexively. The grueling routine frontline workers faced left me humbled. What did they do at home after enduring such strenuous shifts? At least I had the comfort of a hot bath waiting for me at my mother's house.

MR. CHA SEEMED TAKEN aback to see me again the next day.

"Back for more, sir? Thought we'd scared the suit right off you." He chuckled, guiding me to the quality control area, where the conveyor belt transported finished products. My task for the day was to randomly select cans and bottles and scan them for any irregularities or defects.

"After yesterday's deep dive, sir, I bet you can smell a crooked label from a mile away," he said, pushing his nose up like a pig's snout.

The core work at the quality control station remained unchanged, though the environment was different, with the constant whir of the conveyor belt droning in my ears. Metal arms hissed and thunked every few seconds in the distance, releasing rows of freshly packaged drinks onto the rubber magic carpet. The bottles clicked and rattled like they were chortling with each other in uncontainable excitement, marching down the belt. Around me, workers stood spaced about ten feet apart, eyes scanning labels, caps, and fill lines with clinical focus. I quickly got into the swing of things. Then, about ten minutes into my shift, a woman in her fifties yelled out and stormed over to me just as I placed a bottle of Joa back on the conveyor belt.

"Hey, young man! Stop!" Her sharp voice cut through the hum of the machinery like a siren. She slammed a large red button, bringing the conveyor belt to an abrupt halt. Snatching the bottle from the line, she thrust it back toward me. "Look." Deep grooves in her face sharpened as she jabbed at the label. "Can't you see it's off-center? If you're going to be sloppy, don't even think about coming back tomorrow."

Embarrassed, I bowed my head. "I'm sorry. I'll do a better job."

She clicked her tongue—a jagged tsk-tsk—then hit the green button to restart the conveyor and went back to work. Her hands moved with the practiced fluidity of a calligrapher crafting elegant strokes. Her eyes, though framed by the wrinkles of time and toil, held a spark of focus as determined as the gaze of a hawk locked on to its prey.

Even with the repetitive tasks, time passed quickly. When the lunch chime echoed overhead, the workers let out a collective sigh of relief and wandered over—cracking jokes, nudging elbows, and grumbling about what side dishes might be served. But whenever their eyes met mine, they quickly looked away, their expressions turning guarded.

The cafeteria was a far cry from the sleek, brightly lit dining hall at headquarters, where executives debated whether to upgrade the furnishings or reconfigure the layout. Here, the floors were worn linoleum, the walls bare concrete, with narrow windows set high up, letting in only slivers of daylight. The workers lined up with stainless trays, their dimpled compartments glinting like silver under the lights. With practiced speed, the kitchen staff filled each tray with rice, seaweed soup, kimchi, gyeran-mari, and jang-jorim. I walked over to the same empty corner table as the day before and sat down. Just as I lifted the spoon for my first taste of soup, the woman who had scolded me earlier scurried over.

"Sir, I'm sorry. I didn't realize who you were. I don't know what came over me. Please don't fire me." She lowered her head in a formal bow, carefully avoiding my startled stare. Someone must've informed her of my title. A pang of guilt struck me as I imagined her shock. I stood up and bowed back.

"Please, ma'am, you were just doing your job. And you're excellent at it," I said, extending my hand for a shake, which she accepted with a continued bow of her head. Her hands were calloused and swollen. "If you don't mind me asking, may I please know your name?"

"It's Bongja Son, sir."

"Mrs. Son, please do me a favor and join me for lunch. If you would like, please bring your colleagues along as well. I could use some company." I gestured toward the three empty chairs at my table.

Her eyes widened before she trotted back to her table and spoke to three other women her age. Soon, they all grabbed their trays and moved over to my table, then sat down with careful, tentative motions. They shifted in their chairs, glancing at one another. One adjusted her seat multiple times while another fidgeted with her tray.

"Thank you for joining me. It's a pleasure to meet you all. I'm River Jung."

"We know who you are," the woman with a bandanna said, punctuating her words with a sharp flick of her hand. "You are more handsome in person." She let out a sheepish giggle, cut short by an elbow from the woman next to her. "Sir."

"Thank you. Please, no need to be overly formal. I imagine you have children my age."

"My oldest daughter is getting married in two months," Mrs. Son said shyly, her earlier intensity nowhere to be seen.

"Congratulations. You must be so proud."

"Thank you. Her fiancé is an assistant manager at the largest car dealership in town. If you ever need a new car, let me know. I'll make sure he gives you a great deal. He listens to whatever I say!"

"Except when you tell him to get more exercise," the woman in the bandanna chimed in, setting off a round of laughter.

"At least he eats everything I cook, unlike your picky son-in-law." Mrs. Son shot back, grinning. More laughter followed.

Through the rest of lunch, we shared jokes, stories, even jabs—the kind of banter that let me loosen the tension in my shoulders and forget who I was supposed to be. It struck me that this was the first time in a year I had felt free from the pressure to maintain the facade everyone expected of me. Was this what leadership was supposed to feel like? Not commanding a room, but being invited in? Maybe, after all, it wasn't about being unassailable, but about letting others see what lay beneath—what moved me—when my defenses came down.

IN THE FOLLOWING MONTH, I immersed myself in each facet of factory life: loading and unloading, assembling and sorting, picking and packing, lifting and stacking. I mastered operating a pallet jack without constantly bumping it against my foot. I also joined the workers for skewered chicken gizzards during their happy hours, where they bombarded me with, "Do you have a girlfriend? Do you want some introductions?"

Through my close work with frontline workers, I developed a deep, enduring bond with them. The Korean word *jeong*, pronounced like my last name, encapsulated this connection—one that had no direct English equivalent. *Jeong* encompassed the depth of love, loyalty, and belonging. It could only be cultivated over time, through shared experiences, mutual care, and emotional ties. Experiencing *jeong* with them taught me that human connections could transcend social boundaries.

On my last day working at the factory, I headed home earlier than usual. My mother's face lit up at the sight of the freshly baked kkwabaegi, twisted Korean donuts, in my hand. We settled into the dining room, savoring the crispy, chewy donuts with warm milk.

"Is it true that using SOL's trucks to deliver emergency kits during national crises was your idea?" I asked, recalling a conversation I'd had with one of the truck drivers.

"I brought it up to your father after Typhoon Vera," she said, covering her mouth as she chewed kkwabaegi. "I saw all the trucks driving around with empty containers after making their deliveries and just sitting idle in the evenings. So I thought they could be better used if they doubled as emergency vehicles. I did not think your father would take it seriously, but I am glad he implemented the idea."

The typhoon had left six thousand people homeless in 1986. Thanks to her suggestion, SOL no longer just helped people quench their thirst—they also helped communities rebuild in the aftermath of disaster.

"I've also learned that you visit the factory and warehouse workers on major holidays with gifts. They really appreciate you."

"Oh, there is nothing to make a fuss about. I just wanted to show my deep gratitude. Without them, who would be up at five a.m. delivering products during Chuseok or Lunar New Year? They sacrifice their holidays to ensure SOL's success."

"I didn't realize how much they revere you. To them, you're like a celebrity. What other surprises do you have up your sleeve?"

My mother grew up in a poor part of Seoul, torn by the Korean War. Like my father's tragic childhood, hers had its own share of hardship. My grandfather died during the war, before my mother's first birthday. She barely got to know my grandmother either, who spent her days selling whatever she could at the market. But my mother wasn't entirely alone. My aunts and uncle, still just children themselves, adored her. They recognized her academic gift early on and began bringing her discarded newspapers and worn schoolbooks left on stoops—anything they could to feed her hunger to learn. In a village where literacy was scarce, each scrap was a treasure that revealed a world beyond her own.

My grandmother passed away just after my mother graduated from elementary school. My aunts dropped out of high school and began working to support her and my uncle. Before long, my uncle dropped out too. Yet my mother's determination to continue her education never wavered. Carried by the sacrifices of her older siblings, she pressed forward. Her acceptance into Ewha Womans University—rare for a woman without wealth or connections—was nothing short of a miracle. After marrying my father and leaving her studies at Ewha unfinished, my mother felt she had lost her sense of self and direction. But when I was born, she poured herself into motherhood—never asking for recognition, only wanting to give.

I watched her, trying to reconcile the woman of grace and strength before me with the girl who had come from so little and made it all the way here. She looked down, swirling the milk in her glass with both hands wrapped around it. "What other surprises do I have?" she repeated. "Well, there's a lot that I've never told you. Do you remember much about how you ended up leaving Korea in middle school? It was me, not your father."

Contrary to what I had believed, it was my mother who suggested to my father that I study in America. My father had no idea that

American boarding schools welcomed promising students from around the world. My mother had seen my potential early on. She had felt that I wouldn't be able to fully realize it within the confines of the Korean education system and the strained dynamics of our family.

"It was the hardest decision of my life. I slept in your room for months after you left for America. What kind of mother willingly lets her only son leave home at eleven? It broke my heart every time I thought about you, alone out there. There were moments I almost brought you back. But I had to be strong." Her voice faltered as she grabbed a napkin. I thought she would use it to dab her eyes, but she held it in her hand before placing it back on the table. "Even though it was an excruciatingly difficult decision, seeing the man you have become today, it was the best choice I could have made."

"I'm grateful you sent me to America," I said, my head lowering. *I never would've met Deborah if you hadn't.* A bittersweet smile tugged at the corners of my lips as the irony of the thought lingered.

THE NEXT MORNING, returning to the polished headquarters, nostalgia for the factory crept in—my coveralls, my nonslip boots, the sarcastic banter, the hum of the conveyor belt, the beep of the forklifts, and even the humble bowl of seaweed soup from the cafeteria. I couldn't wait to go back soon.

As the elevator ascended to the top floor for the monthly executive review, a newfound energy surged through me. Stepping into the pristine conference room, however, I sensed the collective weight of the team's gaze.

"Where has he been?" Mrs. Lee's whisper to Mrs. Kim was audible over the murmur of discontent. The air was thick with tension, as the product and marketing executives occupied one side of the room while the operations and distribution executives sat on the other.

Taking my seat at the head of the table, I offered a smile, which was met mostly with blank stares and furrowed brows. Mr. Cho coughed dryly and took a sip of water, while Mrs. Lee and Mrs. Kim exchanged another quick, subtle glance. The only one to smile back was Mr. Kangster.

I proceeded to make my announcements. "I have two directives to share this morning. First, I acknowledge your concerns about the cafeteria's condition. I also understand that my father previously supported the renovation. However, I believe that allocating our resources and budget to remodel it is no longer justifiable. Therefore, I will not be approving the proposal. Instead, I plan to redirect the budget toward improving the conditions at our factory and ware-house in Anyang. Once we achieve meaningful gains in employee safety and productivity as a result, I want to allocate more funds to expanding improvements to other factories and warehouses. Mr. Cha will take charge of this effort."

As I scanned the room, I met a wave of disappointed expressions. Mrs. Lee's mouth opened slightly, as though she considered speaking up, but she quickly closed her mouth and leaned back.

"Secondly, all salaried employees at headquarters must spend two days working at the Anyang factory before the end of June. Failure to comply will result in the forfeiture of quarter-end performance bonuses."

The room erupted into a cacophony of murmurs, complaints, and objections.

"There will be no exceptions," I said, turning to Mr. Kangster. "That includes the CFO."

He gave me a thumbs-up. "Your father would've supported this decision, sir."

7

RIVER

Winter 1995

I had never been fond of Christmas. After so many years away from my family, the holiday came to mean desolation more than joy. Until I met Deborah.

It had been her favorite holiday, though spending our first Christmas together hadn't been part of the plan. She left for home a few hours after we gave ourselves to one another. I stayed on campus, where the silence turned cavernous without her. With most students gone for the break, the absence of voices and motion felt even sharper on Christmas Eve. To keep the emptiness from swallowing me, I went for a walk and wandered all the way to Central Square. Christmas lights blinked half-heartedly as a few procrastinators hunted for last-minute gifts, their urgency at odds with the square's tired cheer. While searching for a place to eat, I passed a travel agency window advertising a last-minute flight to LA for ninety-nine dollars. The only catch was that I would have to take the first flight out on Christmas morning and return on the last red-eye flight that night. But with the time difference, I would land in LA by 9:00 a.m. and have the entire day with Deborah. I couldn't resist the opportunity to see her, even if for twelve hours. Without telling her, I booked the flight.

I arrived at her doorstep just as her family was about to open presents on Christmas morning. As soon as she heard my voice, she came running, screaming, "Look what Santa just delivered!"

That day, surrounded by her love and her family's kindness, Christmas took on a new meaning for me. I began to understand why she saw the world with such optimism. Her family embodied warmth and glee, their laughter spilling into every corner of the home—even over minor mishaps that might have frustrated others. There was no pretense, only an easy contentment that surrounded them. And they loved Deborah endlessly, as I did.

Her father was a chemistry professor at Pomona College, and her mother taught music at Mt. San Antonio College. They had met as teenagers at McGill University and grown up side by side—through shared lecture halls, late-night poutines, and summers without air conditioning. After her father completed his PhD and secured a position at Pomona, they married and moved to the greater LA area, where they had lived ever since. Watching her parents sing carols together, I envisioned Deborah and me, aged and wise, sharing a scene just like this decades later.

Later that morning, after the carols quieted, Deborah and I retreated to a sunlit nook by the window.

"I made this for you." She handed me a white gift box. "My first attempt at knitting."

I opened the lid, not knowing what to expect, but paused when I saw the soft wool peeking out of white tissue. Beneath it, a hand-knit scarf waited for me to drape it around my neck. I reached in, careful not to tug or crease it, and lifted it free. It was lighter than it looked. And warm. Very warm. I folded it in my hands like a treasure, pressed it to my nose, and breathed in deep, picturing her fiddling with knitting needles, pulling threads through the loops, hour after hour. Then I wrapped it around my neck, letting its love sink in.

She beamed at me, waiting for my response—until her smile faltered, replaced by wide-eyed horror. "Oh no!" she yelped.

It was only then that I noticed the rest. The scarf was supposed to feature a gingham pattern in cream and maroon, but the checkered design had turned into an eclectic mix of mismatched shapes and sizes. It was also a bit short, making it look like I was wearing a fluffy bow tie.

"I thought I'd finally gotten it right, but I guess not!"

"This is the most beautiful scarf I've ever had. I'm going to wear it every day," I said, running my fingers over the cozy fabric.

"Even in the summer?"

"Even in the summer."

"Ooh, I can't wait to see that. I'm going to get you matching swim trunks so you can wear them with the scarf at the beach!"

"Will you knit the trunks too?"

"With pom-poms."

~

FIVE YEARS LATER, I donned the scarf as I walked into the empty SOL office on Christmas morning. While my mother had invited me to join her and my aunts on a holiday trip to Jeju Island, I had chosen to spend the downtime preparing for the new year instead. Just as I thought SOL's business was stabilizing—Joa was regaining market share, and the two major divisions were finally coalescing after my push to foster *jeong*—new challenges kept emerging.

Two issues, in particular, gave me immense headaches as I reviewed the annual planning memo. The first was the company's outdated promotion policy. It rewarded age and tenure over merit—and we were bleeding talent because of it. Competitors dangled better titles and broader responsibilities, and our top talent left. In any workplace, motivations—conscious or not—boiled down to a simple question: "What's in it for me?" For ambitious employees, company success wasn't enough. Not if their own careers stalled. When senior staff clung to coveted roles, it left rising performers disillusioned. Several told me that they appreciated the turnaround I was leading, but they had to look out for their own futures. I couldn't blame them. Loyalty had limits, and we were testing them. If we failed to address it, we'd keep losing the very people we needed to win.

On the product side, even after phasing out Spark to focus on Joa, we struggled to attract younger consumers who favored our competitors' newfangled products. To them, Joa was something their parents drank. We had a few new flavors in the pipeline, but it was uncertain whether they would be enough to change that perception.

By midday, I had assessed all viable options, yet no definitive path emerged. I got up from my desk, picked up the scarf Deborah had given me, and walked over to the window. Outside, the winter streets of Gangnam lay deserted. Remnants of last night's trash sat scattered along the curbs, waiting for collection. Christmas pulled love indoors, around shared meals, around warm blankets, into a pocketful of sanctuaries—even if only for a day.

I could almost see Deborah at home, curled up with coffee on the sofa as her parents unwrapped presents, her sisters' giggles and teasing about gift choices reverberating through the living room. That smile, that laughter—so vivid in my memory—tore at me. I looked down at the scarf. Then I whispered into the silence, "Merry Christmas."

8

RIVER

Summer 1996

During my first two years at SOL, I abandoned any semblance of a social life. The pressure of keeping the company afloat—and proving I deserved to lead it—consumed me. Every conversation outside work felt performative, like I was pretending to be someone who hadn't spent long days in the office firefighting. Even at company events, where laughter and lightness filled the venue, looming business decisions—and the unbearable longing for Deborah—crowded my mind. I stayed just long enough to thank the team before making a discreet exit.

Some of the affluent families my father had lined up as potential matches for me eventually reached out to my mother. Invitations to social soirées followed—each laced with ulterior motives. But she knew better. After witnessing the pain I had endured with Deborah —and likely sensing my unwavering love for her—my mother shielded me from the noise. Over the phone, she would respond with a wry chuckle, "He works too much to be any fun, I am afraid," then quickly change the subject. Had she pushed, I might have shown up to those extravagant banquets in sweatpants, rambling nonsense—or nothing at all. The news outlets would've had a frenzy: "SOL's Young CEO: Out of His Depth in Boardrooms *and* Ballrooms."

~

PETE and I had caught up a few times over the phone last year. After college, he had thrown himself into his first manuscript, chasing the passion he had carried for years. While his sisters and cousins followed the well-worn paths of business and politics, he had always dreamed of becoming a writer. Back in college, I would often see him in the dorm or around campus, hunched over a notebook, scribbling fugacious thoughts, half-formed ideas, and imaginative takes on the mundane. But during our last call, he admitted something he hadn't before: a brutal case of writer's block.

"It's been weeks. Maybe months."

"I'm sorry to hear that. Is there anything I can do from seven thousand miles away?"

He sighed. "I don't know. The words just aren't there. I keep thinking about chucking the whole manuscript."

"I've always seen a gifted writer in you. One of a kind in the making. You've got this. I mean it."

"Thanks . . . but the whole thing's just . . . demoralizing. I don't know if I can do this."

"Could a change of scenery help? Come visit. I would love to show you around Seoul."

"Maybe," he said after a pause. "Yeah, maybe."

About six months after that call, he arrived in Seoul, one of the final stops on a three-month tour of Asia. I spotted him immediately as he walked through the gate at the airport, though his hair now brushed his shoulders and his beard had grown into a dense thicket that covered half his face. Even with two years and a new look between us, he smiled the same way—a slight crook on one side, eyes twinkling behind his glasses. The moment he hugged me, it felt like we were back at Harvard, trading dry humor or debating whether anyone ever really changed. I supposed the jury was still out on that question.

That night, we wandered through the bustling streets of Apgu-jeong, heading toward one of my favorite restaurants. It had been a while since I had walked these streets without rushing. With Pete beside me, it felt as if I were seeing it all for the first time. There was a symphony to it, a harmony in the tumult, that I hadn't noticed before. A steady stream of people swirled around us, cars wove through intersections, and neon signs flared above the sidewalks. Every movement seemed choreographed, as if the city danced to the guidance of an unseen conductor. Amid this strange and beautiful chaos, sleek glass towers rose beside austere concrete buildings, built in haste and practical to a fault. Yet somehow, they were full of character, their facades decorated with signboards for dentist offices, cram schools, and hair salons.

"Seoul feels more like Berlin in spirit than Bangkok," he said. "There's no tropical ease. Just a restless tension between old and new."

"That's a perceptive take. Seoul has this understated edge. Definitely not what most tourists expect."

As we approached the restaurant, the scent of barbecued meat and garlic drifted toward us. The doors swung open, and heat, smoke, and commotion rushed out to welcome us. Salarymen packed nearly every table, grilling meat, clinking glasses, and airing grievances about their bosses. The moment we headed to a table, the noise dipped, and all eyes swiveled to Pete. Although South Korea had opened its domestic market years ago, foreigners were still a rare sight, especially those who were not associated with the US military. In a restaurant full of suited Koreans, Pete—with his long hair, thick beard, and casual T-shirt—broke the uniformity.

As we took our seats, people continued to stare, their whispers just loud enough for me to catch snippets.

"Is that white guy a singer? Only rock and rollers sport hair like that."

"That Korean guy speaks English fluently. Must be his translator."

"Wait, that's Mr. Jung, the young CEO who avoided military service."

I shifted uncomfortably, but Pete—usually so reserved—seemed to thrive in the unexpected spotlight. He flashed an exuberant wave at our wide-eyed audience, who quickly turned away and stopped gawking.

"I thought they were going to ask for my autograph."

"They're waiting for you to sing first."

"It's coming. Just need a few shots of soju first," he winked.

I shook my head, half-laughing. "Anyway, tell me all about your adventure so I can live vicariously through you. Technically, my job counts as my military duty, which means I'm not allowed to travel overseas, at least for another year or so until I've fulfilled it." I poured his inaugural glass of Joa.

After taking a sip, he gave two thumbs-up. "Very refreshing!"

For all his typical contemplative demeanor, he was chatty during dinner. It seemed as if three months of solo travel had unlocked a dormant loquacious nature within him. He regaled me with stories from his peregrination, which had begun in Jakarta and taken him through five different countries in Asia. He raved about the best bowl of laksa he'd had, at a tiny hawker stall in Kuala Lumpur, and how he had gotten lost on his way to Hanoi, only to stumble upon the enchanting city of Hoi An. He also recounted how, while watching the sunset in Cebu, the journey had sparked creative ideas, inspiring him to rewrite his manuscript from a fresh perspective. His tale, told through his infectious energy, temporarily erased the loneliness that had plagued me.

"Your turn now," he said, munching on kongnamool—marinated soybean sprouts. "What's it like being the youngest CEO in Korea?"

"Where do I begin . . ." I exhaled, flipping kalbi on the charcoal grill with tongs. The kalbi sizzled, sending a symphony of crackles and pops through the air. "Most days, I just feel like a clueless kid with a fancy title." I grumbled about the never-ending problems piling up, the skepticism about my ability to steer the company, and the ongoing struggle to build my confidence in the midst of it all.

"The past two years have been a complete blur. If anything, it's only getting harder."

"That sounds brutal. Sorry, my friend."

"Thanks . . . but even with the challenges, I'm constantly learning. I feel like I've grown a lot. It's been a journey full of invaluable life lessons." I placed some freshly cooked kalbi from the grill onto his plate.

"I don't know how you do it. Here I am, traveling the world and eating all this amazing food!" He wrapped a piece of kalbi, roasted garlic, and shredded radish kimchi in crisp lettuce. He opened his mouth wide and popped the whole thing in. His eyes fluttered like he had just sunk into a hot salt bath.

As we feasted, he updated me on our friends. Kate was understudying in *WonderFool*, the acclaimed musical, eagerly waiting for the lead actress to lose interest and return to Hollywood. Abigail remained at Windsor, dreading each workday and contemplating quitting soon. Tom had climbed the ladder at his father's real estate firm in Boston. Amy and Jack, who had started dating senior year and ended up at Columbia Law School together, were now engaged—a development that left me wistful. Hadn't all our friends been sure that would be Deborah and me?

The mountains of food gradually disappeared from the table, but my appetite had long wandered elsewhere. I twiddled my chopsticks, watching Pete devour his naengmyeon—cold buckwheat noodle with pear and radish in icy broth.

"So . . . have you heard . . . about her?" My voice wavered, my words caught between hesitation and hope.

"I was wondering when you'd bring that up," he said, finishing his last bite. "After graduation, she cut ties with everyone. We tried calling to see how she was doing, but she never returned our calls. It was like she wanted to erase any connection to our circle. Everyone else stayed on the East Coast, while she went west. Maybe that distance made it easier. I am sure she's doing well at UCSF. No news is good news, right?"

I absentmindedly grabbed a burnt piece of meat from the grill with my chopsticks, then placed it on my plate without any intention of eating it. For the first time since he and I had reunited, silence stretched between us. I rested my chopsticks beside the bowl. He studied me, running his fingers through his beard.

"Well, what would you like to do tonight?" I asked, checking the time on my watch.

"Where do introverts go to sip something strong and lament every life choice?"

That night, I drank more than I ever had before, only to reaffirm my revulsion for alcohol—the bitter taste, the loss of control, the physical pain that followed. Still, it felt like the kind of thing people with broken hearts were supposed to do, as if drowning the pain in alcohol might numb it. It didn't work, though. No amount of alcohol could mend what was broken. Amid the ache, however, I found solace in Pete's presence. A reminder that having a friend like him could assuage even the deepest wounds.

9

RIVER

Winter 1997

T he events of 1997 served as another lesson on how quickly life's unpredictable currents could alter one's fortunes. The year opened with a false sense of promise. Our new product launches aimed at younger generations soared to wild success. Tabon, the low-calorie drink infused with vitamins, became an overnight sensation after an unexpected boost from a popular boy band. Although we never paid them royalties, tabloids caught them holding it at concerts, speculating about what they were drinking. Within weeks, corner stores were selling out of Tabon faster than we could stock them. Another new drink, Ayra, a versatile canned Americano served hot or cold, also gained popularity among college students and young professionals burning the midnight oil. These were the kinds of wins we needed—desperately—after three grueling years. That spring, the mood at SOL bloomed with euphoria, as giddy and buoyant as the cherry blossoms outside. Yet the optimism quickly faded. Certain aspects of life were beyond our control. In fact, I didn't think SOL would survive beyond 1997.

By the time spring turned to summer, Asia's financial stability began to crumble. Months of uncertainty around the weakening Thai baht came to a head when Thailand's foreign reserves collapsed. Panic surged, rapid and uncontrollable. The financial crisis swept across Asia, hitting Malaysia, the Philippines, Indonesia, and Singapore in rapid succession.

By late summer, the South Korean won started to depreciate sharply against the US dollar. Whispers of impending bankruptcies among major Korean companies ignited, spreading like an inferno. Even before the public caught wind of it, Hanbo, a major player in the steel industry, declared bankruptcy. Subsequently, another company followed, and another. It felt like watching a roller coaster plummet with no brakes.

I was well aware that my father had accumulated substantial debt over the years to drive aggressive expansion. Twenty million dollars of debt, to be exact. It had been one of the many concerns that kept Mr. Kangster and me awake at night for the past three years. My father had believed that SOL's growth potential justified this level of debt. In a growing economy, he might have been right. However, he couldn't have anticipated that this debt issue would spiral out of control due to an exogenous financial crisis of this scale.

Our limited international presence shielded us from the level of foreign currency risk that plagued other companies. The challenge was that the debt was due in December, and with the weakened financial market and banking sector, few—if any—banks were willing to refinance our maturing debt. At the beginning of the year, we thought we had secured a deal with the Commercial Bank of Seoul, with whom we had a banking relationship spanning decades. But as the won continued to plummet, the bank battled for its own survival. Every newspaper predicted their imminent shutdown.

Unfortunately, we didn't have enough cash reserves to pay off debt by year-end. If we couldn't repay it, we would either have to sell the company at a fraction of its fair market value or declare bankruptcy, ending more than sixty years of SOL's history. All this, on my watch.

~

AT OUR OCTOBER BOARD MEETING, the somber mood clashed with the oblivious flamboyance of the fall foliage bursting outside SOL headquarters. All the board members, including my mother, attended. I had also invited Mr. Kangster and our general counsel, Mr. Heeju Byeon, to provide additional guidance.

"What do our private equity partners think?" Mr. Kangster asked, after walking us through the financial scenarios and the limited options we had. He glanced between Jason Choo from LCK Capital and Alex Kim from Infineon Capital. The two partners scrupled, each waiting for the other to speak first. Eventually, Jason exhaled and broke the silence. "Well . . ." he murmured, his gaze drifting around the room.

Born in Minneapolis, he had gone to Dartmouth for undergrad and earned an MBA from the University of Chicago. Upon completing business school, he relocated to Korea to begin his career at LCK and quickly advanced through the ranks. With his crew cut, frameless glasses, and slim build, he projected the kind of spreadsheet precision he demanded from everyone around him.

"LCK has always believed in SOL's potential. We'd love to be a good partner and double down on the company," he said. "We're willing to pay off the entire twenty million dollars of debt in exchange for additional ownership in the company."

His response landed squarely within one of the scenarios I had anticipated. I rubbed my chin with my left hand—a signal Mr. Kangster and I had prearranged as a cue to proceed.

"Thank you. We're grateful to hear that," Mr. Kangster said. "I'm curious to hear what kind of terms you're considering." He had often reminded me, especially when I was eager to make a rash decision, that every deal had a catch. It was always in the details.

"We can get into the specific terms if this is the direction Mr. Jung wants to pursue," Jason said, glimpsing at me as I tried to decipher his intentions.

"Let's cut to the chase," Alex interrupted, drawing attention from the group. "It's already getting late, and I'm starving."

Alex, a former swimmer at Northwestern, was in his late forties and no longer as physically fit as he once was. His Korean wasn't fluent, so he often relied on Jason for translation, particularly with longer statements full of business jargon. While he lacked Jason's intellectual sharpness, he had a remarkable ability to bulldoze complex deals to completion.

Jason removed his glasses, wiped them with his handkerchief, and put them back on. "All right. We'd like an additional twenty percent ownership in exchange."

"Twenty percent? Are you saying the company is only worth a hundred million dollars?" Mr. Kangster snapped. "When you invested in us over five years ago, you valued us at two hundred million dollars. Since then, our business has grown, and we've successfully fended off international competitors. And our new products show real promise. SOL should be valued significantly higher now than it was five years ago. So why has our valuation been cut in half?"

"Do you have any other options?" Jason shrugged, almost belittling Mr. Kangster, and turned to look at me. "We're ready to wait and see what other options become available."

An uneasy quiet settled over the group. The boardroom seemed to hold its breath, as if submerged underwater.

My mother, usually a reserved observer at the quarterly board meetings, raised her hand, disrupting the stillness. "Since I'm not as financially savvy as you gentlemen, let me clarify," she said, looking around the room. "LCK and Infineon will pay off SOL's twenty million dollars of debt due in December. In return, they'll gain an extra twenty percent stake in the company. This would reduce River's and my combined share from seventy-five percent to fifty-five percent, while LUK's and Infineon's stake would rise from twenty-five percent to forty-five percent. Is that what's being proposed here?"

After Jason translated her statement for Alex, everyone nodded.

"But there's one more condition." Jason paused, ensuring he had our full attention. "LCK wants to replace the current CEO with one of our choosing. We need an experienced CEO to realize SOL's full potential."

Silence reclaimed the room, wrapping it in an all-encompassing hush. I stared at Jason. He met my gaze and tilted his head. A wave of heat crept up my neck. My mother, eyes closed, looked as if she were meditating in a temple under siege. Mr. Kangster, visibly shaken, rose from his chair, walked to the wall, and leaned against it.

"Jason," I said, snapping the room out of its thick layer of shock. "Since my appointment as CEO over three years ago, I've helped streamline our product line, successfully launch new products, and boost company morale to an all-time high—at least before the financial crisis. What exactly would a new CEO do differently?"

Jason averted his eyes and let the silence stretch.

"That says enough." I turned to the others. "Time is of the essence. I would like to make a decision tonight. Can we break for now and regroup in two hours?"

As Jason and Alex exited the boardroom, Dr. Nam, Mr. Kangster, and Mr. Byeon approached me and my mother.

I raised a hand, stopping them midstep. "Gentlemen, could you give us a moment alone?"

They exchanged brief glances before excusing themselves. In the empty boardroom, I settled into a chair beside my mother, who sat as if she were listening to the wind move through tall grass. Her unexpected equanimity caught me off guard.

"Mother, what's on your mind?"

She fixed her gaze on mine, letting the pause harden into discomfort. "Are you happy?"

"Happy? What do you mean?"

"It's a simple question."

"No, it's not. I haven't had a single night of peaceful sleep or a proper day off for the past three years. My every waking moment has been dedicated to keeping SOL afloat. And now, I might be the one to end our family legacy. So thinking about my happiness feels like a luxury."

"I see." Her eyes sagged at the corners. "Do you remember when I used to take you to the Buddhist temple as a child? You would play with the rescued dogs in the courtyard while I meditated."

"Yes . . . I would barge into the meditation room and ask when we were going home." I replied out of courtesy, though my thoughts raced ahead, impatient to comprehend her intentions. *Please, Mother, get to the point,* I urged silently.

"One of the universal truths that Buddhism teaches is this notion of impermanence, where all things are constantly changing. Our suffering happens when we hold on to things that are not meant to be permanent. We can stop suffering by letting go of attachment."

She closed her eyes, seemingly gathering her thoughts, then opened them again. "Over the last three years of watching you step up and lead SOL, I was so proud. You have done an impossible job."

"Thank you, but how is this Buddhist teaching relevant here?"

"Every day, I watch the pain digging deeper into you. Staying here, making that sacrifice. Your father and I pushed you into this. We imposed our desire to preserve SOL's legacy on you. Against impermanence. I cannot shake the guilt that you have suffered too much for it. I thought you would move on from Deborah, find joy again. Maybe with someone new. But that pain, it still follows you." She averted her eyes, trying to mask her tears, but she quickly brushed her emotions aside. "You are so young, yet you are trapped in this cage. It anguishes me to see you carry such a heavy burden of guilt. I worry it will consume you. Then what?"

"I still don't follow where you're going with this, Mother."

"When Jason made his proposal, I questioned whether surrendering was the right thing. Not to Jason, Alex, or the financial crisis, but to my own attachment to SOL. Maybe it is time to let go. I do not want to place the weight of saving SOL on your shoulders anymore. It was never your responsibility, and I was wrong to make it that way. You have suffered enough. I want you to live your life." She placed a hand on my arm, but I pulled away.

"This all feels dramatic. If this is how my time at SOL ends, then why did I give up Deborah in the first place? Why did I choose this path at all? Stepping down now would mean losing both SOL and Deborah. Has everything I sacrificed been for nothing?" A surge of anger burst out of me.

"No, River." She pressed her lips together and looked me straight in the eye. "We will not lose SOL. You and I still hold the majority share, and we can bring in a new CEO to carry on the legacy. Because of the work you have done, SOL is in a much stronger position. And with twenty million dollars of debt paid off, the company is going to be on solid footing financially. This could be a positive outcome for employees and shareholders, even if it feels like a crisis right now. We would not be here without the painful decision you made three years ago—and the sacrifices you have made since. Do you understand what I am trying to say?"

I rose from my chair and walked to the window, struggling to process what she had implied. I wanted to hear her—tried to—but resentment gnawed at me. Resentment for choosing family over Deborah, only to fall short of my obligations three years later. I couldn't just leave the past behind and pretend to live in the present. How could I? I had already lost Deborah. And now, I was about to lose the family legacy too. How was I supposed to keep going after that?

Still, worn down and knotted up inside, the idea of letting go—of letting life take me wherever it pleased—seduced me. It felt almost like relief. But that felt like resignation. *Giving up.*

Tangled in my thoughts, I turned toward my mother. She sat there in silence, her expression pained. What lay behind it? The crisis at SOL? A grief she bore alone, hidden from view? Or was it my pain —my suffering—that she carried as her own? I realized then: all she wanted was for me to find the joy. Not fix the business. Not salvage the family legacy. Just me. Just for my heart to heal, to be whole again. And as clarity bloomed, something inside me gave way. I no longer saw just my mother, but a woman who had spent a lifetime putting everyone else's needs before her own. There she was again, ready to set aside her devotion to SOL—her duty, her pride, her loyalty—all for the sake of her son. Even after all the years she had spent supporting my father through SOL's endless ups and downs. Even after the tireless way she had fought—invisibly but fiercely—for its people, for its future, through every crisis. She was prepared to surrender the legacy she had championed for decades, just to let go of her son. In that moment, I began to understand what she meant about impermanence and suffering. Not completely, but enough to surrender, if only a little.

That small surrender moved me to reach for her and wrap her in an embrace. Her ribs rose against mine as she exhaled. For a long moment, neither of us spoke. Then I pulled back slightly to look at her. "Do you know what Deborah used to tell me whenever I was in doubt?"

She tilted her head, brows knit.

"She would say, 'You do you, darling!' " I mimicked the playful way Deborah would swing her arm.

My mother squeezed me back with surprising strength. "I see why you loved her so much."

"I still love her. I'll never stop loving her."

WHEN EVERYONE RETURNED, the boardroom felt like a courtroom—muffled, tense, waiting on a verdict no one wanted to hear. I rose from the table and fixed my eyes on Jason and Alex. My heart pounded with adrenaline, but I knew what I had to do.

"Jason, Alex," I said, my voice steady but firm. "As long as I am the CEO, the final decision is mine. Are we on the same page?"

They each acknowledged with a single nod.

"Here is my counter to your proposal. First, I will accept the twenty percent additional shares in exchange for the twenty million dollars of debt payment. Second, I will also agree to step down so that SOL can have a new CEO, per your proposal."

As the words left my mouth, Mr. Kangster released an anguished sigh. Dr. Nam and Mr. Byeon exchanged startled glances before lowering their heads.

"But under one condition. I get to choose the CEO, not you. And you must trust me that I will appoint the best leader who will ensure that your forty-five percent shares, and my mother's and my fifty-five percent shares, will be worth significantly more in the future. Our financial interests are aligned in this regard." I looked around the table, letting the gravity of my words settle in.

Jason leaned back in his chair, arms crossed and lips pursed, while Alex drummed on the edge of the table with his fingers, studying me intently.

"If you don't accept this offer, I will take it elsewhere. Another deal might leave you in a worse position, and if nothing else comes through, bankruptcy is the only way out. That means we all lose—my mother, me, everyone here, and the employees. If it comes to a fire sale, I will make sure SOL does not fall into your hands. I would rather give it away to a competitor for a dollar than let you have it. So take the deal, or we all go down together. I want your answer now." My heart pounded, but I remained unyielding as I locked eyes with Jason and Alex.

Jason scribbled something on a piece of paper and showed it to Alex, who responded with a tap of his finger on the table.

"Fine. You've got the deal. So tell me, who do you have in mind?" Jason asked, leaning forward, his body angled toward me.

"Mrs. Sooin Jung. My mother. She will be the new CEO of SOL."

ALTHOUGH MY MOTHER had never completed college and lacked formal business training, I had come to realize that she was the soul of SOL. Most employees, especially those in operations, held her in high regard and had deep respect for her. With over thirty years of experience observing my grandfather and father, she possessed an intimate knowledge of the beverage industry. Whenever I faced difficult decisions, she would subtly steer me in the right direction with her razor-sharp intuition while modestly downplaying her own expertise. It was as if she could sense problems before they even emerged. With her at the helm as CEO and Mr. Kangster overseeing the finances as CFO, SOL was in trusted hands. While I might have been young and inexperienced, I knew exceptional talent when I saw it. And my mother was exactly what SOL needed.

By December, South Korea received a fifty-eight-billion-dollar bailout from the IMF, the World Bank, the Asian Development Bank, and various other countries. This marked the largest rescue package in the IMF's history. While many Korean companies still grappled with ongoing bankruptcy or restructuring, SOL had successfully managed to pay off its debt and maintain family control.

The employees, though initially surprised, welcomed my mother as the new CEO. Several women's groups in South Korea applauded the move, as she became one of the few female CEOs in the male-dominated Korean business world. However, the media continued to question her lack of business experience and college degree, labeling it as another instance of family power and nepotism due to poor corporate governance at SOL. That was the nature of the media: a friend one day, a foe the next.

10

RIVER

Spring 1998

Just before her inauguration as SOL's new CEO, my mother took me to the hillside where my father, grandparents, and other ancestors rested. The day my father passed felt like only yesterday, with nearly four years lost to memory. Would he have been proud of what I had achieved at SOL if he were still here? What would our relationship have been like?

As if sensing my thoughts, my mother placed her hand on the headstone. "*Yeobo*"—a Korean term a wife would call her husband—"I wish you could have seen everyone at SOL last week," she murmured, brushing the dust from the headstone, her touch reminiscent of how she used to smooth the lint from my father's suit before he left for the office in the mornings. "They were proud when they said farewell to River—employees in the office, in the factories. So many came to me to say how your son's dedication and commitment inspired them. They looked at him like he was one of their own. He won them over with his heart, just like you had done before him."

She shifted her gaze to the zelkova trees across the hill, their limbs bursting with fresh shades of green after a long winter's hibernation. "Because of River, SOL is stronger now than when he first took over. And it is time to let him take on whatever comes next in his life. Can you do that for him?"

Her words wrapped around my heart. Though directed at my father, they felt as though they were meant for me. A message too delicate to deliver outright. Perhaps she was still shy when it came to expressing her love for her son.

We walked back down the hill, the midday sun warming the earth beneath our feet. Forsythia lined the trail and swayed in the breeze. My mother extended her left arm, her fingers grazing the canary-yellow blossoms. Watching her soaking in the vastness of the field, I could feel the serenity those glorious flowers brought her.

"Forsythia has meant a new beginning to me," she said. "After the Korean War, winters were harsh. We had nothing but our summer clothes and a handful of rice. I wondered if I had any spirit left to endure. But when the forsythia bloomed in spring, it felt like the world was offering a promise. That better days were waiting to unfold. Hope."

"Hope . . ." I exhaled, my breath folding into the chirping of magpies around us. "There were moments in the last few years when I questioned whether hope was even real."

"Of course it is real," she said, her grin small but sure. "Many in business think hope is for the weak. They prefer strategy and well-laid plans. Things they can control and measure. But when those plans fall apart, what keeps us going? What inspires us? Hope is the nucleus of the heart. Of love."

"Did you just say *love*?" I asked, half-teasing. "I don't think I've ever heard you use that word."

"I was young once, like you. Romantic, even," she said, letting out a cackle. "I could still teach you a thing or two about love."

"Are you sure? Did you and Father even say 'I love you' to each other?"

"Are you asking if we loved each other because we never said it?"

"I know there was love between you. But as a kid, I never understood why you fought so much."

"We didn't mean for you to carry that. We just didn't know any better."

"I understand," I said with a small nod. "But that's not why I brought it up. I see it differently now. The arguments—the ones with screams and tears—might have been your love language. You fought to keep each other's priorities straight. If you didn't care, you would've ignored each other. But you cared fiercely. You were a team when it mattered most. Like when SOL faced trouble. You acted as one, without hesitation. That's what your love looked like . . . I think." I turned to study her face, but her expression remained hidden as she gazed ahead along the trail. "When I was in college, my love for Deborah was so ferocious it felt like my heart would burst. Yet I struggled to say *I love you* at first."

A smile tugged at my lips as I remembered the night I finally said the words to Deborah—in the hidden corners of Lamont. "But once I started, I couldn't stop. Almost like an incantation. I said it so much it began to feel out of place. One day, I suggested we find a subtle way to express our love in public. We brainstormed a few creative ideas, but in the end, we settled on a simple hand squeeze. Our secret language. It let us say *I love you* without words." I turned to my mother, reached out, and gently squeezed her tiny hand. "Like this."

She looked at me, eyes wide, tears shimmering. "Like this?" she responded, squeezing back.

THE DAY after my mother's inauguration as CEO, I packed my suitcase and headed to the airport. She was already deep into her first day—visiting factory workers across the company—so Mr. Kangster came to see me off instead. Perhaps also to spare my mother the sorrow of watching her son leave again.

"I got you some rice cakes for the plane. Your favorite snack, sir." He handed me a small bag. "So how do you feel, sir?"

"How do I feel . . . ? Well, I feel a thousand times lighter, not having to answer, 'Are you sure about that, sir?' "

Mr. Kangster and I chuckled simultaneously. To the strangers at the airport, we might have looked like a father and son.

"Frankly, there's a bittersweetness to leaving. The last four years felt like military training in leadership and management. I've learned so much from you, the other executives, and, of course, my mother. I'm grateful to you and will dearly miss working with you and the team."

"We will miss you, sir. But I have to say . . . I have never seen you this relaxed. You look like a real twenty-something for once, ready to take on the world. Though technically unemployed, sir."

"Unemployed has never felt good. I feel liberated just thinking about all the possibilities out there. A fresh start. This is the first time in years that I feel excited rather than scared or stressed, even though my future is more uncertain."

"I can't wait to see where you go from here, sir. So—what's the plan in San Francisco?"

"I want to build something of my own with all the money I've saved by not paying rent. Something separate from my grandfather's legacy and my father's work. What exactly that will be, I'm not sure yet."

"But why San Francisco?"

"Haven't you heard about the internet? Smart people are flocking to Silicon Valley. A modern gold rush. I want to be where the action is. Please ensure SOL invests properly in the internet. People will be buying Joa online soon."

"Are you sure that's the only reason? Isn't UCSF—"

"No comment."

We shook hands before pulling each other into a hug. Without a second glance, I boarded the plane, the memory of my first flight at eleven stirring within me. Back to the land of hope. The land of dreams.

PART III

2001 — 2011

11

RIVER

Fall 2001

W e were all born with the gift of dreaming. A gift that no one could ever take away. Yet few ever dared to use it to its full potential. Some held back to spare themselves the pain of disappointment. Others turned their backs on dreams entirely, insisting they never aligned with reality. In the end, most traded the gift for something more certain. But for me, dreaming had been a sustaining force in my existence. Even in my darkest hours, that simple act had been my light. It carried me through the past three years in San Francisco. The elusive hope that I could start anew, build something from nothing, and, most of all, that I might see Deborah again.

~

THE MONITORS BATHED the deserted desks in a cold, dark gray glow. Mismatched chairs sat askew, abandoned. Forgotten mugs rested cold on tables, half-moon coffee stains marking their bottoms. Fluorescent yellow and pink sticky notes adorned the walls like scraps of abstract art. On the whiteboard, half-erased graphs and scribbled plans blurred together in a messy spectrum of color. The space resembled a TV drama set, built for a temporary scene, then left behind. There were no voices, no footsteps. Just the distant groan of the building settling into night. The clock crept toward 10:00 p.m., but I didn't get up. Instead, I turned back to my screen.

The senior associate at the law firm had replied to the revised term sheet. The sharp edges of words sliced through my exhaustion. His message was blunt—no pleasantries, no preamble: "River, the five-year noncompete clause is a nonstarter. If we can't resolve it, we shouldn't move forward."

I had to bite back the urge to correct him that it was *me*, not *us*, who would have to face the consequences of this deal. I knew he was looking out for me. He was doing his job, stuck in the office, just like I was. But the truth was, his edits moved us further from the deal, not closer. And I couldn't help but wonder how much his firm would charge me for the privilege of being pushed in the wrong direction.

MarsEdge, the start-up I had been building for the past three years, was on the brink of implosion. With two months of cash runway remaining, the survival of our twenty-person company hinged on one thing: sealing the deal with Archstone. Our cutting-edge technology for mining unstructured data had both threatened and fascinated them. To keep us within arm's reach, Archstone dangled a lifeline. They offered to fund us for the next three years if we met the ambitious milestones we had agreed upon.

However, Archstone, a global giant with its hands in diverse industries from agriculture to automotive, demanded a noncompete clause that could block us from selling our solution to the industries we aimed to target. In effect, they could control our company's fate, making it impossible to market our product on our own. They were not a charity. They were the hyenas of the industry. Their game involved befriending their prey and devouring it when the guard dropped. With the recent devastation of September 11 and the tech-bubble collapse, they knew our access to other funding sources had become nonexistent. We were cornered, and they reveled in keeping us there.

If we didn't accept the deal, we would die. If we did, we might survive, but in a vegetative state, our vocal cords ripped out. The image of MarsEdge fading into oblivion jolted me harder than any electric shock.

My cursor hovered over the reply button—then the office phone rang, its shrill tone disrupting the silence. It had to be Jeff. I picked up, already picturing him slouched on his bed, biting his nail, his leg shaking restlessly.

Jeff Hemmings was indelible. Standing at six feet, six inches, and appearing even taller due to his slender build, he often reminded people of a daddy longlegs. To me, he moved more like an amphibian, lacking any discernible core muscle. At times, it seemed as though he was still mastering the coordination of his arms and legs. When anyone asked if he played basketball in high school, he would squint and say, "Never touched a basketball in my life."

I met him three years ago, about four months after I had arrived in San Francisco. He walked into a diner looking less like a tech founder and more like someone who had wandered in from a week of sleeping rough. A ragged Caltech hoodie, stained with grease, hung off his frame. The jeans were torn at the knees—not for fashion, but from age and wear. His unruly auburn hair looked like it had met a lightning bolt instead of a comb. And those alien toes splayed out of flip-flops, as if they had forgotten how to live inside shoes.

"Hey, dude, are you River Jung? Let me guess. Lake and Ocean are your siblings." He guffawed, yanked out a chair, and squeezed himself into it. His long legs brushed against mine beneath the table.

"Nice to meet you too. And no, I don't have siblings." I kept my tone cordial, though an edge of annoyance slipped through. An awkward pause ensued—the one that often blanketed the air when two strangers with wonky chemistry met.

Finding a technical co-founder for my start-up had proven to be less like choosing a business partner, more like searching for a spouse. Building something from nothing with someone from a different world was a gamble. Choose wrong, and it could feel like a bad marriage: painful, messy, and expensive to unwind. So the search became an exhausting dance of evaluating, courting, and second-guessing.

I had already met several candidates through mutual introductions. Most candidates were brilliant, but they were either arrogant or lacked authenticity, all trying to emulate Steve Jobs or Bill Gates. I couldn't imagine navigating the daily tribulations and spending long hours in the office with them.

Out of desperation, I placed a classified ad in *San Jose Mercury News*. To keep costs down, I kept the word count to a minimum: "Tech co-founder wanted. Big idea." Among the handful of responses, Jeff's stood out: "Caltech '95. Dangerous."

During our first meeting, he fidgeted with his fingers, bit his nails, and scratched his back with his freakishly long arms. All the while, he rattled off his thoughts at warp speed. No small talk. No fluff. Every exchange felt like a verbal sparring match. Strangely, his directness—his lack of filter—invigorated me. I could say exactly what I thought without fear of judgment. Then, somewhere along the way, he started articulating the business plan I hadn't even written yet. And I found myself leaning in. I kept reminding myself of all the red flags: he didn't look the part, and he didn't act it either. But there was an ineffable gravity to him I couldn't resist.

In the end, what sealed the deal was when he told me—without irony—that he was an extrovert, "a social butterfly." I stared at him blankly. But he was serious: "I'm Myers–Briggs ENTJ. The dictator. You must be an INFP. You look like a mediator."

Even though I hadn't disclosed much about myself during our first meeting, he had assessed me accurately. I reluctantly flashed him a sign of admission.

"Holy shit! We got a dictator and a mediator here. As far as start-up co-founders go, we're a perfect match, dude." He broke into a wide smile. I must confess that he had a nice smile. And I liked his face—sharp green eyes; thin, well-defined lips; and a nose with classical symmetry.

A few months later, Pranab Singh, our first engineering hire, asked Jeff why he had decided to start MarsEdge with me.

"River picked me when no guy or gal wanted to be my co-founder. That's all that matters, even though he's weird as hell."

"I'm the weird one?"

"For real, dude. You talk like someone stuffed *The Wall Street Journal* into your mouth. And you dress like a Korean preppy. All formal and shit."

"It's called style. You should try it sometime."

While we were busy debating nonsense, Pranab silently swiveled back to his screen, probably questioning his decision to join Mars-Edge in the first place.

What had started off as an awkward first encounter turned into an extraordinary friendship I hadn't even known I was ready for.

Now, hearing the phone ring in the silence of the office, I didn't need to wonder why he was calling. It had to be about the deal. I sighed and picked up. "Jeff, you just couldn't wait until morning."

"Hey, River. It's me, Pete. Sorry to call so late. I tried your apartment first, but no one answered. I figured you were still at the office."

Pete? It had been nearly three months since I had last spoken to him. Earlier in the year, he had secured both a literary agent and a publisher, and since then, he had thrown himself into perfecting his debut work.

"What a surprise! How are things?" I forced a smile into my voice, though the fatigue bled through.

"Good. Still in Boston, finalizing the book. Drowning in edits at this point. I've lost track."

"You've come so far. I will be first in line when it hits the bookstore."

"Ah, the pressure." He chuckled. "It's more nerve-racking to think about people close to me reading it than strangers. Especially someone who devours books the way you do."

"Don't worry. I only judge writers for misusing the Oxford comma."

"Why am I not surprised? How's everything going at MarsEdge?"

"Ups and downs, as usual. Mostly downs."

"But you love chaos."

"It's the other way around. Chaos loves me." I let out a soft laugh, but the weariness showed underneath. "It's past midnight where you are. Everything okay?"

"Yeah. You know me. The night owl. Hey, listen . . ." A long pause followed before he resumed. "It's about Deborah."

Deborah—a name that would whisk me away to heaven, plunge me into hell, and then rescue me back to heaven, in an endless, feverish loop.

My pulse throbbed as if invisible hands had closed around my neck. "What about her?"

"How should I say this . . ."

"Just say it."

"Well, it looks like she's been in Boston, not San Francisco."

"Sorry?"

"I just had dinner with an old high school friend. He's a third-year psych resident at Mass General. He got to talking about his colleagues, and, well, her name came up."

"Are you sure it's the same person?"

"Yes, it's her. Deborah Noe. She's a psychiatry resident at Mass General now."

"But I thought . . . what about UCSF? I'm so confused."

"I didn't know she was in Boston either. None of us did. You know how she cut ties after college. We all just assumed she stayed in San Francisco, doing fine at UCSF. No one knew she'd gone to Mass General for residency." His voice was heavy, as if he had done something wrong. As if it was all his fault.

"Wait—you're telling me she hasn't been in San Francisco these past few years, since I moved here?"

"I guess so. I'm sorry, River."

A chilling sensation swept through me. For the past three years, I had lived in an apartment near UCSF. Each day, scanning the campus and city streets, I felt certain our paths would cross again. Though it never happened, I held on to the idea that it was only a matter of time—any day, any moment. And yet, all this time, she had been in Boston.

IN THE WEEKS THAT FOLLOWED, the revelation that Deborah had been in Boston tormented me. It was as if I had been walking through a mirage, all that time spent searching, waiting—wasted. Perhaps we were never meant to find our way back to each other.

Meanwhile, the deal with Archstone screeched to a halt. The continued decline in the stock market spooked their board of directors, putting the deal on hold indefinitely. Worse yet, we had less than a month of cash runway left. We frantically searched for other funding sources, but not a single person returned our calls.

A week before Thanksgiving, we shut down MarsEdge. This venture was supposed to be my redemption, a way to move past the death of my father and my breakup with Deborah. I had left my mother and SOL behind in Korea, hoping to rediscover myself through this new beginning. For three years, I poured my heart and soul into this company, determined to escape the grip of my past and move forward. Failure couldn't be an option. But it became the only one.

On the last day of MarsEdge, Jeff and I bid farewell to the Edgers who had faithfully followed us on our moonshot journey. Some voiced their feelings of betrayal. Others feared facing unemployment amid some of Silicon Valley's worst market conditions. Regardless, most expressed gratitude for the start-up experience and the camaraderie we had built.

After the last Edger left, Jeff and I sat on the carpet of the empty office. The silence settled like dust, broken only by the whisper-thin sound of our breath.

"Do you remember the day we moved in?" I asked.

"Don't go there. We swore we'd never speak of those fucking rats again."

"No, not rats. But your scream."

When we had opened the door, a family of rats had greeted us with a surprise party. Jeff had squealed and bolted for the exit. I hadn't known he had that many octaves in him.

"I'm still in goddamn therapy because of that day." He chuckled and handed me a bottle of vodka.

I opened it and took a cautious whiff. Then a small sip—only to spit it out a second later. It tasted exactly like it smelled: rubbing alcohol.

"Lightweight." He shot me a frown and snatched the bottle from my hand. "So what now?" he asked, then took a swig.

"When do you think a day begins? When we go to bed or when we wake up?"

"Obviously, it starts when we wake up."

"I see it differently," I said. "Every journey begins with a dream. For some, it plants the seed. For others, it feeds the fire. Either way, the day begins when we close our eyes. When we dream."

"Dude, what the fuck are you talking about? A day starts when we wake up. Period. But fine. What's your point?"

"My point is this. I believe we need to dream again so that we can restart. We shouldn't give up just because we failed the first time. We have nothing to fear."

Even with the constant fear of failure, my experiences at SOL and MarsEdge had equipped me with an unbreakable shield to confront seemingly impossible challenges head-on. Over the past few years, fear hadn't deterred me from pursuing what I wanted. It had become something I managed whenever it flared, no more, no less.

"What do you suggest, then?"

"We've been at this for three years, nonstop, twelve-hour days. I think we deserve a break. But after that, I would love to dive into something new with you. If you're in, of course."

"Yeah, man. Who else would put up with you? You need me," he said, his voice rich with that familiar, easy confidence. Then, after a pause: "Hey, what about your other dream? Are we moving to Boston or what? I'm up for a change of scenery if it means helping you chase it."

I dropped my gaze, feeling the weight of his eyes on me. "I don't know. I just don't know anymore."

He studied me for a moment, then rested a hand on my back. "You know what fixes everything?"

"Are you about to say something vulgar?"

"Nah, dude. I'll save that for tomorrow."

"Then what?"

"Pizza," he said, getting to his feet. "Heck, I'll even let you put your disgusting pineapple on it. Just this once."

He offered his hand and gave me a firm tug. No lecture, no pity— just Jeff, knowing exactly what I needed.

I took one last walk around the office. Once full of life, it was now as nondescript as a brown cardboard box. I hoped the next souls to inhabit this space would find a kinder fate. Though life, it seemed, had no room for kindness. At least not for me.

12

RIVER

Winter 2001

After MarsEdge collapsed, I visited my mother in Korea for the first time in three years. She was buried in year-end work at SOL, but still found a way to come home each evening and cook for me. When I protested that she shouldn't interrupt her schedule, she smiled and said, "Cooking for you makes me happy. This is how I take care of myself, too."

After a few days of rest in her care, I left her apartment and began backpacking across the country with no real plan. In Gimje, I disappeared into the frozen, solemn rice fields. The horizon stretched wide and fallow, relieved of its duty to bear lush, golden abundance. A landscape at rest—a pause between seasons—unlike the barren space inside me, hollow and unmoving. In Busan, I wandered through the chaotic beauty of its sprawling fish market, where young couples leaned in close, sharing bites of bubbling stew, their laughter rising with the steam. They stole glances at me as I drifted past alone. And in that moment, loneliness pressed in like dusk settling over the harbor. In my last leg, I hiked along the jagged cliffs of Donghae, and suddenly I was back at a weather-beaten cove in Massachusetts—a place I hadn't stood since college. There, at the edge of the shore, something broke loose inside me. I wailed, pouring out all the rage I had been holding in. At myself. At life. The wind howled with me, and the gulls circled overhead as if they understood.

During those months of reflection, the choices I hadn't made haunted me more than the ones I had. I had always approached life with relentless intensity. Whether it was my studies or my career, I left nothing unfinished, no goal untouched. But with Deborah, I had let too many years slip away—passive, waiting for life to unfold instead of shaping it myself. In doing so, I betrayed not just my principles, but something deeper: my very soul.

Yet beneath the regret, one truth stood firm. I wanted to see Deborah. Not eventually, but now. I couldn't leave it to chance any longer. Whatever the outcome, I had to stop living in this uncertain space between past and possibility. It was time to face the fear, the guilt, and the shame that had kept me frozen for so long.

13

RIVER

Spring 2002

Spring had been my favorite season in Boston. When the city stirred from winter's slumber, the shift—from muted gray and brown to an explosion of color—felt nothing short of miraculous. It wasn't just the azaleas, camellias, and magnolias that lit up the streets with their coruscating hues. It was the people, too, flooding every corner of the city in garish short sleeves. The air still bit with cold, but they moved through the streets like sun-soaked vacationers, willfully ignoring winter's last tantrum.

Even with my longstanding love for Boston in the spring, I hadn't returned since 1994. The pain was too sharp. And yet, here I was finally.

～

THE YELLOW TAXICAB I took from the airport crawled through the early-morning traffic and onto Storrow Drive. Despite the eight-year gap, the scene before me felt strikingly familiar. The Charles River danced with the early light, its path dotted with industrious runners.

As the cab curved along the water, the city's tangled, nonsensical roads came into view, and the Hancock and the Pru rose abruptly against the otherwise demure skyline. Lining Storrow Drive, the familiar brownstones stood—ageless and watchful after all these years. Then, there it was: Mass General. I didn't know which building Deborah worked in or whether she was there at all. But just the possibility was enough to stir something tight and breathless inside me.

The cab dropped me off at a stately building in Back Bay, where dog walkers and joggers wove between commuters clutching coffee. I lugged my suitcase through the entrance and into the muted but refined lobby. Pete stood beside the doorman, already waiting. I almost had to do a double take. An Ivy League cut, neat with pomade, now framed his face, replacing the shaggy hair that had rarely met a hairdryer. The browline glasses that had been his unmistakable trademark were gone, revealing eyes unshielded, like a sky rinsed clean after rain. The beard had vanished, drawing the eye to a jawline that sharpened the angles of his face. The untucked linen shirt looked like it had been tossed on without a second thought, yet it fell to just the right length over his crisp stone khakis—casual on the surface, but too polished to be chance.

"Welcome back to Boston! You must be exhausted from the red-eye flight." He enclosed me in a full hug. His body felt firmer, no longer soft around the edges.

"Who are you and what have you done with my dear friend?

"Didn't I tell you I got a twin brother?"

"Wow, you look . . . debonair."

"You think?" He gave a bashful smile. "I guess I'm finally growing up, with the book deal and all. Anyway, so good to have you back. Come on in!"

His three-bedroom condo evoked a pristine luxury hotel suite, rather than a home marked by daily life, cluttered with laundry piles, chipped plates, and knickknacks hoarded from forgotten trips. Light flooded the living room through wide windows overlooking the Public Garden. Abstract black-and-white photos of body parts—

indistinct as male or female—stared out from the walls. Even the air smelled curated, steeped in cedarwood and leather.

"Whenever we talked on the phone, I pictured you in a cramped room, hunched over your Remington. But your place makes my apartment look like a college dorm," I said, accepting the glass of water he handed me. He motioned for me to sit on the Scandinavian-style sofa that anchored the living room.

"It belongs to my family," he said, settling in beside me. "My oldest sister lived here when she worked in Boston, but she moved to DC last year, and it's been empty ever since. I'm staying here temporarily just until I can get my book out. I know it sounds kind of privileged . . ."

His voice held a trace of sheepishness. There was a conscious effort in it—a desire not to let his family's wealth speak too loudly.

"It's a beautiful place. And you're making the most of it."

"I am grateful. It's given me the headspace to focus on finishing the book."

"Is it almost done?"

"In the final stage. Starting to feel a little anxious."

"That's exciting. I can't wait to read it."

"By the way, my friend mentioned that the psych residents are doing their rotation at McLean this month, not at Mass General."

"McLean?"

"It's the psychiatric hospital tied to Mass General. They've got a campus out in Belmont."

"That's good to know. I would hate to make the same mistake again—showing up at the wrong place and waiting, as I did for the past few years," I said, my gaze drifting toward the window.

"So . . . are you sure about this?"

"I think so." I smiled, my fingers tracing the rim of my glass. "I know how selfish this must seem—showing up like this after all these years. She might not want to see me. But I have to see her. Maybe it's the only way I can end the waiting."

"Well, whatever happens, I'll be here." He rested his hand on my shoulder. The gesture was small, but it grounded me.

GRAND, prewar brick buildings rose amid manicured lawns and bushes heavy with spring blossoms. McLean looked less like a hospital and more like a bucolic New England prep school. The winding paths and the serenity of the grounds lulled me into a strange calm, as if I had stepped into a sanctuary removed from everyday worries. For a moment, I slowed my pace and breathed in the floral morning air, letting the equanimity of the atmosphere settle over me. But as I approached the main building, the ephemeral peace evaporated the instant I remembered what lay beyond those walls. A flood of doubts swept in. My feet almost betrayed me, fear whispering sweetly in my ear to turn back, to walk away. Still, I reminded myself that facing her—whatever the outcome—was more merciful than living with the torment of regret. I drew strength from it and opened the door.

At the reception desk, a middle-aged woman in a carnation cardigan chatted with a stout doctor in a white coat. She let out a coy laugh at something he said, and he smiled and straightened a little, appearing pleased to have gotten a laugh.

I cleared my throat, and their conversation broke off as they turned to me. "Sorry to interrupt, but I'm here to see Dr. Deborah Noe."

"Do you have an appointment?" the receptionist asked.

"No, I'm an old friend of hers, just in town for a short while. I thought I would drop by to say hello."

"She's busy with patients. But lunch break's coming up soon if you wanna wait around. I can't tell ya where she'll be during lunch, though."

Was this what I had expected? I had spent weeks rehearsing the moment, playing through a hundred versions in my head. But now that I was here, my thoughts tangled into knots. I ran through my options: wandering the halls, waiting in the cafeteria. Ultimately, I decided to wait outside, willing to bide my time and prepared to stay as long as necessary. It felt less intrusive that way, and perhaps less likely to draw unwanted attention.

The McLean quad was serene, the kind of place that offered calm even in the face of distress. Between the main hall and the cafeteria across from it, a small pond shimmered under the late-morning sun. A few empty benches dotted the lawn, arranged as if standing silent guard around the water. I settled onto one, angled to keep the main entrance and a few side doors in view.

The soothing scent of lilacs floated through the air, but my nerves stayed taut. I pulled a worn paperback from my jacket pocket, hoping to distract myself, but the words blurred into a haze. I read the same line over and over, unable to move forward. My mind was split in two —one part tethered to the page, the other flicking anxiously toward the buildings around me. Down to the book. Up to the doors. Back again.

Just then, a figure appeared in the doorway of the main building. She moved with effortless grace, her dark-brown hair cascading down her back like midnight silk, bouncing with each step. A crisp white blouse hugged her frame, the neckline revealing the soft curve of her neck and shoulders. Slim black pants accentuated her long legs, and black pumps clicked against the pavement. But it was her face—her eyes—that stole my breath away.

Eight years of regret and longing melted away in an instant. People often said that memories had a way of deceiving us, casting illusions over the past. Yet she appeared even more transcendent than when I had first seen her at Annenberg.

With slow, deliberate movements, she approached an empty bench by the pond. After settling into her seat, she pulled out a small Tupperware container—likely her lunch—but instead of opening it, she remained there, her gaze fixed on the placid water.

From my bench several yards away, I was transported back to those enchanting moments on campus, watching her from afar, mesmerized by the elegance in how she engaged with the world. The same love I had carried for her all those years tightened its grip on my heart. This unrequited love that refused to die.

After all these years, here she was, just a few paces away. I got up and took a step forward. My knees trembled with a raw anticipation that threatened to collapse me. Each step toward her felt like wading through quicksand, the ground beneath me shifting. The lush grass muffled my movement, but a frantic symphony of pulse clamored within me.

When I finally reached her, my mind went blank. I sat beside her, as if the bench had claimed me, as if it had been waiting for me. She didn't turn to acknowledge me. But her startled reaction and blanched complexion made it clear she was aware of my presence. We remained quiet, accompanied only by birdsong and the distant hum of footsteps and voices drifting across the lawn.

I turned to look at her face. Her sparkling eyes, pearl-like skin, and tulip-petal lips still left me breathless. I wanted to tell her how radiant she was—more than I had remembered. How I had counted the days until this moment, imagining it day and night over the last eight years. How I had never stopped loving her. But the words didn't come out. Instead, I managed, "Deborah." The dearest seven letters.

Her gaze stayed fixed on the pond, her chest rising and falling in rapid, uneven breaths. The space between us grew heavier, weighted by years of unspoken words.

I exhaled a deep, shuddering sigh. "I cannot believe I'm finally seeing you again."

At last, she turned to me. "What are you doing here?" Her eyes brimmed with tears, and the sight of the first one spilling down her cheek hit me like a blow.

"I came to see you."

"You came to see me? After eight years?"

"I suppose so . . ."

"Suppose so? So you got up this morning and said, 'Oh, why don't I just drop in and say hi?' You had the audacity to just show up . . . like you could walk into my life whenever you felt like it?"

Her words sliced through my heart. All the years apart, all the pain and longing, came crashing down between us.

"Eight years!" she yelped, her voice cracking as a sob overtook her. "Do you have any idea what I went through? And now here you are, like nothing ever happened. What kind of person does that? Is this some kind of game to you?"

"Deborah, please . . . I missed you."

"No, River. You don't just show up like this after all these years just because you missed me."

"I'm sorry. Please forgive me for what I did and for all the pain I have caused since."

"There's nothing left to forgive. But you still haven't answered my question. Why are you here? Why now?"

"I wish I could offer you an answer that makes sense."

"Great. So you don't even know why you're here. Just an impulse."

"No. Not an impulse. For eight years, I've lived with the guilt of breaking your heart, never knowing how to ask for your forgiveness. I kept searching for the right words, the right moment. But nothing ever felt like enough. What happened back then . . . I was grieving, confused, and immature. And I was a coward."

"You *were* a coward? You still *are*. And a liar."

"I fully deserve that. But the truth is, not a single day has passed when I didn't think of you. You've always been my North Star, guiding me even in your absence."

In the breathless pause that followed, I wrestled with the turmoil rising in my chest, words catching in my throat. I swallowed hard, forcing past the lump as the words scraped their way out. Then I began—recounting those turbulent years at SOL, full of setbacks, exhaustion, and near-misses. I hadn't meant to burden her with any of it, but the story poured out, unfiltered.

"Those years in Korea without you . . . they left me undone. I barely recognized who I had become. Leaving SOL was supposed to bring clarity. A fresh start. But with you oceans away, that new beginning felt impossible. I had to be closer to you, breathing the same air. That's why I came back to America. Even when I told myself it wouldn't matter, that it wouldn't change anything, I couldn't shake the need. All I knew was that you were in San Francisco. So I moved there and searched, hoping not just for absolution, but to see you. Even if only from afar."

As my heart released the heavy words I had been carrying, she kept her gaze turned away from me, her breath shallow.

"I lived a few blocks away from UCSF, often loitering around the campus, hoping to catch a glimpse of you. I combed through the school directory, even the yellow pages, but your name never appeared. I should've noticed the signs. But I kept thinking . . . if I just waited one more day, I would see you again. I watched those years vanish before my eyes."

What was I hoping to accomplish by dredging up all these past stories in my rambling soliloquy? Was this just a reckless attempt to unburden myself? To offload the weight of my past onto her so I could feel lighter, even at her expense? Probably. But more than anything, I wanted her to see me again. To remember the flawed person she once saw so clearly. The one she had accepted just as I was, both the good and the bad.

"When I finally learned you were in Boston, not San Francisco, I realized how my own internal guilt, shame, and fears had held me back all these years, keeping me from the only person I've ever truly loved. I couldn't let them hold me back any longer. I couldn't waste another day. That's why I'm here."

Her face twisted with something between anguish and emotion she hadn't yet made sense of, lips parting with words that never came.

"Deborah . . . please look at me. Just once."

She turned slightly toward me but avoided my gaze, as if meeting my eyes might stir feelings she wasn't ready to confront.

"I've never stopped loving you. And I'm still desperately in love with you. Every day, I've carried the darkness of how I hurt you, how I let all that time slip away without doing everything I could to make it right. I don't know how to forgive myself for that. But I can't imagine facing the years ahead without you by my side . . . I am here to ask you for a second chance. No matter how long it takes to earn back your love."

I reached out, my fingers brushing against hers.

Then I saw it.

The platinum band, the diamond so bright it almost burned my eyes, nestled on her finger. It had been there all along, hidden just beyond my peripheral vision, wrapped unapologetically around her finger. I stared at it, and in that moment, the world fell into a crushing silence, as if every sound had been suddenly smothered. My mind spun, struggling to process the overwhelming reality of what I had just realized. My breath hitched, ragged and erratic, as I swallowed the guttural cries clawing their way up my throat.

"I'm getting married . . ." Her faint voice tore through the fog of my delirium. "I should get going." She dabbed her tear-filled eyes with the back of her hand and stood up abruptly. Her movements were stiff, her hands fumbling for her bag, fingers trembling as they clutched the straps. She slung it over her shoulder with a sharp, jerky motion. With her back turned, she walked away. Her shoulders sagged, her head lowered, each step heavy yet rushed. The distance between us stretched like a stifled scream, unrelieved, unending.

When she disappeared into the building, my eyes fell on the untouched Tupperware she had left behind on the bench. I picked it up, paused, then cradled it to my chest.

14

RIVER

Fall 2002

Amonth after that encounter at McLean, Deborah completed her residency and moved to LA to start a new chapter at Cedars-Sinai. Around the same time, she married George Starfield, a radiologist from California. Pete shared the news with an apology in his voice and a sadness he could barely conceal.

His words struck like a second blow. Would it have stung less if I had stayed in the dark? I couldn't extricate my emotions enough to answer. My heart, shattered beyond recognition, had lost the ability to discern jealousy from grief, anger from resignation. All I knew was the gaping void where hope used to be and the bitter ache of realizing I had no place in the life she had chosen.

My mother had told me time healed broken hearts. Even the ones that felt irreversible. But how much time did she mean? A few months, a handful of years? Or was it something closer to decades? Could any stretch of time ever ease the pain I would have to live with? Even an eternity?

∼

LIFE HAD its own distorted sympathy. It wounded deeply, then turned around to offer a consolation prize, convinced it could heal the hurt it had caused.

Since returning from Boston, I had been working with Jeff on our second start-up, Charis. We wanted to continue developing and enhancing the unstructured data technology we had created at Mars-Edge. We knew our technology was groundbreaking, but it was too esoteric. It lacked a compelling daily use case. Something that would let people experience its power firsthand and make the value proposition undeniable. Without that tangible demonstration, its potential remained hidden.

This time around, Jeff and I asked ourselves what specific daily problems we wanted to solve leveraging our proprietary technology. Serendipitously, during a weekend excursion to Muir Woods in June, we bumped into another hiker—an anthropology researcher at UC Davis. She shared with us a staggering statistic that over 50 percent of Americans reported feeling lonely. The aftermath of September 11 still engulfed the nation. The economic downturn following the tech crash only deepened the weight. Fear and uncertainty crept into the corners of daily life, opening the door to loneliness.

"Loneliness kills. It's as lethal as smoking. It even leads to premature death," she had said.

Her revelation resonated deep within me. With eight years of loneliness etched into my soul, I knew its insidious power all too well. I saw it in Jeff too. Abnormally tall, geeky, and highly opinionated, he had limited options for his social circle. Though he acted unfazed, I recognized how it surfaced unexpectedly, sneaking past his defenses and catching him off guard. It was in the droop of his shoulders, in his eyes fixed on the wall when he believed no one was watching. Loneliness was becoming a national epidemic, an invisible plague, and we believed our technology could offer a revolutionary solution to combat it.

We became enamored with this new problem, fueling our enthusiasm for our second start-up and dispelling all the apprehensions we had carried from our first failed venture. We reached out to three of our former top engineers, who had joined large but sleepy software companies shortly after MarsEdge imploded. Over a fancy dinner of two-dollar tacos, we convinced Pranab, Lea Kincaid, and Steve Cortland to join Charis. Although they would have to work for a paltry salary in exchange for a large amount of early employee stock options until we raised our seed funding, they decided to take a chance on us again.

In my eight-hundred-square-foot apartment, Jeff and the three engineers started working on building the beta product, a platform to enable social connections among lonely people. In the meantime, I focused on creating a business plan and investor presentation.

As we neared the public launch, I spent all my time on raising capital. The market had improved from the previous year—when investors wouldn't even bother to return my calls—but securing funding remained an uphill battle. The deadline of the public launch was looming over me as I headed to my meeting with Innoplan Ventures, one of the most prominent funds in the game, boasting a track record of multiple billion-dollar successes.

After I had waited nearly fifteen minutes past the scheduled time in an ostentatiously large conference room, a venture partner and his associate strolled in leisurely. They sported a similar look: dress shirts and vests, matched with jeans for a more laid-back touch.

The partner settled into his seat. "Are we waiting for the CEO?"

I politely corrected him that I was the CEO.

"Oh, interesting," he remarked, jotting something down in his notebook. Perhaps, he was writing, "Will he grow into the role?"

Even though I had delivered the same pitch nearly a hundred times, a flutter of nerves still settled in my stomach. With two pairs of eyes fixed on me and the screen displaying my presentation, I started by outlining the problem we aimed to solve.

"There are over four billion people struggling with loneliness worldwide. Research indicates that fostering human connections can profoundly assuage this isolation. Despite the proliferation of communication tools, people still find it challenging to form meaningful relationships and combat loneliness."

Next, I introduced our solution. "We tackle this critical issue with our technology. Charis uses advanced matching algorithms and a robust data infrastructure to connect individuals experiencing loneliness. When users log in, they're instantly paired with another member facing similar challenges. From there, they can choose to stay connected with a small, familiar circle or meet new people for fresh perspectives. To ease the friction of getting started, we offer gentle prompts—conversation starters designed to spark genuine dialogue or help guide the conversation when it stalls. Most importantly, all of this happens within a private, secure environment where users feel safe opening up. Our goal isn't just to create emotional connections. It's to nurture lasting, meaningful relationships."

I then highlighted how we differentiated from existing solutions in the market. Finally, I detailed our financial projections and the amount of capital we sought to raise. While presenting, I paid close attention to nonverbal cues. Were they leaning in or smiling? Were they creasing their brows? Were they yawning or checking their watch? Based on their body language, I adjusted my pitch's pace and volume. After the presentation, I answered their barrage of questions flying at me at a hundred miles per hour.

"How is this different from dating services?"

"Dating services would be equivalent to trying to put out a fire on the Golden Gate Bridge with a fan. Our platform's scope and application are specifically catered to people dealing with loneliness."

"How do you make money?"

"Right now, our focus is on delivering an exceptional user experience. Once we have built a substantial user base, we believe there will be numerous channels to generate revenue from business partners."

"What does it cost to acquire a user?"

"Almost nothing. Our user growth will be driven by word of mouth. As more users find solace in our platform, they will naturally bring in others, creating a flywheel effect."

"What will you do with the funding?"

"We'll build a world-class team to solve this complex problem. Not just the smartest minds, but people who are hungry, resilient, and passionate. People who understand loneliness not as an abstract concept, but as something they've lived through themselves."

"What is your exit strategy?"

"I'm not thinking about that. I'm here to build a next-generation company to make this world a less lonely place."

Eventually, the question I dreaded most arrived. "Have you received a term sheet yet?" In essence: Has anyone made an offer? Most venture firms, despite their claims of being contrarian and risk-taking, often behaved conservatively. And rightfully so. It was an impossible job to predict the next breakout success when hundreds of entrepreneurs knocked on their doors daily, each claiming to be the real deal. As a result, firms were hesitant to commit unless others had already shown interest.

No surprise with Innoplan. At the end of the meeting, the partner said, "The market feels too niche for us. It's not something we're interested in right now. But give us a call when you have the first term sheet on the table."

I thanked them for their time, packed my backpack, and walked out of their conference room with my tail between my legs.

Over the past three months, meetings with other investors had followed nearly identical patterns. It was like watching the same horror movie and getting shocked by the same scene every time.

Nevertheless, Jeff remained steadfast, insisting he had faith in my ability to secure the capital. He would act out a scene from *Jerry Maguire*, bouncing around my tiny apartment, flapping his lanky limbs, screaming at the top of his lungs, "Show me the money!" Yet no one did.

BY THE END OF OCTOBER, we publicly launched the beta version of Charis, targeting users of various message forums focused on mental health topics. It was an immediate hit, far exceeding our expectations. Our servers crashed multiple times, especially in the evening, when lonely people started connecting with one another. The unexpected surge of demand left Jeff and our three engineers in a constant state of crisis management. We urgently needed more engineers and servers to keep pace with the growing demand. Unfortunately, we had no money.

There were times I wanted to ask my mother for another loan, but she had already helped me several times during MarsEdge's darkest days and again to kick-start Charis, and I still hadn't repaid her for any of it. I was self-conscious and terrified of becoming the privileged son who constantly fell back on his mother. Jeff felt the same way. He had grown up in the Midwest in a middle-class, hardworking family where both his parents had respectable jobs in the public sector. He wasn't willing to ask to borrow from their retirement savings. Some might have argued that money was money, whether it came from family or institutional investors. However, we didn't want to commingle personal relationships with finances.

Truthfully, I was on the verge of asking my mother for help one night after witnessing the worry of our founding engineers. The silence from investors was starting to wear me down, and I wasn't sure how much longer I could hold out.

"Hello, Mother."

"My son! Always a joy to hear your voice. I just got out of a morning meeting with Mr. Cha. Remember him from the Anyang facility? The one who trained you at the warehouse?" Her voice was warm over the phone, almost cheerful, as if she could sense she needed to uplift my spirit.

"Of course I remember him. The tough guy," I said, settling into the old couch.

"So how are you doing? I can tell you've got something on your mind."

"Nothing's on my mind. All good."

"Are you sure? Do you need some—"

"No, Mother, really. Our early users seem to love what we're building. I feel optimistic."

"That is good to hear, but remember, there is no shame in needing help. Even Steve Jobs did not do it alone."

"I know." Weariness seeped into my voice, but I still couldn't bring myself to admit the truth. My pride—my recalcitrant determination—kept the desperation at bay, even as it sat heavy on my chest.

"And you know . . . you can always come back to SOL if you want to."

"I cannot see myself doing anything but building Charis," I said, glancing around the dim apartment and at the clock. "It's getting late here. Please tell Mr. Kangster to stop saying, 'Your husband wouldn't have done that, ma'am.' "

"I can't take that joy away from him." She let out a soft laugh, but it quickly dissolved into a sigh. "In a way, I wonder if Charis is saving you. It seems like the burden and hardship of building Charis are somehow alleviating the suffering you still feel after Deborah's wedding."

Her words landed softly, calm and full of love and wisdom, as if she had already reached Nirvana. Long after the call ended, her comment kept circling in my mind. Was she right? That Charis had been my oxygen, keeping me from drowning in the past? If Deborah and I had stayed together after college, would I still have chosen this all-consuming path of building MarsEdge, then Charis? I could've been like so many others, climbing a more predictable corporate ladder, sheltered from the heartache of start-ups that, ironically, had been the force driving me forward.

IN CONTRAST TO MY STRUGGLES, Pete finally published *Night Eyes*, the novel he had spent years crafting. A historical fantasy, it imagined a world where Churchill's Dunkirk evacuation had failed. Critics praised it as a masterpiece in the making—meticulously researched, rich in detail, and told in an evocative voice. Within weeks, *Night Eyes* soared onto *The New York Times* bestseller list. An influential talk show host lauded it as the book of the century. Many suspected it would win multiple awards by the end of the year.

I was thrilled to reunite with him during his visit to San Francisco for a book signing on his national tour. The bookstore buzzed with bursts of chatter and the occasional chirp of excitement from rows of fans clutching their copies like prized treasure. I spotted him near the front, surrounded by a small crowd—mostly women, young and old—hanging on his every word, lips slightly parted with anticipation. He looked just as urbane and fit as he had last spring. When his eyes found me across the room, his face lit up. With a quick apology to his admirers, he broke away and jogged over.

"There's my rescue mission. You have no idea how glad I am to see you."

"I finally get to meet a celebrity on his red-carpet tour. Congrats, my friend."

"Thanks." He grinned, then glanced back toward the crowd as they began settling into their seats. "My team's got me on a short leash. But—here." He reached into his bag and handed me a hardback. "Saved this for you. First edition."

A month before the launch, he had asked me not to buy the book. He said he wanted to give it to me in person. And now, here it was. I held it in my hands, savoring the heft of it—his years of sweat, tears, dark hours, all bound into something real. Something lasting. He watched me for a beat, then smiled. "Go on. Open it."

I flipped open the book to find my name printed on the dedication page: "For River, whose encouragement turned my doubts into stories." A surge of emotion hit me—surprise, gratitude, and loyalty intertwining inside of me. My eyes lingered on the inscription, the words blurring as I fought back tears.

"Pete . . . I don't know what to say."

"You don't need to say anything."

He was right. Some moments didn't need words. I let the feeling wash over me, careful not to let my tears drop onto the page. When I looked up, he met my gaze with a warmth that said he understood—how much his friendship meant to me, and how grateful I was.

"Sorry," I said, wiping the page, then my eyes. "I might've gotten a few tears on this special copy."

"Don't even worry. I've got hundreds more."

I burst into laughter, and he joined in without hesitation.

"So how are you holding up? How is Charis?"

"Still fundraising. I have stopped counting the number of rejections."

"That must be exhausting. Have you talked to Abigail about it?"

"Abigail? No, I haven't spoken to her since Harvard."

"You should reach out to her, at least to catch up. She's now a partner at Lamarr Ventures. Still living in New York City, but she travels to San Francisco frequently." At that moment, a woman called out his name, tapping her watch. His expression tightened into a frown. "I'm so sorry, but my team is waiting for me."

"Please do your thing. We'll catch up later. Thank you once again for the book."

WHEN I GOT BACK to my apartment, I emailed Abigail, letting her know I had gotten her contact from Pete and had been in the Bay Area working on my second start-up. By the time I grabbed a glass of water, her reply was already in my inbox: "Heading there on Thursday. Lunch in Palo Alto?"

I FOUND myself feeling oddly nervous about meeting Abigail, despite having known her since I was fourteen. Perhaps it was the years that had passed, or maybe it was the fact that she was a venture capitalist. And sooner or later, I would have to ask her to invest in Charis. Friends, but with different power dynamics. Would she feel uncomfortable with me pitching to her? And if she turned me down, how would that affect how I saw her, or vice versa?

I arrived at the restaurant ten minutes early to calm my nerves. The restaurant was lively, even though it was still early for the lunch rush. The scene looked familiar—young guys in hoodies on one side and middle-aged men in Patagonia vests on the other. It seemed I wasn't the only one seeking investment. As I scanned the room, I spotted her already there, scribbling with intensity, untouched by the noise that filled the room. In the sea of men, she stood out like a symbol of defiance.

"Abigail?"

I tapped her shoulder, and she turned around. Meeting my eyes, she smiled. Not a big, toothy smile, but with both lips tightly closed. We exchanged a restrained, polite hug before I took my seat across from her. She exuded the same confidence I remembered—every inch poise and understated sophistication. Her icy-blue eyes, sharp nose, and flawlessly tied blond ponytail, with not a strand out of place, gave her an air of refined assurance. She looked like a woman at ease in her own skin, unapologetically herself, with no need for an affectation.

"You look well. Like a real man."

"I suppose I've grown up a little," I said with a half-smile.

Over lunch, we caught up on the last eight years since college. I filled her in on my time at SOL and, later, MarsEdge. I walked her through the missteps as well as the breakthroughs—how each shaped the next chapter.

She listened without interrupting, occasionally brushing her cheek and murmuring, "Fascinating."

When I asked how she was enjoying her work, she shook her head and smoothed her hair with a practiced gesture, pausing before responding, "The past two years in tech have been brutal. I still like what I do, but love it? I don't know. I'm still trying to figure that one out."

As we finished up our lunch, she stared at me, raising her eyebrows. "So are you not going to pitch me your new start-up?"

I dithered before responding, "Only if you promise me that our friendship won't be awkward afterward."

"Oh, River, you're too sweet," she said with a simper. "Do you know how many bozos from Harvard reach out to me for money, thinking I'd say yes because we went to school together? And when they don't get what they want, they turn into irascible children, calling me all kinds of names. Would they do that to male venture partners?"

She slammed her palm against the table, startling the two guys seemingly eavesdropping at the next table.

"So no, your pitch won't change a single thing. Plus, you were different from these children even when I met you at Andover. More authentic. With more spine than most. Stubborn, though. So tell me what you've got."

Summoning my courage, I began to articulate my story. I spoke about my years of struggling with loneliness and how, through soul-searching, I came to see it as an unrecognized pandemic. I shared the path Jeff and I took—driven by a shared passion to confront that crisis—and how we built a solution using our proprietary data algorithm. I told her what I hoped Charis could become: a way to make the world a little less lonely. While I articulated my vision, she listened intently, looking straight into my eyes. She had a deluge of astute questions, all of which I already had detailed answers to. When I wrapped up my pitch, she nodded slowly and rested her face against her palm, deep in thought.

"I'm lonely too. And I have been for a long time. I'm glad you're doing something about it. How much are you raising?"

"About two million dollars."

"Two?"

"Yes, but I'm just looking for a lead investor who would give me a term sheet, even if it's for twenty-five thousand dollars. Or ten thousand dollars. I can use it to go back to all the other investors I have talked to and try to get them to join the financing round." I forced confidence into my voice, but my body betrayed me, curling inward with hunched shoulders. My conviction in the product we were building at Charis remained resolute, yet wave after wave of rejections had taken its toll.

"Don't waste your time. I'll do the entire round. I'll sync with my partners this afternoon and send you the term sheet tonight." She jotted something in her notebook, then lifted her espresso cup and took a sip nonchalantly. No smile. No hesitancy.

"What about a proper investor pitch to your partners?"

"I invest in the founder, not some twenty-page presentation. You single-handedly turned around your family business in Korea. You negotiated with those vultures and saved the company during the Asian financial crisis. Then, you left that job with your own conviction. You restarted your life from scratch, building MarsEdge from nothing. Almost every tech start-up imploded last year, so it's not entirely your fault that it didn't work out. And even after that, you're back at it again. You just don't give up. You're like a cockroach during Armageddon. You'll survive anything." She signaled the waiter for the check.

"Like a cockroach? Thank you?"

But what I meant to say was that I felt seen for the first time in a while. After numerous critics had dismissed Charis's potential and regarded me as an unproven founder despite the grit I had demonstrated at SOL and MarsEdge, her encouraging words felt like vindication.

"I saw you in action when we were in school. Once you love something, you never give up. You're all or nothing. That's the kind of founder I want to back. Are we done?" She signed the bill and rose to her feet. I glanced up at her, still dumbfounded by the events of the last hour. Her expression remained impassive, like a blank canvas. "By the way, why did you name your company Charis?"

"Charis in Greek mythology represents beauty and grace. It's our symbolic commitment to help and empower people who suffer from loneliness," I said, omitting the fact that it was Deborah's favorite Greek goddess.

"Love it. I know you're going to make it big. It's *when*, not *if*. I'll be in touch. Au revoir."

No hug. No handshake. As cool as an Arctic glacier.

THAT NIGHT, after receiving the term sheet, I reflected on what she saw in me and Charis. I had often heard the aphorism, "It's not *what*

you say but *how* you say it." But with Abigail, it was her words themselves that made me feel cared for. She recognized the entirety of my
successes and failures and deemed me deserving. I had overcome
countless setbacks to reach this point. I had built a product I was
proud of and convinced her that my idea was worth the two-million-
dollar risk. Just the thought of that financial commitment triggered
the familiar pangs of imposter syndrome, but I quickly brushed them
aside. I had traveled this road before, and I was no longer an inexperienced boy. Even Abigail had called me "a real man."

How would Deborah have felt about me taking the investment
from Abigail's firm and working closely with her? A moot point.
Silly me.

15

RIVER

Winter 2003

During Thanksgiving break of our senior year, Deborah and I decided to stay in Cambridge and spend the holiday on campus. With no means to prepare a proper meal, we ended up at a tiny diner—the rare spot still open that night.

It was mostly quiet, with its few patrons sitting alone at scattered tables, each preoccupied in their own solitary Thanksgiving. A blind man sat alone in the far corner, savoring his meal: turkey, stuffing, mashed potatoes, cranberry sauce—the works. As he left, he approached our table and said we spoke to each other like two souls who had been waiting lifetimes to find each other. "A rarity in this world," he added.

As soon as he walked away, I looked at Deborah, puzzled. "How could he hear us?" He had been seated at least thirty feet away, and we hadn't spoken above a whisper.

She explained, with that brilliance of hers, a phenomenon called *cross-modal neuroplasticity*. "It works like this. When someone loses a sense, like sight, the brain doesn't just give up. It rewires itself. The parts that used to handle vision get reassigned to boost the other senses. Like hearing or touch. Isn't that amazing?"

"Interesting . . . I think my heart does something similar. Whenever you're away, it rewires itself to love you in new ways. Let's call it *cardioplasticity*."

"*Cardioplasticity*? You may have just coined a new theory, darling. I might have to disappear more often. Purely for research purposes, of course."

Back then, I couldn't have known how much our conversation would matter. But in 2003, her words returned, as other parts of me bloomed around the hollow left by my fractured heart.

EARLIER IN THE YEAR, Jeff and I secured an office lease near the Powell BART station. Although it bordered the Tenderloin area, infamous for its high density of drug dealers and addicts, the bargain rent was too good to pass up. The central location also made commuting easier for our employees. We knew it would be sketchy at night, but it had just enough charm for us to call it our first home. When we initially moved in —fortunately for Jeff, no family of rats welcomed us—the space seemed enormous. But as we kept hiring, it felt like the office shrank daily.

In late spring, I reached out to Cynthia Sharpe, the former head of HR at MarsEdge. She had moved on to greener pastures, but I tried to recruit her back to Charis as our vice president of HR. Though the renewed mission to help the lonely resonated with her, she declined my invitation. The scars of MarsEdge still clung to her. So I resorted to unconventional measures. I flooded her inbox with her favorite Emily Dickinson poem, sending it every day for a month.

On the thirty-first day, she called me, likely out of sheer exhaustion. "River, what the heck?"

"Charis needs you. Jeff and I need you."

"You're either the most persistent CEO or the most unhinged spammer. You're lucky I like Dickinson."

She joined six weeks later and immediately focused on getting the culture of the company right. Many people mistook culture for things like perks or a happy work environment. But she believed it was defined in Charis's unseen moments. She would say, "What we do when no one is watching. That's culture."

Culture became an invisible force shaping how we operated at Charis. Even as the company expanded at breakneck speed, we continued to refine the values and principles that guided our actions. After the heartbreak of shutting down MarsEdge, I was determined to get even the smallest details right and to avoid experiencing that same pain again.

Building a fledgling start-up like Charis and running an established company like SOL might have seemed worlds apart, but they shared a critical common thread: walking a tightrope. Both required navigating a minefield of decisions. One wrong move, one poorly timed decision, and the consequences could be catastrophic. But that was where the similarities ended.

At SOL, there had been at least a baseline of trust and market influence. People knew what it was. That brand recognition opened doors with relative ease. Meetings with key customers, partners, and banks didn't require hours of explaining what it was, what it did. Résumés from top-tier graduates flooded in. The allure of partnering with and working for a historic company like SOL persisted.

Yet that machine was slow. Meetings begot more meetings, followed by a parade of presentations—each one feeding the illusion that the collective act of slide creation might somehow solve real problems. The obsession with slide decks never ceased to amaze me. It was as if intelligent people had been trained to perfect the art of making slides with buzzwords and acronyms rather than bold decisions.

In addition, conformity was king. Standing out or taking risks was viewed with skepticism. Titles, turf—"my team," "your team"—and the politics of career advancement took precedence over taking daring steps forward. Decisions were made at the speed of a tortoise race and, once made, were met with such resistance that implementing change felt monumental. As Mr. Kangster often said, it was like trying to make a semitruck do a U-turn on a narrow, uphill, one-lane road. Nevertheless, when that truck finally completed its slow, painful U-turn, the momentum that followed was unstoppable. The sheer power and inertia of SOL, once set in motion, was unlike anything I had ever experienced.

Start-ups, on the other hand, operated under a different set of rules. At Charis and MarsEdge, there was no safety net. Each day was a struggle, especially with the incessant tick of the cash burn. It was a sobering reminder that failure was never far off, perpetually looming just months, weeks, or even days away. But there was an innate freedom in that. Decisions were made fast and without the drag of corporate bureaucracy.

At Charis, Jeff had a saying: "POP—Progress over perfection." He said it so often the team started calling him our "pop star." It was all in good fun, but the phrase became a rallying cry. Whenever someone hesitated, overthinking a launch or second-guessing their work, someone else would call out, "Just pop it!" If something was ready—even if it wasn't perfect—we "popped" it and launched it. And if it didn't work, we didn't wait for a quarterly review. We pivoted the next day. We had no choice but to move fast. Survival demanded it, just to keep the company alive for one more day. That urgency drove every decision.

As a result, hiring at Charis required a different set of lenses. To succeed in the unforgiving start-up world, we needed rebellious people who found ways to make things happen with whatever they had, often turning limitations into opportunities. Those rare breeds understood something fundamental: the company might not exist tomorrow. Even so, they showed up each day and gave their all, accepting lower pay now for the chance at greater rewards in a future that was anything but guaranteed. More work, less pay, and no stability. Who in their right mind would sign up for that?

Yet some still did, risking their careers on such an unfavorable proposition. They were the ones with something to prove, driven by a chip on their shoulder, an underdog's fire, and a belief in the mission that made the sacrifices feel worthwhile. I supposed I was one of them. But what was I trying to prove? What kind of chip was I carrying? These questions often invaded my thoughts, especially when I sat alone in the empty office after the team had left for the day. Was this still about Deborah?

CHARIS ENDED its first year with a sixfold growth in its user base. Jeff and I had hoped for a threefold increase, which would've made us ecstatic. But six times!

We had underestimated how many people were lonely—and how differently loneliness could manifest, from fleeting emptiness to chronic depression. Charis attracted a wide spectrum of individuals who didn't need clinical care but still longed to alleviate the ache through human connection. As adoption grew, we quickly adapted to meet our users' evolving needs. We refined our matching algorithm to better reflect the varied forms of loneliness—pairing some with light, low-pressure check-ins, and others with deeper, more sustained relationships. We also upgraded our screening engine to block bots, scammers, and abusive behavior, making Charis safer and more welcoming than generic chat apps. The results were clear in our data: users spent hours on Charis, unlike the seconds or minutes typical of other platforms.

Abigail, now a board member alongside Jeff and me, was her usual self. "What would it take to replicate this result next year?"

"You mean, aside from a miracle?" Jeff raised an eyebrow. "Let's see. Maybe a big fat cash cannon, a few engineer clones, and a margarita machine to numb the freaking panic every night." He chuckled, eyeing Abigail, then me, as if we were all in on some inside joke. I kicked his foot under the table before he could say something even worse.

Her expression gave little away, but there was no mistaking her excitement. She offered to lead our next Series A financing round with a ten-million-dollar investment at a seventy-million-dollar valuation. In that instant, the thrill of momentum overpowered the uncertainty of the start-up journey. At least for however long ten million dollars would carry us.

The excitement extended beyond our office walls. Since late summer, Jeff had been dating Michelle Tan, a public elementary school teacher—caring, compassionate, and endlessly patient. Of all places, their connection began on the Charis platform, matched by the algorithm late one night. They clicked almost instantly, surprised by how easily vulnerability flowed between them. She told him she often felt lonely, caught between long days in the classroom and a lifetime of putting others' needs before her own. He shared his own loneliness, rooted in feeling misunderstood for his expressiveness— his blunt candor, his penchant for debates. When she told him she wished she had his courage to speak the truth so freely, he blurted out, "I love you already."

It wasn't until their third date that she discovered he was one of the masterminds behind Charis. She thought he was joking at first— even tested him by asking how the matching algorithm worked. He proudly launched into the details, showing off a bit of his technical brilliance. Then she teasingly accused him of gaming the system to match with her.

I learned all this one afternoon at Golden Gate Park, when he invited me to a picnic to meet her for the first time. As we grazed on the charcuterie she had packed, he recounted every moment with wide-eyed detail, like a feverish kid narrating his favorite movie scene. She watched him with a small shake of her head, equal parts amused and adoring, a smile never leaving her face. And of course, he couldn't resist asking her the ultimate Jeff question: her Myers– Briggs personality type.

"INFP," she said.

"No shit! So is River! Now I'm gonna have two identical partners. One for work, one for outside of work. That's fucking fate."

He thought it was hilarious and brought it up to anyone who would listen. Michelle and me? Not so much. But regardless of their differences, he was right. They did look as if fate had brought them together. Through his relationship with Michelle, I began to see new sides of him. He spoke slower, stood taller—not that he needed to—and walked with a pronounced spring in his step. I would catch him smiling for no reason, even in the middle of tense meetings. She brought out a joy in him that was impossible to ignore. Oh, and she stood just four-foot-ten. Opposites did attract.

"Yo, Michelle and I are gonna watch a movie tonight. You wanna join?" Jeff stood over me as I reviewed the Series A investment agreement.

I put down my pen and looked up at him. "As a third wheel? That's a hard no."

"Dude, it's Friday. You can't be reading your legal bedtime stories in the office. That's why you've got no date."

"Save your pity. I've got plans. Pete's in town. I'm meeting him tonight."

"Wasn't he just here last week or something?"

"I'm sure it's some kind of book or movie deal he's working on." I shrugged. "Anyway, have a great time. Oh, and if it's a romance movie, take notes. You need to level up your game. For Michelle."

"Cool. Then queue up some comedy specials and take notes yourself. You need the help. For all our sakes."

PETE HAD BEEN TRAVELING to San Francisco regularly throughout the year, with his visits becoming even more frequent as winter approached. I hadn't asked him outright, but the thought crossed my mind more than once. Was he seeing someone? As far as I knew, he hadn't had any serious relationships. Anytime I brought it up, he brushed it off, saying he was too busy with his book or hadn't found "his Deborah" yet. But with his skyrocketing fame after the block-buster success of his book—and his powerful family background—I wouldn't be surprised if he were on the list of the most eligible bachelors now.

The moment I stepped inside the restaurant, the rhapsodic

strains of Greek music welcomed me. The aromatic tang of oregano, garlic, and olives wafted from the kitchen. Every table, draped in white linen, was filled with guests mid-conversation, their laughter rising and folding into the jovial thrum. I spotted Pete at a corner table, engrossed in the menu. His right leg shook visibly, and his back was hunched. A rare departure from his normally calm, easygoing exterior.

We started with the usual updates—me sharing news about the Series A fundraising, and him discussing the potential movie adaptation of *Night Eyes*. While we chatted, he wore that familiar, gracious smile. But something was amiss. His eyes flitted restlessly—from his glass to his utensils, to the menu, and finally back to mine. Beneath his voice, there was a subtle undercurrent I couldn't quite place.

"I don't want to be presumptuous, but it seems like you have something important to tell me."

"Yeah. I've been carrying it for a while."

"Would you like to share it with me?"

"Of course. I'm just . . . struggling to get the words out. I don't know how to start."

"It's okay. I'm listening."

"Well . . . I'm . . . I'm seeing someone in San Francisco."

"Pete! That's exciting. I mean, really exciting. Who's the lucky lady? I can't wait to meet her." I smiled broadly, genuinely joyous for him. But the tension in his posture hadn't eased.

He dropped his gaze to the water glass in his hands, his fingers tracing patterns in the condensation. "Um . . . it's *him*, not *her*. His name is Jeremiah," he said, looking up at me slowly.

Jeremiah? It took me a second to process—more than it should've. How had I missed it before? With that surprise came a slow, heavy guilt. I had been so wrapped up in my own world—Deborah, Charis —that I had overlooked the signs, the subtle hints he might have dropped, hoping I would notice. How many times had he tried to open up, only for me to be too distracted, too engrossed in my own life, to see him clearly? The thought of him navigating this alone, without my support, twisted my gut. He had been there for me in critical moments. And I had failed him when he might have needed me most.

Yet despite the initial surprise—despite the sting of my neglect—joy surged, carried by a wave of unrestrained love for him. Tears welled in my eyes, for our friendship and for the privilege of witnessing this moment in his life.

"Pete . . . that's beautiful . . . truly . . ." My voice cracked, tears finally dropping down. "What a gift."

Relief flooded his eyes. His whole face brightened. And the tension in his shoulders melted away. "I hadn't mentioned anything about coming out to you. I frankly didn't know how to bring it up."

He had long felt different from other guys and assumed that, with time, an interest in women would come. Then, while working on his first book, he met a fellow writer named Mark at a workshop. Though the relationship didn't last, their connection upended something fundamental in him. It opened a door he hadn't dared approach before: the permission to stop hiding, and the courage to embrace his full self. Still, he kept that part of himself secret from his family and friends. He feared that coming out might cause serious rifts. On top of that, he was preparing to publish *Night Eyes*, and the last thing he needed was emotional fallout just as his debut was about to launch.

A turning point came during a book tour last year, when he met Jeremiah. In the flurry of signing books and shaking hands, he hadn't realized he had left his phone behind. It wasn't until someone shouted halfway down the block that he turned—and saw Jeremiah hurrying after him, waving it in the air. Reflecting on their initial connection, he said, "I finally understood what you must've felt when you saw Deborah. Now, I believe in love at first sight." His relationship with Jeremiah in the ensuing months illuminated what it meant to be seen and loved for who he was beneath the surface. "Jeremiah taught me that the shadows I had been carrying were my own," he said. "That the cost of staying hidden was greater than the risk of being seen."

When he finally found the voice to come out to his parents, the doubts were still there—even in the seconds before he spoke. "But they didn't even flinch," he said. "My mom just held my hand and said, 'Thank you for trusting us. We love you.' And my dad—he got up and hugged me. That was enough."

A few weeks before our get-together, he proposed to Jeremiah during a camping trip in Mendocino. It was just the two of them amid the towering redwoods, and for a moment, he said, it felt like he owned the world. Since then, he had been struggling to find the appropriate way and the right moment to share the news with me, and here he was.

He also mentioned that Massachusetts was on track to become the first state to legalize gay marriage. With this development in mind, he was hoping to hold their wedding in Cambridge sometime next year. He envisioned a small ceremony in front of city hall and wanted me to be his man of honor to witness the marriage.

"It would be a real privilege. I'm so happy for you and Jeremiah."

I got up, walked over to him, and hugged him tightly. An unbreakable thread connected us. An extraordinary friendship that had blossomed from a tiny dorm room thirteen years ago.

"By the way, it was Mark who encouraged me to do the whole makeover," he said as we sat back down.

"That explains it. When I visited you in Boston last year, I couldn't believe it."

"I didn't want to change my style at first. But he was persistent. Once I got used to it, though, I started to appreciate how I looked and felt. Honestly, if it weren't for his guidance, I doubt I could've won Jeremiah's heart with my scruffy look."

"He would've still fallen in love with you. You're one of the most beautiful people I know. Even with the Sasquatch beard."

"I actually miss my beard. It made me feel like Hemingway." He touched his chin, as if his old beard were still there.

I chuckled, shaking my head. "So are you going to tell me about Jeremiah? I want to know every detail."

"How much time do you have?"

"For you, my friend, all night. I'll even drink something other than sparkling water."

That night, I learned that one way to heal a broken heart was to watch my best friend madly in love. It was a reminder that even in my darkest places, hope could still find me in the most unexpected moments. That even a fragmented heart could feel something more than just pain. The real lesson was to hold on to those glimmers of light for as long as possible.

16

RIVER

Winter 2004

I n 2004, I learned something unexpected about myself: weddings moved me to tears. Not just misty-eyed. Full-on bawling. Shoulders shaking. Maybe it was the splendor of love at its brightest. Or maybe it was the reminder of the love I had lost. Whatever it was, my tears seemed to understand before I did. That it was okay to feel it all, okay to let it wash over me.

The wedding of Pete and Jeremiah at Cambridge City Hall in the summer was a celebration filled with love and joy. As they had wished, the ceremony was small and intimate. Jeremiah's best friend since elementary school stood by his side, while I took my place beside Pete. Throughout the ceremony, Pete and Jeremiah clutched each other's hands like they couldn't let go. Even later, during the toasts and photos, they kept stealing glances, almost afraid they would wake up from it.

Following the wedding, they settled into an industrial loft near Seaport Square. Jeremiah had just completed his assistant professorship at UC Berkeley and relocated to Boston to start his new role as associate professor at Emerson College. Pete, meanwhile, continued working on his newest book. Watching them start their life together stirred the possibility of a second chance I thought I had lost. I didn't know what might turn it into something real. But it was enough just to feel it flicker.

That summer also coincided with the celebration of the Olympics in Athens, Greece. It brought back vivid memories of 1992, when Deborah had introduced me to the grandeur of the Olympic Games. After long days of work and study, we would find ourselves at a tiny restaurant in Harvard Square, drawn in by their irresistible three-dollar happy hour featuring our favorite potato skins and deviled eggs. There, amid the clatter of plates and the chatter of summer school students, we would watch the Barcelona Olympics unfold.

"What amazes me most are the stories," she had said. "The trials, the physical and mental battles . . . and still, they rise. The athletes aren't just chasing medals. They are confronting their own demons and pushing the boundaries of human potential. Then one person breaks a record, and suddenly, the floodgates open. It's like the whole world wakes up and says, 'Wait, we can do that?' "

I watched her—the light in her eyes radiating outward, the conviction in her voice filling the small space between us.

"I see that in you too," she said. "You've got that magic for something extraordinary. Go show them the way."

Show them the way.

Had her words taken root in my mind and shaped my path all along without me realizing it? At that time, I couldn't decipher what she meant or what she saw in me. But after MarsEdge and now Charis, I saw the parallel. Building a start-up demanded the same unyielding drive as an athlete striving to defy the odds. At the start, people doubted the vision, calling it unrealistic or too risky. A dream unlikely to materialize. Yet proving them wrong brought a shift, like flipping on a hidden light switch in a pitch-dark room. One breakthrough and suddenly others would follow, turning the once-impossible into everyday reality. Success in entrepreneurship, much like in athletics, was about redefining conventional beliefs about what could be achieved.

Did love work the same way? Could conviction, courage, and grit transform unrequited love into reality?

THROUGHOUT ITS SECOND YEAR, Charis experienced exponential growth. Over the summer, we had more than six million active users on the platform, and by the end of the year, we were quickly closing in on the ten-million-user milestone.

Additionally, we raised forty million dollars in Series B financing led by Lamarr Ventures and Infigen Ventures, both eager to elevate the importance of mental health. To our astonishment, investors valued Charis at well over $250 million, even though we didn't yet generate any revenue.

It helped that the economy had roared back. The US homeownership rate had soared to an unprecedented 70 percent. It seemed like anyone, regardless of their financial means, could get a mortgage. Watching demand for new housing continue to climb, I couldn't shake the feeling that I was missing my chance to buy a house. But the logic didn't add up. Savings rates were at an all-time low, while consumer debt was skyrocketing. A red flag that my college economics classes had warned me about.

It wasn't just consumers overspending. Money was pouring into Wall Street, with private equity firms snapping up businesses using massive amounts of debt. Several of those firms made eye-watering offers to buy SOL from my mother. But true to her shrewd nature, she trusted her instincts and turned them down. She often said, "If something seemed too good to be true, it probably was." And yet the revelry showed no sign of stopping.

WITH CHARIS'S stratospheric growth and popularity, Jeff and I gained media attention. Being an introvert, I tried to dodge the barrage of interviews. My experience at SOL had shown me that even the most amiable reporters could turn menacing once the initial luster wore off. Jeff, on the other hand, thrived on it.

During a media-day event our marketing team had organized, Joshua Torvik from *Forbes* posed the last question. "As you know, less than one percent of start-ups eventually make it. How do you guys navigate through all the challenges? I'm sure every problem is uncharted and there is no textbook on how to build Charis."

Without missing a beat, Jeff replied, "Nothing fazes me. Even in a crisis, I'm in my Zen. River, on the other hand, tends to be paranoid all the time. Dude needs to smoke some weed and chill out." He nudged my shoulder, grinning. The room erupted into laughter.

I shot him the familiar "Not this again" look, one he had grown all too accustomed to.

"River, do you agree with Jeff's take?" Joshua turned to me.

"Let's just say one of us reads the fine print. And if you think I'm intense now, imagine me high. You don't want to see that." A few deliberate claps sounded from the front row. "But I get it . . ." I paused, contemplating my next words carefully. "We all want certainty. But life's only constant is its unpredictability. Have you heard of impermanence in Buddhism? The idea that nothing stays the same. I would love to say I've embraced it, but honestly, I'm still working on it."

THE UNPREDICTABLE HAD a way of lurking around the corner and showing up uninvited. Like that time in late October, when I ended up on a panel at REWAKE—the largest mental health conference of the year, spanning three days at the Ainsworth Hotel in Chicago.

When my PR team had first pitched the speaking opportunity, I hesitated. It was our busiest quarter, and I was neck-deep in hiring our first head of revenue to shape our monetization strategy. At the same time, we were preparing to launch a major product feature that would let users seamlessly organize in-person meetups. Adding to the chaos was my own inner struggle. The last week of October brought a sense of unease. Fourteen years on, Halloween decorations still reminded me of that first walk with Deborah, casting me into a melancholy mood.

Regardless, the PR team believed that my participation could elevate our brand recognition among potential business partners. So I reluctantly consented to join the panel: "Loneliness in the Digital Age—Are We Doomed?"

The REWAKE event buzzed with energy. Mental health practitioners and company reps filled the space, eager to showcase their solutions. Booths lined the perimeter, alive with demos, branded swag, and banners marking their ground like territory.

My panel, scheduled near the end of the first day, drew a full house. Emily Owens, the host, led me through a series of questions, exploring emerging trends in mental health and the impact of technology on care.

As the session wound down, her smile turned elvish. "In your recent *Forbes* interview, you said Charis was born out of your own experience with loneliness. Now that Charis has become a success and touched millions of lives, would you say loneliness is a thing of the past for you?"

I glanced around the room, feeling the pressure of every gaze on me. "If I'm being honest, I'm still lonely. That's one of the driving forces behind my commitment to building and growing Charis. Our work is not finished. I want to continue making a positive impact on millions more people around the world."

"Interesting. What do you think is still causing your loneliness? And if you could wave a magic wand, what would make it go away?"

Her question caught me off guard. Was that even appropriate? Flustered, I stared at her. She leaned forward, hands clasped beneath her chin, eyes fixed on mine. I turned back to the audience, searching for composure. Suddenly, Deborah's smile surged in my mind, striking me with intensity of a burst of light. My tongue felt twisted, like it was choking the words, and it took all my strength to pry my mouth open.

"If it were that simple, Charis wouldn't exist. Thank you for having me today." I stood, shook her hand, and stepped down from the stage. Without looking back, I made my way through the conference room, past the lobby's polished marble, and out the doors of the Ainsworth. Ahead of me, Lake Michigan stretched wide, glinting under a pale sky, vast like an ocean.

No matter how hard I tried to push thoughts of Deborah away, she remained like the moon in daylight. Hidden, but always there. Smiling, teasing, seducing—a thousand expressions, shifting like the phases of the moon. But those thoughts didn't always stay buried. A whiff of Trésor on the BART train, or a woman in an oatmeal beanie with brown eyes—any of it could bring her to the surface and bring me to my knees. An invisible weight would clamp down on my chest, stealing my breath until I nearly passed out. The psychotherapist I saw after Deborah's wedding called it post-traumatic stress disorder. She warned that dwelling in the past would deepen my depression, while imagining an improbable future would stoke my anxiety. She gave me tools—breathing exercises to stimulate the vagus nerve and progressive muscle relaxation. But no matter what I tried, panic stayed close. With Deborah, there was no past, present, or future. Just a continuous loop of longing and suffering.

I SKIPPED the conference dinner and stayed in my hotel room to catch up on work. But the room soon felt suffocating, its opulence doing little to mask the growing sense of confinement. I needed a break— from the room, the silence, myself. I grabbed my sport coat and headed for the door.

The brisk evening air greeted me with a damp edge, cutting through the panic that hadn't fully let go. I let my feet guide me through a ravine of buildings. Light spilled from their windows like lanterns. Halloween decorations crowded storefronts: pumpkins with crooked grins, faux cobwebs made of cotton, a skeleton stretched out in a coffin letting out a coarse groan. Overhead, a gray-purple sky seemed to infuse the night with a sense of mystery. Step by step, my breath slowed, the heaviness inside me beginning to scuttle away.

On my walk back, I passed a narrow bar tucked beneath a forest-green awning. I rarely went to bars, but a stream of live piano music drifted out and tugged at me in my unguarded state. I paused, surprised by the falter in my steps. My mind urged me onward, but the melody—alluring, intimate—held me. Against my instincts, I gave in, letting it guide me through the door.

Inside, the dimly lit room barely contained the grand piano that dominated the floor. Couples sat close at tiny tables, watching a tuxedo-clad pianist coax melodies from the keys. I took a barstool tucked into the corner and ordered a glass of seltzer. For a moment, the music offered refuge from the sentimental thoughts. But the pianist seemed to conspire against me, launching into "When a Man Loves a Woman." The lyrics threaded their way into my defenses. Memories came flooding back. Deborah and I used to play that song endlessly on her Discman—one earbud each—sharing unhurried stretches of our weekend trips. We would watch the scenery roll by, the music wrapping around us. Back then, I was certain I would forsake my own well-being for Deborah, just like the man in the song did for his woman. Yet in the end, I lacerated her heart instead. That truth pulsed like a raw wound.

As the song ended, the bartender asked if I had any song requests. I entertained a few options that paralleled my mood. I was about to respond when a familiar voice interrupted, "Could you request 'Clair de Lune,' by Claude Debussy? And gin and tonic, please?"

I looked over my shoulder, almost instinctively, and my mind stuttered as my vision narrowed to a single detail I couldn't make sense of. There she was, standing like a fragment of the past brought to life. The unpredictable, capricious, ever-fluctuating whims of life. With her silky dark-brown hair resting on her shoulders, lips like ripe raspberries, and those deep-brown eyes, she was as stunning as ever.

"Is this seat taken?" She touched the chair next to me. Before I could respond, she pulled it out and settled in. Then, turning to me with an intrigued glint in her eye, she pointed at my glass. "No skim milk tonight?"

I froze, words caught in my throat.

"Aren't you going to say hello?"

"Hello, Deborah," I stammered. "What are you doing here?"

Her smile, the one that had refused to fade from my mind, now stood before me, real and alive. I glanced at her hand resting on the bar. A diamond ring reflected the dim light. It stung, but that had been a well-worn pang.

"I watched you on the panel this afternoon."

"You were there?"

"Emily threw a few curveballs, but you handled them well."

I blinked, trying to place her. "How did I miss you?"

"I was standing in the back, hiding behind the crowd. Figured I'd spare you a live meltdown."

"You were probably right. And my PR team wouldn't have been thrilled." I let out a nervous laugh. "So—are you here for the conference?"

"Proudly representing Cedars-Sinai."

"Finally, a doctor. Your childhood dream."

At that moment, the pianist cut in with the opening notes of "Clair de Lune." It was Deborah's favorite classical piece in college. The time we spent together—lying in her dorm room, listening to this very song, and dreaming about our future—felt as vivid as if it were yesterday. She had explained that the song was based on a poem by Paul Verlaine—a meditation on the human soul. "It evokes water in the natural world," she had said. Like water, the soul shifted shape to fit the container it occupied. The walls around it could press in, guiding its form, and the surroundings might influence its temperature or flow. But none of that touched its essence. Only what was poured in could change the soul's flavor. "Each person has the autonomy to decide what goes into their soul. Yours is sweet and savory," she had said, caressing my cheek. I hadn't thought about that in years until now. What had I been feeding my soul in her absence? What flavor would it carry now?

We sat in silence, immersed in the song. She closed her eyes and swayed faintly, as if the melody lived inside her. I had longed to gaze at her like this, even if for a few seconds. Her presence, the scent of her, and the delicate touch of her hand accidentally brushing mine seemed to dissipate years of sorrow I had accumulated.

When the song ended, she opened her eyes and applauded. I noticed a hint of moisture at the corners of her eyes. It was barely perceptible, but I never missed a detail when it came to her.

"Wasn't that beautiful?" she asked.

"Yes. It stirs something in me every time. I wish there were a word for how music moves through you."

"You and your obsession with vocabulary." Her smile lingered, but slowly dimmed. She glanced away, blinking once, then again. "That day at McLean, when you showed up out of the blue . . . I was . . ." She trailed off, her words hanging in the air.

"I shouldn't have just shown up like that. I was wrong to be there."

"Oh, River . . . that was just you being you. Extreme."

Extreme. Someone had asked her in college how she would describe me. After a thoughtful pause, she had said, "River's extreme. It's like he's driving a car with his foot all the way on the gas. He never cruises." I used to take pride in that. Hearing it again now, I wasn't so sure.

"Life . . ." She dabbed the corner of her eyes with a napkin, then forced a smile. "I never imagined this is how we'd meet again—if we ever did."

"You used to say you loved life's unpredictability."

"I still do. Though, as I've gotten older, I've learned it has a cruel side too."

"Sometimes it feels like life's making it up as it goes."

"Doesn't it? But what if it's not life that's uncertain? What if it's just us? We're always in motion, asking why things happen or what comes next. Maybe we're better off learning to live with all of it. The beauty, the cruelty, and everything in between." Her eyes wandered, lost in the distance. Then, with a quick inhale, she turned back to me. "Sorry. Got a little philosophical there."

"Please don't apologize. You've always had an introspective way of looking at life. I can already tell you're a phenomenal psychiatrist."

"And you've always had a way of flattering me." She ran her fingers through her hair—a self-conscious gesture she used whenever she didn't know what to do with a compliment. "Speaking of flattery, your company's everywhere now. Charis . . . I like the name."

"You're kind to say that. What do you think of what we're building? Be gentle, though."

"I think it's compelling. You're democratizing mental health access, especially for those who don't need a hospital visit or can't afford basic care. But I do wonder if users will get the right guidance from strangers and what that might lead to in the long run. To help, you need to understand someone's background and deepest secrets. Will users be willing to share that?"

"You raise valid points. But you might be surprised. Many of our users feel more open with strangers. There's something about the distance that makes it easier. They don't have to wear a mask or pretend to be someone they're not."

"I get that, hotshot. Just don't replace people like us with machines in the future. I've got hefty medical school loans to pay!"

We chuckled into our drinks and let the laughter settle between us.

"Hey, Deborah."

"Hey, River."

"Would it be out of line if I invited you to join me for an evening stroll? As old friends, I mean."

"Right now?"

"No, in ten years."

～

WALKING beside her felt like sliding into an improvised jazz medley. My steps were light, my shoulders lifted, as if something tight had unshackled from my chest. I couldn't remember the last time I had felt this way—present, giddy, almost youthful again. Before we left the bar, I had paused. What did I hope to gain from this? I didn't have a clear answer. Only an urgent desire to stay in her orbit a little longer. Being with her was, in essence, my real answer to Emily's question during the panel session: "If you could wave a magic wand ..." Now, walking beside Deborah, I didn't need a magic wand.

"Remember our first walk fourteen years ago?" I asked.

"You mean, 'purr-fect?' "

"Hey, I never pretended that humor was my superpower."

"Has it gotten any better?"

"It's still in beta testing."

"I think it got worse."

We shared a knowing smile, the kind that came only after an inside joke that didn't need explaining.

"So ... I saw that picture of you and your executive team in one of the magazine articles. I was surprised to see Abigail standing next to you. Or maybe surprised isn't right. It was more like, 'I knew it!' "

"She's important to the company. But not like that. When no one else would invest in us, she took a chance."

"You sound suspiciously defensive."

"It's just work and friendship. Nothing more. Besides, I'm still ..." I faltered, almost crossing a line before quickly recovering. "Anyway, how is work? What's it like being a psychiatrist?"

"I love what I do. The hours can be brutal, but it's rewarding to help patients. What makes psychiatry so fascinating is the intangible nature of the mind. You can't see it on an X-ray or fix it with surgery. People come to me with their deepest secrets. Not many professions get that unguarded access."

"Knowing you, I'm confident you'll be running the entire hospital soon."

"Ha! I don't even know if I'd want that. But is that what you've been dying to ask me? My work?"

"You know me too well." I let out a small laugh, hands lifting briefly in mock surrender. "How's married life?"

"There you go. Sounds like you've gotten slightly better at asking for what you want."

"I'm still learning. Evolving."

"Aren't we all?" She grinned. "So, my marriage . . ." Her smile faded slightly. "It's good. George and I make a great team. Being physicians, we have this tacit understanding of each other's work. Our schedules are chaotic, but we make it work."

"What's George like?"

"What's he like? Let me see . . . he's social, easygoing, talkative. Loves football, loves having friends over for barbecue, and he's got this thing for collecting bourbons. He's hands-on. Fixing things around the house, cooking, you name it. Oh, and there's his fancy car that just sits in the garage. He's always waxing it, staring at it, but never driving it. Life with him feels . . . stable."

"I'm glad to hear that. He sounds wonderful." I forced a big smile, though envy chafed like sandpaper on bare skin.

"Look at this!" She paused halfway across the DuSable Bridge to take in the view of the Chicago River. The green water reflected the streetlights like floating gold leaflets.

"I have an idea. Please come with me." I took her hand, and she let me without hesitation. I guided her to the end of the bridge, then down the stairs to the Riverwalk, where we could get closer to the water. "You can see it better from here."

The city's skyline shimmered above, its lights rippling across the surface below like a film projected on a screen.

"Magical," she said. "It's like the buildings decided to go skating."

We settled on a bench by the river, the susurrus of the night folding around us as we wandered through the stories of our lives. With the street lamps lighting her face like a spotlight on a stage, she spoke about how moving back to LA had reconnected her with old high school friends. They had become the community she had missed during medical school and residency. The kind of people who dropped by with a bottle of wine or planned last-minute outings. She also talked about the joy of traveling, especially the impromptu weekend trips that didn't require much planning or budget. Just a packed bag and a good paperback. I asked if she had ever made it to Korea—something we used to talk about back in college. Her expression shifted. "Yes, but it was a short trip." Before I could ask more, she pivoted, brushing past the emotion. She still ran almost every day, sometimes with New Kids on the Block in her ears. And as always, she liked to remind me she could run circles around me.

"Are you sure about that? I want a rematch."

"Yeah? Why not now? I could beat you even in heels." She bumped her shoulder against mine as laughter sparked between us. "Enough about me. Tell me what's going on in your world. And don't worry. I won't probe you about any wild kiss scenes this time."

"Good, because there are way too many of those." I gave a sheepish chuckle. "Where should I start . . . want to hear about my co-founder?"

"Sure. I'm ready for the gossip."

"Jeff came into my life right after I settled in San Francisco . . ."

I told her how we first met through a newspaper ad I had posted. Total opposites. An improbable partnership. Yet something clicked. I talked about the chaos that followed—the ups, the downs, the unexpected journey of building not just one, but two companies together. About how we balanced each other, challenged each other, and somehow made it work. I shared stories—his quirks; his towering height; his girlfriend, Michelle; her empathy; and her not-so-towering stature.

"I like Jeff already. You two sound like a great team."

"He and I complement each other, despite the constant quarrels. Sometimes, though, I wish I could duct-tape his mouth."

"If you're fantasizing about duct tape, it means you actually care."

"True. I'm grateful for him. Building a company feels like a microcosm of life. It's messy. Never a straight line. And it's not easy to navigate without an understanding partner."

"Careful. If your partner outside of work hears how much you love Jeff, she might get jealous."

"No risk there. I'm in a committed relationship with Charis."

She shook her head with a laugh. "Still the same River, I see." Her eyes drifted toward the water as the laughter faded into something gentler. "I always imagined you following an extraordinary path. Going against the grain."

"I never saw this coming. And sometimes, I wonder if I would've ended up here if you and I—"

"We can't know that, can we? Life moves only forward, even when our hearts keep pulling us back."

"You're right . . ." I swallowed the discomfort and quickly steered the conversation elsewhere. I told her about my mother in Korea— how she was upending the traditional authoritative leadership model with her inclusive and empowering approach. And about Pete and Jeremiah's wedding, one of those rare days that reminded me what contentment felt like. Deborah listened as if I had the entire stage, with her as my sole audience.

"I can see how much you care about the people in your life, but you haven't shared much about how you're doing. Tell me, how are you doing?"

"I'm doing well."

"You don't sound so sure."

"I'm sure. I keep myself busy. I start with a workout before heading to the office. Staying physically fit helps with mental performance at my job. Most nights, I eat dinner at my desk and stay at the office until around midnight."

She stared at me, aghast. "Are you serious?"

"I mean . . . sure, there are nights I get home early enough to unwind. I'll read. Put on some music. Sometimes jazz. Sometimes hip-hop. Depends."

"No, no. Not that part."

"Then . . . what?"

"What you just described is what you do, not how you're doing."

"Yes, and I am doing well."

"No, River." She shook her head. "Let me be direct. Are you happy?"

"Are you?"

"Of course I am. But don't deflect my question like it's a media interview. Just tell me. Are you happy?"

"Am I happy?" The word *happy* pulled the breath from my lungs. My mother had asked me the same question once, hadn't she? And still, after all these years, I struggled to answer it. "Well . . . building a company from scratch is exhilarating. And I take real joy in seeing Charis succeed. That makes me happy, I think."

"You think? You *feel*, not *think*, happiness. Tell me, you really don't have a girlfriend?"

"Aside from Charis?"

"I'm serious!"

"No girlfriend at the moment."

"What about before? Have you met anyone since—"

"No. Not yet."

"Not even a casual date? In Korea? In San Francisco?"

I shrugged.

"That's impossible."

"I just haven't had the time."

"But how? You said you felt lonely during the panel earlier, and in all those interviews you've done over the years. So why not?"

Her question stayed there, like a stain that wouldn't scrub out. I turned toward the river, unsure of how much to give away. Could I allow myself to open up to her, a happily married woman? What good could possibly come of it, for either of us? Yet despite the tempest churning inside me, I felt an irresistible compulsion to finally speak the words I had buried for so many years.

"Because of you . . ."

"Because of me?"

"I still haven't gotten over you."

She opened her mouth to respond, then paused. Instead, she leaned back, her hand resting lightly against her chest.

"I'm sorry for crossing the line. I know you're—"

"I don't understand. What you and I had was a decade ago. I'm not the same Deborah you used to know."

"I get that time has reshaped us."

"Then why?"

"Why what?"

"I mean, why haven't you been able to get over me?"

"I wish I knew. Sometimes I wonder if I'm just attached to a memory. An old version of you. But when I see you—like at McLean, and even now—I know it's not just nostalgia. My love for you has been real. It still is. Even if we have both changed, my heart still feels like it belongs to you. All of you."

"But . . . I'm married now. Doesn't that mean anything to you?"

"I know I shouldn't be saying this to a married woman—and I hate myself for not holding back—but I would give anything to live the life we once dreamed of. Back in your dorm room, planning it all."

Her brows lifted, then knit together. She twisted the ring on her finger, slowly, lost in thought. A heavy silence stretched between us. I tilted my head toward the star-speckled sky. Back in college, we used to sit beneath these same stars, wondering if they could see us—if they knew our love was meant to last forever. But we weren't those same students anymore. I was just a fool, still haunted by feelings for someone who now belonged to another life.

"It's ironic," she said at last. "You started Charis trying to make sense of your ghost. And I went into psychiatry to mend my own heartbreak. And yet here we are, still trying to untangle the same questions we help others work through. Loneliness and all."

"Do you get lonely too?"

"Loneliness is part of being human, isn't it? Some just get better at managing it. Or masking it." A flicker of shadow crossed her face. Like it escaped before she could catch it. "I do think about those days at Harvard. They come back when I least expect them. But I try not to let them stay too long."

"What does our time together mean to you?"

"They're memories. Glorious ones." She exhaled.

"They're more than memories to me."

"But we don't get to change what happened."

"Right. But I still carry them. They live inside me. They bleed into every part of who I am."

My words hung in the air. Her eyes clouded with sadness and trepidation. My heart clenched at the sight, already regretting the weight I had placed on her.

"You should know . . ." She blinked hard, her voice catching with hesitation. I held my breath, bracing. "George has been talking about starting a family soon. We've both been so busy that we haven't had time to plan for it. But I'm thirty-two. George is almost ten years older than I am. Time seems to fly faster each year." She turned to face me and reached out to take my hands in hers, as if I were a feeble child. "Do you understand what I'm saying?"

A family?

A sharp tear ripped through me. Life had a way of introducing new kinds of pain. I turned away, unsure where to even look, or what to do with my hands.

In the background, a worker at a small café was closing up, but their music continued to play. Through the outdoor speakers, "The Look of Love" filled the air. Diana Krall's voice held the confession I couldn't give voice to. A single glance, and Deborah would have seen it all—the love I still carried, too deep for words. Maybe this was what she had meant back in college—that the unspoken could carry more weight than words. That love, in its truest form, didn't always need to be spoken.

"River? Will you please say something?"

I turned back to her and caught the way her eyes searched mine —tender, yet tinged with ache. Instead of answering, I stood and gently pulled her to her feet, her hands resting in mine. A faint blush colored her cheeks, and for a moment, hesitation flickered in her eyes. Still, she stood beside me, uncertainty lingering, before I drew her into my arms.

"Deborah," I whispered. "Dance with me."

She lowered her eyes, shy at first, and leaned into me. Her delicate frame fit perfectly against mine, her hair brushing beneath my chin. We let the music guide us, swaying slowly as if we were back on campus, just teenagers again. Once we settled into the rhythm, she nestled into me, her head resting against my chest. I breathed in her scent, letting it fill the depths of my being. In that suspended moment when time blurred—caught between the past and the present—my soul was sweet and savory again.

17

RIVER

Spring 2006

In 2005, four million babies were born, and she was one of them: Adeline. Deborah's daughter. Pete had learned about her from a mutual physician acquaintance and called me with the news on New Year's Eve morning, just as I was stepping out of my apartment.

A gloomy, rain-drenched chill enveloped the empty city. I still wore the scarf Deborah had knitted for me. Its once-soft threads had faded, frayed at the edges after more than a decade of winters. Yet it remained one of the few artifacts I had of her. It wrapped me in a nostalgia of love that still felt alive, even if far-flung and inconceivable.

On the walk to the office—now on the posher Spear Street—I pictured Deborah cradling Adeline, caressing her tiny forehead and nose. Even with the frigid drizzle falling around me, my heart swelled with warmth for her. And yet, it still hurt. Sharp and unrelenting. I paused midstep, unwound the scarf from my neck, and approached a bare-limbed tree near the curb. Its brittle, barren branches shivered in the rain. I tied the scarf around its thin trunk and stood there for a moment, my fingers resting on the knot. Then I turned and walked away, the cold settling on the back of my neck.

Spring in San Francisco arrived with a dusting of pastels, not the riot of color found in Boston. Instead of a landscape in bloom, a lone fuchsia bush spilled over a fence, and a jasmine vine spritzed its subtle perfume into the air. There were no crocuses pushing through frost, no muddy footprints from children trailing behind melting snow in the park. The days stretched longer, but the fog didn't seem to get the message from the sun.

While the city entered the new season inconspicuously, Charis marched in roaring. The past year had been a whirlwind of milestones. With over thirty million users and rising influence, our trajectory had outpaced even my boldest expectations. At the center of it all was Naomi Maes, whose impact reshaped our path. I had first encountered her several years earlier at a leadership conference while she was employed at another company in the mental health industry.

"No VP title automatically makes someone a leader if the team doesn't want to follow. Leadership cannot be assigned. It must be earned through action," she had stated during one of the breakout sessions. Her words resonated with me. Too many executives mistook titles for leadership, believing their own hype while their teams saw through the facade. Despite the varied experiences I'd had at SOL, MarsEdge, and Charis, one lesson remained constant across all three: true leadership transcended title, status, and age.

She defied the stereotypical macho image often mistaken for leadership. Instead, she embodied the qualities I admired: astute self-awareness, genuine care for others, and an unrelenting drive to refine her craft. Her presence stayed with me long after the conference.

Although she wasn't ready to leave her position at the time, my persistent outreach spanning several months—no Dickinson poems involved this time—eventually convinced her to join Charis early in 2005. With her sharp strategic mind, she spearheaded our monetization strategy, built a top-tier sales and marketing team, and implemented the systems we needed to scale. Her ability to inspire—and to consistently deliver results—became a new benchmark for excellence. She never needed to command. People followed her willingly. In doing so, she transformed Charis from a start-up held together with Scotch tape into a polished, profitable business.

It had been an easy decision for me to promote her to chief operating officer in March, handing her the reins of day-to-day operations. If anything were to happen to me, she would be the obvious choice as my successor. Charis, undeterred by the insurmountable challenges of rapid growth, felt unstoppable.

In April, I received an out-of-the-blue call from Abigail. She told me she was stepping down from Lamarr Ventures and resigning from her board seat at Charis. "It's finally my time," she said. The news hit me like a wave. I hadn't seen it coming. She had barely hinted at exploring other paths, let alone leaving altogether. When I asked about her plans, she shared her vision to support incarcerated women by offering legal advice, education, and job opportunities to help them reintegrate into society. She believed many had been wrongly imprisoned due to financial struggles. The stigma they encountered when reentering the workforce only deepened their challenges. She didn't have a full plan, but what she carried was rarer: conviction and courage. And in her voice, I heard a goodbye with no turning back.

Her words stayed with me long after we hung up. Part of me wanted to celebrate her next chapter. I was proud of her for following her heart. But another part couldn't help but feel a wound, as if something foundational had shifted beneath Charis. She had been instrumental in the company's success from the start. And on a personal level, her unwavering belief in me—through every high and low—had been the steady presence I came to depend on. Only then did I notice the invisible constancy she had been in my life these past few years. Something I had taken for granted, never realizing it had been borrowed time.

When she came to San Francisco a few days later to finalize matters with Charis and her other portfolio companies, I offered to take her to dinner. But she had back-to-back meetings until 8:00 p.m., so she suggested we meet for coffee near the Ferry Building instead.

After wrapping up work, I headed out. Downtown in the evening lacked the bustling energy of New York or Seoul. It was as if the city had spent all its gusto by sundown, retreating into the night to recover. The Ferry Building stood solitary against the cool breeze. It seemed to wait for morning, when its marketplace would stir back to life with visitors seeking coffee, artisan cheese, or something in between.

Abigail arrived ten minutes late, dressed in her signature New York chic, though a trace of fatigue muted her usual composure. Her hair, typically immaculate, hung loose around her shoulders, and her steps, usually quick and purposeful, now carried a subtle weariness as she drew closer. We greeted each other with amiable pecks on the cheeks. I suggested we find somewhere warm, but she shook her head. She had been sitting all day and needed a stroll to clear her mind. Not wanting to keep her out too late, I offered to walk her to her hotel. She considered it for a moment, then nodded, almost relieved.

"So how do you feel?"

"It hasn't hit me yet," she said, her voice flat and her face devoid of expression. "Today's been so hectic that I didn't have a chance to digest."

"Well, I'm excited for you. I cannot imagine anyone else tackling such a critical issue."

"Thanks." She offered a smile, but it didn't quite reach her eyes.

We crossed Fremont Street in silence, weaving through the flickering headlights of impatient drivers. I caught a glimpse of her, shoulders drooped, walking at a slower pace than usual. Had something happened to her earlier? Sensing her mood, I decided to shift the topic.

"Do you ever think back to Andover's orientation week? I find myself doing that now and then. 1986 feels like a whole other lifetime."

"What about it?"

"I remember feeling intimidated. There were so many ambitious kids from all over the world. The campus felt overwhelming. Then, on my way to the first cluster meeting, I saw you. Just prancing around. You looked so confident, like you owned the place."

"Confidence is a camouflage for panic."

"Then your panic was way more convincing than mine."

Her eyes warmed, and for a moment, the strange heaviness that had hovered between us seemed to lift.

"Do you still remember how we first met?"

"The breakfast club."

"You remember," I said, flashing a grin.

"We were so young."

"And a little lost. Just Tom, you, and me at Commons before the rest of the campus was even awake. For days, we sat alone at separate tables. Then one morning, Tom walked over to me and asked if we were socially allergic. After that, we went straight to your table and just sat down. But you barely looked at us. Didn't say a word."

"That doesn't sound like me."

"Right. You were the life of the party." We exchanged knowing grins. "Jack eventually joined our table. Then Kate came along and dubbed us the Breakfast Club. That's when you finally spoke— quoted the movie, said something about being awkward—and we all just stared at you."

" 'We're all pretty bizarre. Some of us are just better at hiding it,' I think."

"That's it. We really were bizarre in our own ways."

"We still are." She shrugged, a shadow of something—*regret? hesitation?*—passing across her face.

As I glanced at her, my thoughts drifted back to those early days. In the blur of memory, I could see the fourteen-year-old Abigail again. All these years later, that same look of determination and poise was still there.

We walked the rest of the way in silence, the sentiment of reminiscing giving way to something harder to name. When the lights outlining the silhouette of the hotel appeared ahead, our steps slowed. A few paces from the entrance, I stopped and turned to her. "I just want to thank you for your support. I don't think Charis would be where we're today without your help. And I'm also grateful for our friendship all these years."

She lowered her gaze, letting out a deep sigh before facing me. "Is that all?" Her question, delivered in a stern tone, took me by surprise. Her eyes, rimmed with smudged mascara from a long day of marathon meetings, met mine. They glistened with a sadness and defeat I had never seen in her before. Did my comment come off as disrespectful? Or did I leave something important unsaid?

"Sorry. I'm not sure I understand."

"Of course you don't," she said, her voice edged with bitterness. "We've known each other for twenty years. Have you ever felt anything for me beyond just being a good friend and working partner?"

Her stare was biting, and the tears she tried to hold back finally began to spill. In all the years I had known her, not once had I seen her shed a single tear. I froze, my mind scrambling to process the implications of her words. Was this what Deborah had meant all along? That Abigail viewed me differently from others? She had dated plenty of eligible bachelors before, so I had brushed off Deborah's suggestion as a passing whim. Just ephemeral feelings, nothing more.

"I still don't follow . . ."

She shook her head, sorrow overtaking her face. Her pale, almost translucent skin flushed pink. "I know what people say about me. I'm the ultimate ice queen. But have you ever considered that I might want to be loved? Truly loved? I've waited for you. Stupidly. Illogically. It never made sense, yet I kept falling for you. In high school. In college. At Charis."

Her voice grew louder, filled with a raw desperation. Her words tumbled out in a flood of emotion. "But it was always Deborah. Deborah! Goddamn it, River! She's married now. She has a child. You're sick. Completely, utterly broken, beyond saving. And even then, I would've taken the scraps of your heart reserved for her. Do you know how pathetic that makes me feel? Me. Supposedly *the* ice queen."

She started pounding her fists against my chest. I stood still, letting her release all she had kept buried inside, each strike a testament to the hurt I had caused. I had been so consumed by Deborah —by my own pain—that I failed to see what was right in front of me. Guilt tore through me. I hated myself for all the ways I had overlooked her, diminished her, made her feel invisible—for how blind I had been to her suffering. When she finally stopped, I pulled her into my arms. Despite all her strength to resist, she felt fragile. She wept, her sobs echoing with heart-wrenching intensity. I held her tighter, wishing that somehow, in this moment, her broken heart could begin to heal.

"I'm sorry," I whispered, smoothing her hair in an attempt to comfort her.

She lifted her gaze to meet mine. "I'm exhausted. I felt like you could see through me, but you never saw how I felt about you because of Deborah. I don't believe you'll ever get over her. Tell me I'm wrong."

"Abigail . . ."

The urge to alleviate her pain was overwhelming. To tell her she was wrong, to offer some vague promise I wasn't sure I could keep, to kiss her and pretend, just for a moment, that it could lead somewhere untouched by grief. Was it because I knew what that kind of hurt felt like? Was it guilt for being the one who had caused it? Or maybe— just maybe—buried beneath it all was something more: a feeling for her I hadn't dared to explore until now. But how would I know for sure? For the first time in a long time, I found myself unsure of what my heart desired.

As I wavered, she released a laugh that came out like a sigh. "I thought so." She looked at me one last time, her hand trembling as she caressed my cheek. "I hope we both find the love we deserve someday." She leaned in and kissed me. A gossamer touch. Then, after a final, lingering look, she turned and walked away.

18

RIVER

Fall 2008

I t was in the calmest times that we were most exposed to life's menace. Even when the Charis ship sailed smoothly, I couldn't shake the gnawing paranoia. My mind stayed on edge, constantly scanning for unseen dangers. After weathering a storm of setbacks at SOL and MarsEdge, I had learned how swiftly tranquil waters could turn treacherous. That dread shadowed my thoughts, even as the company celebrated the monumental success of 2007. Unfortunately, the hurricane I had feared was just around the corner, gathering force, waiting to strike with a fury far worse than I had imagined.

Winter arrived prematurely that fall, not in temperature but in the heavy atmosphere that gripped the country. It was as if a blizzard had blanketed the entire nation without a single flurry of snow. When New Century, the largest subprime lender, had filed for bankruptcy the year before, it triggered a tsunami of failures. The aftershocks only worsened in March, when Bear Stearns was sold off in a fire sale, propped up by a thirty billion dollars of Fed financing.

The unstable macroeconomic climate shook Charis to its core.

For most of the year, Naomi and I traveled across the country, meeting with our business customers and commercial partners. We fought to keep their confidence intact in the face of an imminent financial downturn. But what none of us knew was how severe or long-lasting it would be, or the full extent of its impact.

Charis was in an increasingly precarious situation. User numbers had surged over the past year, spiking as people sought connection amid growing uncertainty and isolation. Yet our revenue, ironically, had dropped. Most of our revenue came from licensing fees paid by enterprise clients who provided our customized products as part of their employees' mental health benefits. We also generated revenue by offering data and analytics to clients seeking insights into broad mental health trends. However, with the impending recession, these clients began to tighten their belts, cutting back on spending—even on services like ours, which were designed to help in exactly these moments. Naomi and I tried to persuade them of the value we could bring during tough times, but it was like preaching to a crowd that had already boarded a plane and taken off.

Then came Armageddon.

Just after Labor Day, Lehman Brothers had filed for bankruptcy, erasing generations of legacy in a single stroke. The following day, the Federal Reserve unveiled an eighty-five-billion-dollar rescue package for AIG. From that moment on, the markets spiraled into a free fall, with no bottom in sight. Charis's revenue nose-dived right along with it.

Declining revenue led to profit loss, which meant our cash burn was escalating far beyond what we had planned for the year. Amid the turbulence, I urged the team to focus on what we could control. But inside, I was flailing, unsure where to steer us next. It felt like the road ahead had vanished behind a wall of fog, with no horizon in sight.

Three weeks before our quarterly board meeting, Aisha Khan, our CFO, called Naomi, Jeff, and me into the conference room. She was a veteran in the finance world, having navigated both the chaos of early-stage start-ups and the rigor of large public companies. Petite in frame yet commanding, she carried herself with unmistakable authority. The instant she spoke, her resonant voice shook the room. Pens stilled and all focus gravitated toward her, as if every word landed with a significance no one dared overlook.

As soon as we sat down, she cut straight to the point. "Guys, our revenue is down over sixty percent. Our cash burn is climbing dangerously fast. At this rate, we'll be out of money in eighteen months—if we're lucky. And if the recession drags on for more than two years, we're done."

A stifling air blanketed the room, amplifying every creak of a chair and the mechanical whir of the building's HVAC system. Jeff stared out the window, maniacally biting a fingernail. Naomi perched on the edge of her seat, head sinking into her hand.

"Should we start charging users?" Aisha finally broke the silence, glancing around the room. "I know we've always said Charis should be free and accessible to everyone, but these are desperate times. We need to consider it."

"They'll fucking revolt," Jeff muttered, rubbing his face. "It's gonna be a total shitshow."

"Yes, but if Charis goes under, that's worse," Aisha said, locking eyes with him.

"Maybe we only charge for select features," Naomi offered, turning toward me. "Position it as a premium tier."

I shook my head. "That still undermines what we stand for. Every feature we've built is meant to be open, to help anyone, no matter their situation. People come to Charis at their lowest, sometimes right after losing a job. And now we're going to ask them to pay just to connect with others in the same boat? That's not the kind of company I want us to be."

Aisha leaned forward, her voice firmer now. "If you're not willing to explore that, we're left with two paths. And they're not either-or. They're both-and. We need to slash costs in line with the revenue decline and raise more capital, even if it means accepting unfavorable terms. Are you prepared for that? Cutting roles, laying off people we've worked with for years?"

"No, I'm not." I let out a long breath. "But I'm also not okay with charging our users, especially when so many are struggling."

Aisha gave a small shrug. "Well, you're the CEO." She turned to Jeff and Naomi. "Are you two aligned?"

They nodded. But I saw it—the flicker of doubt in their eyes, the beat too long before answering. Like they were still trying to convince themselves this was the right move.

Aisha began cutting non-payroll expenses wherever possible— renegotiating contracts, terminating unnecessary services, anything to reduce our cash burn. She also instituted an immediate hiring freeze. The announcement sent shock waves through the company. At the monthly town hall, hands shot up in unison during the Q&A.

"Are we expecting a layoff?"

"If layoffs do happen, which departments will be hit the hardest?"

"Why did we hire so many people in the first place?"

We addressed their concerns to calm those fears, but the unease only deepened with each passing week, dragging morale down with it.

In the meantime, I reached out to our investors, hoping to raise more capital. But they struggled with their own internal challenges in the unfolding financial crisis. Desperate, I reached out to outside investors I had cultivated relationships with over the years. But the response was the same: uncertainty and reluctance. This was a real crisis. How had we gone from celebrating key milestones to facing an existential threat within just nine months?

AT THE BOARD meeting a few weeks later, the room felt heavy with tension. The board, now composed of representatives from three venture capital firms and two industry experts in addition to Jeff and me, agreed that we needed to go beyond trimming non-payroll expenses. There was no other viable option for Charis but to follow the path other companies had already taken: layoffs.

The suggestion landed like a blow, the bile curling in my stomach as I struggled to hold it down. I couldn't shake the painful memory of having to let go of the entire team at MarsEdge. Yet the risk was irrefutable as we faced a bleak choice: either cut now and give the company a chance to survive, or risk losing Charis altogether.

THE NEXT MORNING, I arrived at the office lobby, my skin pallid and my eyes sunken. Fitful sleep and an erratic appetite left my spirit feeling even more depleted. The shame of impending layoffs consumed me. I could hardly bring myself to acknowledge the team, who subtly gauged my energy. Passing through the hallway, I caught a few of them whispering or abruptly cutting off their conversations, lowering their gazes to avoid my eyes.

As I sat down at my desk, an unexpected call awaited. A remotely familiar voice reverberated from the other end.

"Hey, buddy, Jon Estes here. Long time no talk."

The CEO of Archstone. In a flash, I was transported back to my final weeks at MarsEdge. I could almost feel the cold silence when he had ignored my calls and emails. Finally, his secretary had delivered the devastating message: the deal was off.

"Jon, it's been a while."

"The market's a bloodbath. Survival of the fittest, right?" He guffawed.

What a cruel, tone-deaf way of describing the crisis. I pictured him lounging by the pool, a cigar dangling from his lips, his skin slowly turning orange, and his chest hair singeing under the cheerful sun, blind to a nation shivering in the dark.

"What can I do for you?"

"Well, word on the street is that you're looking for capital. If that's the case, I think there's a partnership opportunity here." His voice brimmed with enthusiasm, as if he were presenting a sacred gift. But venom crawled just beneath the surface. Archstone had played friendly before, only to back businesses into a corner and decimate them.

"Yes, we are looking for capital," I said, keeping my tone firm, "but I'm not sure if we're interested in revisiting the Archstone terms. As I recall, your deals come with a lot of handcuffs."

He let out a low whistle. "It's just business. You know how it is. Nothing personal, buddy."

Call me buddy one more time.

"If you want to cut to the chase, here it is. We'll buy you guys out. Charis fits squarely into our mental health strategy. I'm prepared to offer you a billion dollars. Flat. No strings attached. We acquire you outright, and you and your team work for me. With our distribution channels, we'll unlock instant revenue synergies. You'll be unstoppable under our brand."

"Did you say a billion dollars? With clean terms?"

"Yup. A billion buckaroos. The market's crumbling, but I'm doubling down on you. You in?"

For a moment, the words just hung there as my brain struggled to catch up. Something didn't add up. *What am I missing? Where is the catch?*

"I appreciate the offer. But I'll need to discuss this with my board before we make any decisions on the next steps."

"Get back to me by the end of the week. This is my cell. Call me anytime, buddy!"

After hanging up, I sat back, feeling as though he had thrown me a surprise party. A billion dollars. In the midst of financial chaos, it represented a lifeline. Yet, strangely, I felt no excitement—no flutter of nerves or rush of adrenaline—just an unnerving calm. Almost an ungrateful calm. How had a billion dollars come to feel like nothing more than a hollow figure on a page? Maybe it was because I knew what came with it. The compromise of what we stood for. The loss of our mission. I hadn't poured my heart into every waking moment of Charis just to hand it over to a soulless corporation like Archstone. Did they even care about the people we were trying to help—the lonely, the vulnerable?

Regardless, I called my executive assistant. "Carmen, could you please help schedule an emergency board meeting? And please find Jeff, wherever he is. We need to talk immediately."

THE NEXT FEW days were a pandemonium. To maintain confidentiality about the potential sale, Jeff, Naomi, Aisha, and Cynthia each selected just one trusted person from their respective teams to help analyze the critical data needed for the board's deliberation. It was a staggering amount of work for such a small group, but we powered through the nights, making sure all the details and scenarios were accounted for.

When we finally presented our findings to the board, we laid out the numbers, the pros and cons of the deal, and all the factors that needed to be weighed before making a decision. Archstone's offer thrilled the three investor board members, eager to cash in. Jeff and I, however, were still uncertain, torn between the financial relief and the potential loss of autonomy as well as its implication to millions of our users. The two independent board members worked to provide neutral perspectives, aiming to help Jeff and me think clearly.

Meanwhile, we moved swiftly to interview investment bankers who could advise us on the potential deal. Their role was to ensure Charis was properly valued and, if necessary, help us shop the company around for better offers. They would also coordinate the many moving parts, from finance to accounting to legal.

With deals drying up due to the financial crisis, the sheer size of this potential transaction had major investment banks salivating. The fees alone were highly lucrative, making this a prime opportunity for them. When the board sat down to interview the candidates, I had one question. "What should we do?"

Banker after banker walked into the boardroom, eager to earn our business. One of them was Doug Avons from Windsor Pearson. He didn't seem to remember that years ago, when I was just a college student interviewing for a summer internship, he had brushed me off as "not the right cultural fit." Now here he was, polished to a shine in a tailored suit and slicked-back gray hair, pitching me like we were old fraternity brothers.

"River, don't you see?" he said, flashing that sleazy grin. "The Archstone offer is a once-in-a-lifetime opportunity. Especially in a market like this. You and Jeff? You'll walk away with generational wealth. I mean, that kind of security? You don't pass that up."

He wasn't alone in that sentiment. Nearly every banker we spoke to echoed the same pitch—urgency, inevitability, the glitter of a big exit. But Richard Mancini from Sterling Greenough stood apart. Where the others leaned on charm and polish, he showed up in a plain sweater beneath a rumpled blazer, his hair tousled—not by product, but by a morning spent getting kids out the door. He looked more like a tenured professor than a dealmaker. And yet, there was a sharpness in his eyes—a clarity and intellect that cut through the noise.

"The billion-dollar offer undervalues Charis by a huge margin," he suggested. "If you can ride out the financial downturn for the next two to three years, Charis will easily be worth ten times that."

Some of the board members scoffed at his bold prediction.

"You think Charis could be worth over ten billion dollars?" Paul Serta from Finerra Ventures asked, his words quick and clipped. "It's a great company, but that's astronomical."

Richard remained calm, unfazed. He turned to me. "River, you've said that nearly fifty percent of people are lonely. That's four billion people globally. Charis currently has fifty million users and is growing each day, especially with the hardship people are facing. You've barely scratched the surface. Yes, your revenue is down significantly, but once the economy recovers, you'll be a force to be reckoned with. Jon Estes is a shark. He isn't offering a billion out of kindness. He knows he's getting the bargain of the century."

Jeff tapped his pen on the table. "Hey, banker man, aren't you shooting yourself in the foot here? If we walk away, your firm doesn't earn a dime."

"I'm well aware of that. But my job is to give you the right advice, not the advice that benefits me or my firm."

Richard's contrarian stance set a tension in the air that didn't dissipate even after he left. A stir of conversation moved through the boardroom as members leaned in, each engaging in a side exchange with the person next to them.

"Well, River, you should take the deal. You've already declined the strategic option to charge users and address the revenue shortfall—against our advice. Don't make two bad decisions in a row," said Andrew Montgomery, the Lamarr partner who had replaced Abigail, breaking the lull in the room.

"I concur." Paul raised his hand.

"Yup, I'm on board," Barbara Duffy from Infigen chimed in, giving a thumbs-up.

Andrew raised three fingers. "That's three votes." He turned toward the independent board members. "Sarah? David? What about you two?"

Sarah Neilson looked around the table. "I'd like to hold my vote until we hear from River and Jeff. Their input is crucial."

"Agreed," David Burgess said. "River and Jeff are the ones with the most at stake. Charis has been their baby from the start. I believe it's important to hear what they have to say."

Having built multiple companies themselves, Sarah and David understood that founders and investors often had different motivations. All eyes shifted toward Jeff and me. We exchanged a glance—one that carried years of understanding.

"Board, please give us a day to sleep on it," I requested. "We'll reconvene tomorrow morning with our thoughts."

The three investors conferred reluctantly, their faces filled with disappointment. We had until morning to decide the future of Charis.

WHEN WE HAD FIRST STARTED WORKING TOGETHER ten years ago, Jeff had introduced me to walking meetings. At the time, I was convinced that important discussions needed the privacy of a closed room. But he believed otherwise. Walking, he explained, boosted creative thinking by over 80 percent—something about the change of scenery and the physical activity igniting new ideas. Plus, being outdoors lowered tension and helped us make better decisions. Over time, I became a believer. That was how we ended up trudging up California Street—one of the steepest, longest streets in San Francisco—in the middle of the night.

"What the fuck, man? When I said a walking meeting, I meant a nice stroll along Embarcadero, not a full-blown workout," he said between huffs and puffs.

"I feel more creative when my body is strained."

"Screw creativity. I need a cardiologist right now." Drenched in sweat, he looked like an ostrich meandering through a savanna. I couldn't suppress my grin, though my thoughts were a tangled mess. "Dude, stop smiling at me. Every time you smile like that, my life gets more complicated. What is it this time?"

"I keep thinking about what Richard said. And I agree. If we sell to Archstone, they'll flood the platform with ads, strip out the unprofitable features our users love, and dismantle everything we've built. Our community won't stick around for that. It'll unravel fast. Charis will implode."

"Yo, but if we don't sell, you know what that means."

"I know," I said, dreading the thought.

"What do you think Abigail would've said if she were still on the board?"

"Abigail? Why are you bringing her up?"

"Because she wouldn't have blinked in a moment like this. She called bullshit when we were killing it, but never flinched when shit hit the fan. She showed up when it counted. Like when we were bleeding on the floor. I fucking loved that about her." His expression grew serious, his pace slowing. "I never understood why she left. She could've stuck around as an independent board member even after leaving Lamarr. Damn shame, if you ask me."

I stayed silent, lost in thoughts of Abigail—her sharp insights, her ability to distill complex situations into clear action steps. And the way she looked at me in those tense meetings, as if her unflinching eyes could strip away the layers of my mind and expose the thoughts I kept hidden, even the ones I didn't know I had.

"Well, she's not here. What do you want to do?"

"I don't know, man," he said, taking in the expansive night view of the city that enveloped us. "Look, I know it's hard with the financial crisis and all the crap. I'm not heartless. But isn't building a start-up supposed to be fucking impossible? If we're honest with ourselves about why we started Charis, the answer seems clear. If we focus on our why, we stay the course and do whatever the fuck it takes to help millions more people out there. Even if we fail in the end, we keep swinging the goddamn bat. Plus, if Archstone acquires us, they'll fire most of us anyway. Redundancies and the usual bullshit."

"Go big or go home?"

"Fuck yeah. Do or die."

I stared out toward the lights dotting the houses below. Many of our employees lived in those homes nestled beneath the hills. Could they understand the gravity of what Jeff and I had just discussed? Or the upheaval about to disrupt their lives? Guilt and shame had already entrenched themselves in the darkest corners of my soul.

THE NEXT DAY, David and Sarah both supported our decision, so with four to three votes, we turned down Archstone's offer to buy Charis for a billion dollars.

"A huge mistake," Jon snarled over the phone. "We'll come after you and fuck you up."

"That's the Jon I remember," I said. "Bring it on, buddy." Then I hung up.

I HAD BEEN A VIVID DREAMER. Not just in the sense of daydreaming about my future, but in the surreal dreams I had at night. Dreams had been more than random images or experiences. They were visceral, almost like an extension of my waking life. An integral ritual my soul undertook while my body rested.

The night before the layoffs, I had one of those immersive dreams. I was sitting naked on the toilet in the middle of an exhibition space, confined by four glass walls. The employees at Charis looked at me in contempt from outside. I scrambled off the toilet, frenetically searching for a towel or anything to cover myself. Suddenly, Deborah emerged from the crowd, her eyes locked on mine, her face as blank as an empty page. Then I woke up in a cold sweat, still gripped by the embarrassment. It didn't feel like a dream. It felt like a warning. Like I was being watched. Dissected. Judged. Could dreams somehow bleed into reality?

That morning, as I got ready, a splitting headache ripped through me. The pain was so excruciating, it had me clutching my head and writhing on the floor. The room spun as my headache clamped down like a bear trap. I barely managed to pull myself together and get dressed for the office. Just before stepping into the all-hands meeting to deliver the dreaded announcement—a 45 percent reduction in Charis's team—I threw up in the bathroom. In the wall mirror above the sink, a pale, green-faced man with gaunt, protruding cheekbones stared back at me. I stumbled a step back. Was that really me? Somewhere along the way, I had regressed. And I hadn't even noticed. Walking to the podium, knees weak, I felt the strain of hundreds of anxious eyes fixed on me. Each person seemed to carry a slim hope that maybe the news wouldn't be what they had feared.

I had rehearsed the statement crafted by HR and legal. They had urged me to project strength, to rally the team with visions of future success. Like a fearless general wielding a giant sword, leading us into the unknown. As I spoke, though, the words felt empty, clashing with the turmoil inside me. I felt like a felon, not a general. I wanted to abandon my prepared remarks and speak from the heart, unscripted. To say how sorry I was, and to mourn with the team for the loss this decision would bring. But it didn't matter, because their minds had already raced ahead to the fallout—what this meant for their careers, how they would pay the bills, how quickly they could find something new. My words were merely background noise to them. By the time I finished, my body shuddered, my shirt was soaked through, and my head throbbed, flashes of light flickering behind my eyelids.

The decision gutted me. Years of trust collapsed as employees voiced their devastation—dismay, anger, remorse. Cynthia later shared a torrent of damaging feedback about my leadership that had surfaced. The sting of their words cut deep, mirroring the collective anguish surrounding me.

Mr. Kangster had once pulled me aside after an especially controversial call: "Sir, the role of a CEO is to make the tough decisions. The ones no one else is willing to make." It was meant to comfort me, to remind me that leadership wasn't about pleasing everyone. "If everyone agrees with you," he added, "you're probably not doing your job, sir." Yet in moments like this, I found myself yearning for a life free from the weight of leadership.

When people talked about starting a company, they obsessed over whether their product was differentiated, whether the market was big enough, or whether they could secure the capital to grow. Rarely did they acknowledge the deeper, more personal toll. The invisible suffering. What if a founder had to fire employees who had poured their hearts into the company from the start? Or lay off someone just back from paternity leave—not because they were incompetent, but because the founder had to shift direction? Or what if the whole team —the ones carefully chosen and nurtured—left, taking others with them, all because the founder's choice shattered their trust? The shame and guilt would persist, invading the mind long after the decision.

Was I good enough? Was I even a good person? How could I call myself a responsible leader when my choices demolished other people's lives in the pursuit of my vision? Should I continue the journey despite it all just because I unequivocally believed in my dream? The self-doubt would become relentless, shadowing each waking moment with unbearable loneliness.

These were the dark sides of entrepreneurship no one warned

about. Just like the unseen challenges of falling in love. Love, much like entrepreneurship, was romanticized for its magic, excitement, and joy. But the emotional debris—heartbreak, disappointment, and the slow burn of resentment—rarely made the headlines, obscured by the fantasy of happily-ever-afters. In many ways, building a company resembled falling in love. Both were beautiful and bold. But both had the power to break a person.

19

RIVER

Spring 2010

In December 2009, Jeff and Michelle tied the knot on a beach in Penang, Malaysia—a destination they had chosen after stumbling upon a fantastic deal and turning it into a full-blown escape. Most of us at Charis hadn't had a proper break in ages, and the trip offered a rare moment to breathe. Pete and Jeremiah—by then, honorary fixtures in our Charis circle—also came along for the celebration. Pete had recently launched his third book and was more than ready for the chance to disappear for a while. The timing, for all of us, felt like a kind of rejuvenation we desperately needed.

The wedding unfolded like a living panorama. Turquoise waters and lush green hills of Batu Ferringhi framed us, while the sunset cast a dreamy haze. Palm trees swayed in the evening's first breath, carrying the mellow acappella of waves breaking on the shore below. I had never pictured Jeff in anything other than stained hoodies, but there he was at the altar, looking as dashing as a prince in a fairy tale. As he watched Michelle glide down the aisle, a broad smile unfurled across his face. One hand rose to his chest, then to his cheek, before returning to his heart. When their lips finally sealed the vows, it felt as though life, just for a moment, had retreated from all its darker sides.

Even amid the beauty, laughter found its place. Jeff's family towered at over six feet, while Michelle's family averaged around five feet. The poor photographer's biggest challenge wasn't the lighting or getting everyone to smile. It was inventing new geometry just to fit them all into the frame. Later that evening, just before the speeches, Michelle dragged me into the bouquet toss with her bridesmaids. She threw the bouquet straight at me, while the women around me made no effort to intervene. In my surprise, I blundered and dropped it, earning some good-natured boos. Pranab shouted, "Throw him a term sheet. He'll catch that with both hands!"

By the time I gave my best man speech, I had already wiped away a few tears. "Jeff is the only guy I know who can build a world-class software application with his eyes closed. But when we go out to dinner, he somehow forgets his wallet. And every time, he orders the most expensive thing on the menu."

From the crowd, Michelle chimed in, "He didn't bring his wallet to our first date either!"

"You still married me," Jeff shot back, flashing that proud, mischievous grin. "Final sale. No returns."

A wave of laughter swept through the guests.

"But seriously, Jeff . . . I'm so grateful you answered my ad and showed up that day." I smiled at him. "Thank you for bearing with my quirks and chaos all these years. You've always carried me when I couldn't stand on my own. I love you like the brother I never had, though I'm glad we never had to share a bed growing up."

He shook his head, but I caught the glint of tears in his eyes. Then I turned to Michelle, my own eyes beginning to well. "Jeff is the most loyal person I know. You'll never have to wonder where he stands. He's already there at your side. Probably with snacks. And he'll keep standing by you. Not just in this life, but in the next. And the one after that."

The rest of the night blurred into dancing, stories, and the glow of a celebration in full swing. But eventually, our much-needed reprieve in Penang came to an end. The music faded and the grind resumed. We were back in the trenches, fighting to keep Charis alive.

When Jeff returned from his honeymoon, he walked into the office with two topics he treated like breaking news.

"Dude, Abigail was supposed to come to the wedding, but she bailed last minute over some bullshit conflict. Seriously, what the hell?" He leaned against the edge of my desk, shoving aside a pile of papers that tumbled to the floor. "You know anything about that?" he mumbled through a mouthful of chips, scattering crumbs across my desk.

"No," I grumbled, swiping at the crumbs and stooping to gather the papers.

"Didn't you and Abigail, like, grow up together or something?"

"We haven't kept in contact."

A fragment of our last encounter surfaced—her tears, her frustration, the raw vulnerability of her love. It pulled at my heart unexpectedly. Before the spiral began, I caught myself and turned my gaze back to him.

"So what was the other thing you wanted to say?"

A cheeky simper spread across his face, eyebrows dancing with amusement. "Yo, I can't believe you weren't into any of Michelle's single friends at the wedding. We worked so hard to hook you up."

I let out a deep sigh. "How many times do I have to explain this to you? My heart doesn't work that way. It has to find its way, not be forced."

"Yeah, I get that, but you don't even try."

"I'm busy. Do you have a point?"

He looked around, as if checking for eavesdroppers, before lowering his voice. "What about your, uh, needs, man." He pointed his finger at my pants with a smirk. "I bet Taoist monks get more action than you do."

"Oh, come on. We are not having this conversation in the office."

"Dude, all I'm saying is, you're all bottled up. You gotta release them from time to time." He undulated his hand through the air, rising and falling, oblivious to the way my jaw dropped. Then, he slapped my shoulder with his potato-chip-stained hand and strolled away, his long, flowy strides radiating the confidence of a newly married man.

The truth was, I had tried.

There was Lauren Park, an old classmate of Naomi's at UC Berkeley. She had founded Murphy, an HR software company serving small businesses. Not too long ago, she had walked away from a long-term relationship—one she was finally ready to leave behind. Naomi thought we shared more than a few similarities. "A kindred heart," she called it.

Our first date was a half-day hike through Tilden Park, surrounded by towering redwoods and the sweet, heady scent of eucalyptus. Sunlight filtered through the dense canopy, threading its way between the shadows. The cacophony of birds resembled an elementary school orchestra rehearsal, a confusing racket to untrained ears. Chipmunks timidly peeked out from the bushes, then darted across the path as if propelled by a slingshot. Though my mind buzzed with nerves—how to show up, what to say—I found unexpected pockets of equanimity in the vastness of nature.

Unlike many outspoken CEOs I had met in Silicon Valley, Lauren had the demeanor of a worldly life coach. She wore barely any makeup, spoke softly, and walked slowly, pausing to touch the plants along the trail, almost like a butterfly flitting from one flower to the next.

For all the serenity of the setting and her peaceful presence, something in me remained out of sync. Our conversation stayed polite, but it lacked fluidity. Not because of Lauren, but because of me. Earlier that day, Naomi had reassured me it would be like riding a bicycle, but it felt more like trying to play tennis after a decade off—where every swing missed the ball. My questions seemed to fly out of bounds, while my answers got stuck in the net. I spent more time scrambling to retrieve missed shots while Lauren patiently waited on the other side. I couldn't shake the feeling that I should've practiced more before stepping onto the court with her. Maybe I had convinced myself I was ready when, in truth, I wasn't there yet.

"So, River, I feel like we spent more time discussing strategies to optimize user funnel conversion than getting to know each other," she said as we stood in the parking lot after the hike.

"I'm sorry about that. I don't know how to talk about myself beyond Charis. I feel like my mind is continually consumed by the company," I said, staring at the ground and absently scuffing my shoe against the pebbles.

"Is that all? Because it feels like something else is holding you back. Something deeper than work."

I pondered her words, stretching the silence that followed. "You're right. I think I've been pretending with you. Not intentionally, but subconsciously." The confession surprised me, but I was grateful she had given me the space to say it. "I was heartbroken once. Maybe I still am. Healing has been slower, more paralyzing than I ever imagined. Naomi keeps telling me to put myself back out there, but clearly, I fumbled it with you today."

"Yeah, I figured as much. But you must know that hearts aren't fragile like glass. They aren't destined to remain broken. They're more like iron in the fire, softened by pain, bent by sorrow, and somehow, with each strike, forged stronger than before." She held my gaze for a moment, then offered a faint smile. "In any case, good luck with your search. Whatever you're looking for." She gave one last glance, then slipped into her car and pulled away.

Naomi had later chided me, "How can you blow up a date like that? Do you know how many guys are after her? You're hopeless!"

She was right. I was hopeless. New love never seemed to land in my heart. It circled in loops before vanishing into the dusk. Each date after Lauren felt like I was chained to a post underground, with a string just long enough to reach the stairs—but never the door. The harder I tried to push forward, the tighter it pulled, tying me to a past that refused to stay behind.

∿

In early spring, Charis's revenue had begun to rebound, and our user base had grown to nearly a hundred million. To sustain that momentum, our business development team ramped up efforts to partner with entertainment companies, seeking collaborations that could connect more lonely people through emotionally rich content. With so much riding on these deals, I found myself spending more time in our Santa Monica office.

For almost a month, I flew into LA every Monday morning, stayed at a local hotel, and flew back on Friday evenings. But with no real commitments waiting for me in San Francisco—just a minimalist studio filled with books, CDs, a few electronics, and not even a plant —Carmen, my executive admin, arranged a short-term rental in Santa Monica. She figured it made more sense to live closer to the action until the deal closed in a few months. It was also cheaper than flying back and forth every week.

But when I saw the rental address on the map, my breath hitched. It was only ten miles from Cedars-Sinai on Beverly Boulevard, where Deborah still worked. I knew this because I sometimes checked her profile on the hospital's website. Unhealthy, I knew. But it held me together when the missing got too loud.

During the first week at the rental, the compulsion to drive over to Cedars-Sinai for a glimpse of her was potent. It was a reckless temptation—one neither of us needed. Each time the urge surfaced, I fought it back, reminding myself that showing up unannounced would only disrupt her life. Nevertheless, life had other plans.

I had quickly established a satisfying daily routine as I settled into working from the Santa Monica office. Mornings began with invigorating runs along the beach, where the salty sea breeze and powdery sand provided a refreshing change from the San Francisco city hustle. My drives to the office, whether through palm-lined streets or with ocean views, offered a vivid contrast to the urban landscape I was used to. In the evenings, I frequently found myself in Koreatown, savoring the rich variety of Korean cuisine. Having access to authentic flavors quickly became my favorite perk of working out of Santa Monica.

My rental unit was a significant upgrade from my San Francisco studio. Situated on the top floor of a modern three-story condominium, it featured a rooftop terrace with an ocean view. Evenings were my time to unwind there, reading, writing, or listening to music. Somewhere in that new flow, I felt more relaxed than I had in years—something both my mind and body had been pleading me for. Amid the calm, the idea of relocating to Santa Monica crossed my mind multiple times. But the thought of living so close to Deborah's work was a Pandora's box I was terrified of opening.

One new routine I had picked up was visiting the local library on Saturday afternoons. While most people were at the beach—drawn to the sun and sea just minutes away—I found solace in the stillness of the nearly empty library. Surrounded by shelves, I would lose myself in a book, cocooned in that rare, undisturbed space that felt like mine alone.

That afternoon, as I was about to leave the library, I heard the fluting voice of a girl reading aloud in the children's section. Drawn by the sound, I glanced over. The girl was sitting on the floor with her legs crossed, engrossed in the pages of *Where the Wild Things Are*, by Maurice Sendak. She wore a yellow sundress adorned with ice-cream cone prints and looked to be around four or five years old. She read with impressive fluency for her age. Her pronunciation was crisp and deliberate. The words rolled off her tongue with ease, her voice rising and falling with the cadence of the story. It was as if she were on stage, her dainty intonations caught by a hidden microphone. *Who is she reading it to?*

My eyes wandered to a woman standing behind the girl, partially obscured by the bookshelves. Her back was to me as she browsed children's books. Though her visage remained hidden, the lithe silhouette of her spine and the serpentine arc of her waist—every line burned into my memory—sent my heart skipping a beat. Could it be her? Or just years of yearning birthing a phantom? It wouldn't be the first time. A cruel trick of the mind, showing up on random occasions. Madness. A roar rose in my ears as I waited for her to turn, to reveal the truth. Time thickened, the air congealing around me, until the need to know became unbearable.

Holding my breath, I took a hesitant step closer, desperate to catch a glimpse of her face. Just then, the girl finished the story, and the woman turned, her attention fully on the girl.

"That was beautiful, Adeline," she said, her voice filled with adoration. "Can you read Mama another book?"

Deborah. There she was, completely unaware of my presence. She approached and lowered herself beside her daughter. I froze, transfixed by the sheer beauty of the moment unfolding before me. A daughter reading to her mother with such tenderness, the mother reveling in the simple joy of her child's voice. My heart overflowed with affection, watching them with a love so intense it brought unshed tears to my eyes.

I inched a few steps closer, careful not to intrude, yet helplessly drawn into the tide of their love. That was when Adeline noticed me. She paused, offering a shy little wave, her dimples appearing as she smiled. Her eyes twinkled with the same innocence and joy that reminded me so much of Deborah.

"Sweetheart, why did you stop?" Deborah glanced at Adeline and turned to see who her daughter was waving at. When she saw me, her eyes widened and her hand flew to her chest, as if she had seen an apparition. "River!" She gasped and sprang up from the floor, her hair flaring out behind her like wildfire. Adeline giggled, amused by her mother's dramatic reaction.

"What are you . . ." The words tangled in her throat as she smoothed her T-shirt with a shaky hand and tucked a loose strand of hair behind her ear. Clad in a simple T-shirt and sweats, with no makeup to hide behind, she looked celestial in her natural beauty.

"Sorry to surprise you like this." I stepped back, resisting the impulse to hold her in my arms.

"What are you doing here?" she asked, her hands fluttering. "I mean, how did you find me?"

"I didn't find you. I found myself here."

"You're not making sense."

"I know how it looks, but this wasn't planned."

"Then?" She planted a hand on her hip.

"I've been working out of the Santa Monica office for the past few weeks. My team arranged a temporary place a few blocks from here."

"And you just happened to be here."

"Right . . ."

"Of all places. On a Saturday. At my daughter's library."

"I've been coming here every Saturday. You know my love for—"

"Books, I know. So how come I never saw you before?"

"I'm not sure. I still don't fully understand how life works." I let out a small smile, but her expression didn't change. Instead, she examined my face, then let her eyes travel down to my shoes and back up again, as if deciding whether to believe me—or perhaps measuring how I had aged since we last saw each other in Chicago.

"How long are you in town for?"

"Two, maybe three months."

"That long?"

"I can make it shorter—if that's easier."

"No, I didn't mean it like that."

"I will stay out of your way. Avoid the library."

"Don't. Please don't. I just . . . I wasn't expecting this."

A silence settled between us as we both cast our eyes downward. The desire to invite her somewhere, anywhere, just to catch up on the years between us, was overwhelming, but it felt inappropriate— almost outright wrong—to make that request, especially in front of her daughter. Maybe the right thing to do was to pretend none of this had happened and to retreat into the safety of distance.

"I probably should get going. I didn't mean to disrupt your day."

It took every ounce of restraint to turn away, even as all of me begged to stay just a little longer. Still, I walked away without waiting for a response, the sound of my footsteps echoing in the library.

Outside, I let out a deep sigh, surprised by how my heart didn't ache as much as I had anticipated. Was I finally healing? Or was it the joy and warmth from witnessing the tender moment of Adeline reading to Deborah that had filled my heart so completely, leaving no room for pain?

Just as I stepped off the curb, I heard Deborah's voice behind me: "River, wait!"

I turned to see her running out of the library. I paused, taking in her approach—hurried yet composed, like a ballerina late for a recital.

She stopped a few feet in front of me, catching her breath. "You really are the master of surprises. What am I going to do with you?"

"I'm sorry. I didn't mean to make things uncomfortable for you in front of your daughter. I must've seemed creepy, watching you like that."

Her eyes softened, though only for a moment. "How have you been?"

"Good, I think."

"You think . . ." Her eyes drifted to the books in my hand. "Still married to your romance novels?"

"You got me there."

"Oh, River . . . you're impossible." She let out a half-hearted laugh.

"I can't help it," I said, adjusting my grip on the books. "By the way, your daughter is a gifted reader."

"Thank you. Adeline is special. Quite mature for her age."

"Like her mother."

She raised an eyebrow. "Are you saying I'm old?"

"Sorry. I meant you were already on another level in college."

"Just messing with you."

"You got me again." A blush crept across my cheeks. "How about you? Are you doing well?"

"Yeah . . . I am doing well."

Her voice held a tremor I didn't recognize. The Deborah I had known rarely wavered, always quick with a word, sure in her step. Maybe the years had reshaped her. Or maybe it was this moment, unprompted and unguarded, with her daughter waiting nearby and too much left unsaid between us.

"After so many years, all I can manage is a surface-level, customary question." I gave a dry laugh.

"What happened to your disdain for small talk?"

"I know. I'm just struggling to say anything meaningful. There are a thousand things I want to ask you, to share with you. But right now, my mind is blank. Not with panic, just . . . quiet. Like all I want is to stand here, in front of you, and let the silence say what I can't. And be okay with that."

"You really haven't changed much."

"Still a work in progress."

"Well . . ." She let out a slow breath and glanced toward the library. "I should get back to Adeline." She hesitated, then turned slightly. "Meet me at Rosalie tonight. Say, ten? George is away at a retreat, and Adeline will be asleep by nine thirty. Mary, our au pair, will watch her. Rosalie at ten. Okay?"

Without waiting for my reply, she rushed back inside the library. I stood there, still untouched by the pain I had braced myself for.

As the setting sun painted fiery shades of apricot and goldenrod across the ocean—like remnants of a dying fire—time seemed to sink into a quagmire. My mind raced with thoughts about the upcoming rendezvous with Deborah. I wondered what our conversation would be like. Would we stick to safe topics like work and the mundane routines of life? Or dare to explore the forbidden, the enduring love I still harbored for her? An evanescent, illicit scenario did cross my mind, one that could shatter what she had built for herself and her family. A shiver passed through me, chased swiftly by shame. I pushed the thought away, appalled it had surfaced at all.

Rosalie was an upscale bar on the ground floor of Hotel Vitality, buzzing with life on a Saturday night. Bartenders moved like pantomimes behind the counter, tossing bottles and shaking tumblers with theatrical flair. Waitstaff weaved between tables with the spatial awareness of dancers, balancing trays of flamboyant cocktails that barely swayed. As I approached the polished marble counter, a couple vacated the two coveted corner seats facing the beach. I slipped into one and waited for Deborah before ordering a drink.

Around me, people relaxed into their Saturday night like it was a ritual. A tranquilizing wave of unfamiliar lo-fi music floated through the air, fusing with the undertone of laughter and clinking glasses. Yet the calm didn't reach me. Ten minutes passed, and though I scanned the room repeatedly, she was nowhere to be seen. Maybe getting Adeline to bed was taking longer than expected. My colleagues with kids often shared stories about their children's ingenious stalling tactics before date nights.

At ten fifteen, with still no sign of Deborah, a man in a hotel uniform approached me. "Are you River Jung by chance?"

Puzzled, I confirmed.

He introduced himself as the hotel concierge and said there was a call waiting for me. Instantly, my stomach knotted. Had something happened on her way here?

I followed him to the concierge desk by the entrance, anxiety building with each step. The black phone receiver lay face down on the desk. I grabbed it instantly.

"Is everything all right? Are you safe?" The words tumbled out before I could even confirm it was her on the line.

"Yes, I'm fine. I didn't have your number, so I didn't know how to reach you. But I can't come tonight."

Her words hit me, enervating my body, but relief followed. For a moment, I had feared something far worse. "It's okay. I'm just glad you're safe."

"I shouldn't have asked you to meet me tonight. I wasn't thinking clearly at the library. Sorry."

"You don't have to apologize. I could've said no."

"Why didn't you?"

"I don't know. Maybe I wasn't thinking clearly either."

The line stayed quiet, a beat of hesitation crackling through the phone. Then, a stifled sigh broke the silence. "River . . ." She said my name like it hurt to say it. "I can't have you showing up in my life every few years like this."

"I never planned for it . . . but it feels like life had other ideas."

"Like what?"

"Like putting me in front of you again to test what I would do."

"Have you still not found anyone?"

"No, not yet."

"Why not?"

"I don't know . . ."

"What do you mean you don't know?"

"I don't know how."

"You don't know how? Come on. You're a famous tech CEO. The media's obsessed with you. Half the world would kill for a chance with you."

"What does that have to do with me finding someone?"

"Everything! You could have someone smart, kind, beautiful . . . anyone you wanted."

"Not anyone. I can't have you." I winced and shut my eyes, wishing I could reel the words back in. "Sorry. That came out wrong."

"River." Her breath hitched like she was trying not to cry. "You can't do this to me."

"Do what to you?"

"This. You still orbiting around me."

"I'm not—"

"What do you want from me? What are you waiting for?"

"Nothing."

"That if you wait long enough, we'll somehow end up together?"

I shook my head, unable to form a single word.

"All because of what we had in college?" Her voice cracked. "Is that what this is?"

"No. It's not that."

"Then what? Why are you still there?"

"Because . . ." I shut my eyes, steadying my breath.

"Because what?"

"Because love isn't a switch I can turn off."

"I've moved on, River. I'm a wife. A mother."

"I know that."

"But you're still stuck in the past. Still wishing."

"I'm not still—"

"Let me ask you again. Why haven't you let me go?"

"Deborah . . ." I held the phone tightly to my ear, as if I could pull her closer through it. The sound of her breath flooded into me. "This love—whatever's left of it—is all I have of you. Why can't I just hold on to that?"

"Look what it's doing to you. I can't be the shadow that keeps you from the light. Seeing you like this . . . it tortures me. I want you to live your life without looking back. I want you to be happy. Happy, River."

Her voice carried the same sorrow and desperation I had once unleashed. The kind that had filled my own words on that fateful day in Korea, when I had shattered her heart, our future, and every dream we had imagined. All of it, undone.

"Will you let me go? Even the version of me you're still holding on to?" She waited—breathless, hoping maybe I would say the thing she needed to hear. "Please, River. Can you do that? For me?"

"Yes." I forced the words out. "For you."

"Thank you," she whispered on an exhale. "I have to go. Take care." Her voice was faint. Like she was already halfway gone from my memory.

The line went dead. I kept the phone pressed to my ear, even as the disconnect tone droned on. The room tilted and spun. A shrieking beep filled my head, drowning out every thought. Unbearable pain shot through my spine, radiating out like an unrelenting wave. This must've been how she had felt when I had hung up on her in Korea. What I had done to her came back like an undertow, dragging me under. Beyond absolution. Beyond atonement.

20

RIVER

Summer 2011

Even the darkest winters surrendered to spring. As ordinary as it sounded, it was one of life's undeniable truths. Amid life's unpredictability, this certainty provided consolation, reminding me that there was still hope for healing my heart.

Back in February, Jeff and Michelle welcomed their first child, Ollie. Naturally, people speculated about his size. Would he take after Jeff's towering frame or Michelle's petite build? But Ollie arrived perfectly average-sized, with a head full of dark hair and cheeks as plump as castella cake. Given Jeff's unconventional, often unruly ways, I used to wonder what kind of father he would become. Turned out, he was a wonderful one. Devoted. Present. Even after long days at the office, he would stay up late rocking Ollie to sleep, bleary-eyed but beaming, energized by the small, sacred moments only new fathers understood. He would recount them to me the next day, the frequency of his once-revered f-bombs notably reduced. There was something innocent about this new chapter of his life, and I cherished being there to witness it. And yet, an inexplicable mixture of affection and bitterness welled up inside me. Admiration for his joy, shadowed by the pang of being outside an experience I hadn't lived but still felt deeply.

AT CHARIS, the bet Jeff and I had placed during the financial crisis turned out to be right on the mark. As the economy slowly recovered, a strange paradox emerged. With the proliferation of the internet, social media, and mobile apps in recent years—all designed to foster connections—people found themselves feeling more isolated and lonelier than ever. As a result, the user base at Charis surged to three hundred million. It was the kind of growth that former customers and business partners could no longer ignore. They came back in droves, and the company not only regained its lost revenue but also returned to profitability.

Archstone launched Penia in the fall of 2010, an attempt to create their own Charis competitor. The name, derived from the Greek goddess of need, felt like a deliberate jab, standing in contrast to Charis, the goddess of grace. My team got a kick out of that. One joked, "The letters *A* and *S* are next to each other on the keyboard. Imagine if their marketing team hits the wrong key and spells that on the launch materials. Penis instead of Penia!"

Fortunately for them, the marketing push was typo-free. They threw millions of dollars into the launch. Celebrity endorsements, Super Bowl ads, and billboards plastered in every major city for months. But despite the flashy marketing, and the name spelled right, Penia flopped. Their platform was buggy and clunky, and users saw no reason to abandon Charis. We had prioritized user needs as the core criterion in our decision-making process. Archstone, on the other hand, seemed more focused on their own bottom line. I was tempted to call Jon at Archstone and congratulate him after the flop of Penis—*I mean, Penia*—but I decided against stooping to his level of gamesmanship.

Inc. magazine featured Jeff and me on their April cover, with a title that I opposed but they ran with anyway: "Solidudes." It was Jeff's suggestion, and the editorial team loved it. The two of us on the magazine cover appeared almost unrecognizable compared to how I had perceived myself and Jeff. In my mind, we were a mismatched odd couple bruised by the grind of building something from nothing. In the photo, however, we projected a polished maturity that masked our quirks, idiosyncrasies, and insecurities. The magazine labeled us as gurus on loneliness, a designation I had been uncomfortable with. When Truman Su from *Inc.* asked for my perspective on loneliness as an expert, I found it challenging to articulate my views.

"Loneliness doesn't discriminate. It seeps into all kinds of lives, in all kinds of ways. It's impossible to generalize and define what loneliness is because each person experiences it differently. I cannot explain your loneliness—why it happens, what triggers it, or how it feels—better than you can."

Truman wasn't buying my response. He pressed further. "Then tell us about your own experience with loneliness." He shuffled through his notes, as if verifying something I might have mentioned earlier.

"For me, the loneliness I experience doesn't follow any set rules. It doesn't wait for the dead of night in an empty room. Sure, that happens, but more often, it sneaks up on me in moments I would least expect. For example, when I'm surrounded by friends on Christmas, strolling on a sunny Saturday afternoon, dancing on the dance floor at a wedding ceremony, or even during a high-stakes board meeting when a life-or-death decision is on the table for the company. Oddly enough, as access to information through social media and apps becomes more ubiquitous, I find myself encountering those unexpected lonely moments more often. Like when I see a photo of my dear friend's daughter blowing out her birthday candles. There is a bittersweet taste in witnessing such vignettes through a screen."

"It's a paradox, isn't it?" Truman said. "More connected than ever, yet somehow lonelier."

"Exactly. That tension—between external appearances and internal truths—is what we're trying to address."

As I shared my thoughts with Truman, I couldn't help but reflect on the irony of it all. This concept that Deborah had once brought up in Chicago many years ago. I had dedicated a decade to building Charis, with the goal of helping others overcome loneliness. All the while, my own loneliness followed like a scar that refused to fade. Only sharpening with the years.

"Yo, Truman, don't let River drag you into his sob story," Jeff chimed in, leaning back in his chair and crossing one leg over the other. "You wanna know how to beat loneliness? Find yourself a damn good life partner. It's the most important decision you'll ever make. Luckily, I've already got mine. Now I'm on a mission to find one for River, so he stops sounding so fucking morbid all the time. Make sure you include his email in the article so the ladies can reach out."

He always had a way of distilling complicated issues into easy-to-digest advice. If only his advice were as easy to execute in practice.

As FINANCIAL MARKETS began to recover, the board of directors at Charis suggested we consider an IPO. Given the significant time, preparation, and resources required, they thought it would be wise to start the process now so we would be in a strong position by the first quarter of next year.

An IPO, or initial public offering, was when a private company like Charis offered its shares to the public for the first time. Before going public, a company was privately owned by its co-founders, its employees, and a group of investors. Going public meant selling a portion of that ownership to anyone who wanted to buy shares on the stock market.

For start-ups like Charis, an IPO represented a major milestone. It provided a substantial influx of capital to fuel future growth; offered early employees like Pranab, Lea, and Steve the opportunity to cash in on their stock options; and allowed investors to see a return on their investment. It also boosted the company's credibility and visibility. But above all, an IPO represented a Cinderella tale, embodying the tears and heartaches the entire team had endured through an unending string of failures. A defining moment where the underdogs triumphed against the odds.

The first step the board recommended was to start interviewing investment bankers to lead the IPO process. Bankers played a key role in going public, acting as intermediaries between the company and potential investors. One of their primary responsibilities was underwriting the IPO, meaning they would buy a large portion of the company's shares and resell them to the public. This ensured the company raised the necessary funds while managing the risks associated with the stock not selling.

I told the board there was only one investment banker I wanted to work with day in and day out.

"We should consider all options, including more seasoned bankers," Paul said.

"No, Paul. The board can help me with selecting co-managers, but I want him to be our lead underwriter," I said, meeting Paul's gaze and the other board members' stares with unyielding conviction. For once, it felt liberating to say exactly what I wanted. Finally, I had learned.

"THIS IS RICHARD MANCINI." I could hear the pleasant surprise in his voice when he picked up. We traded the usual updates, settling into the easy banter of old friends. He shared his thoughts on the economy, then talked about his sons—how they were doing in school, how fast they were growing up. I told him Charis had done well after the financial crisis, and that Jeff had gotten married, had a son, and was learning the ropes of fatherhood.

"It's amazing to hear how resilient you and Jeff have been. It's a real testament to Charis's success. Sounds like you came out even stronger."

"Thank you. That leads me to why I called."

"How can I help?"

"We're thinking about going public early next year, and I want you to be our lead banker on the IPO. You were the only one who stood firm and recommended we do the right thing during the tough times. I trust you'll do the same for us now."

"I'd love to be on board and help!"

"Just to set expectations, we are not aiming for that ten-billion-dollar valuation you once projected, but we believe it'll be well above the billion that Archstone lowballed us with."

"I understand. But I still believe you'll get there eventually. Half the population is lonely. And now, even more so with this social media craze."

We discussed the next steps and wrapped up the call. While the market conditions for next year were unpredictable, my path forward was clear: focus on what I could control, and ensure that Charis reached its pivotal milestone. At times, winning in business was easier than winning in love.

21

RIVER

Winter 2011

The unrelenting march toward IPO became my most potent painkiller. Whenever the sharp, persistent ache of loneliness returned, I drowned it in work. More meetings. More deadlines. More pressure. Chasing something tangible, measurable, rewarded—it was easier than asking why the loneliness kept resurfacing, or what I wanted to do about it. So I let the work become the story I told myself. A convincing decoy, just believable enough to keep the questions I had buried at bay. But life had a way of seeing through the reality I had constructed. Eventually, something broke. A fracture in the fabric of the everyday. And in that rupture, I was forced to pause and confront what I had long avoided.

For the past six months, Aisha, Naomi, and I—alongside a battalion of teams—had worked to prepare Charis to go public by next spring. Richard and his team at Sterling guided us through the entire IPO process, from drafting the prospectus to navigating a complex web of regulatory requirements. Every step brought us closer to the moment we had spent years building toward.

As we approached the final stretch, I traveled across the country meeting with potential investors to introduce them to Charis. The goal was to build familiarity so that, when it came time to pitch the actual IPO, they would already have a strong sense of the company and its potential.

The Denver leg was supposed to be straightforward—fly in, present to investors on repeat, fly out—until a blizzard grounded all flights, turning the airport into a chaotic sea. After a grueling day of investor meetings, my hope of catching the last flight back to San Francisco vanished.

"It's a zoo out there," Carmen said over the phone. "I've been calling every hotel, but everything near the airport is fully booked. The only place with any vacancies is Hearthstone Grand downtown."

"Hearthstone?" I groaned. "In this weather, that's at least an hour away, not to mention extravagant. Are there any practical options?"

"Live a little, for heaven's sake!" she chided, but I could hear the smile. "It's the only place with any rooms left. Plus, think of the luxurious bath salts, the fluffy robes . . . a long, hot bath is exactly what you need after a day like this."

"All right, Carmen, you win. A hot bath it is."

"See? Was that so hard?" she teased. "And don't worry about the airport scramble. I've already booked you a black car. Door five, 8:20 p.m. That's how you make five-star lemonade out of a snowstorm."

I weaved through throngs of travelers, all scrambling for information in every direction. Exhausted parents lay sprawled across the floor, their folded strollers leaning against poles and walls. Children draped themselves over chairs with the weary scowls of people much older, kicking at their parents' suitcases. Overstuffed bags and abandoned carts turned the walkway into a makeshift obstacle course. The recycled air was pungent with the mingled scents of fries, pretzels, popcorn, ice cream, beer, and damp clothes. Overhead, hurried cancellation announcements echoed through the terminal in a flat, robotic voice. Then, amid the disarray, I saw her—standing by the exit door, head down, engrossed in her BlackBerry. Her once shoulder-length hair, often tied in a ponytail, had been replaced with an elegant Italian bob that framed her face. A black trench coat cinched at the waist, a water lily scarf softening the modern precision of her boots and tights. Poised. Unmistakably herself.

How long had it been? Five years? The shock sent my heart racing, a torrent of memories flickering through my mind like an old kinetoscope film—our teenage years at Andover, mock interviews at Harvard, whiteboarding sessions at Charis, our last stroll down in San Francisco. I quickened my pace, my eyes fixed on her familiar profile.

"Abigail Fields?"

She turned around, momentarily startled but quickly regaining her composed demeanor, the same coolness I remembered so well.

"River Jung. Of all the people to run into," she said, a subtle curve tugging at her lips.

My chest swirled with nerves and wonder. The cacophony of the airport seemed to fade, replaced by a coiled energy. We stood there, hesitant, each of us waiting for the other to speak. Then she let out a long sigh. "Isn't life so bizarre?"

"It sure is. Just like us," I said. Was I supposed to hug her? Uncertain, I kept my arms at my sides. "I take it your flight got canceled too?"

"Yeah, I was just trying to arrange a car service."

"I have one picking me up in about five minutes. If you're heading downtown, or wherever, I can give you a ride."

She peered outside before meeting my eyes. "Under normal circumstances, I'd say no. But I've been traveling for three days straight and don't have the energy to deal with the line."

"I will take that as a yes."

I grabbed my suitcase and waited as she gathered her things. Without another word, we fell into step and headed for the exit. A gust of frosty wind hit us the moment we stepped outside. The black SUV already waited, and the driver came over to help with our luggage.

Once we settled in the warmth of the car, I turned to her. "Where to?"

"Hearthstone Grand."

"I'm heading there myself."

"I thought the River I knew was loyal to budget hotels."

"I still am, but Carmen insisted."

"Carmen, the legendary EA. Sounds like she's still taking good care of you." Her eyes followed the ponderous snowflakes drifting down and the molten glow of sluggish traffic outside. On the windowpane, her reflection shimmered, her features rendered almost ethereal.

"I've read about your work from time to time. What you're doing for incarcerated women is remarkable. The kind of change society needs. And the name of your organization . . . New Beginnings . . . I like it a lot. It reminds me of my mother's favorite forsythias in spring."

"Forsythias . . . that's an interesting connection." Her gaze lingered on the snow-covered landscape, her breath creating a small oval of condensation on the window. She lifted a finger and absently traced the fogged glass. The tawny ambient light in the car brushed the fine line of her hand. My eyes flicked to the rest of her fingers—no engagement or wedding ring. As if sensing me, she glanced over and caught me watching her. I quickly pretended to study the window button before turning back to meet her gaze. She tilted her head ever so slightly, gave a small shake of her head, and offered a whisper of a smile. "Were you checking me out?"

"I was just . . . wondering how you've been."

She turned toward the window, tracing her finger on the glass again. "I've been fine." Then, with a subtle shift in tone: "So—Andrew from Lamarr mentioned you're preparing to take Charis public. Congrats."

"I wasn't sure if you had heard, but thank you."

She gave a nod, settling into the supple leather of the seat with an almost regal composure. Her hands, clasped gently in her lap, were steady and calm. Yet beneath that impeccably polished exterior, I saw a fragility that tugged at my heart. It was there in the subtle tremor of her fingers, the way her eyes held a hint of loneliness. A loneliness that mirrored my own. That juxtaposition of composure and the ache just under the surface—that raw humanity—made her captivating.

The drive to the hotel stretched over an hour, the snow still falling boundlessly. When we stepped into the hotel, the opulent lobby cocooned us in soothing air, permeated with the scent of indefinable, expensive fragrance. We checked in at the front desk and headed to the elevator. *Say something,* I urged myself, but the words seemed to dissolve into the dark cloud of my mind. After five years of void, how could I put into words the way I had failed to see her as someone who belonged in my heart? How could a handful of words, spoken in seconds, undo the years of hurt?

"So here we are," she said. "It looks like you haven't changed a bit."

"What do you mean?"

"Still overthinking every word. Always a beat too late."

"I tend to approach most things in life seriously."

"Too seriously."

I forced a smile, hoping to allay the tension, but she didn't return it. "As strange as it may sound, standing here by the elevators, I've often wondered what I would say if we ever crossed paths again—"

Just then, the elevator pinged, interrupting me, as if it were advising that this wasn't the time or place for something so delicate.

She stepped inside and leaned against the mirrored wall. "Join me in my room."

Her invitation caught me off guard, but before I could process it, something in me followed—pulled by a force stronger than thought. We stood in silence as the floors ticked by. When the doors parted, I trailed behind, head lowered, still unsure what I was doing. My heart raced as we walked down the hallway. At her door, she turned the handle and went in, leaving the door ajar. After a brief pause, I entered. Almost reverently.

She moved around the room as if she had been living there for months. With practiced ease, she opened the bar, poured a bottle of white wine into one glass, and filled another with sparkling water.

"I hope you haven't picked up a drinking habit. That would be disappointing." She handed me the glass, the restless bubbles dancing and chasing each other upward.

"No, no alcohol for me still."

She walked to the sofa by the window, where downtown Denver lay blanketed in snow, streetlights scattered like orange syrup over shaved ice. After a sip of wine, she settled into the cushions. "Are you planning to drink standing up?"

I removed my coat, hung it next to hers in the closet, and took a seat beside her. Unsure where to look, I let my eyes wander around the room.

"So, continue," she said.

"Pardon?"

"You were saying how you're a serious person. And that you've been contemplating what you'd say if we ever bumped into each other like this."

"Oh, that . . ."

"Go ahead. I'm all ears." She leaned back against the sofa, her posture relaxed yet attentive.

"Would you prefer the original version? Or a revised one that might suit the current moment more appropriately?"

"Let's start with the original."

"All right." I cleared my throat. "I was going to say something like . . . Oh, hi, Abigail. What a surprise. You look—wow—fantastic. I've read about New Beginnings. I admire your work. Really impressive and inspiring. Congratulations." As soon as I said these words, I took a long sip of the seltzer, letting the cool fizz tickle my tongue. I felt her gaze pressing on me, but my eyes stayed fixed on the glass, as if it could shield me from the discomfort.

"That's it? You already kind of said that in the car, minus the 'You look fantastic' part. I was expecting more from someone who was once regarded as the greatest romantic on campus."

"Apologies for disappointing you, but you asked for the original version," I said, turning to her with an attempt at a lighthearted smile. "I'm happy to offer you the revised version."

"Let's hear the second draft," she said, leaning closer. Her expression was inscrutable, but the glass tilted slightly in her hand.

I bit down lightly on my lip, searching for the right words. "I'm feeling incredibly vulnerable right now. I don't know what might come out of my heart. And that scares me."

"That's a better start. Continue."

"The truth is . . ." I took a deep breath. "It's been a long, painful journey trying to move on from the past. I've often asked myself if my heart even deserves a second chance. A new beginning. Like the name of your company. But that second chance still hasn't come."

She sat still, her eyes steady, inviting the rest of the truth.

"Over the past five years—since that night I realized the pain I caused you—you've drifted through my thoughts from time to time. Not casually, but with tenderness. And each time, I dismissed the feelings that stirred, unsure what to do with them. But earlier today, when I saw you at the airport, something shifted. Walking over to you felt like taking that first tentative step on a foot that had been broken and trapped in a cast for far too long. Then, during our ride here, I caught myself stealing glances, even when I tried not to. Like a teenager nursing an old crush, still hoping it might bloom."

Her eyes glimmered at the word *crush*, a guarded flash of affection not yet ready to surface.

"I thought my heart had been frozen. Hopelessly barren. But since seeing you, being with you tonight, even with just a few words between us, something is stirring again. This unfamiliar desire—confusing, terrifying, and maybe even a little hopeful—is rising in me. All at once. And . . . I can't help but feel that you're at the very center of it all." My voice faltered, suspended in the raw tangle of emotions.

She let her gaze drift around the room with a weary sigh, her hand lifting to her collarbone for a quick, instinctive touch before settling back in her lap. Her shoulders eased slightly, as if releasing something she had been holding in.

"That night in San Francisco, I didn't know where my heart was—if it even existed at all. Maybe this is my way of making up for it, even though it took five years and a snowstorm. Maybe this is how I find my heart again." I smiled faintly. Not at her. Not at myself. Perhaps at the strange turns life had steered me toward. "Being with you right now, I can barely make sense of the thoughts and emotions moving through me, unfolding inside me. But I know they're real. And I can't turn away. I want to lean in, follow wherever this might lead. And if you're open to it, I would love the chance to discover what this could become . . . with you."

She let my words settle between us. Her eyes strayed to the window, returning to me in fleeting, searching glances before slipping back to the darkness beyond the glass.

Did I regret what I had just confessed to her? No, it had been so long since I had experienced anything this visceral. I wanted to grasp every thread of emotion igniting my body. Even if she dismissed my confession as impulsive, I was ready to accept the consequences. For in that moment, I realized that hope had never left me. It had always been there, buried deep, yet fiercely vital.

At last, she set her drink on the side table and turned to face me. Her eyes lingered on mine, not with doubt but with an expectant tenderness, as though waiting for the rest of my heart to speak. In their depths, I could almost see my reflection.

"Is it going to be all or nothing?" she asked.

"I don't know any other way. My feelings are raw right now, so I might say something I'll regret tomorrow. But even so, this is my commitment to you. You'll have my all—good and bad, but extreme either way—if you're willing to explore it with me. Whatever 'it' is." I reached for her hands. The moment our fingers touched, a charge of electricity coursed through me.

She glanced down at our lightly joined hands. "Let me sit with it. It's unexpected for me too," she said, her fingers tracing lightly over mine. "In the meantime, tell me what you've been up to."

I opened up about the excruciating pain, shame, and despair I had endured during the financial crisis and the wave of layoffs at Charis. I told her how I had wished she were still in my life then, as a confidant to help me navigate those dark times. I also shared my disappointment that she hadn't attended Jeff and Michelle's wedding. Then, though hesitant at first, I recounted the chance encounter with Deborah and her daughter in Santa Monica. How my presence that day had caused Deborah immense torment, and how, ever since, I had been trying to let her go. Finally, I spoke of my determination to see Charis through its upcoming IPO, and how much it would mean to the team after years of tireless work and heartbreak.

In turn, Abigail shared her own journey. She had poured her heart into launching New Beginnings, speaking about the highs and lows of building something from the ground up. Despite the struggles, she felt her work was a true calling. Something she couldn't imagine walking away from. She also confided in me about her engagement to Scott Penrose Jr., which began four years ago. They had met through her brother, who had played squash with Scott at Princeton. But life, as she put it, had kept getting in the way, leading them to postpone the wedding time and again. Two years ago, they had realized that their engagement had been built on shaky foundations. They parted ways amicably, though it came as a great disappointment to both families. As for Jeff and Michelle's wedding, she hadn't attended because she was navigating the aftermath of that breakup.

While sharing her stories in a self-deprecating yet endearing way, she laughed more than I had ever seen before. Her laughter was feathery and elusive yet magnificent and addictive. Was it the occasion that brought out her laughter, or had I not allowed myself to see this side of her before? I also hadn't laughed this much in years.

As we talked through the night, losing track of time, the loneliness that had worn down my heart began to subside. In its place, I felt a deep desire to hold on to this moment, this feeling of connection.

"Do you think someone like me deserves a second chance?" I asked, my heart emptying years of guilt, resentment, and regret in a single breathless moment.

"Everyone deserves a second chance."

"How does it work?"

"Just like every journey of life. You take one step at a time and see where it leads. But that first step takes courage. It has to come from here." She placed her hand on my chest.

At her touch, the thimble I had worn around my heart began to loosen—then slipped away entirely. No longer caged, my heart thundered, sudden and startling, as if to reclaim the years it had stayed dormant. I drew her into my arms, her body unfurling like she had been waiting to let go.

"I would love to give a second chance a try with you, if you're willing to grant it to me. If this is not the right moment, I'll wait as long as it takes," I whispered.

She looked at me for what felt like the entire snowstorm. Then, without a word, she kissed me with a healing grace that awakened something deep within me. Something I hadn't known was still alive. With that kiss, my heart was stitched back together—whole again, stronger than before, as if every crack had been reforged into something antifragile.

The night was pitch dark, yet the snow fell brightly, drifting down like a bouquet of edelweiss. In that serene moment, my life began to recover its vibrant colors.

PART IV

2012

22

PETE

July 2012

Throughout my writing career, I never enjoyed writing hospital scenes. Even on my best days, they brought me too close to life's fragility. Yet here I was, not just writing about it, but living it, breathing it.

The hospital room was dimly lit. The metronomic beeping of the heart monitor punctuated the gloom. The off-white walls loomed with a clinical coldness. Various medical devices—whose functions I couldn't begin to name, or understand why there were so many—encircled the bed. Needles and tubes lined the veins in his thin arms, like stakes clipped to the withering stems of a dying orchid. How his once-robust body had deteriorated into this strange torpor astonished me.

He told me that his brittle limbs reminded him of trees stripped bare in winter. That his vision blurred like wandering through San Francisco's foggy streets at dawn. And that he feared the smell of the sickness inside him—a sour trace of decay—might repel even those who loved him. Even so, in his failing body, in this somber room, gratitude and peace radiated from him. His eyes, though sunken, still burned with the same fervor I had seen in him since we first met at eighteen. The dreamer I had known for two decades never left him, even beneath the shroud of illness.

"So, River, I've spent the past few weeks taking notes and chronicling your life story. But I'm not sure I fully understand it. Tell me, my friend . . . what is the cure for loneliness?" I opened my laptop and notebook again. Pages and lines of text scrolled past—quotes, reflections, questions. A lifetime recorded, and still, the heart of it eluded me.

He turned and met my gaze. "Thank you for letting me share the memories still alive in me. And for bearing with me as I've tried to weave them together."

"Hearing them was a gift. I write to capture the light and the dark of what it means to be human. Through all our years of friendship, I saw both in you. Extraordinary stories, all carried in a single soul. Thank you for trusting me with them."

"I must admit . . . I was hesitant at first when you asked to write about my life. But after some reflection, I'm grateful it's your voice giving those memories and lessons a second life for someone who needs them. Someone still trying to find their way through loneliness."

"I'll write your story with all my heart. You have my word."

"I know you will." A thin smile ghosted across his face. "So . . . the cure for loneliness . . ." He let the thought linger in the space between us. "For a long time, I believed life was angry with me. But it wasn't anger. It was patience, waiting for me to see clearly."

"And what was it waiting for you to see?"

"That opposites aren't always at odds."

"If not at odds, then what—complements?"

"Sort of. Have you ever noticed how light disappears in a room full of glitter, but blazes in shadow? How hope hides in certainty, yet blooms in despair? What we call contradictions often live side by side."

I didn't know where he was taking me, but I wrote it down anyway, trusting the meaning might come later.

"In a similar vein . . . to understand loneliness—life itself, really—means seeing death not as life's opposite, but as its reflection."

"Death?"

"Yes. Death."

"But you didn't mention anything about death in your story. I mean, aside from that anthropologist's point about loneliness causing premature death. You're not saying—"

"That loneliness made me sick? No . . . and I'm not lonely anymore. But that's the strange thing about death. It rarely visits our thoughts, even though it's always nearby. Until it suddenly stands before us."

"I'm confused. Are you saying the cure for loneliness is death?"

"Sorry, I didn't mean to confuse you. That's not what I'm saying," he said, a small laugh escaping before it broke into a painful cough.

I set down my pen, reached for the cup by his bed, and guided the straw to his lips. He took a sip, his throat working with effort, as if even swallowing drained what little strength he had left. His fingers brushed the edge of the blanket, reaching toward me. I wrapped my hand around his.

"What I'm trying to say is . . . I've come to believe life and death aren't opposites, but two mirrors facing each other, each holding the same truth in a different form. I used to want nothing more than to live life to its fullest—all or nothing—oblivious to death's presence. Now, my thoughts linger on how I want to die beautifully instead."

"But you've lived your life beautifully. Why should your ending be any different?"

"It shouldn't. And that's what I'm trying to say." His lips curved into the softest smile—worn, but resolute—and his eyes brimmed with tenderness.

I stopped typing, the words on the screen scrambled as I tried to piece together what he meant. I set my laptop and notebook aside, letting my heart hold his words instead.

"Just like life, death is a savior, not an interloper or an afterthought. If my goal had been to die beautifully, not just to live fully, I might have made different choices. Instead of dwelling on my guilt and shame—or trying to conquer them—I could have learned to forgive myself, to be kinder to myself, and to love myself just as fiercely as I loved everyone else. And I might have healed the ache of loneliness sooner." He drew in a shallow breath, a faint tremor passing through the hand that held mine. "I believe that the answer to loneliness is to give a second chance. Not just to others, but to ourselves. Fully. Unconditionally. No matter what we've done, what we're holding on to, or what we fear—all the things loneliness feeds on. It's about trusting that we all deserve a second chance so that we can find beauty in our final moments too. Free from loneliness."

23

ABIGAIL

August 2012

Pete sat beside me on the narrow sofa. River lay across from us. Motionless, unresponsive, his spirit fading, but still present. At least according to the monitor next to his bed.

"Whenever you're ready," Pete said, giving me space.

"I'm not sure about this." I glanced at the blank page on his laptop. The cursor blinked. Patient. Expectant. Almost like a heartbeat. "I'm private. And I don't think of myself as a storyteller."

"I understand." He placed his hand on my shoulder. "But as I've been working on the draft, I keep coming back to the same thing. Your voice is missing. It's what River's story needs to bring it to life."

"To bring it to life . . ." I lowered my chin, my gaze drifting over the sterile floor. "Kind of fitting, isn't it?"

"It sure is."

"Okay." I let the discomfort settle—then stepped through it. "I don't have anything prepared, but I trust you'll find the story in it."

He gave a small nod.

"Where would you like me to start?"

"Maybe after the reunion in Denver. River said that's when you helped him find his second chance."

"Denver . . ." The memory lifted through me, warm and aching. "The snowstorm lasted longer than expected. We ended up stuck at the hotel for another day. I won't go into the details. I'm not comfortable sharing that. But I will say this. I found love in Denver." I blushed, tears already filling my eyes. *Hold it together, Abigail.* I dabbed my eyes with the edge of my cardigan sleeve. "When the snow finally cleared, River went back to San Francisco, and I returned to Brooklyn. We both had demanding schedules. He was preparing for the IPO, and I was visiting incarcerated women across the country. Our work kept us apart, but we talked whenever we could. Between meetings and flights. Stolen moments."

"What kind of things did you talk about?"

"Just ordinary, everyday things, mostly. But even then, our conversations were open. No disguise, no pretense. Just vulnerable and unfiltered. Maybe that's why we connected so quickly. So deeply."

"You two are the paragons of intensity." A small smile tugged at his lips, almost involuntarily.

I returned his smile. "In between our phone calls and the times we met in person, he wrote to me."

"Emails?"

"And letters. The good old-fashioned kind. With stamps."

"Still about mundane things?"

"Whatever was on his mind."

"Would you mind sharing an example? Any quotes I can use? Only if you're comfortable."

I wavered for a moment, then reached for my handbag on the table. "I carry one of his letters with me. It's short. More like a poem." My fingers brushed against the inside pocket, and there it was. I pulled out a neatly folded piece of paper, the ink smudged, River's wild handwriting sprawled across it. He wrote with inconsistent legibility, with font size and style shifting from line to line. One *a* would look like an *o* in the next sentence, as if the letters had minds of their own. Until I'd gotten used to it, it took me multiple tries to decipher his handwriting. He'd crafted a labyrinth of words—meant, perhaps, for me to get lost in.

> *Dearest Abigail—*
> *Is the love I feel any less*
> *Sacred because it has arrived the second time,*
> *Enduring because it has only just begun,*
> *Fervid because it lives in the thick of life?*
> *How can I compare what is never meant to be measured?*
> *The love I feel is enough.*

As I read the letter to Pete, memory transported me to the moment I'd first opened it, standing by the mailbox. I could still smell the faint trace of his cologne on the paper. I could still taste the same delicious ache of his words. And I could still feel his love. Every thread of it.

"Thank you for sharing it," Pete said, his voice low, as if careful not to interrupt whatever I was still lost in.

My thumb pressed along the edge of the paper, holding me back from returning to the present just yet. Then, slowly, I tucked the letter back into the small pocket of my bag and resumed my story.

"He came to visit me almost every weekend, no matter where work had taken him. Or me. And then there was the time he drove seven hours from Pittsburgh. Left a meeting halfway, just to bring me chicken noodle soup after hearing I had the flu. He skipped a full week of investor meetings and stayed until I got better. Then, of course, he caught the flu himself. So we stayed in for days, wrapped in blankets, watching movies."

"Let me guess. Romance movies."

"Of course. It's River we're talking about." I let out a shaky laugh, pressing my palms to my cheeks. "Anyway, he really meant it when he said his love was all or nothing. It wasn't about grand gestures or extravagance. It was a collection of small details. Things I didn't even notice about myself. He was relentless. Always asking what I was thinking, what I was feeling. Like he needed to live inside my mind.

And he remembered it all. Every word, every touch, every expression I thought had gone unnoticed. Even the unremarkable, throwaway ones. It was dizzying. Spellbinding. I didn't know what to do with that much love. But I didn't want it any other way." I closed my eyes for a moment and took a slow breath. "Then, it happened."

Pain surged through me like flame as I thought back to that day. "The IPO of Charis in early March was a huge success. The story and mission resonated with the public. He invited key employees and investors to the New York Stock Exchange to ring the opening bell. During the celebration, he mentioned feeling nauseous. Headaches, blurred vision. He brushed it off as euphoria and exhaustion. He even joked that maybe love for me had blinded him. But I couldn't ignore the signs. He was sweating constantly, retreating to a corner to cradle his head when he thought no one was looking." I shook my head, a bitter sigh escaping. "Later, I found out he had been dealing with persistent headaches for a while. Not just months, but years. But he always shrugged them off. Dehydration, fatigue, stress, he said. Never bothered to see a doctor."

"Yeah . . . I saw him deal with those headaches a few times over the years. They were brutal," Pete said, pinching the bridge of his nose. "I told him to get them checked out more than once. Still don't understand why he never listened."

"Did he ever bring it up when you interviewed him? Why he didn't go to the hospital sooner? I never asked. I didn't want to make him revisit old decisions."

"No. He didn't say a word about it."

"I guess we'll never know." I paused, my mind suddenly blank. "Sorry. Where was I?"

"The celebration at the New York Stock Exchange."

"Right. The hard part."

"The hard part."

"So . . . on our flight back to San Francisco, he said he wanted to close his eyes for a few minutes. But when the plane landed, he didn't wake up. At first, I thought he was just deeply asleep. But after calling his name and shaking his shoulder a few times, I knew something was wrong. I barely remember the day that followed. The ambulance ride to the hospital, the nightmares that came after." I pressed my temples hard, bracing myself for what I had to say next. "When the doctors at UCSF diagnosed it as stage four glioblastoma, I didn't understand what that meant. They couldn't say when it had started or pinpoint the cause, but it had spread too far for any treatment or surgery to work. They gave him six months at most. Brain cancer? How? He was only forty! He exercised every day. He didn't smoke, drink, or even touch caffeine. How could this happen to someone like him?"

My hands clenched into fists, nails biting into my palms. It felt like those moments were unfolding all over again.

"I prayed it was some kind of mistake. A cruel joke. We all did, didn't we?"

Pete nodded, silent.

"I reached out to every neurologist, neurosurgeon, and oncologist I could find. I know you were doing the same. Calling in every favor, searching for anything that might give us hope. I had always believed there was no problem without a solution. But this time . . . there was no miracle."

I brought a hand to my eyes, willing the tears to stay put. But they broke through, tracing hot lines down my face.

"We can resume later, if that's easier for you."

"Sorry. I just need a minute."

"I understand. Please take all the time you need."

I sniffled and wiped my cheeks with the back of my hand. I never liked crying. The mess of it. The helplessness. The not knowing how to stop. Still, the tears kept coming, defying every effort to hold them back. Another sweep across my cheeks. A deep breath.

"Are you okay?" Pete's eyes hovered on mine, uncertain, the crease in his brow deepening.

"I'm okay now."

"We don't—"

"I'm good. Really." I sat up a little straighter, forcing myself to meet his eyes. "In late March, he stepped down from Charis and

passed the reins to Naomi. I took a sabbatical from work. With whatever time he had left, we wanted to cherish every moment together.
Throughout April and May, he put on a brave face. He smiled
through clenched teeth. He refused to let the pain show. But his
strength was declining noticeably. Some days, he could barely eat or
move, and he'd whisper apologies, even when I begged him not to.
Then, one morning, he suddenly said he felt amazing. I thought . . .
maybe this was the miracle I'd been praying for. We rented a convert-
ible and drove along Highway 1 with no destination in mind. We
talked for hours. We even sang together."

"River is a terrible singer, though."

"Almost as bad as his humor."

We chuckled, the sound small but full of understanding.

"Sorry. I didn't mean to interrupt. Please keep going. You're doing
great."

"Thanks." A quick inhale; then I pushed forward. "Unfortunately,
by the time we reached Fort Bragg, his pain returned. He slammed
the car to a stop and ran into the bushes to vomit. I tried to follow, but
he waved me off. My heart shattered all over again. On the way back
to San Francisco, he sat motionless in the passenger seat, his face
twisted in pain. As we crossed the Golden Gate Bridge, he confessed
that he might run out of time before getting to know everything
about me. That he didn't want to die before then. Then he cried. I'd
never seen a man cry like that before. And something in me broke,
too. I'd been holding it all in. For him. For us. But . . . I couldn't be his
peaceful place in that moment."

Pete paused his typing and looked up, as if ready to comfort me.

I caught his eye and offered a tiny, unsteady smile, even as my
eyes shimmered with unshed tears. "After we got home, I settled him
into bed. As I wiped the sweat from his face with a towel, he asked
how he envisioned our future if he could live longer. I didn't know how
to respond, so I stayed silent. He said he'd share how he imagined it
when the time was right. But I forgot to ask him about that later, so I
never found out . . ." *What did you want to tell me, River?* I shielded my
face with both hands, resting my forehead against them. Tears

streamed between my fingers, and I felt myself folding inward, the grief pulling me in with force.

Pete's hand landed softly on my back. Hesitant at first, then steady —his presence quiet yet full of care. I took a ragged breath until the room came back into focus. He handed me a tissue, and I pressed it to my face, laughing a little as I wiped my eyes and nose. I didn't know why I laughed. Heartbreak did that sometimes.

"By June, his condition had deteriorated significantly and required full hospitalization. Do you remember how adamantly he refused? He's so stubborn, isn't he?"

"He's the world's most stubborn man."

With matching sighs, we shook our heads in shared exasperation.

"On his first day in this room, he spoke to me about Buddhism. About impermanence and the need to surrender to it. I asked him how to surrender, but he didn't explain. Instead, he smiled and stroked my hair. The day before he lost his voice, he prayed that I find peace once he was gone. That I accept his passing as part of life's impermanence. Now, in these final days, as I sit by his side, all I feel is gratitude. Our time was short. Far too short. But the love we shared made it enough. I'd trade anything for those fleeting, unforgettable moments." I stared at the floor, vision smudging at the edges, and waited for breath to come back. When I finally looked up, Pete's gaze lingered on me, his eyes glassy with tears.

"Abigail . . . you've undersold yourself. Honestly, I half expected you'd give me a few of those sharp, no-nonsense remarks like you did back in college. Instead, my wrist is cramping from all this typing."

We burst into hushed laughter, even as tears spilled from our eyes.

"There's one more thing." I steadied my breath, mustering the courage. "I've come to realize that loving River meant embracing every part of him, including his love for Deborah. During our time together, he never mentioned her. But I knew he still loved her. And you know what? That was okay with me."

I let the silence settle, unsure what Pete would say—if anything.

But he pulled me into a hug. I let my tears soak into his shoulder, finding a moment of solace in his embrace.

I EXCUSED myself from Pete and stepped out of River's hospital room. Standing in the hallway, I pulled out my phone. My hand trembled with each digit. As the ringing echoed in my ear, I held my breath. Part of me hoped it would go straight to voicemail. But instead, her voice came on, unguarded.

"Dr. Starfield speaking."

"Deborah, this is Abigail Fields."

"Abigail?"

"We went to college together."

"Yes. Of course. It's been ... decades. How—"

"Listen. River has only days left."

"Excuse me?"

"Glioblastoma. UCSF Medical Center."

24

DEBORAH

August 2012

— Diary Entry —

I meant it when I told you I loved you first.

It was during Harvard's Visitas Spring Admit Week, when all the newly admitted prospective students gathered on campus to get a taste of the school before making their final decision. Sanders Theatre was a zoo of nervous energy. Wide-eyed students jostled for seats, their voices ricocheting off the high ceilings in sharp bursts. That's when I saw you. Flanked by a boisterous group of girls and boys, you were absorbed in your reading. Was it Kafka's *Metamorphosis*? There was something about the way you conjured your own haven of tranquility amid the chaos, as if the ruckus didn't dare disturb you.

I settled into a seat diagonally behind you, close enough to steal glances without being noticed. Every so often, one of the kids next to you would lean in and say something, and you'd respond with a *Mona Lisa* smile—then return to your book. My eyes traced the line of your jaw, the way your dark hair framed your face, the graceful movements of your hands as you swept your hair aside. Those sensual yet strong hands. I blushed, startled by the illicit thought of what it might feel like to have them hold me.

The post-welcome chaos subsided as organizers herded us into tour groups. Fate smiled on me, as you and I ended up in the same one. I hung back, covertly watching as you moved through the campus. I felt like a secret agent on a critical mission. You didn't look like you belonged there. Other boys wore sweatshirts, team jerseys, jeans, and sneakers. The unofficial high school uniform. But you stood apart in navy slacks, a light-tan sweater, a herringbone sports coat, and brown leather shoes. Like you'd stepped straight out of a fashion catalogue. It wasn't just your clothes. It was the way you carried yourself, an unpretentious poise that drew every eye. Unforgettable.

When I got back to LA, I couldn't stop thinking about you. I didn't even know your name. We had all worn name tags, but you hadn't bothered with yours. It would've ruined your snazzy jacket. I kept going back and forth in my mind, trying to make the decision about college. All throughout high school, I had assumed I'd follow my sisters to Stanford. My parents, of course, encouraged it, wanting me close. But a part of me wanted to carve my own path, far from them. Then I had this irrational hope—just a tiny bit—that I might run into you again if we both ended up at Harvard. It was a silly thought. But, in the end, it was Harvard.

When I arrived on campus in the fall, I searched for you, hoping you'd also made the same decision. My heart sank when I didn't find you on Welcome Day. But two days into orientation week, I finally spotted you in Annenberg, sitting with the same group of students from Visitas. My heart soared.

But approaching you—that was another story. I couldn't just walk up to a boy and start flirting. What would that say about me? After all, in high school, the boys had pursued me. I had my own dignity to maintain. As luck would have it, I ran into Tom Wood, one of the guys you were often with. I hadn't realized we'd met years ago at Space

Camp. He'd shot up a foot since then, his baby face long gone, nearly unrecognizable. That opportune encounter landed me an invitation to your table at Annenberg. It was then I learned your name, uttered so softly I almost didn't catch it. I had imagined you to be aloof, maybe even arrogant, but you were unexpectedly shy. You barely made eye contact. That only made me more curious. Was it disinterest? A girlfriend—Kate or Abigail, perhaps? You looked so polished on the outside, yet you were reserved, almost unaware of your own mystique.

After that initial encounter, I was determined to find a way to talk to you again. Despite my efforts, our paths rarely crossed. With no shared classes and different dorms, Annenberg became my only hope. Even then, you were elusive, scarfing down your meals and escaping before I could engage you in conversation. Later, I overheard Kate mention that you spent most of your time at Lamont. She also confirmed you didn't have a girlfriend. "He's married to books," she said.

One evening after dinner, I decided to follow you to Lamont. Discreetly, of course. I kept my distance, watching you from the shadows of the bookshelves, completely engrossed. It was an all-consuming crush. I told myself to stop. "Deborah doesn't chase boys." But a month into our first year, you still barely acknowledged my existence. Even when we ended up at the same table in Annenberg, you rarely said a word to me. Finally, I couldn't take it anymore. I broke every rule I had about dignity, pride, and letting boys make the first move.

It was Halloween, a night for masks and mischief, and I was ready to take a chance. Arriving before you, I staked out Lamont. The moment you walked in, I sprang into action, feigning nonchalance as I walked toward you. I was certain you saw me, but you began to turn away, as if to avoid me altogether. What was wrong with you? Panic flared and I called you. Only then did you stop.

A blush crept up your cheeks as you stumbled over my name. It was such a contrast to your suave composure around your friends. Were you always like this with girls, or just with me? The thought that I might be the cause of your nerves was flattering, more than I cared to admit. Still, my heart skipped a beat when you agreed to join me for a walk around the Square. I had half expected a polite brush-off, but you were full of surprises.

That evening unfolded like a magic carpet. The way you spoke—with such sincerity and passion—wasn't a performance designed to impress. It was your way of being, your heart laid bare. And when it was my turn to speak, you hung on to every word, making me feel like the only person who mattered. I never wanted that night to end.

The days that followed our dreamy night dragged on in agony. I had felt a spark, something real, but you acted as if nothing had happened. Frustration built up inside me. Just as I was resigning myself to the idea that it'd all been some transient illusion, I ran into you during a morning jog along the Charles. And then, it happened. You asked me to brunch. Maybe I hadn't been wrong after all. Boys did chase Deborah!

When the waitress at that restaurant assumed we were a couple, a jolt of warmth rushed through my chest. Was fate giving us a subtle nudge? The whole afternoon enraptured me, as if the world had shrunk to just you and me. Like out of a romance movie. The crisp air, the golden leaves, and the way you looked at me. I nearly kissed you when you bought me that beanie on Newbury Street and said I was *resplendent*. It's my favorite word, still to date.

Back in my dorm, I couldn't wait to recount every detail to Amy and a few friends from down the hall. I told them how you'd kissed my eyebrow instead of my lips, leaving me bemused. They giggled, but reassured me. You might just need a little nudge. Maybe you weren't all that experienced with dating. But when I mentioned your first kiss with those European college girls, their eyes widened in shock.

What kind of nudge would you need? While walking along Brattle with some friends that evening, I stumbled upon something I thought might be perfect. *The Art of Love*, by Ovid. Given your love for books, I thought it would make a thoughtful gift. I rushed to Lamont, fantasizing about your hands cradling the small of my back, you kissing me with a feral intensity. Makes me blush even thinking about it now. But to my dismay, you weren't there. I told myself I'd wait five minutes—just five—but that became ten and, before I knew it, twenty. For a boy! What had become of my pride?

That night, I never expected you to come all the way to Hollis and shout my name from the courtyard. It was both mortifying and flattering—your voice reverberating through the space, grabbing the attention of every girl in Hollis. Straight out of *Romeo and Juliet*. I shrank into the shadows, torn between wanting to hide and being drawn in by your daring proclamation. Finally, Amy, bless her heart, pulled me to the window, forcing me to confront the burning spectacle you were orchestrating.

Then you started to sing. Singing! Of all the things I had expected, this wasn't one of them. Your voice, a melody that spiraled above the cheers and applause, transformed any hint of embarrassment into an irresistible pull. Everything else seemed to fade into the background. In that moment, I realized that being with you meant embracing life in its fullest—every unexpected twist, every raw emotion. And you proved me right. People often say "Never say never," but with you, it was an exception. You could never get enough of me, never approached anything about me halfway. Your world revolved around me, and I was the center of it all.

Do you remember how relentlessly you showered me with compliments? *Ravishing, marvelous, gorgeous.* Your words wove themselves into an endless hymn that still lingers in my mind. Your declarations of *I love you*, whispered in crowded hallways or shouted across spaces, haunt me in unguarded moments. But for you, even words weren't enough. Your love overflowed onto paper, spilling into notebooks and scraps you'd hide in my bag, under my pillow. Little fragments of your heart scattered everywhere. And that secret handshake of ours? That silly yet intricate ritual we exercised bounteously. It was your way of reminding me how unyielding your love was. Even now, I catch myself squeezing George's hand the same way. Almost habitually. And when I do, the guilt comes rushing in. The guilt for George, and for our memory.

Our fights, though rare, incinerated with a passion that mirrored our love. Your jealousy, a stupefying niggle to your usual composure, would erupt whenever another guy breathed in my direction. That overprotective streak, though sometimes maddening, was inexplicably endearing. "I'm fine," you'd say, your voice strained, your eyes betraying the turmoil within. But beneath the frustration, I recognized a fierce loyalty. A flawed but exquisite love that, instead of driving us apart, only made me fall deeper for you.

Let me clear the air about something. After your unforgettable serenade—and the relentless teasing from my dormmates—I ran into Abigail. "Don't break his heart," she said. Her icy glare was unsettling, leaving me cautious of your friendship with her. I know I'm not the jealous type, but she had this glacial enigma—intimidating yet captivating, like the aurora. Years later, watching her beside you on a news broadcast, stunning in that navy dress during Charis's IPO, brought those buried feelings rushing back. Perhaps it was the way the two of you seemed to embody a rare, mesmerizing intensity. A connection that felt almost predestined. Still, despite the stab of jealousy it sent through me, I'm grateful she was there to celebrate that momentous milestone with you.

But I digress. The truth is, I loved you first, River. With all my heart. I'd relive those four years at Harvard in a heartbeat. You showed me who I was, what it meant to be loved. And while my love for George and Adeline is profound and irreplaceable, it's a different kind of love from my love for you. Each love is unique. Not to be compared.

∿

THERE ARE a few more things I want you to know.

Our final semester. Your call from Korea shattered my world. But let's not get into that. There's no need to reopen the darkest chapter of my life. Besides, that's not why I brought it up. What I never told you is this: I couldn't let go. I couldn't accept that this was how our story ended. A month before I embarked on the laborious journey of med school, the ache for you turned into a physical need. On a whim, I booked a flight to Seoul, armed with nothing more than the name of your company. It was a desperate gamble, with my heart on the line.

Early the next morning, I stood outside your headquarters, nerves raw and heart pounding. But at the last second, I faltered. I couldn't bring myself to face you. I was terrified. What consequence was I scared of? You rejecting me again? Me forgoing my future in the US? I retreated to a café across the street, my eyes glued to the SOL building. When you finally emerged at 7:45 a.m., the sight of you cut through me—not with admiration but with anguish. Your cheekbones were gaunt, your hollow eyes radiating profound grief, as though sleep and sustenance had abandoned you long ago. Your once-sure steps wobbled. You looked as broken as I felt.

Instinct took over, and I lunged toward the door, desperate to reach you, to cradle you. But before I could act, a throng of protesters surged forward, their shouts piercing the air, their fingers pointed like accusations. A riot. Mayhem. You recoiled, shrinking before my eyes into something almost unrecognizable—a little boy lost in an adult suit. The moment froze me in place, confusion and heartbreak paralyzing me. What was happening?

Later, back in my hotel room, the grim reality unraveled on the English-language news channel. SOL was under siege. The headlines screamed of nepotism, condemning your CEO appointment as an affront. They derided your exemption from mandatory military service, your "privileged and entitled" life. Each word was a dagger, not just for you but for me. Was this the weight you'd alluded to? Why did you face this storm alone, when I could've been there to help you shoulder it?

The flight back to the US blurred by in a haze of exhaustion and unanswered questions. Could I have thrived in Korea? Orbiting your twelve-hour workdays, living in the shadow of your burden? You feared I'd waste my time and talent waiting for scraps of your presence and that, eventually, I'd grow to resent you. Now, after ten years of marriage and navigating the sandstorms that come with it, I can't help but wonder how our life in Korea would've unfurled. Never

mind. What's the point in relitigating it now? But you must acknowledge that my love for you was more than strong enough to weather
the calamities of marriage and life itself.

There's another secret I've carried all these years. My final year at
UCSF. Match Day for residency loomed, that fateful day when you
discover where you'll spend the next chapter of your life. My future
hung in the balance. At the time, I was in an on-again, off-again relationship with George, who was working at Kaiser Permanente in
Oakland. He kept me grounded through the chaos of medical school
—perhaps even served as a shield against the ghost of you. It wasn't
the kind of love that stormed in and upended my world. And he
knew. Still, he urged me to stay in California. So did my parents and
sisters. Even logic itself. UCSF, Stanford—the doors were wide open.

Then, one winter afternoon, as I finalized my rank list, a headline
flickered across the TV and stopped me cold: *The IMF Approves Financial Bailout for South Korea.* Back then—and even now—the word
Korea always made me pause and turn. The segment spotlighted a
handful of companies that had weathered the Asian financial crisis;
SOL was among them, held up as a rare success. It also mentioned
your resignation and the transfer of leadership to your mother. Then
the image on the screen changed, and there you were—sharp suit
and tie, square jaw, dark hair—stepping out of SOL's headquarters,
greeting those around you before disappearing into a waiting sedan. I
called out, "Wait, wait!" at the screen. The past I thought I had buried
clawed its way back to the surface—years of anger, resentment, and
deliberate forgetting. Yet I couldn't deny the truth: you were still
there, still haunting the vast corridors of my heart. It was an
upheaval, shaking the seemingly solid ground of my life.

What did your resignation mean? Were you coming back to
America? Where in America? Boston? Your roots were there—
boarding school, college, memories that tied you to the past. I told
myself it was foolish, but a tiny ember of hope refused to die. It was
irrational, I knew, but the pull was undeniable. I needed to be in that
city of romance, just in case, against all odds, fate intervened.

The night before the residency rankings were due, I made a

drastic decision. I rewrote my list, trading my top California choices for hospitals in Boston. It was a leap of faith, ignited by a glimmering possibility. Match Day arrived. The envelope. Mass General. Shock rippled through the room. George, my parents, my sisters—their faces displayed disbelief and concern. They'd witnessed the wreckage of my heart, and now, I was willingly returning to the scene of old wounds. Yet beneath the trepidation, a thrill coursed through me. This was my chance to rewrite our story. A grand, cinematic reunion worthy of the silver screen. Not some predictable Hollywood ending, but a breathtaking plot twist. Our story was destined to be legendary.

When I arrived in Boston to start my residency that summer, I searched for you everywhere, like a frazzled mother with a lost child —Harvard Square, Boston Common, Newbury Street. My eyes combed every crowd, seeking your dark hair, your kind yet piercing eyes, and those sensual lips. One Sunday morning, I even took the T to Revere Beach, hoping against reason that I might find you strolling along the shore. An inconceivable pilgrimage, propelled by desperate hope. Yet each adventure ended the same: with the blunt torment of disappointment.

Those were the pre–social media days. No quick answers, no digital breadcrumbs to follow. My searches yielded nothing but stale news reports, your name still strapped to SOL. With every passing day, that gauzy hope unraveled a little more, threatening to deplete me. What if you never came back in the first place? The admonishments of my family droned in my mind, growing louder with each failed attempt. I had proven them right.

Thankfully, the first year of residency was a crucible, thrusting me into the fire of long hours and ceaseless demands. There was no time for heartbreak, no room for residual regrets. Survival became the only goal. Yet certain subconscious habits are hard to extinguish. Somewhere in my second year, almost on autopilot, I found myself typing your name into the browser. No expectations. Just a reflex. This time, something new appeared: MarsEdge. My curiosity flared as I clicked the About page. And there you were. In an instant, the heartache, the despair, and that dormant thread of longing erupted, detonating like stray dynamite. But San Francisco? Of all places? Why? How had we missed each other? I mean, how? What if I had stayed at UCSF? Would we have met, found our way back to each other? The questions scorched me in an inferno of what-ifs. Life's atrocious irony got the last laugh.

During my final year of residency, George came back into my life. By then, I had almost accepted—perhaps even surrendered to—the cruel notion that life had no intention of letting you and me end up together. I had clung to an improbable hope for so long, only to finally convince myself that moving on was the only mercy left. Yet when George proposed on one knee, I wavered. Was he the love of my life? I only knew the love I had with you. Could two loves exist? Could my love for George deepen—maybe even eclipse what you and I once had? Despite these doubts, after what felt like hours of keeping him on his knees, I finally said, "Yes." It was about time.

Then, two months before my wedding—in the middle of planning a future with George—you finally reappeared. Eight years of silence, River. And then, just like that, boom.

When I stepped out of the main building and saw you at my usual lunch spot, I froze. For a moment, I wondered if my mind was playing tricks on me. *Is it really you?* I stumbled to the bench near the pond and sat down, barely breathing. Then, you came over. It was really you.

The sight of you sent a shock wave through me. Fury, confusion, desire, all at once. Even in my anger, you were as magnetic as ever. Time and hardship had only sharpened your features, intensifying your presence. Every old feeling—the pull to be loved by you, the aching thirst to be yours—came surging back, refusing to be ignored. I had to resist the urge to hold you, to erase the last eight years with a single kiss. But fear rooted me to the spot—fear of the unknown, fear of destroying the life I had built in your absence. What if you'd come back sooner? What if I'd never met George? Could you and I have found our way back to each other? Would I have called off my wedding if you'd asked me to? I don't know. Life is a merciless master. It forces us to make impossible choices and haunts us with the paths we didn't take. Isn't it sadistic, the way it taunts us with riddles we'll never solve?

Even after I married George, you invaded my thoughts, slipping in at the most ordinary moments—while shampooing my hair, folding laundry, or sitting in a car wash. Would our paths ever cross again? What would I even gain from such an encounter? These questions felt wrong, almost unfaithful, yet they surfaced, unbidden, to irritate me.

Then Chicago happened. You know, I wasn't supposed to be at that conference. My department chief had a last-minute conflict, and I, the honorary stand-in, found myself staring at your name on the program. Charis had become a buzzword in our field. Some saw it as a competitor; others, an ally. Never in my wildest imaginings did I think it would become the backdrop for our reunion. For a fleeting moment, I considered canceling. But the logistics made it impossible. Or maybe I subconsciously yearned for that fugacious chance to see you again.

Throughout the conference, I'd eluded you, ducking into side rooms whenever I caught a glimpse of you. I had no intention of attending your session. Yet at the last minute, a traitorous impulse seized me, and I snuck into the back of the room. Catching sight of you on stage, I forgot how to keep my balance. You looked the same— but different. Still double-take handsome, but more distinguished now. More assured. The way you listened to questions as if your eyes captured each word, the way you leaned in when you spoke, I couldn't look away. But beneath the charisma, there was something dark. A shadow the River I had known in college never carried. When you spoke about suffering from loneliness, something in me broke open. I nearly shouted your name from the crowd and ran up to the stage just to hold you. But I drew in a breath instead. As the session neared its end, I hesitated, torn by the impulse to see you up close. Before I could move, though, you rushed out of the room, vanishing into the crowd.

I spent the rest of the day scanning a tide of unfamiliar faces, hoping to see you again. But you were gone. A dejection settled over me, as if something unresolved had disappeared even further out of reach. Why hadn't I said hello when I had so many chances before?

That night, as I sat through dinner with a group of psychiatrists, images of you on stage clashed with the soporific conversation around me. Maybe you'd be back the next day. Or maybe you were already gone, on your way to San Francisco. My thoughts kept drifting back to you, unyielding. After dinner, I wandered off alone, hoping the cool night air would clear my head.

As I passed a dimly lit piano bar, the opening chords of "When a Man Loves a Woman" snared me. The music rooted me to the spot. Remember that day on our way to Rockport? The song playing, you'd asked me to complete the sentence, "When River loves Deborah . . ." Unprepared, I'd stared in silence. Then I'd blinked and said, "Deborah will know?" You'd considered my answer for a moment, then smiled and nodded in approval.

And in that moment, there you were. Not just in my memory, but sitting alone at the bar, your profile traced in the bronze glow. My breath caught. Was I hallucinating? But it was you. Every instinct begged me to turn away and leave the past undisturbed. But my feet refused to move. The trepidation gave way to an unrelenting curiosity. How had you been—especially after the way I had walked away, leaving you alone by the pond at McLean? Had you found someone else? I had to know. I couldn't let this moment escape me, not again.

As I sat beside you at the bar, doubts plagued my thoughts. What was I doing—to you, to myself? Was this a reckless, selfish indulgence? Yet for a few stolen hours, we were back in college, the years dissolving away with each shared laugh and reminiscence, summoning an irrational hope. Could we, after all this time, salvage something? A friendship, maybe?

Then I saw it—the way you looked at me—that same steadfast love, untouched by time or distance. For years, I had imagined you fulfilled and happy, your devotion earned by someone worthy, someone who could reciprocate the depth of your love. Instead, you stood there, your heart still tethered to me, your love still unwavering in its intensity, your spirit bound to a past that could never be reclaimed. I'd become a barrier keeping you from finding happiness with someone else. What impossible dream were you holding on to? That life, in some twisted miracle, might rewind the years and bring us back to each other? That we could rewrite our story, erasing the pain, the mistakes, and the choices that led us here?

The thought was as intoxicating as it was devastating, tempting me to betray everything I had built, everything I had convinced myself I wanted. The explosive yet understated yearning in your eyes rekindled that familiar, infectious rush within me. The gravity was so strong that, just for a moment, I wanted to relinquish the resistance and whisper, "Yes, River, you may take me. I'm yours."

As you held me in your arms, swaying to Diana Krall's song playing in the background, I let myself imagine throwing away my life—everything—for the chance to be with you again. But fear held me back—fear of betraying George, fear of being hurt again, fear of life's wrath and punishment that might follow. Fear is the most persuasive saboteur of them all.

Back in my hotel room, with the walls closing in, the irreversible finality of our story crushed me. And I wailed. For your loneliness. For the ghost of us. Still, my commitment to George refused to let desire take the lead. You see? When he and I began dating, I confided in him about you—about how irreplaceable our love had been, how you broke my heart, and how I was still trying to heal. He was there for me. And yet I betrayed his heart when I left San Francisco for Boston, chasing after the delusional hope of finding you. Even then, he waited—for me to let go, for me to choose him instead—until, at last, I did. Perhaps we were two wounded souls seeking solace, offering each other a lifeline through second chances. Our bond was built on trust, forged in the shared act of healing one another's broken hearts. The thought of jeopardizing that foundation—of betraying the sanctuary we'd created—filled me with a suffocating guilt. Especially then, with the dream of a child beginning to take shape in our lives. Do you understand the weight of that? I hope so.

After I came back from Chicago, I wore a brave face and forced myself to move on, once more. The arrival of Adeline was exactly what I needed. Yet raising her—especially those first three years—was searing. Nothing could've prepared me for the bone-deep exhaustion of motherhood. And the persistent postpartum depression, an undertow George couldn't comprehend. "How can you be so moody when we have such a beautiful daughter?" he'd ask, shaking his head. I knew he meant well. But in those moments, I couldn't help thinking about how your words used to buoy me. What if it'd been you? Would you have understood? Would you have kept the promise that I'd always be your priority? I know they're unanswerable now. Meaningless, really. But I ask them anyway.

Finally, let's talk about Rosalie. I owe you an explanation, don't I?

You had an uncanny way of surprising me. I was both disoriented and elated to see you when I ran into you at the library in Santa Monica. George and I were struggling then. Even the strongest marriages have their fault lines. It's not conflict that corrodes a marriage. It's the comfort that hides complacency in plain sight. Like lead poisoning. Unnoticeable until it's too late. Every marriage goes through those moments—ennui, lulls, doldrums—and ours was no exception. Trust me. Even if you and I had been married, we would've faced our own inevitable struggles.

I was in a place where every part of me felt breakable. And I craved a kind of undivided affection and impassioned love. The kind we had in college, when even a brief separation felt like physical pain. And you appeared, as if you'd been waiting for that exact moment. Immaculate timing.

I, of course, was completely unprepared. When you saw me in my wrinkled T-shirt and sweats, I was mortified. I hadn't even bothered to brush my hair or do my eyebrows that day. I had always hoped you'd remember me as the young and exuberant Deborah. But there I was—rumpled, sleep-starved, barely put together—like I'd rolled straight out of bed. And you? You looked like you'd rolled out of a photoshoot. Like time had decided to run in reverse for you. So unfair.

Yet there you were, gazing at me with that same intense desire—as if I were gliding down a red carpet, as if I were something divine.

How could you still look at me like that? It was exhilarating and surprisingly familiar. Like a forgotten part of myself had been awakened. That evening, I spent hours preparing—choosing the right outfit, applying makeup, and obsessing over what I'd say and what might follow. A whirlwind of dizzying thoughts flooded my mind, and I savored the heady anticipation. Still, Adeline's simple question —"Where are you going, mama?"—filled me with a sharp pang of conflict.

Just before I walked into Rosalie, my phone rang abruptly. It was George. More immaculate timing. Twice in one day. He'd called to talk about the problems we'd been facing. I told him it wasn't a good time, because I was about to meet a friend.

"At this hour? Who?" he'd asked.

"An old friend," I'd said.

To my surprise, he shot back, "Is it River?" I was astounded. Why would he even mention your name after all these years?

He explained he'd spotted you reaching for pastries one morning at a café near the boardwalk. He'd recognized you instantly. He knew you were the CEO of Charis. By then, your face was everywhere—on magazines, news channels, all of it. He also confessed that he was an active user of Charis. A revelation that made me ponder: Had he wrestled with loneliness too?

He didn't say it outright, but your sudden appearance must have rattled him. He told me he couldn't stop wondering what had brought you to Santa Monica. But whatever the reason, in that fleeting moment as he watched you, he understood why I had once loved you with every piece of my heart. It was something about your soul, he said. He's spiritual that way.

"Should I be worried?" he asked. I hesitated, unsure of how to respond. Then, he said the words that undid me. "Even if you do something you might regret, I will still forgive you. If we can't forgive each other, what's the point of love? Just don't forget to be home before Adeline wakes up in the morning."

He had rarely said the right words in turbulent situations, but in that moment, he did, clearing away almost all the fog within me.

Despite the compulsion to be with you, I couldn't bring myself to do it. I just couldn't. I stood there outside, tears streaming down my face. I finally called the hotel. The concierge went to get you, and I watched from a distance as you answered the phone. I could see the sharp pain on your face when I told you I couldn't come. But it was when I asked you to let me go—to erase me completely—that it broke you. The way you struggled to hold back your own tears, looking up at the ceiling. The way you grabbed your hair with your hand. The way you almost collapsed onto the floor. And for a moment, I hesitated, on the verge of changing my mind. Yet I hung up the phone, turned around, and sprinted away in my heels.

After that day, you persisted in my thoughts for weeks. I mean, months. Even after I had asked you to disappear from my life, every walk around Santa Monica held a sliver of hope that I might bump into you. What a hypocrite I was! But I never saw you again. As time went on, my longing for you dissipated slowly, swallowed up by the endless responsibilities of being a mother, a wife, and a psychiatrist.

Was this how you felt after your father passed in Korea? The love you had for your family, the weight of responsibility, the sacrifices you had to make. The impossible choices. I saw myself in the same predicament. George and Adeline. Or you. How can one make such a life-altering decision? How does one bear the weight of its consequences? But like George said, if we can't forgive each other, what's the point of love? Please forgive yourself, and forgive me, River.

And now, here we are, meeting one final time.

I'm furious at life. I never anticipated this would be our final encounter. When daily tribulations weighed me down, I'd daydream that you might reappear in my life years from now—maybe four or five years down the line, like you had at McLean, in Chicago, and in Santa Monica. A chance encounter at a resort, perhaps. Me with my family, you with your family. Would the two families even dare to have dinner together? George would eagerly share his house-renovation projects with Abigail while you and I exchanged awkward glances. Can you imagine that? Maybe you'd have a daughter too, one Adeline would eagerly take under her wing as a big sister. Would you still look at me the same way even then? Would that be too inappropriate? Of course ...

These little fantasies, however far-fetched, were my way of holding on to the remnants of our love. Yet if I had known this was how our paths would cross in the end, in this lifeless hospital room, would I have made the same choices? Would you have?

— End of Diary Entry —

25

DEBORAH

August 2012

I could no longer write.

It was as if every truth I had carried for years had spilled across the pages, blurred and smudged by my own tears. I rested my pen and closed the diary, sealing the bittersweet memories within. Writing had become my ritual back in medical school—a way to release anger, pain, and longing. Each word untangled the knots of my fractured heart, allowing me to breathe again. Some years, I filled multiple diaries. Others, barely one. I kept them all hidden, even from George. My only secret. But this diary—the one I had just penned—should I leave it here, in this room with River? What would be the point? Perhaps for my own survival?

I got up and moved closer to River's bed. The mechanical sounds of life support filled the hospital room, yet his presence felt over-whelmingly muted, as if he were suspended between a heartbeat and a held breath. His eyes stayed shut, his breathing faint and erratic. I sought any sign of life on his frail face, one that seemed almost unrecognizable, yet it was unmistakably him.

"I don't know if you can hear me," I whispered in his ear, my voice breaking. "But please, River, you must know, even though I could never say it. I loved you with everything I had. I still love you, and I always will. I'll never stop . . ." My breath caught in my throat. I drew in a deep, shaky inhale and closed my eyes, letting the memory of that day pull me in. "I can picture our first walk, that Halloween. When we talked about *Love Story*, we wondered what it would feel like to lose the love of your life so early. I told you that finding true love would be worth it, no matter how it ended. I take that back now. I don't want this to be our ending."

I opened my eyes to look at him again, but tears blurred my vision, spilling down to the blanket. "Do you remember? I wanted to become a jazz singer? You told me how much you'd love to hear me sing one day. And I jokingly said it would only happen if it were your dying wish. 'Your dying wish!' What was I thinking? So many regrets." I buried my face in my hands, my body trembling as sobs racked me. But I fought to steady myself, determined to follow through on my words. "Life has a cruel way of shaking us up just when we think we've found our footing. But whenever it does, this is the song I turn to . . ."

I closed my eyes, remembering all the beautiful moments when River made me smile. I began to sing "Smile," by Nat King Cole. The lyrics carried an everlasting promise—that even through pain, light could still break through. My promise to River.

As I surrendered to the final notes, his fingers brushed against mine. Startled, I quickly gripped his hand. "River, it's me, your Deborah. I'm here. Can you hear me? Please, say something."

He didn't respond, but his fingers squeezed mine with the last of his strength.

Our secret handshake.

26

DEBORAH

September 2012

Koreatown in LA slumbered in the serene morning light, with shy sunbeams replacing the gaudy neon from the night before. The trendsetters' flamboyant footsteps had vanished, giving way to elders dawdling and workers spraying water on storefronts.

She'd asked to see me. Just that. No explanation. No context. The greatest irony? The meeting fell on the very date I first met River at Annenberg. Only now, he was no longer here. I took a deep breath to calm my nerves before stepping inside.

Natural light filled the airy café, its white walls, corner plants, and light oak tables creating a peaceful atmosphere. The scent of fresh coffee mingled with the hum of new-age music playing in the background.

I found River's mother already seated with a gentleman near the corner windows. I had seen her in pictures in the media, highlighting her servant leadership in the Asian business ecosystem. Her diminutive yet resilient presence, like a solitary willow tree weathering a storm, struck me. As soon as they saw me, they rose and bowed in greeting.

After we sat down, the man spoke first, his English polished. "Dr. Starfield, it's nice to meet you finally. I'm Joonan. But please call me Mr. Kangster," he said and quickly clarified that it was a nickname River had given him. "I'm here to help translate for River's mother."

"Please call me Deborah," I said, giving a small bow.

River's mother studied me, as if she was curious about what River saw in me. Though her face was kind, it carried the weight of a grieving mother, her eyes deep with sorrow. My shoulders stayed tense. The question still lingered. Why had she asked to see me? She began speaking in Korean. Her tone, mellow and tranquilizing, bore an uncanny resemblance to River's. As she spoke, she reached out her right hand toward me. Unsure of what she needed, I instinctively held her hand in both of mine.

Then, she wept.

Emotions needed no translation. Though I didn't understand her words, the depth of her pain and grief was unmistakable, her anguish coalescing with my own. Tears welled up in my own eyes, and soon, I found myself crying with her, sharing a moment of unspoken sorrow.

As the sobs slowed and breath returned, she reached into her bag and pulled out a delicate silk handkerchief embroidered with the rose of Sharon. With the same tenderness I remembered in River, she leaned forward and wiped the tears from my face. She placed the handkerchief on my palm, then clasped my fingers around it, as if transplanting a piece of her heart. It was such a simple yet familiar gesture. Something River would've done.

Mr. Kangster turned to the window, hiding his expression, before opening his lips. "River's mother wishes to extend her deepest condolences, first and foremost. She understands that you're a married woman with a daughter. Her intention is not to intrude but to fulfill her role as the mother of someone who once meant a great deal to you . . . so that River's final wishes are delivered as he intended."

At his words, my breath caught for a moment. What could River's final wishes be? Still reeling from the shock of his passing, I was unprepared to face more news about him.

"River loved you deeply. His mother understands why now that she's met you in person. She said it's the compassion in your eyes. An untainted soul, like an angel," Mr. Kangster said. "She regrets the burdens she placed on River at such a young age. When he returned to America in 1998, she was certain he would find you and rekindle what the two of you had, but that never came to pass. She carries immense guilt for the loneliness that shadowed his life for so long. But she's also grateful to you for showing him what real love is, what it feels like . . ."

He paused, giving me the space to wipe my tears with the handkerchief.

"As you know, River didn't want anyone else at his funeral, opting for a simple cremation. However, I understand that Abigail, Pete, you, and a few of his close friends and colleagues held a small gathering to celebrate his life. His mother is thankful for that. We also met Jeff in San Francisco before coming here. He's very tall! And funny," he said, chuckling, placating the heaviness that hung between us. "River's ashes were spread in the Pacific Ocean, as per his wishes. He wanted to ensure he could visit both America and Korea in the afterlife. So if you ever miss him, all you have to do is go to the beach and look out at the ocean."

I nodded, unable to speak, my gaze already drifting toward the window. I swallowed hard, but the lump in my throat refused to move.

Studying my face, Mr. Kangster continued. "Most importantly, we're here because River left three things for you. The first is this." He lifted a shopping bag and handed it to me. Inside was a medium-sized box, carefully gift wrapped. I held my breath, unsure of what I was about to uncover. "Please go ahead."

With trembling hands, I slowly unwrapped the paper. Inside was an old box. My heart lurched as I opened it, revealing a stethoscope. I lifted it from the box and held it in my hand. My fingertips brushed over a faint texture—an inscription engraved on the metal ear tube: *Hear my beating heart.*

I slipped in the earpieces and closed my eyes. The silence was heavy, yet I could almost hear River's heartbeat, just like when I had lain beside him in that tiny dorm room bed.

"River's mother found it in his room and kept it all these years. He'd gotten it for you in college, to celebrate your acceptance into medical school."

I set it down on the table, then gently brushed my fingers over the engraved letters. My mind drifted back to those nights in my dorm room, mapping out our future. River, working to support me through medical school, and then me returning the favor while he triumphed business school. A cozy starter home in Cambridge, filled with laughter. Holidays spent in a whirlwind of family visits to LA and Korea, three to five daughters in tow. Exhausted, but happy.

"The next thing . . . it requires some explanation." From his briefcase, he pulled out a presentation deck, along with piles of paper. "River held substantial ownership in SOL. In the event of his passing, the beneficiary was his mother, ensuring that SOL remained under family control. Four months before his death, River sold some of his SOL shares—just enough to retain family control. In exchange, he used the proceeds to establish a nonprofit foundation for underprivileged youth. This presentation has the details, but let me summarize."

His voice moved through the room with calm precision, but beneath the table, my fingers curled tight against my lap.

"The foundation's mission is to promote literacy among youth, encouraging them to fall in love with books in this age of screens and apps. River also wanted to provide mental health services to them. His plan was to establish sanctuaries in underserved neighborhoods. In these spaces, children could read, receive tutoring, and speak with therapists."

"That sounds incredible," I said, a swell of pride filling me at River's ambition. "It's exactly the kind of thing he would dream up."

"Yes, but there's more. It's also a safe haven for aspiring musicians to test new material before stepping onto bigger stages. It's for those who dream of performing but never had the chance. And anyone can come, enjoy the music, and lose themselves in a good book," he said.

"Books and music . . . River's vices. But I'm sorry, what does this have to do with me?"

"Well," Mr. Kangster said, "River also donated half of his fortune from Charis to the foundation. I won't tell you the exact amount, but given his net worth, it was staggering. And . . ." He swallowed hard, the click in his throat loud in the tense silence, his Adam's apple bobbing up and down. "He left the foundation under your name. He wanted you to have it. He often spoke of the hours you spent together in libraries and how you dreamed of singing jazz on stage. He believed you were the perfect person to grow the foundation and achieve extraordinary things with it . . ."

Mr. Kangster paused mid-sentence, watching as I drew in a sharp breath, hand instinctively rising to my chest.

"You may decline the offer as well. We understand you have many obligations, including your family. But River already assembled a competent team to handle the day-to-day operations to support you. Your role would be to oversee major initiatives. So it won't take too much time away from your current commitments, unless you wish to be involved more proactively. It's yours. You are the boss, after all."

Both River's mother and Mr. Kangster looked at me intently, trying to gauge my reaction. Words escaped me, leaving me lost in a swirl of confusion and shock.

"I don't know what to say . . . please let me think about it and discuss it with George. What's the name of the foundation, by the way?"

"I was wondering when you would ask," he said with a warm grin. "The foundation is called Unspoken Words."

"Unspoken Words . . ." I murmured, my eyes locking with River's mother's. And then, I saw them—River's eyes, gazing back at me with that same intense yet tender warmth that used to make my world dissolve into a blur. "River . . ." I choked out his name, an outcry escaping my lips. The floodgates within me burst open, unleashing a torrent of grief I had held back for years—hidden from George, from Adeline, from myself. It poured out, a deluge of sorrow and longing, an untamed expression of the love I had buried deep within my heart.

River's mother rose from her chair and walked over to me, wrapping her tiny frame around mine. She spoke softly in Korean, soothing me as if I were a hurt child. While I tried to regain my composure, Mr. Kangster began speaking again. River's mother stayed close, her hands gently holding mine.

"There's one final thing he left for you." He reached into his pocket and pulled out a small, weathered book bound in faded orange leather. *The Art of Love*, by Ovid. My first gift to River. It transported me back to that chilly but sunny winter afternoon in Harvard Square, sharing an almond croissant, with a cappuccino for me and warm skim milk for him. Our laughter echoed in the corridor as we debated the book's satirical nature. Could one learn how to love from a book?

Through my tear-blurred vision, I clutched the book to my face, drawing in its distant scent. As I did, a folded piece of paper slipped out and landed on the table. My breath caught. I let it sit there a moment before daring to pick it up. Then, carefully, I reached for it and unfolded it with unsteady hands.

You taught me the art of love: sometimes, what's left unsaid means more. —River

27

ABIGAIL

September 2012

R iver once told me that he never understood why people called love a game. He believed that in love, there were no winners or losers, no universal rules, and sometimes, it took only one person to keep it alive. Now that he was gone, I understood. Even without him in this world, I remained in love. Alone. Love could play alone.

After my sabbatical and bereavement leave, I finally returned to work. My parents and friends insisted I wasn't ready, that I shouldn't rush back. But I needed something—anything—to keep me going, to drown out the emptiness.

New Beginnings occupied a modest prewar building in Brooklyn's Dumbo neighborhood. Its mismatched furniture and well-worn rugs were a far cry from the sleek designer chairs and polished floors of Lamarr Ventures. Still, I felt more liberated in my dilapidated office.

When I arrived, Julia, my assistant, hurried toward me. "It's good to have you back. My deepest condolences."

"Thank you."

Another condolence, another reminder of the unfillable void. My eyes drifted to the desk, now buried under a mountain of folders, each one direly waiting for my review.

"I know you've barely walked in, but there's something important I've been waiting to show you." She hesitated, eyes skittering with a wild urgency she couldn't contain. Her jittery demeanor and the unease in her body language set me on edge.

"Sure, go ahead," I said, feigning a genial tone.

She handed me a plain manila envelope. Yet she held it with the exaggerated care of someone handling a vial of poison. I took it from her, noticing tremors in her hands.

Inside, I found a small sealed envelope alongside two pieces of letter-sized paper—one an official document, the other . . . a handwritten note. River's handwriting. My pulse quickened. Julia, apparently sensing the intensity of the moment, stepped back and left me alone.

I sank into my chair. The papers burned in my hands, but I couldn't bring myself to look. After a few deep breaths, I finally perused the official letter.

Charitable Donation in the Amount of Twenty Million Shares of Charis Common Stock, Owned by River Jung, Transferred to New Beginnings. For Every Woman Who Deserves a Second Chance.

I gasped, my hand flying to my mouth as the paper fluttered to the desk. Twenty million shares of Charis. At the current stock price of fifty-four dollars per share, they were now valued at more than one billion dollars. It couldn't be true. I forced my eyes back to the letter, counting the zeros again and again. Then, at the bottom of the page, a few words were scrawled in River's penmanship:

When no one else believed in Charis, you were the true believer.

A wave of dizziness washed over me, leaving me lightheaded and breathless. With hands that barely obeyed me, I reached for the second sheet of paper. River's handwritten letter. Just before reading it, I had a change of heart and grabbed the small envelope instead.

The tiny envelope crinkled between my fingers as I opened it. A black-and-white photo slipped out, landing in my palm: River and me, seated across from each other in *The Phillipian* newspaper room, circa 1989. *Why this photo?* River had imbued even his most spontaneous gestures with clear intent and purpose. There had to be a reason.

In the photo, River and I looked impossibly young, untouched by the burdens of life's future twists. Though formal, there seemed to be a natural flow between us. I wore a determined expression, but now I could see the faint shimmer of something fragile behind it. My hair, nearly white in the photo, was styled in the infamous high-volume look of the late '80s, full of bounce and perfectly controlled waves. My head was held high, and my fist lay clenched on the table as if the weight of the world rested on my words. On the other hand, River wore a gentle expression, his dark hair, kept longer, falling naturally over his forehead, his eyes alive with curiosity and warmth. He leaned in—one hand on the table, the other resting on his chin—listening with the rare attention he reserved for such moments. No one had ever listened to me like that before. Or since. I continued staring at the picture, grainy with the passage of years.

Then, there it was. The memory from that late evening. I'd asked him a question in the middle of proofreading an article. "You always talk to me as if you can see straight through me. What do you see in me?"

"What do I see in you?" he said, his eyes softening at the corners. He glanced away for a moment, thoughtful, then looked back at me. "A luminous presence."

A luminous presence? I froze, cheeks warm, the words still resting on my lips. When I asked him what he meant, he replied, "Well, when I watch you out on the lacrosse field scoring goals, or hear you speak about gender inequality, I see someone tenacious, with so much conviction, passion, and courage. I find you inspiring. And I'm not just saying that to make you feel good. I have the utmost respect for you."

"You really see me like that?"

He nodded. "I do. That's the truth. Every word of it."

After a coquettish exchange of glances, we turned our attention back to the editorial, an invisible thread of fondness lingering between us in the quiet.

What stayed with me wasn't just what he'd said. It was the way he'd looked at me. I didn't remember him ever looking at anyone else like that. Except for me, and of course, Deborah. The tender affection was there, even if he might've been too young to recognize it back then. Now, looking back through the eyes of someone who had loved deeply—and still did—I could see it. That rudimentary yet sweet and innocent seed of love. Even if it was minuscule, it must've occupied a tiny space in his heart for decades, waiting for a spark to ignite its growth someday. For many, it might've remained buried and hidden, unacknowledged for a lifetime. But River and I were fortunate to uncover it and let it bloom. How precious and delicate . . .

Is that what you saw in the picture, River? If you could go back and tell your younger self where life would take us twenty-three years later, would you have fallen in love with me back then?

I wiped my tears with a tissue and turned the picture over. On the back, it read:

Time heals everything. Except '80s style.

His terrible humor. A laugh bubbled up through my tears, and I held the small photo close to my chest.

Finally, with my pulse racing, I turned to his letter, penned in hieroglyphic handwriting that seemed to have a mind of its own. Like a honeybee buzzing in endless loops, following patterns only trained eyes could decipher. The letter seemed to thrum with his presence. I let the breath go—and began.

My dearest Abigail —

I love you. And I miss you.

I wonder where you might be at this moment. Are you in your apartment, sipping coffee and watching the sunrise? Or in your office, navigating through an endless stream of meetings? No matter where you are, please know that I am with you right now.

I once read that most people live to eighty. So when I was approaching forty, marking the end of my first half, I contemplated the second half of my life. Would it be filled with more remorse? Or could I somehow find a way to begin again? I worried it might be the former. Another forty years of emptiness and suffering.

Then you appeared out of the snowstorm, both literally and metaphorically. Since that moment, my vision for the second half of my life transformed from one of loneliness to one filled with joy.

These past few months with you have been among the most glorious surprises of my life. For so long, I believed life was a cruel force, luring us with beauty only to reveal it as illusion. But you have shown me that life's beauty is not a trick. Rather, it is something we must allow ourselves to continuously discover, even if it means confronting our deepest fears and enduring unthinkable pain. You have helped me realize that love, the purest expression of life's beauty, is boundless. That we are born with an infinite well of it if we choose to let it cascade freely. That has been your gift to me.

After our long drive along the coast that magical day, I never had the chance to tell you how I envisioned our future together. The thought of a life shared with you filled my heart with an endless sense of love. I would have cherished each moment breathing the same air beside you, discovering every layer of who you are, and witnessing all the beauty that finally emerged after years of darkness.

But in my dreams of our future, it was not all sunshine and rainbows. I imagined not only the splendid moments, but also the lackluster routines that come with real life.

I pictured myself: selectively hearing what I want to hear, walking away during conflicts, ignoring your calls, leaving chores dispropor-

tionately to you, or arguing who's right when all you want is a hug and an apology (you're always right).

Those flashes of frustration when you might question, "Who are you?" The petty squabbles that feel monumental at the time but later dissolve into, "What were we even arguing about?" I yearned for that flawed, yet beautiful experience of being human with you.

Because it was in those moments—when things got hard, messy, or unbearable—that I imagined love would have deepened most. They would have reminded me never to take you for granted, to pay closer attention, to really see you. I wanted to show you that my love was not just for the sunny days—that it would have shone brightest in the arguments, the compromises, the reconciliations. And through all of it, I would have made sure you felt like the most important person in my life. Even as time wore on, even as our hair turned argent, I would have found small ways—every day—to show you how much you were loved.

That was my dream.

My love, Abigail, although my second half has been cut short, yours is still overflowing with possibilities. If we believe in second chances at love, we must believe in third chances too.

Would you take a chance on living out all the moments I once dreamed for us?

As I write this last letter, I realize my story is a happy ending, thanks to you.

ACKNOWLEDGMENTS

Building my start-up tested me in ways I never imagined. There were crucible moments so intense I sometimes doubted I would make it through. In those times, I turned to meditation, long-distance running, or coaching sessions. Anything that promised a relief. But when the weight of my responsibilities pressed down on me in the stillness of the night, those practices often felt just out of reach.

Then, on a particularly dark night, while the house lay quiet, I escaped from bed, opened my laptop, and began to write. I did not know what I was writing. Only that something needed to come out. So I poured whatever rose from my heart onto the blank screen.

The next night, and the night after that, I kept going. Not because I had time, but because I had to. Strangely, writing did not drain me. It energized me. It steadied me. My job at work remained just as demanding, but I moved through it with more clarity, more equanimity, and less suffering.

Over time, what began as catharsis turned into something more. It became a way to explore the love I carry inside me: the unbreakable love I have for my wife, the fierce loyalty I hold for my family, and the relentless devotion I pour into my company.

I came to realize that writing is not so different from building a business. Both demand perseverance and courage. Both ask me to let go of things I have dedicated countless hours to. Both force me to face the voice of doubt. And both are acts of love. Too hard to pursue for any reason other than love.

This book exists because of the people who reminded me there is so much love in life.

To Linda: Even before I wrote a single word, you believed in me. Throughout this journey, you encouraged me, supported me, and even took our three daughters away on weekends so I could disappear into writing. There were nights I hovered over the Delete key, just as I had in some of my hardest moments as a founder. And in those moments of doubt, you came to my rescue. You have been my anchor, my savior, and my greatest teacher of love. I could not have finished this book without your unwavering love. Every one of these ninety thousand words is for you.

To Migyu, Minnie, and Lara: I am endlessly thankful to you. From shaping the blurb to sanity-checking plot turns to helping with the title, your insights made this better in ways I cannot fully explain. You asked to read the manuscript, but I could not bring myself to share it until now. I was too terrified of what you might think. I hope it meets your expectations.

To my parents: You have kept my writing from elementary school all these years. You thought I was the greatest poet and probably still do. I would not be here if you had not let me hop on that plane to America to discover myself. I hope there is a Korean translation of this book someday so that you can read it.

To my parents-in-law: Thank you for accepting me as your own son, even when I came with nothing but a heart full of love for your daughter and a lot of growing left to do. I'm grateful for your love.

To Boyong and Yongseok: You've always been my biggest supporters, even when I wasn't the best version of the older brother you deserved. Thank you for always seeing the best in me.

To Liz and Marian: I'm deeply touched that you believed in this story even before reading a single word. Your faith means more than I can ever express.

To Mindi Machart: Your editorial brilliance helped shape this book from an amateur's attempt into something I can dare to share with the world. Thank you for guiding me through both the chaos and the craft.

To Aurelio Perez: Thank you for reading through the early, unpolished drafts, and offering feedback with such generosity, even amid your own packed schedule. Your candor and care have made me a better writer.

To AJ Brustein and Jeremy Burton: Thank you for the resolute spirit and unwavering tenacity it took to build something from nothing. You are among the rare friends who truly accept me, faults and all. I think of you whenever I eat pizza.

To Lori Macias: Thank you for the invaluable leadership lessons, caring mentorship, and steadfast guidance over the years. So many of those insights have been woven into this story.

To all present and past Whammies: Thank you for your heart, your grit, and your conviction in what we could build together.

To Richard and Janet Hart: Thank you for your unflinching belief in me for nearly twenty years. Your support has been unconditional.

To my board members and investors: Thank you for standing by me as I chased what often felt impossible.

To Py Seo: Thank you for guiding me through those early days in America. You were there for me when everything was new and uncertain.

To Mrs. Douglass: Thank you for teaching me English and encouraging me to write daily when I first arrived in America. You lit a spark I did not know would carry me here.

To Steve Herscovici: Thank you for recognizing my potential when I was still finding my footing. Your belief gave me the confidence to grow into it.

To Carmen Rosales: Thank you for the care and kindness you showed me during those long hours in the office. Rest in peace.

To Millie: Thank you for being my most loyal office mate, through every draft, every sigh, and never once demanding a treat.

This book was written in the stolen moments of my life, between raising a family and running a company. It was born of love. Love for my wife, my daughters, my extended families in South Korea and America. Love for my company. Love for my friends. And love for the stories that refused to stay silent in my heart.

To everyone who believed in me even in my darkest moments, thank you for being my sunshine.

ABOUT THE AUTHOR

Yong Kim was born in South Korea and immigrated to America alone at the age of fifteen. He earned a mathematics degree from the University of Chicago, a master's in statistics from Harvard University, and an MBA from Harvard Business School. He began his career as an economic consultant and investment banker before discovering his passion for entrepreneurship. Today, he is the founder and CEO of Wonolo, a leading workforce solution backed by top Silicon Valley investors. He is a devoted husband and father of three daughters, splitting his time across Philadelphia, Boston, and San Francisco.